Sawyer sucked in a breath. Her wisp of gown was so sheer, so delicate, it made Sawyer think of a pretty blush upon her soft cheek. He could see straight through the pale pink gown. He could see the dark roundness of her nipples and the dusky shadow between her breasts.

"I—" he said, still staring at her breasts, "I guess you're trying to breast—I mean rest. *Rest!*" He drove his fingers through his hair, damning his slip of the tongue. Barely taking his eyes off her body, he turned to go.

She stood up. "You can stay if you want to." He turned around to face her. He studied her breasts again, then drew his gaze down lower.

Her lips were parted slightly, like two pink petals almost about to open. They looked so soft, and sweet like sugar. And her breath smelled like the lemon tea she'd been drinking when he'd come into her room.

Pink petals. Sugar. Lemon. What man could resist an exquisite combination like that?

Also by Rebecca Paisley

A Basket of Wishes
Heartstrings

Bed of Roses

Rebecca Paisley

A Dell Book

Published by
Dell Publishing
a division of
Bantam Doubleday Dell Publishing Group, Inc.
1540 Broadway
New York, New York 10036

The trademark Dell® is registered in the U.S. Patent and Trademark Office.

ISBN: 0-440-22157-9

Printed in the United States of America

Published simultaneously in Canada

June 1996

10 9 8 7 6 5 4 3 2 1

OPM

I didn't have a little brother to hang my dolls off doorknobs or pester me to get out of the bathroom. Or sneak into my room to read my diary, irritate my boyfriends, tell on me to Mama, or any of the other things little brothers are famous for doing to their big sisters.

I didn't have a brother at all, little or big.

But I have a brother-in-law.

This is a man who knows me as well as a real brother would. I can look my worst in front of him, make demands of him, and spill all my emotions into his lap. This is a man who adores my sister, my nephews, and takes care of my mother as if she were his own.

This is a man who has shown exceptional courage and character by not only accepting my outrageous family, but by continuing to love us all throughout the years.

Tommy Howe, I don't care what the law says. You are my *real* brother, and no judge or court in the land could ever convince me otherwise.

With all my love and all my gratitude, I dedicate *Bed of Roses* to you.

And a special, heartfelt thank-you to my editor, Mary Ellen O'Neill, who patiently waited for this book to be completed, who has become a true friend to me, and who is undoubtedly trying to prepare herself for the next whirlwind that comes to all editors I work with. Love you, Mary Ellen. You're the best, darlin'!

Lost Kiss

I am to you a drop of darkness
Spreading across the holy waters
Of a glittering morning soul.
How can one delay the destiny of dawn
By letting slip the translations
Of the stars in my chanced upon part
In the bejeweled constellation
That prophesies us.

I wonder of this curious thing
That lingers in the taste of a kiss.

That first gingerly conceived kiss
Sweaty palmed contact of two trembling leaves
Sweetness tainted of nervousness
And glazed by the soft madness of anticipation
Like two roses touching in the breeze
Two fearful hearts starting to believe.

Perhaps I seek that bold five-hundredth kiss
Seduced by sweet celebrations of champagne
And difficult to pronounce French dishes
It tastes like two warm hands
Clasped together in a certain prayer
Asking that they part as albatross wings
Beating to the rhythm of one heart.

Wandering the raven nights within your hair
Cut from the canvas of elusive dreams
I am so anxious for the freedom in your eyes
Longing to quench a burning noontide of life
To pencil the glory of my dawn for her . . .
She of eyes lost upon a sky of gems.

To stay a prophet of forgotten suns
Wrapped in pretty crepe paper
Bound in mesmerizing twists of fate
Can only keep me from giving . . .
                    That fairy tale kiss
And seeing all the seasons
In the perfect creation of two lost souls.

—Scott Shou

one

"You cannot turn three eccentric old men back into the skilled gunmen they used to be, Zafiro." Sister Carmelita dropped the sack of flour she'd brought to Zafiro from the convent and took a seat on a weathered barrel. Folding her arms over her stomach, she slipped her hands into the sleeves of her coarse brown habit and shook her head. "Such a thing is like trying to turn raisins back into grapes."

"There is no other way, Sister." The words were hard for Zafiro to speak. Her heart pounded frantically, her mouth was dry, and breathing seemed all but impossible.

She hadn't felt the horrible dread in years. But the fear was upon her now, a deep, paralyzing apprehension that never failed to alert her to danger. "Something is going to happen, I tell you. Something very bad. I do not know when it will happen, but I have had the feeling for over a week and it grows stronger."

"But perhaps it is not Luis, *niña*," Sister Carmelita cooed, reaching out to smooth Zafiro's long black hair. "Perhaps—"

"H-he pr-promised he would find me, Sister."

"Oh, Zafiro," the nun murmured, shaken by Zafiro's fear-induced stutter.

"He swore. Luis did. Swore that he would find me no matter how long it took. And he is a man who will stop at nothing to get what he wants."

Sister Carmelita didn't answer. She could only dwell on the sheer horror of Luis's crimes, most of which she and the nuns learned about through tales brought to them by the weary travelers who stopped at the convent for shelter and what little food the sister house could provide. Luis and his gang had killed scores of people, some of them innocent children.

"Sister?" Zafiro pressed. "You know that I am right, don't you?"

Silent prayers for Zafiro's safety threading through her mind, Sister Carmelita looked up at the beautiful young woman. "I am sorry that I could not bring more food to you, Zafiro," she hedged. "Things are very difficult for everyone. Usually the villagers have many things to share, but this year has been hard."

Hard, Zafiro thought. *Impossible* was a more suitable word. "Yes, I know, Sister. But you know we thank you very much for what you and the nuns do for us."

"Yes, and—"

"But we were talking about Luis, Sister."

Realizing Zafiro was not going to forget the subject, Sister Carmelita gave a resigned nod. "Many years have passed since he swore to find you." She tried to comfort Zafiro. "You were only a child then, and he has not found you in all that time, not even with the help of his men. It is possible that he has forgotten or given up—"

"Forgotten how many times I sensed danger before it arrived to harm us?" Zafiro shook her head. "Sister, you do not know how many times I knew when to tell Grandfather to move us before trouble found us. I still do not understand this instinct that I have that tells me when danger is approaching, but it has never been wrong. Now Luis has his own gang. With the help of the devil himself he and his men have managed to escape every attempt to catch them. But their luck cannot last forever, and that is why Luis will not stop looking for me. With my gift, with the strange sense that I have for seeing a dangerous situation before it . . ."

She broke off, frustrated by her inability to make herself clear to the nun. "Listen to me, Sister. Luis has not given up trying to find me. Tomorrow, next week, next month . . . I do not know when he will come, but somehow, some way, Luis will find where I hide because he and his gang *need* me."

Brushing her hair out of her eyes, Zafiro walked a few feet away from the nun and gazed at the thick pine and oak forest that surrounded La Escondida, the hideaway home her grandfather, Ciro, had built to safeguard his gang of aging outlaws. To conceal them from the law, for they all were still wanted for their crimes of the past.

But La Escondida also sheltered *her*. From Luis. Her cousin was an evil that haunted her dreams at night and her thoughts during the day.

Zafiro bowed her head and caressed the large sapphire that hung between her breasts. If only her beloved grandfather were still here. He'd know what to do. But Ciro had died two years ago. Jaime, her father, was gone too, struck down by Luis's bullets when Zafiro had been but a little girl.

Now she was left alone with the remaining members of the Quintana Gang, with the two elderly women, Tia and Azucar, and with Ciro's final whispered instructions:

"They have no one but you now, *chiquita*. You will be strong. Strong and bold as the Sierras themselves."

His words clinging to her thoughts, Zafiro raised her head and looked up. Beyond the woods rose the majestic Sierra Madres, and the sight of the beautiful mountains eased her agitation.

How she loved the Sierras. Their towering snow-capped peaks. The steep slopes of their edges, and the multitude of cool, clean streams that flowed through the deep canyons and rocky valleys.

The hard, unyielding Sierras had endured through centuries. As Ciro had instructed her, she would be like these mountains. Nothing would wear down her resolve.

She turned toward Sister Carmelita again. "To teach old men skills they have forgotten, Sister," she began, "it will not be easy. But I am not a soft nut."

"A soft nut," Sister Carmelita repeated. "That is another of the American expressions you like so much?"

"Yes." A soft nut, Zafiro thought. That didn't sound right. "A nut that cannot be smashed? I am a hard nut? How does it go, Sister?"

The sister shrugged.

So did Zafiro. "It does not matter. What I mean is that no one will crack me. Especially now, when we are in such danger."

Sister Carmelita didn't miss the fire of determination that flared into Zafiro's startling blue eyes. She was a stubborn one, Zafiro Maria Quintana.

But tenacity would not transform three bumbling grandsires into proficient, able-bodied men. "You forget one important thing, Zafiro. To teach, one must know how to do what one teaches. You know nothing about guns and shooting. Ciro did not allow you to handle the weapons. Perhaps that was a mistake, but what matters now is that you cannot teach your men something you have never done."

Zafiro realized the nun had a valid point, but refused to admit defeat before she'd even begun. "What I meant to say is . . . is that I will *help* them remember their skills. I will not stop or rest until I have succeeded. You know the saying: I will burn oil at midnight until they are the men they used to be."

"Look at them, Zafiro," Sister Carmelita demanded, popping up from her seat on the barrel. "There. By the fence Maclovio is staggering along."

Zafiro turned and saw Maclovio. Her eyes narrowed with exasperation. "Another bottle. I just took one away from him this morning, and now he has another!"

Weaving alongside the broken fence, Maclovio raised his bottle toward Zafiro, smiled, and then drank deeply. At age sixty-eight he was the youngest of the Quintana Gang, and there had been a time in his life when his proficiency with horses had been unmatched. Indeed, he'd put on numerous exhibitions through the years, performing his astonishing equestrian tricks in front of crowds. The shows brought in hefty sums of money, none of which Maclovio had ever kept.

All of which he'd given away to orphanages, missions, or other worthy charities.

Now Maclovio was a drunk. Most of the time he was a fun-loving, good-natured drunk, but sometimes liquor made him mean. Testimony to that were the holes he'd kicked in the sides of the barn, all the broken fences, and the hanging door he'd tried to pull off the woodshed. Zafiro had nearly torn the mountains apart searching for the contraption he'd fashioned to make his liquor, but she'd never found it.

She hated that he drank, for although the years were

certainly catching up with him, he remained big and strong for his age. There were many heavy chores around La Escondida that he could perform. Drunk as he always was, however, his size and strength did Zafiro no good at all.

"He is not looking where he is going," Sister Carmelita said. "The tree—"

"Maclovio, the tree!" Zafiro shouted. "The tree!"

Maclovio walked straight into the thick trunk of the oak. His head fell back over his shoulders; his bottle slipped from his hand. A moment later he crashed to the ground, flat on his back, rendered completely unconscious.

Zafiro sighed. "It is just as well, Sister. If the tree had not knocked him out, the liquor would have."

Sister Carmelita nodded. "He spends more than half his time in a senseless state. And Pedro spends the same amount of time on his net. Look at him there, *niña*."

Zafiro glanced at Pedro, who sat on his large rock with his knotted rope net spread out in front of him. A string of keys dangling around his scrawny neck, he was busy adding and tying more rope to the net.

Another sigh escaped Zafiro as she continued to watch him work on the net. He claimed he had lost the other one. The first one that had hauled in hundreds of fish.

The one Jesus had told him to throw over the side of the boat.

Pedro believed he was Saint Peter the Apostle. The keys he wore were the keys to heaven. His rock was the same that Jesus had sworn to build His church upon. And if ever Pedro heard a cock crow three times, he dissolved into tears that only hours of prayer could stem.

Sweet Pedro loved to preach. To tell Bible stories. A pity he always got the sacred tales so mixed up.

He was seventy-seven now, the oldest of the Quintana Gang. Once upon a time his expertise with weapons had been the stuff of legends. But the hands that had once handled guns with such precision now tied and knotted rope into a net that was already almost too heavy to lift.

"And then there is Lorenzo," Sister Carmelita said, pointing to the third member of the Quintana Gang as he exited the cabin and walked across the well-swept yard.

"Yes, and then there is Lorenzo," Zafiro echoed, smiling as he sauntered toward her with a ginger-colored chicken in his thin arms.

Lorenzo was seventy-three. In his prime, a lock or safe didn't exist that he couldn't open. Claiming he could hear soundless clicks within catches, bolts, and other sorts of metal fasteners, he could unlock whatever device the gang needed open.

But tiny sounds within locks were not all his sharp ears heard.

The years fell away, and Zafiro remembered all the times she'd bared her soul to Lorenzo while she was growing up. After her father's death. Sometimes she'd sat by the campfire with him while the rest of the gang slept. She'd taken long strolls and gone fishing with him. During those times he hadn't only heard her speak to him with his ears, he'd listened with his heart.

He couldn't listen anymore. Couldn't be her confidant ever again.

Because Lorenzo was deaf.

He slept almost constantly now, drifting into slumber quickly and without caring where he happened to be at the time. And when he awakened it was as though he hadn't slept at all. Indeed, he immediately continued whatever conversation he'd been having before falling asleep.

"You took your nap, Lorenzo?" Zafiro shouted at him when he neared her.

"Lap?" He returned her tender smile with a toothless one of his own. "Yes, you used to sit on my lap, Zafiro, but you are too big to sit there now."

"*Nap!*" Zafiro shouted again, her lips almost touching his hairy ear. "I asked if you had taken your—"

She stopped trying to talk to him. What was the use? Lorenzo never heard anything correctly, no matter how loudly one shouted.

"I have been napping," Lorenzo said. Wiping the remains of sleep from his eyes, he slowly sat down on the ground and leaned against the barrel. "Jengibre was bothering Tia, so I brought her outside with me." Gently, he caressed the hen called Jengibre. "Tia is making tortillas, and Azucar is mending a rip in one of her dresses."

Tia and Azucar, Zafiro thought, her gaze rising to the window of the room the two women shared in the cabin. Precious Tia had done all the cooking and doctoring for the gang while they'd still been in the outlaw business, and declining in years though she was, her culinary and medical skills hadn't diminished. She was seventy-one now, but, provided she had enough food and other supplies, she continued to keep everyone at La Escondida well-fed and healthy.

"I do not know what I would do without you, Tia," Zafiro whispered. "If only . . . if only . . ."

If only Tia could accept the fact that her son was dead, she finished silently, compassion for the woman sweeping through her. Tia had lost her little Francisco to cholera several years before she'd joined the Quintana Gang, but nothing or no one could convince the grieving woman that he was gone.

Indeed, she "saw" Francisco in every man she met.

With the exceptions of Maclovio, Lorenzo, and Pedro, no man was safe from her unfulfilled desire to mother.

And dear, dear Azucar. "Oh, Azucar," Zafiro murmured, another wave of tenderness filling her heart as she contemplated Azucar.

The woman had seen eighty-two years come and go and had spent a little over twenty of those years as a highly successful harlot. When Ciro had met her, however, age had already stolen her beauty and she'd been but a destitute old woman with an empty belly and a bag full of scanty crimson gowns. Ciro's big heart had gone out to her, and the gang had taken care of her ever since.

Special care of her, for Azucar had yet to come to terms with her age. Though her wrinkled skin hung off her limbs in much the same way scraggly moss drooped off thin, dead tree branches, a decrepit woman was not the reflection she saw when she gazed into a mirror.

In Azucar's dark and bleary eyes she was still the young and desirable seductress she'd once been. She continued to wear the scarlet satin gowns that had been her strumpet's garb, and there was nothing she enjoyed more than talking about all the sensual things she would do to the next man who paid for her services.

Through the years Zafiro had learned a great deal about sexual intimacy while listening to Azucar's vivid descriptions of lovemaking. Ciro had never told her a thing about what happened in bed between a man and a woman, and she'd never asked. Who better to learn from than a seasoned lady of the evening?

Yes, indeed, Zafiro mused, her thoughts wandering. When she married she would know exactly what her husband wanted from her on their wedding night. She would know exactly—

Her daydream ended abruptly. *When she married?* Save

Maclovio, Lorenzo, and Pedro, she didn't know a single other man. And since it was quite likely that she would be forced to remain hidden away in these mountains for a good many years to come, the chance that she would ever have a sweetheart, much less a husband, was nonexistent.

"Zafiro?" Sister Carmelita murmured. "Do I see tears in your eyes, my child?"

"Tears?" The very word dried the moisture that had just begun to sparkle in Zafiro's eyes. "I do not have time for weeping, Sister. Did you bring the gun?"

Sister Carmelita slipped her hand into the deep pocket of her habit and withdrew a small pistol. "It belongs to Rudolfo, the farmer who lives near the convent. I promised him I would return it to him. But there is only one bullet in it, Zafiro. Rudolfo, he did not have more to give to me. Poor Rudolfo. He is like many of the other villagers. His livestock have taken sick and died, and his crops do poorly. If I give you this gun you will pray for him?"

Zafiro shut her eyes. *Lord, take care of Rudolfo and us too. Amen.*

She held out her hand, closing her fingers around the gun when Sister Carmelita gave the weapon to her. Staring down at it, she ran her fingers over the cool metal.

"You do not need more than one bullet anyway," Sister Carmelita said. "Your men will not remember how to shoot. Do not do this to yourself, my child. Lorenzo, help me dissuade her from trying to do the impossible."

In answer Lorenzo let out a snore so loud that it startled the birds from the trees.

Holding her head so high that her chin nearly pointed to the sky, Zafiro marched away from the edge of the woods and placed the gun in Pedro's bony lap. "Where is your faith, Sister Carmelita? You are too doubting."

"Yes," Pedro agreed, his gnarled hands caressing the pistol. "You are too doubting, Sister. Just like my good friend Matthew."

"Thomas," Sister Carmelita corrected him. "It was Thomas who doubted."

"Thomas is a tax collector," Pedro argued. "He doubts nothing. Do you know I once saw Thomas bring a dead man back to life? Cain was the dead man's name, and he had a brother called Noah. Noah lived in the Garden of Eden with Moses, who spent most of his time turning water into wine. Moses was—"

"Pedro, please," Zafiro pleaded. "Enough stories. Now, show Sister Carmelita what you remember. Shoot the gun."

Pedro lifted the pistol from his lap and raised his arms. Squinting, he pulled the trigger. The resulting explosion knocked him off his rock, and the bullet he fired ricocheted off a tree trunk, shot a hole through the top of Sister Carmelita's wimple, and finally smashed into the chicken coop. The wooden birdhouse toppled over, its gate swinging wide open. Squawking and flapping their wings, all nine hens raced around the yard.

"*Santa María*, my chickens!" Knowing the barnyard fowl would disappear into the mountain coves if she didn't catch them, Zafiro scurried after them, Pedro doing his best to help her.

With as much dignity as a nun with a bullet hole in her wimple could muster, Sister Carmelita plucked the pistol off the ground and headed toward the hidden exit from La Escondida. "Help her, Lord," she prayed as she slipped through the secret opening within the rocks and thick brush. "You are the only one who can give her what she needs. A miracle."

A week after her talk with Sister Carmelita, Zafiro felt the strong need to visit the convent. Her worries about Luis had increased tenfold, and she knew that while a brief call on the nuns would not completely alleviate her fears, being with the holy women would at least help her to relax for a short time.

After warning her charges to behave while she was gone, she slipped out of La Escondida. As she turned to make sure the hidden entrance to the hideaway was secure, she noticed her pet cougar, Mariposa, stretched out upon a large, flat rock. The great cat gleamed in the sunlight, and she looked more like a gold statue than a living creature.

"Take care of La Escondida while I am with the sisters, Mariposa," Zafiro told the lion. Smiling, she blew a kiss to her pet, then made her way down the craggy slopes. The trip to the convent was much easier and faster upon Rayo's back, but the burro suffered a bruised hoof.

If only Coraje would let her mount him, Zafiro mused as she finally left the pebble-strewn ground and walked into the cool shade of an evergreen forest. But the coal-black stallion had never let anyone but Ciro near him. Now, after two years without being ridden, he was wilder than he'd ever been.

"Five elderly people, a hurt burro, the meanest stallion in Mexico, two lost chickens, and Luis searching the country for you, Zafiro," she told herself aloud, swiping at low-hanging tree branches as she trudged through the pine-scented glade. "And do not forget that there is no meat, that the fences are falling down, that the roof leaks, or that every rabbit in the mountains thinks you have planted the vegetable garden especially for him!"

The burden of worry she bore became heavier with each step she took, and by the time the old Spanish mission came into her view, she felt as though she carried on her shoulders one of the Sierras themselves.

She stopped at the edge of the woods, her gaze missing nothing as she surveyed the area surrounding the convent. She truly enjoyed being with the good sisters, but each time she visited she took the chance of being seen by someone other than the nuns.

No one could know where she was.

Finally convinced she was alone, she made her way to the convent door and rang the bell that hung suspended from a rusty hook in the stone wall. The scent of cut grass caught her attention while she waited for one of the nuns to come to the door. She also recognized the smell of freshly dug soil and decided the nuns had been toiling in their flower gardens this morning.

Other things began to capture her notice as well. The huge statue of the Blessed Mother stood upright in the flower bed. Only last week the granite sculpture had been lying on the ground, too heavy for the nuns to lift. The dead tree was gone too. The one that had been killed by lightning several years ago. Only a smoothly cut stump remained.

And the nuns' quaint little pond was prettier than she'd ever seen it. The good sisters loved to sit on the stone benches around the pond, basking in the sun and watching turtles poke their heads out of the shining water. Sometimes they recited the rosary there too.

Zafiro had made a mental note to help them clean the pond, for the winter months had left the water slimy and filled with leaves and sticks. She was also going to try to mend the crumbling stones that encircled the pond.

The stones she saw now, however, were new, and there wasn't a leaf or twig to be seen upon the glassy surface of the water.

Baffled, Zafiro turned to ring the bell again.

The door swung open abruptly. "Zafiro!" Sister Pilar exclaimed. "How good it is to see you, my child."

The nun's warm welcome drew Zafiro into the foyer and straight into Sister Pilar's arms. Hugging the nun tightly, she closed her eyes and breathed deeply of all the aromas of the convent.

The perfume of lemon oil swirled around her, as did the hot smell of burning candles and wood smoke. She smelled roses, and the soap Sister Pilar used to wash her habit, and apple cake too, which was Mother Manuela's favorite dessert.

The familiar scents were so comforting. The whole convent was, and Zafiro visited as often as she could. To find a bit of serenity. And to hear whatever news about the outside world that the nuns learned from travelers who stopped at the holy house for rest and a bit of food.

"We've been expecting you, Zafiro," Sister Pilar said.

"You have?" Zafiro stepped out of the nun's embrace. "How did you know I was coming?"

Smiling, Sister Pilar closed the door and headed toward the staircase, which shone with the lemon oil rubbed into the wood. "Sister Carmelita told us about your plans to turn your men back into skilled fighters. We knew that it would not be long before you came to seek the peace you claim to find here in the convent with us."

Zafiro was about to argue, but realized the futility of quarreling against the truth. Smiling at how well the nuns knew her, she followed Sister Pilar up the staircase and into a small room on the second floor of the convent.

There she hugged Sister Carmelita, Sister Inez, and Mother Manuela, who immediately offered her a glass of cool water and a slice of warm apple cake.

"Where are all the other sisters?" Zafiro asked, her mouth full of the savory cake, which was a rare treat seeing as how food was in such short supply.

"Some have gone to the village to collect a few supplies that the villagers have for us, some are starting supper, and others are at prayer," Sister Inez replied. "How are the men? They have practiced their skills?"

"Maclovio threw a knife and hit the exact center of the front door."

"Oh, that is good!" Sister Pilar clapped.

Zafiro shook her head. "He was aiming for the weather vane on the roof."

"Oh, that is bad," Sister Pilar answered.

"He was drunk, of course," Zafiro continued, "and then he got mad. After yanking the knife out of the door, he tore several planks out of the porch and smashed one of the cabin steps. Finally, he passed out in the barn and slept with the cow."

The good sisters all made the sign of the cross, silently praying for Maclovio's deliverance from the evils of alcohol.

"Your feeling of danger is still with you, my child?" Mother Manuela asked, taking a seat in one of the ornately carved chairs grouped around a small table.

"It is, Reverend Mother. I try not to think about it, but it is always there. Like a sore that will not heal." Fear rippling through her, Zafiro rubbed her upper arms vigorously, struggling in vain to tame her troubled emotions.

"I am so afraid of the unknown thing that is going to happen that I cannot sleep at night."

"*Pobrecita,*" Sister Carmelita murmured. "Poor little girl." She walked across the room and retrieved a small statue of St. Michael the Archangel from the mantel. Above the mantel hung an ancient sword that she and the other sisters believed was used in the Crusades, when Christian powers battled the Muslims to win the Holy Lands. Sister Carmelita reached up and touched the shining blade reverently before turning back to Zafiro. "Come and sit with us, Zafiro," she said, placing the statue of St. Michael on the table. "Together we will pray for the answer to your troubles."

Zafiro licked a crumb of cake from the corner of her mouth. "I have already prayed, Sister. I have prayed so often and so hard that I am sure God hides when He sees and hears me coming. I have no doubt that He will send me help, but He is sweetly taking His own time."

"Sweetly taking His own . . ." Sister Pilar repeated. "I think it is something about His own sweet time."

"However you say it, He is in no hurry."

"One cannot hurry heaven, my child," the Reverend Mother advised, then bowed her head.

Zafiro listened to the sisters' whispered pleas for a moment before she began to pace around the room. Her bootheels thudded upon the gleaming wooden floor, and the sound made her think of a drumroll, which, in turn, only increased her nervousness.

After a short while of ambling from corner to corner, she stopped by one of the barred windows, gazed out at the beautiful mountains, and saw a huge flock of white birds skimming through the sky. Sunlight kissed their feathers, making them iridescent. Zafiro thought they looked like a silver cloud passing over the mountain peaks.

"A silver cloud," she murmured, her breath fogging the windowpane. What was that American expression about a silver cloud? "Problems are lined with silver clouds," she guessed softly. "For every trouble in a cloud, there is a line of silver."

Well, however the saying went, it meant that for every difficulty there existed a solution.

If only she could find the silver cloud to her difficulties, she mused, lowering her gaze and peering down at the garden below. There she saw rows of newly planted vegetables and a mass of well-shaped rosebushes. The marble statues of various saints sparkled in the sunshine as if just washed, and the white pebble walkway that meandered through the garden was clear of all litter. A huge stack of freshly cut firewood lay piled neatly against the stone wall of the stable, and the sisters' little swinging gate shone with what could only be a new coat of paint.

Just as she'd noticed in the front yard of the convent, everything Zafiro saw in the garden was clean, tidy, and well done.

In the next moment she learned the reason why.

A man walked out from beneath a canopy of oak trees, his arms full of logs. He was shirtless, a black kerchief knotted around his neck, his tight brown breeches hugging every masculine curve he possessed.

Unnerved by his sudden appearance, Zafiro gasped softly and moved away from the window. A man, she thought, lifting her hand to hold her sapphire. How many years had passed since she'd seen a man younger than fifty?

A man, she thought again. A man with muscle and energy.

And youth.

Intense curiosity urged her back to the window. She stood there spellbound, her eyes and her mind memorizing every magnificent part of the man below.

His long, thick hair flowed over his broad shoulders like a river of burnished gold. Hard muscle coiled through his sleek back, bulged in his arms and thighs, and rippled down his flat belly.

He was tall. Taller even than her grandfather had been, and she imagined that if she stood in front of him the top of her head would not even reach his chin.

Unfamiliar yearnings caught her unaware as she watched him throw the logs to the ground, pick up an ax, and begin to split the wood. His tanned skin gleamed with the sweat of his labor; his back and arms swelled with strength. She wanted to feel those hard muscles beneath her palm, to know what his hair felt like slipping between her fingers. She longed to hear the sound of his voice, see his smile, and learn the color of his eyes.

She felt drawn to him in a way she couldn't understand.

"Zafiro?" Sister Carmelita called softly. "Didn't you hear me, *niña*? I asked what you are looking at in the garden below."

"What?" Only vaguely did Zafiro hear the nun speak to her. The man in the courtyard below absorbed too much of her attention for her to concentrate on much more than him.

Still watching him, she felt an almost uncontrollable urge to join him below. "Who is that man down there?"

Sister Carmelita sent a small, knowing smile to the other sisters. "Ah, so you noticed him, did you?"

Mother Manuela rose from her chair, crossed to the window, and looked down. Zafiro, she mused, had not only noticed the man, she'd practically consumed him with her staring.

The Reverend Mother and the other nuns had tried to impress upon Zafiro the fact that maidens were supposed to be shy and reserved, but the strong-willed girl preferred Azucar's advice to theirs. Yet one couldn't blame Zafiro. After all, romantic stories were much more appealing to a young girl's fancy than stern lectures about proper etiquette. And Zafiro had spent a great deal more time with the old lady of the evening than she had with the holy sisters.

"Sawyer came to us five days ago, weary and lost," Mother Manuela explained. "He said he would stay only long enough to rest. In exchange for a room and food he has made numerous repairs, cleaned our pond, and has planted a new garden of vegetables that we pray will thrive."

"And he built a new lamp table for my cell," Sister Inez added. "It does not wobble like the old one."

"He has done a great many things for us," the Reverend Mother said. "In return we have prayed very hard for him."

"Why?" Zafiro asked quickly. "Is he in trouble?"

Mother Manuela looked down at Sawyer again. "When I said that he came to us lost, I meant that he has lost his memories. He remembers nothing but his name —Sawyer Donovan."

"He arrived on a mule he calls Mister and had with him only a satchel of clothing and a small, locked trunk," Sister Pilar elaborated. "And there is something about the trunk . . . He does not seem to like touching it or looking at it."

"What is in the trunk?" Zafiro asked.

Sister Pilar held up her hands in a gesture of ignorance. "We do not know. There is much about him we do not know. He could not tell us where he was from or what he did for a living. All he said was that he had been traveling for a long time. Wandering, with no destination in mind, no plans . . . not even a reason why he was wandering."

"But he is a nice man?" Zafiro queried.

"He is very nice to us," Sister Carmelita answered. "His quick wit and gentle teasing have made us laugh many times."

"But other times there is pain in his eyes," Mother Manuela said softly. "A sorrow he carries in his very soul. After a while the pain passes and he is again the man who makes us smile, but his struggle to force his pain away is a sad thing to see. And I think it must be very frustrating for him to know he has lost a whole lifetime. It is my suspicion that whatever terrible thing caused such torment inside him also took away his memory. He does not remember because to remember would be to relive the terrible thing."

"He remembers nothing at all?" Zafiro asked.

"He has retained many skills," Mother Manuela replied. "It is obvious that he has had a great deal of experience with plants, so perhaps he is a farmer. But he builds as well, so it could be that he has also done carpentry work."

"And he is good with the few animals we have left," Sister Pilar added. "So we know that he has been around livestock. But it is so sad that we do not know more about him. If we did, we could help him."

Compassion for the golden-haired stranger passed over Zafiro like the caress of an unseen hand. What must it be like to have no memories? If Sawyer had a family he could not remember their faces or their love. He could not reminisce about special things that had happened to him, happy things that made him laugh and feel good.

"Stay and have supper with us, Zafiro," Sister Carmelita said. "We have only some bread and a bit of potato soup, but we would love to share our meal with you. And if you stay you can meet and talk to Sawyer."

"Meet him." Zafiro wondered what it would be like to be near the strong, handsome man named Sawyer. "I . . ."

In the next instant, hard, cold reality erased every tender and timid emotion she'd felt. "*Meet him?* Do you forget that I am in hiding? I can meet no one!" She scurried away from the window, suddenly angry with herself.

What was the matter with her? How could she have forgotten to take care? On the contrary, she'd stood right in front of the window for a full five minutes in plain view.

"What if this Sawyer Donovan is one of Luis's men?" she asked. "Or what if he—"

"Zafiro," the Reverend Mother said, reaching out for the trembling girl. "He—"

"He has lost his memory," Zafiro pointed out. "Before he lost it he might have been a cruel man. Maybe he has only forgotten how to be evil. He could find his memories again at any time! When they come back to him, he could be a man who knows Luis. Or a lawman who knows my men are still wanted. I will not take any chances with this Sawyer! He—"

She stopped speaking as the familiar, sickening dread came over her, drying her mouth, pounding through her heart, and causing her to struggle for her next breath. Her stomach coiling into knots, she held her belly as if she would soon double over with pain. "Sis-sisters, he—

Santa Maria, he is the danger that I have known would come! He *must* be!"

"You do not know that, Zafiro!" Sister Carmelita exclaimed, hating the look of utter terror in the girl's eyes. "You cannot be certain—"

Before the sister could finish, Zafiro raced out of the room and sped down the dim hall. She took two steps at a time while descending the staircase and quickly crossed through the foyer. Her heartbeat thundering in her ears, she snatched the door open . . .

And ran straight into a solid mass of muscle.

Gold eyes like a lion's seemed to penetrate her very soul. The man was huge, his form radiating such awesome power that Zafiro felt the insane urge to bow before him.

She backed away from him.

He stepped toward her, then stopped, his stance wide, his shadow falling over her, making her feel tiny, vulnerable.

For a moment terror immobilized her, but in the next second the same terror forced her out of the convent. She fled through the yard and disappeared into the cool darkness of the evergreen glade.

The man with no memory followed. She could hear his footsteps crashing through the brittle pine needles. Imagining his piercing gaze stabbing through her back, she could almost feel his might overcome her.

Santa Maria, he was stalking her through the woods just like the lion she'd compared him to.

Her panic intensified, streaming through her body like liquid strength. She ran faster, flying through the forest as if carried by the angels themselves. Finally the edge of the woods came into view, the sunlight a beacon of hope for escape. Lunging forward, she fairly threw herself toward the pebbled ground around the base of the foothills.

But she didn't make it.

Large, powerful hands suddenly encircled her waist, pulling her back into the shadows . . . plucking her off the ground as if she weighed no more than a baby's sigh.

And at that moment, Zafiro knew in her heart that her leonine captor—whoever he was—would change her life forever.

two

The girl's scream echoed through the hills, sounding like a thousand women being tortured by a slew of savages. Sawyer clamped his hand over her mouth, still holding her tightly with his other arm, still wondering what she'd been doing sneaking around in the convent.

Something hard pressed into his wrist, something that seemed to be attached to the girl's tattered blouse. Glancing down, he saw an extraordinarily large sapphire that hung from a solid gold chain.

A magnificent jewel and a girl dressed in rags?

Sawyer's suspicions deepened. She'd fled the convent like a thief who'd been caught, he recalled. Indeed, surprise and terror had nearly dropped her to her knees when she'd run into him.

"Stop that screaming," he hissed into her ear, "and tell me what you were doing in the convent. Did you steal that sapphire from the sisters?"

She bit into his palm. His own shout mingled with her muffled cries. "Dammit, woman!" Yanking his hand away from her mouth, he continued the difficult task of holding on to her. Remarkably agile and strong, her body twisted in his arms like a dozen angry snakes.

He turned her so that she faced him and winced when she began to slap at his face. Quickly, he caught her wrists and frowned down at her . . .

And went totally rigid. He hadn't seen her clearly in the convent.

He did now.

Her beauty was almost unreal. For one long moment he stood there mesmerized by the snapping fire in her clear blue eyes, the blush of fury on her high cheekbones, the taut pout on her full, pink lips, and the swift rise and fall of her breasts.

He knew nothing but his name; he had no idea who he was, where he was from, or what he'd done in his lifetime. But one thing he did know: the girl who stood before him now, glaring at him with all the fear and hatred he imagined existed in the world, was the most incredibly gorgeous female he'd ever seen.

Only slightly aware of his own actions, he let go of her wrist and reached out to touch her hair.

And Zafiro seized that moment. With all the power her body held, she jerked her other arm from his hold, spun on her heel, and tore up the side of the hill. She fell twice, but made steady progress. Soon the entrance to La Escondida was within her sight.

So was Mariposa. Blending in with her untamed surroundings, the tawny cat crouched amidst a thick tangle of brush, her gold eyes narrowing, her long, sleek tail swishing through the dusty air.

Zafiro climbed past the animal and slipped quickly and easily through the passage that was concealed by boulders, scrub, and a smattering of scraggly trees. She could hear Sawyer behind her, but knew his climb had been more difficult than hers. Not only did she know the exact path to take on the side of the hill, but her ascent had created an obstacle course of sliding rocks and sticks for him to maneuver around.

Hidden by the boulders and brush, she pushed at the wide, heavy wooden doors that led into the hideaway, every part of her relieved to hear the familiar squeaks as the portals swung slowly open.

But just as the squeaking sounds faded away and she crawled inside the rocky walls of La Escondida, another noise filled the mountain air. And then another and another.

A low growl. A gruesome snarl.

A terrible shout.

Sawyer had just met Mariposa.

— ·—■◆■—· —

It took all three men to carry Sawyer into the cabin. They dropped him in the yard three times, banged his head against the front door, and ended up dragging him up the stairs. By the time they finally laid him down on the bed Tia had prepared on the second floor of the house, they were completely out of breath.

And Sawyer was bleeding profusely.

"Where is Zafiro?" Pedro asked, looking all around the small, tidy room.

"She and Tia are finding bandages for his wounds." Staring down at the bleeding man, Maclovio withdrew a flask from inside his shirt and took a long, deep swallow of his homemade whiskey. "Sawyer. That is what Zafiro called this giant. How does she know what he is named?"

"Maimed?" Lorenzo said. "Yes, he is maimed." He sat

down in a chair in front of the window. "He is also big. There is only one man I can remember who was the size of this man. *El Maestro de la Noche.*"

"The Night Master," Maclovio translated. Old memories crept through his mind. "Lorenzo, do you recall the time he stole our gold?"

Lorenzo's loud snoring was Maclovio's answer.

"Lorenzo is right," Pedro said, wiping his sweaty brow. "This man, he is made of nothing but muscle. He is strong as Abraham, and even has the long hair. If we cut his hair he would lose his strength."

Maclovio gulped down more liquor and dried his mouth with his shirt sleeve. "That was not Abraham. It was Samson."

Pedro laid his hand on Maclovio's shoulder. "You are wrong," he said softly and smiled. "I am Peter the Apostle, and I know the Bible better than—"

"You are both wrong," Tia announced as she waddled into the room carrying rolls of cloth strips. Bending, she pressed a tender kiss to the unconscious man's cheek, several of her tears splashing on his face. "He is Francisco. My dear little boy. I have finally found him again."

"He is not a little boy, Tia." Her scarlet gown rustling, Azucar hobbled out of the hall and into the room. Looking down at the man on the mattress, she smiled and placed her gnarled hand over the bulge between his legs. "Leave us," she demanded of all the people gathered around the bed. "What this man has come to me for is not something I will do in front of so many eyes. He is a stallion and will probably want me for the whole night. That is fine with me. As long as he can pay, I can perform."

Tia snatched Azucar's bony hand away. "He is not your lover, Azucar! He is my Francisco, and I—"

"He is like Abraham," Pedro stated once more. "Strong like Abra—"

"But the Night Master is dead now," Lorenzo stated sleepily, just awakening from his moments-long nap. "There never was and there never will be another bandit like him." In a reverent gesture he laid his hand over his heart and bowed his head.

"May God the Father give eternal rest to Night Master's soul," Pedro murmured. Clasping his hands together, he began to pray silently.

"What are you doing?" Zafiro asked as she stepped into the room, Lorenzo and Pedro's solemn demeanors slowing her gait. Instantly, she looked at Sawyer, who lay stretched out on the bed . . . like a corpse. "He . . . he died?" she whispered. "*Santa Maria*, I did not realize that Mariposa's attack was . . . She killed him? But Tia, you said he would heal! You said—"

"He is not dead, *chiquita*," Tia quickly reassured her. "The men, they are mourning the death of Night Master."

"Night Master?" Zafiro stared at her men, her emotions racing from confusion to disbelief and finally to anger. "There is a dangerous man here in La Escondida, and you mourn a thief who has been in his grave for months?"

"Brave?" Lorenzo rose from his chair. "Yes, Night Master was brave. He—"

"If only I could find Night Master's grave," Pedro murmured. "With prayer I am sure I could bring him back to life."

"Bring him back to his wife?" Lorenzo said. "No, I do not think Night Master was married."

Zafiro pushed past the men and handed the medical supplies to Tia—thread and needles, a small pot of salve, and more bandages. "I have told all of you about the terrible feeling of dread that has been with me," she said, her voice so shaky that it made her cough. "C-can you not understand that the fear has come because of this man, Sawyer Donovan?"

Through his drunken daze Maclovio managed to note her genuine terror. He took hold of her trembling hand. "Then why did you have us bring him inside La Escondida? We could have taken him back to the convent. We could take him back right now."

Zafiro looked up into Maclovio's bleary brown eyes. "You can hardly stand up, much less take this Sawyer Donovan back down the mountain! Besides, he has already seen the way into La Escondida. There is no use in taking him back to the nuns."

Maclovio nodded. "We could have left him outside to die."

"Die." Zafiro spoke the word so quietly that she could not hear herself speak. Afraid as she was of the stranger in her house, she could not bear the thought of his death.

Clasping her sapphire, she squeezed it as if she could crush it into a handful of blue powder. "I led him straight to La Escondida. I did not think, and I am very sorry. But I was so afraid! My only thought was to run from him. Now he has seen the secret entrance and knows where we hide. To others, finding La Escondida is like trying to find hay in a needle stack, but I brought this Sawyer Donovan straight to us!"

"I will smash his face," Maclovio declared, pushing up his sleeves and balling his fists. "I will—"

"What is hay in a needle stack?" Pedro asked, rubbing his chin.

Zafiro realized she'd mangled the expression. "I mean that finding La Escondida is almost impossible. But that does not matter anyway. What is important is that this

Sawyer Donovan is the worst thing that has happened to us. Maclovio, stop it!" she shouted when Maclovio pulled back his arm and prepared to deliver a punch to Sawyer's face.

"I do not know a Sawyer Donovan," Tia said. "But I tell you that you do not need to be afraid of my dear Francisco. We must hurry now, *chiquita*. His wounds will fester if we do not clean and stitch them."

"I asked to be alone with this man," Azucar repeated, unfastening her scarlet gown. "It is the pleasure he will find in my arms that will heal him of his wounds."

Quickly, Zafiro stayed Azucar's hand, trying to keep the woman from taking off her clothes. She then grabbed Maclovio's arm as he again prepared to hit Sawyer. "Listen to me, all of you! The only way we will be safe with Sawyer here is if we do not say anything about who we are. He could be a lawman. A bounty hunter who would not think twice about turning you in to the law to be hanged. He could even be an outlaw who knows Luis, or—"

"When he wakes up we will ask him who he is," Maclovio said. "Then I will smash his face and—"

"He does not know who he is," Zafiro replied, still trying to keep Azucar from taking off her gown. "The nuns say he has lost his memory. But he could remember tomorrow, the day after, next week. . . . When and if he remembers, we will be in even more danger. So I do not think I have to explain how important it is that he learn nothing about us. Now," she said, turning Azucar toward the door, "out. Except for Tia, all of you out."

Grumbling and shuffling their feet, Azucar and the men headed toward the dim hall.

Before he shut the door, however, Maclovio stepped back into the room. "But if he knows we are the

Quintana Gang and that we are well-known and feared in two lands, he will be too afraid to—"

"Afraid?" Zafiro shouted the word. "Afraid of what? Of your bottle? Of Lorenzo's naps? Of Pedro's preaching? You will say nothing, do you hear me, Maclovio?"

He drew himself up to his full height, lost his balance again, and began to totter. "I heard you. I am not the deaf one." With that, Maclovio shut the door.

Satisfied, Zafiro turned back to the bed and hurried to arrange the medical supplies on a small table. "I found this whiskey under Maclovio's pillow, Tia," she said, withdrawing a brown bottle from the deep pocket in her skirt. "If Sawyer awakens we will have him drink it so he can sleep again."

"My little Francisco cannot have whiskey. He is too young, but it is good that you brought the liquor. Soak the threads and the needles in it."

Zafiro did as bade, grateful that Tia knew so much about doctoring.

"Now, help me strip him, *chiquita*. His leg is bleeding, but he is a big, strong boy, and I cannot take off his clothes by myself."

While Zafiro watched Tia tug off Sawyer's boots and stockings, she pondered the fact that she was going to see him naked in only moments. She'd seen her men bathe in the stream every now and again during the past years, but Sawyer's body was going to look very different from those of her men.

Her eyes wide with curiosity, she reached for the fastenings at the top of his breeches. When the buttons were opened she saw that he wore no undergarments.

Evidence of that was the thick mat of tawny hair at his groin.

Heat melted through her, a warmth that flustered her

thoughts and aroused that odd feeling of yearning again, that same strange desire she'd felt while watching Sawyer from the convent window.

"*Ayudame,*" Tia ordered, pulling at the waistband of the pants. "Help me."

Her hands and fingers quivering, Zafiro assisted Tia with Sawyer's tight breeches, rolling them over his hips, down his thighs, and finally pulling them off altogether.

"Oh, my little Francisco!" Tia exclaimed when she saw a jagged gash on his thigh, an injury much worse than the ones on his upper torso. "Zafiro, wet the cloths and help me clean his wounds!"

Zafiro didn't move. All she could do was stare.

Naked. Sawyer Donovan lay before her completely naked, his massive frame nearly covering the entire mattress.

Hardly aware of her own actions, Zafiro took a step forward, closer to the bed, branding in her mind her first sight of true male splendor.

His whole body was tanned, his skin lighter than hers, of course, but dark for a white man. She wondered if he spent a great deal of time in the sun without clothing. Bathing, perhaps, or maybe just basking.

The thought stirred her emotions further; she felt moisture trickle down between her breasts.

She'd never seen so much muscle. His shoulders, chest, stomach, legs . . . Not even Maclovio—mighty as he'd been years ago— had been as strong as Sawyer.

Filled with awe, she continued to examine him, her gaze drawn to the area beneath his hips, between his thighs, where his . . .

She thought of all the many things Azucar had told her about the sexual intimacy between a man and a woman. Thought about what a man did to a woman when he bedded her. Thought about—

"Zafiro!"

Startled nearly out of her skin, Zafiro turned and wet several white cloths with the water she'd boiled earlier. Tamping down her heated emotions and silently chastising herself for wasting time admiring a man who might be dying before her very eyes, she forced herself to tend to the cut on the right side of Sawyer's torso. When the wound was clean of all dirt Tia began to stitch it closed. Zafiro then moved to bathe the laceration on Sawyer's chest and another on his shoulder.

After that there was only one injury left to clean. As she examined it she realized it would take much longer to heal than the injuries on his torso. The nasty claw slash ripped Sawyer's inner thigh, starting only a few inches above his knee and ending dangerously close to his genitals. To thoroughly nurse the cut she would have to touch him. Handle him *there*.

Dios mío.

"Tia," she murmured. "The wound—it is very near to his . . . his man parts."

"Man parts? Francisco is only a child."

Sawyer was definitely not a child, Zafiro mused, still gazing down at his masculinity. She glanced at his face again. He was asleep and would never know that she'd touched him. Of course, maybe he'd like for her to touch him. Azucar said men liked to be touched.

Not that she cared a bit about doing something he liked. He could be dangerous, after all, and she certainly wasn't going to try to please a man who posed a possible threat to her and her men.

"Zafiro," Tia said, holding her needle poised above the wound she was stitching. "Clean his leg."

Starting above his knee Zafiro began to wash away the blood and grime, the tips of her fingers soon grazing him in the most intimate manner she'd ever touched a man.

And then he groaned.

She raised her gaze to his face and saw a slight frown creasing his forehead. Had he felt her touch him?

She drew her hand away from him. "He feels, Tia."

Deftly, Tia slipped a last stitch into the wound she'd just finished sewing, then tied the thread into a tight knot. "He is asleep."

"It does not matter. He felt where I touched him."

Tia glanced at his face, but saw no evidence that he felt anything at all. "You imagine things, *niña*, because you are tired. He is so asleep that he would not know if Mariposa attacked him again. Go to your room and sleep for a bit."

"I am not tired." In truth Zafiro was weary down to her toes, but she was always careful not to show her exhaustion. Her charges did what they could to help her, and she would not have them feeling guilty that they could not do more. "I am young and strong, and I—"

"Strong, young people become tired too. All morning you worked in the garden, Zafiro, and then you hauled water from the stream. After that I watched you try to build a new house for the chickens. You could not build it, so you went to the convent and ran from my son, who was probably only trying to catch you to ask where I was. Sleep now, and I will awaken you when I am too sleepy to stay here any longer. Someone must always be with my little Francisco because he will soon have fever. When that happens we will have to take turns keeping his body cool with water."

"We will bathe him?" The thought of touching Sawyer again was not at all unpleasant.

"Only you and I can bathe him, Zafiro. Maclovio, drunk as he always is, would drown him. Lorenzo would fall asleep before finishing. Pedro would only pray over him, and Azucar would rape him. You do not mind to help me with him, do you, *chiquita?*"

Zafiro dropped her cloth back into the basin of water. "Someone must help you, Tia," she answered, and feigned a deep sigh. "If I must bathe him, I will bathe him."

With that Zafiro started for the door, but turned to look at Sawyer one last time.

His eyes mere slits, Sawyer watched her, unable to decide which glowed more brightly—her eyes or her incredible sapphire.

He saw her gaze touch each and every part of him, flowing over his body like warm liquid. And he did, indeed, feel touched. By her gaze and by the sensuous thoughts he knew she was thinking.

Sensuous thoughts about *him*.

A slight smile curved his lips before he slipped into unconsciousness once again.

————— ❋ —————

He didn't know how long he'd slept, but the dimness of the room and the cool air that blew in from the window convinced Sawyer that nighttime had fallen. Someone had drawn a white, soap-scented sheet over his bare body. His head ached, and he felt hot. Too hot, and yet he shivered.

Realizing he had fever, he wondered if he would die. Would it make a difference if he did? Was there anyone who would mourn his death?

He didn't know. Couldn't remember.

He closed his eyes, slept again, and dreamed. A hazy image of a big house with frilly white curtains hanging at each sparkling window drifted through his thoughts. Flowers bloomed everywhere. A man and a woman stood on the porch, and children of various ages played in the grassy yard.

It should have been a soothing scene, but it wasn't. Horror strangled him like two iron fists.

He heard himself shout, then forced himself to wake up. His heart thrashing like something about to die, he opened his eyes.

A tiny woman peered down at him. Bright sunlight illuminated her wrinkles and stark white hair, making him realize that it was daytime again. She wore a red gown that hung off her frame like a piece of cloth draped over a stick, and when she smiled he didn't see a single tooth in her mouth.

She was definitely not the beautiful girl he'd chased from the convent. The dark-haired vixen who had helped doctor his wounds.

"I am here, my anxious stallion," the old woman said. "Here to satisfy all your needs."

Before he could understand what the woman meant, he felt her bony hand caress the top of his thigh. The sheet still covered his body, but her caresses agitated him nonetheless.

What the hell was she doing?

He tried to move away from her hand, but the pain of his injuries was too raw. Indeed, he felt as though someone had inserted strips of fire into various places on his body, most especially his thigh. "Stop," he whispered.

"Stop?" she repeated. "But we have not even begun!"

She bent down to him, her mouth pursed, and he realized she was about to kiss him.

God Almighty, the hag was trying to seduce him!

"Azucar!" another woman shouted.

Totally bewildered, Sawyer saw another woman wad-dle into the room. "Out," he heard her say, and then the old, toothless woman hobbled away, muttering what he was sure was a string of profanities.

The plump woman commenced to bathe his face, neck, shoulders, and chest with cool water. The water felt so good on his hot skin that had he possessed the strength, he would have squeezed the woman's gentle hand in gratitude.

"Drink, my son, my precious little boy."

He drank thirstily when she held a cup to his parched lips, all the while wondering why she called him a little boy.

"Enough now, sweet Francisco," she cooed down to him. "Now, see what I have brought you."

Though his vision was blurry, Sawyer saw her place by his side a slingshot, a puppet, a red ball, and a small wooden box. She opened the box and held it up.

"I have saved these things for you, Francisco, because I knew I would find you again." One by one she withdrew each of the box's contents: a few shiny rocks, a tiny pinecone, a rusty pocketknife; a harmonica, some fish hooks, and a piece of yellowed paper with a childishly drawn picture of a horse on it.

Before Sawyer could begin to comprehend the signifi-cance of the articles she showed to him, he felt con-sciousness slipping away once more. The next time he awakened, the room was dark again.

Another night had fallen.

"So Mary stepped out of the mouth of the whale," he heard a man say. "The journey in the whale's belly had been a difficult one for her, especially since she was great with child."

Slowly, Sawyer's vision cleared. The first thing he saw was a ginger-colored chicken sitting on his chest, a hen who appeared to be trying to lay an egg.

Chickens didn't talk. Someone else had spoken about Mary's journey in the whale's belly.

Sawyer looked up. A man came into his view. His long white hair, beard, and several keys hung over his sunken chest, and a piece of rope belted his white robe.

He looked like a heavenly being. An angel, or maybe a saint.

Dear God, Sawyer swore silently. Had he died and gone to heaven?

No. In heaven one felt no torment, and his injuries still hurt so badly that even breathing was difficult.

And he didn't think there were any chickens in heaven either.

"Mary's husband, Pontius Pilate, also stepped out of the whale's mouth," the man went on, "and together they looked for a place where Mary could give birth. But there were no more rooms in Rome, and so Mary delivered the child inside Adam's ark, where pairs of animals gathered around and watched."

Bewilderment and fresh waves of pain caused Sawyer to close his eyes. He struggled to stay awake, to understand all the oddities that occurred every time he came out of unconsciousness.

He lost the battle, but didn't realize he'd fallen asleep again until bright sunlight stabbed through his eyelids. Daytime. Nighttime. Daytime . . .

He'd lost count of how many days and nights he'd been drifting in and out of consciousness. Slowly, he lifted his hand and rubbed his eyes, trying to clear his vision.

"Good. You are awake."

The sudden sound of another man's voice startled Sawyer into twisting in the bed. Instantly, his action jolted his body with pain so bad that he clenched his teeth. "Dammit!" he swore softly.

"You curse," Maclovio commented. "You must be getting well. Who are you?"

The question, Sawyer mused, was who were all these strange old people he saw every time he opened his eyes?

And where was the young beauty with the black hair and vivid blue eyes?

"I have been waiting to talk to you," Maclovio said. "Zafiro, she does not know I am here, and Tia has gone to boil more water."

The man's liquor-laced breath was almost bad enough to knock Sawyer out again. Looking up, he saw a big, broad-shouldered man with salt-and-pepper hair, whose drunken slur and heavily accented English made him all but impossible to understand.

Lethargy crept through his body. God, he was so tired. Lucid thought seemed an impossible thing to achieve.

"Did you hear me?" Maclovio queried. "Can you talk?"

"In a whale," Sawyer whispered, his weary mind fairly bursting with a tangle of thoughts. "Mary."

"Mary? I am called Maclovio. There is also Lorenzo. And Pedro. Our leader, Ciro, is gone now, and so is Jaime. Luis still lives, the damn son of a bitch."

Try as he did, Sawyer could not connect the man's rambling to anything that made sense. "The mountain lion."

Maclovio pulled a chair close to the bed and sat down. The chair creaked beneath his weight. "Mariposa, she is outside, maybe in the big tree by the barn, or maybe asleep on the rocks. Did you know I never met a horse I could not gentle—except Coraje. Only Ciro could ride that devil. I trained all the horses we rode. I could ride standing up, and people would pay to see my tricks. It is true that you cannot remember who you are?"

Sawyer stared at the man. Jumbled Bible stories, he thought. A fat woman who believed him to be her son— a little boy called Francisco. A hundred-year-old seductress in a scarlet satin gown, a chicken laying eggs on his chest, and now an elderly drunk who had once ridden while standing up.

Sawyer decided he'd been hallucinating for days. The chicken and the bizarre collection of people were but figments of his imagination, brought to life by his raging fever and the pain of his wounds.

Or perhaps he suffered damage to his brain. Maybe during the cougar's attack he'd fallen and hit his head so hard that his mind was impaired!

Dear God. Brain damaged, in a strange house, at the hands of a bunch of imaginary lunatics, and with a vicious mountain lion on the loose.

"Yes," Maclovio continued, "I trained all the horses, and even taught Ciro's stallion to come when he heard a whistle. We were well-known in two lands, Sawyer Donovan. That is why you should think twice before trying to steal from us. Before trying to hurt any of us. Well-known and feared, that was us, the Quintana Gang. Many lawmen and bounty hunters tried to catch us, but no one ever came close. And if you do not believe what I say, I will smash your face and—"

"Maclovio!" Zafiro's voice sliced through the quiet room as she stepped in from the corridor, a basin of fresh water in her hands. "What are you doing here?"

Maclovio bolted from his chair. "I . . . He . . . Tia
. . . Watching over him, Zafiro. And trying to . . . trying to find out who he is. Yes, I am watching over and
interrogating him. You are here now. I will go. But if he
dares to threaten you, call me and I will smash his face."
As quickly as his intoxicated state would allow, Maclovio
weaved out of the room.

Zafiro shut the door, carried the water to the bed, and
wet a clean cloth. As she smoothed the rag upon the side
of Sawyer's face, she glanced at the door and wondered
what Maclovio had talked about while in the room. Azucar, Tia, and Pedro had also visited Sawyer, but none of
them would have said anything of much importance.

It was Maclovio who worried her. While he was in one
of his drunken states, his tongue was so loose that it was a
wonder it even stayed in his mouth.

And Maclovio had looked awfully guilty when she'd
caught him talking to Sawyer.

Deep in thought as she was, a while passed before she
realized Sawyer had opened his eyes and was watching
her. Another moment passed before she also realized that
she had absently pushed the sheet down and was now
sliding the wet cloth over his lower abdomen.

She pulled the sheet back over his chest, cast the cloth
aside, and casually brushed her hand over her hair. "You
are awake. I was washing . . . bathing you. You are hot
with fever, and I am trying to cool you."

He tried to hear what she said to him—the dark-
haired girl with the startling blue eyes—but her voice
seemed to be coming from a hundred miles away. "My
head. I think I fell and hit my head. Seeing . . . seeing
things."

Zafiro understood he was very sleepy. Maybe he hadn't
even felt her bathing his stomach. "Maclovio," she said

down to him. "The man who was just here. What did he say? What did he want?"

"Kiss," Sawyer whispered.

"Maclovio wanted to kiss you?" *Dios mío*, Zafiro thought. Considering Maclovio's drunken state and Sawyer's long hair . . . Did Maclovio believe Sawyer was female?

"The old woman," Sawyer said. "She tried . . . tried to kiss . . . Lay. Lay an egg on me."

"An old woman tried to kiss and lay an egg on you?" Zafiro frowned. Perhaps Sawyer's fever had made him delirious, she guessed, and people often spoke secrets when raving with fever. Maybe Sawyer would say something that would help her understand who he was. "Tell me more, Sawyer Donovan. Go ahead. Let the peas flow out."

He blinked several times, but couldn't quite keep his eyes open. "Peas . . ."

"Yes. You are American. You know the expression. Let the peas flow out. Tell me everything."

He couldn't for the life of him understand why she was chattering about flowing peas. Dammit, if only he wasn't so groggy!

"Sawyer, tell me your brain."

Somehow, finally, he surmised that she was trying to tell him to speak his mind. "A slingshot," he replied, voicing whatever thought came to him. "A boy called Francisco. Red. The toothless hag wore red. But it wasn't . . . it wasn't in an ark. He was born in a manger."

Listening to his mumbling, Zafiro realized he had, indeed, met and listened to the ramblings of Tia, Azucar, and Pedro. "What else, Sawyer? Did anyone else say anything to you?"

His eyes still closed, Sawyer continued to relate whatever thoughts entered his mind. "Blood. She saved the fish hooks. So much blood in the house with the . . . with the white curtains."

Dazed as he remained, Zafiro didn't miss the torment in his voice. "Blood?" Was he recalling a terrible memory, something the nuns believed he wanted to forget? "Blood in the house? Was it your house?"

"He rode standing up. Jaime's gone. Well-known and feared in two lands."

Zafiro made no reply; cold dread sat in her belly like a lump of ice. "Who, Sawyer?" she finally whispered. "Who . . . who is well-known and feared in two lands?" *God, please do not let him say what I think he is going to say!*

Sawyer opened his eyes and saw her eyes staring down at him. Jewels, he thought. Blue as the heart of a flame, the color of those pretty eyes. "Gang," he mumbled. "The Quintana Gang."

Zafiro's heart lurched as if someone had prodded it with a poker. A gamut of emotions twisted inside her.

Shock.

Fear.

Anger.

And finally resolution.

He knew. Sawyer knew who they all were, and now there was only one thing she could do.

Santa Maria.

She would have to kill him.

three

"His fever is finally breaking, *chiquita*," Tia announced. "When he awakens he is going to be able to talk to us. He will still be tired, but he will speak to us normally instead of ranting like he did when he had the fever."

From the threshold of Sawyer's room Zafiro watched Sawyer move his legs and arms. Sweat poured off his face, shoulders, and chest as though he'd only just emerged from a bath.

His health was returning just when she would take his life.

But when would she do it? she asked herself for the hundredth time. Her decision to kill him was already four days old. But the first day she'd been too busy with a second attempt to build a chicken coop. She still hadn't completed the task, and in her opinion one couldn't commit a slaying when one hadn't finished one's chores. The day after that she'd gone to the convent to advise the nuns about Sawyer's encounter with Mariposa and also to have them borrow Rudolfo's gun again. Of course, she hadn't told them why she needed the gun. Telling a group of nuns that she would soon be a murderess just didn't seem to be the right thing to do.

When she'd returned to La Escondida from the convent, she'd seen to all the chores. After having climbed up and down the mountain and then toiled for hours, she'd been too weary to carry off an assassination.

Yesterday had been Sunday. Taking a life on the Lord's day was something she refused to even consider. And today . . . well, today she hadn't found a second of time for the killing. Tia hadn't left Sawyer's room since daybreak, and Zafiro was not going to perform his execution in front of the dear woman who believed him to be her son.

Another dilemma also plagued her. What manner of death would she choose for him? The decision deserved much careful thought.

She had the gun, yes, but what was the most comfortable way to die?

"Now that I know he is out of danger, I go to rest, Zafiro," Tia said. Stifling a yawn, she swept her hair out of her eyes, then tried to swat Jengibre off the bed, to no avail. The chicken merely positioned herself more comfortably within the nest of sheets.

Tia let the hen be. "Zafiro, you will watch Francisco for a few hours and make sure he sleeps peacefully?"

Zafiro couldn't imagine a more peaceful sleep than death. "*Sí*, Tia. I will do what I must to give him a long, long rest. Please go sleep now."

When Tia was gone Zafiro fidgeted with her skirt for a while, then paced around the room, her heart skipping beats every time she concentrated on what she was about to do. Finally, she stopped in front of the window and gazed out at the peaks of the Sierras. "Forgive me, Grandfather," she whispered to the mental image she had of him. "I know you never killed. Not once, and neither did Maclovio, Lorenzo, Pedro, or my father. But there was always another way for you and the men. Some way to avoid spilling blood. For me there is no other way. I must kill this man because I can think of no other way to protect our people."

Her head bowed low, she left the room, but returned shortly and laid an array of items on the floor near Sawyer's bed. As she closed and locked the door, tears burned her eyes.

Santa Maria, she was about to destroy a life. Slaughter a young, healthy, and vitally handsome man who should have at least fifty more years ahead of him.

This day, this beautiful, sunny morning, would be his last.

Drying her wet cheeks with the back of her hand, she sniffled and tried to summon the courage she would need to send Sawyer to his Maker.

"This chicken laid an egg in my bed."

The sudden sound of his voice caused her to shriek with surprise and whirl to face him. "You scared me!" Taking deep breaths to try to slow her pounding heart, she saw him watching her intently.

Had he heard her speak to her grandfather about the killing? "How long have you been awake?"

Sawyer tried to shrug, but his shoulder injury wouldn't let him. Still, he felt better and he realized he was no longer sick with fever.

In fact, he was hungry. "I woke up a few seconds ago when I heard your sniffling. I didn't mean to scare you. I'm sorry."

His apology made her feel worse. He was nice, she mused. Just as the nuns said he was.

It would sure be a lot easier to kill him if he were rude and cruel.

"You're the girl from the convent. Why were you crying?"

"My tears have no business with you, Sawyer Donovan. And do not be nice to me."

He frowned. If her voice had been any sharper she could have sliced steel with it. "Don't be nice to you?"

"That is right. Do not be nice to me."

Her command didn't make a bit of sense to him, but he complied. "All right. Get the hell out of my room to do all your damn crying, woman, and get this blasted chicken out of my bed."

She stared at him, unable to believe what she'd heard him say. *"What?"*

"You said for me not to be nice to you." Grimacing, he touched the thick white bandage on his shoulder. "And considering the way I feel, it's a hell of a lot easier to be mean than it is to be nice."

"You are in my house, and you dare to be mean with me?" She marched toward the bed, stopping a few feet away. "I do not think you have enough pickles in your barrel."

"Pickles?"

"Your barrel needs more pickles?" Zafiro rephrased the question. Oh, how did that expression go? "You are crazy."

Finally, he understood. "I'm one pickle short of a barrel."

"Yes, that is what I said. Now, do not be mean with me in my own house."

"You don't want me to be nice, and I didn't ask you to bring me here, got that? The last thing I remember is being attacked by a cougar, so it must have been your own decision to bring me into your home and—"

"If you had not chased me from the convent, none of this would have hap—"

"I thought you'd stolen—"

"Well, I did not steal anything—"

"How was I supposed to know—"

"*Basta!* Enough! I will not listen to you say one more word!"

Her shouting quieted him, but not because her anger intimidated him. Actually, he couldn't have cared less how mad she was.

It was his preference to study her in silence that induced him to cease arguing with her.

And study her he did.

Standing in the middle of the sparsely furnished room, she rocked back and forth on her heels. Her ebony hair flowed down her body like melted midnight, the ends of those thick tresses curling around her gently rounded hips. Her breasts strained against her white blouse. They weren't overly large, but her shirt appeared to be too small for her.

"You are staring at my breasts."

Her immodest statement made him smile. "Sorry."

"You cannot help it. Azucar said that men like to do that, so I think that it is a liking you were born with. Men also like to touch and taste women's breasts. I know everything there is to know about lovemaking."

"Oh, really?" The conversation seemed highly improper, but if it didn't bother her, he certainly wasn't going to let it bother him. "What else do you know?"

"Everything Azucar told me."

"I see. So who is this authority on lovemaking, your beau? Husband?"

Zafiro raised one eyebrow. "Azucar is a woman. A very experienced woman. Her name means 'sugar' in Spanish. I do not think there is anyone in the whole world who knows as much about lovemaking as Azucar, but it would take me too long to tell you all the things she has explained to me."

Sawyer decided that if Azucar—with all her experience—was as beautiful as this dark-haired girl, he'd like to meet her. "I'll be in this bed for a long time. You could tell me a little bit, couldn't you?"

"You will not be in the bed for much longer." He'd soon be in his grave, she thought.

She had to tell him. He had every right to know his fate. Drawing herself up to her full height she prayed he wouldn't notice how her knees were shaking. "You are going to die."

He smiled again. "I have to admit that I've had better days, but I don't think I'm going to die."

"You are." Pretending there was something in her eye, Zafiro quickly wiped away another tear.

Santa Maria, she had to get hold of herself! She was her charges' sole protection, and who was more important, after all? This stranger, Sawyer Donovan, who had never done a thing for her? Or her people, who had taken care of her since her mother left her in their care when she was a newborn?

"You are going to die, Sawyer Donovan. I want you to die, and for that I am very sorry."

Her admission stunned him into a long moment of silence. "If you wanted me to die why did you bring me here and sew me up? Wouldn't it have been easier to just leave me on the mountain and let that cougar and the vultures—"

"I did not sew you up. Tia did."

Sawyer decided that Tia was the plump woman with the motherly demeanor. "She might have sewn me up, but you did your share too."

"That was before. Things have changed. Your life, it does not have the value of a pile of peas now because—"

"Peas." Hadn't he heard her mention peas before? "What is it with you and peas? I remember you saying something about them . . . I don't know. A few days ago, I guess. Something about letting the peas flow."

"Yes, that is what I said. To let the peas flow means to tell what you are hiding."

"Spill the beans. *Beans.*"

"Peas, beans, or even radishes . . . What does it matter? A vegetable is a vegetable—"

"And the expression you just tried to use is *not worth a hill of beans.* My life is not worth a hill of beans."

"It means the same . . ."

"Maybe. But the way you said it didn't make sense."

She bristled. "Do you make funny with me?"

He ignored her irritation. "No, I am not making fun of you. Who are you, anyway?"

She ignored his question. "A cat died from being curious, you know."

"Curiosity killed the cat."

She nodded. "Whose cat was it?"

"What?"

"Whose cat—"

"No one's cat. It's only a saying."

She couldn't understand why anyone would make up an expression about a cat who didn't even exist, but she had more important things to do than try to untangle such twisted logic.

She had to put Sawyer to death. Her heart skipping beats again and her palms so wet with perspiration that she could not even dry them in the folds of her skirt, she walked nearer to the bed and pointed to the various articles she'd arranged on the floor.

Sawyer looked down and saw a knife, a long piece of rope, a bucket of water, and a gun.

"Choose your death, Sawyer Donovan. I can shoot you, stab you, hang you, or drown you. Or," she added, spying his pillow and slipping it out from under his head, "I could suffocate you. It is your death. You choose."

Her announcement shocked him. "You . . . You're going to kill me? Why?"

"Because you know who we are." Visions of Sawyer leading Luis to La Escondida filled her mind, causing her to shudder inwardly. Even the possibility of Sawyer turning her men in to the law horrified her.

She bent and picked up the knife, a long, rust-covered dagger with a handle cocooned in old spider webs.

Sawyer eyed the knife. What with his injuries, could he stop her if she lunged at him in the next moment?

God. Beautiful though the woman was, she was deranged. His apprehension deepened. "Look," he said, his gaze moving back and forth from her eyes to the ancient blade in her hands, "I have no idea who you are, so—"

"You try to blind me with fleece." Zafiro tapped the flat side of the knife on her palm. "You *do* know who we are, because Maclovio opened the sack and the cat jumped out."

"Maclovio?"

"Again you try to be as dishonest as a carpet. You talked to Maclovio only four days ago, and after that you spoke our name. You are only grabbing at hay because you do not want to be killed. You know we are the Quintana Gang. Because you know, you must die."

"Who?"

"The Quintana Gang!"

He searched his memory for some clue as to who the Quintana Gang was, but continued to feel more confused by the second. "I don't know any Quintana Gang."

Zafiro didn't reply; she merely looked at him. Her gaze traced the chiseled planes of his face: his high cheekbones, long, straight nose, and sharply defined jawline.

Tia had washed his hair earlier, and now, as it lay spread over the mattress and his massive shoulders, it shone like antique gold. Zafiro longed to touch it. To feel how thick it was and to see how it looked sliding through her dark fingers.

He blinked, his action drawing her attention to his eyes. She'd never seen eyes such as his—golden, flecked with warm brown.

Instinct told her that those eyes could coerce a woman into doing anything. Anything at all.

The thought quickened her breath and loosened her thoughts. "You are the handsomest, youngest man I have seen in ten years," she said softly. "I . . . part of me wishes I did not have to kill you. But . . . but life, it is not roses to sleep on, and I cannot keep my cake if it is in my belly."

He stared at her so hard that his eyes stung. "I'm trying to pull the wool over your eyes, someone let the cat out of the bag, I lie like a rug, I'm grasping at straws, life is no bed of roses, and you can't have your cake and eat it too."

She stared straight back at him. "That is what I—"

"No, it's not what you—"

"You will be a dead man in only minutes, and you would waste the last of your life arguing with me, Sawyer Donovan? You have more nuts than a fruitcake!"

"*You're* the one who's nuttier than a fruitcake, woman! God Almighty—"

"It is good that you are saying your prayers. Make your peace with God Almighty, pick your death, and I will make the necessary preparations to kill you."

He heard her voice tremble and knew then that the notion of killing him was truly abhorrent to her. There might just be a way out of his predicament yet, he mused. "Please," he said, reaching out to hold her hand, "don't kill me."

She felt like curling her fingers between his. But, of course, she didn't, because one didn't caress one's murder victim. "You are making this harder for me." She yanked her hand from his grasp.

"Harder for *you*? What about *me*?"

"It is supposed to be hard on you. You are the one who is going to be killed."

If he didn't still feel slightly nervous he'd have found her explanation amusing. But he remained wary because his would-be killer was definitely daft, and daft people were unpredictable.

He tried to think of another way to dissuade her from murdering him. "I want to be drawn and quartered."

"Drawn and quartered?" She wrinkled up her nose as she pondered his wish. "Will that kill you?"

"After being drawn and quartered I'll be as dead as a doornail."

"What is a doornail?"

He decided not to explain a cliché she'd turn around and mangle anyway. "Never mind. Just draw and quarter me."

She gave a slow nod. "All right. But first tell me what it is."

"Four horses pull and tear off my two arms and two legs."

Zafiro couldn't suppress a violent shudder. "We only have Coraje and Rayo, our horse and burro. Coraje, he will not allow as much as a gnat to get near him, and Rayo suffers a bruised foot. Besides, to be drawn and quartered, it sounds very painful. I do not want you to feel any pain. I only want you to die."

Her explanation was the stupidest thing he'd ever heard. Glancing down at her weapons again, he spied the gun. "The sound of gunfire's so loud. Deafening, actually."

Zafiro looked at the gun she'd had Sister Carmelita borrow from Rudolfo again. This time the pistol was fully loaded. "You will not realize that you have gone deaf because you will be dead. Besides, you will only hear the gunfire for half a second."

"Too long. I refuse to be shot, and that's it."

She nudged the pistol away with her foot and made a mental note to return it to Sister Carmelita as soon as possible.

Sawyer looked down at the various killing instruments again. "I've never liked the feel of something tight around my neck. I can't even button the top button on my shirts."

"But you were wearing a bandana."

"It wasn't tied tight though. It was so loose I barely felt it."

Zafiro kicked the rope across the room.

"I'm already slashed to ribbons. Do you think I'd enjoy being cut into again?"

She laid the dagger on the table under the window.

"Feathers make me sneeze. I can never sleep with my nose too near the pillow."

She booted the pillow under the bed. "There is only the water left. Please put your head in this bucket and drown."

She might as well have asked him to please pass the salt, so nonchalantly did she give his death order. He tried to sit up, wincing when bolts of pain shot through his injuries.

Carefully, he laid back down. "Starve me to death."

She shook her head. "I have been hungry many times, and I can tell you that an empty stomach is painful. You must drown."

"I deserve one last meal." While she went to get his food he'd escape, he decided. Even if he had to drag himself out of the house on his hands and knees, he'd escape. "A really big meal. Eight courses, plus dessert."

"First you want to starve to death, and now you want to eat?"

"Yes."

Zafiro sighed every bit of air from her lungs. "If you keep stalling you will die of old age before I have the chance to kill you."

"Do you expect me to hurry along my own execution? Bring me some . . . some lobster." He smiled inwardly, daring her to find a lobster in the middle of the Sierras. "Yes, lobster to start. Once I've finished that I'll tell you what else I want."

"Lobster?"

"You do know what lobster is, don't you?"

Zafiro remembered eating lobster whenever she and the gang journeyed through small towns near the gulf. "Where do you think I will get lobster in these mountains?"

Nowhere, he answered silently. "I'm not going to die until I get some lobster."

Zafiro glared at him, her patience so sorely tried that she no longer remembered to feel sorry over having to kill him. "Do you know what I am going to do? I am going to shoot, stab, drown, hang, and suffocate you all at the same time!"

"Fine, but I want my lobster first."

"*Fish!* That is the closest I can come to lobster! You will eat it, and then you will die!" With that, Zafiro turned on her heel and marched out.

Sawyer waited until the sound of her bootheels faded, then pulled off his covers and slowly, painfully, sat up and placed his feet on the floor. Looking around the room, he wondered where his clothes were.

He'd have to escape naked. His legs shook as he began to stand, and it took every bit of strength he had to fight off waves of dizziness.

Familiar sounds hit his ears just as he took his first step away from the bed. A growl and a snarl. His body completely rigid, he strained to hear the noises again.

A mountain lion slunk into the room. Stopping a few yards from the bed, she crouched, her gold eyes narrowing, her hindquarters moving from side to side as she prepared to spring forward.

Sawyer felt every drop of blood drain from his face. Words whispered through his mind.

You will be a dead man in only minutes. . . .

The girl with the long black hair had apparently decided to allow the cougar to finish him off.

He had no time to think. To shout. To prepare himself for his gruesome death.

He fell back into the bed.

And the great cat flew toward him.

Holding a tray that held a steaming bowl of fish stew, a freshly baked loaf of bread, a big red apple, and a glass of milk, Zafiro walked down the hall toward Sawyer's room. During the time it had taken her to catch the fish and prepare the meal, her temper had cooled.

Now, as she smelled the aroma of the fish stew, she wished she'd been able to accommodate Sawyer and give him his lobster. After all, who could blame him for wanting the taste of his favorite food in his mouth while he took his dying breath?

His dying breath.

"God," she prayed, "please give me the strength to commit this horrible sin."

A sigh escaped her when she realized the content of her prayer. Asking the Lord for the courage to execute a murder was probably a sin all by itself.

Arriving at Sawyer's door, she entered the room . . . and almost dropped the tray of food.

There lay Sawyer, on the bed, right where she'd left him. Only he wasn't alone. Indeed, he seemed to be thoroughly enjoying his company: Mariposa.

The sleek cougar lay stretched out beside him, her eyes closed in contentment, her long tail leisurely beating the mattress as Sawyer scratched her ears.

"Nice kitty," Sawyer said, smoothing his hand down from her ears and across her back. "Nice little kitty."

In response Mariposa leaned her head back onto his shoulder and licked his chin with her long, rough tongue.

Watching, Zafiro realized she'd never known the cat to take to a stranger so quickly. The cougar was even wary around the nuns, all of whom she'd known for three years. Bewildered by her pet's abnormal behavior, she set the tray on top of a small bureau and crossed to the bed. "What did you do to her?"

Sawyer noted the disbelief in her gorgeous blue eyes. "I didn't do anything to her. She came in right after you left. I thought you'd sent her in to kill me, but all she did was jump on the bed with me. When I realized she wasn't going to have me for lunch, I held out my hand, she licked it, laid down, went to sleep, and that was that. I went to sleep too, and she woke me up only a few minutes ago by rubbing her head on my arm."

Zafiro wanted to believe he was lying, but the truth—in the form of a very content cougar—lay stretched out right before her very eyes. Mariposa liked Sawyer. And maybe, in her own mountain lion way, she was trying to apologize for attacking him.

Animals possessed an instinct that told them who was friend and who was foe. Mariposa, apparently, had belatedly decided Sawyer was a friend.

Zafiro folded her arms in front of her waist and deliberated. Who was *she* to contradict the instincts of a wild animal? Yes, her own instincts had been warning her of a coming danger, but wasn't it possible that Sawyer was not that danger?

Mariposa obviously thought so. The cat was purring and had now maneuvered her body over Sawyer's stomach.

And not only had Mariposa decided to like Sawyer, but Sawyer had chosen to pardon the cougar for attacking him. Wasn't a man who could forgive an attempt on his life a man who could be trusted?

Yes.

So if the peril she anticipated was not Sawyer Donovan . . .

It had to be Luis.

Zafiro closed her eyes and pressed her shaking fingers against her temples, trying in vain to subdue the horrible premonition of danger. But it built steadily inside her, warning her in no uncertain manner that evil was soon going to find her.

"Did you hear what I said?"

Sawyer's voice broke through her grim preoccupation. Opening her eyes, she looked at him blankly. "What?"

"I asked you if this cougar is your pet," Sawyer repeated, rubbing his fingers up and down the cat's soft belly. "And the chicken too." He pointed to the ginger-colored hen who nested between the vee of his legs. "She's laid another egg, I think."

Nodding, Zafiro took a deep breath, and then another and another. Slowly, her feelings of fear faded and she was once again able to concentrate on Sawyer. "The chicken, she is Jengibre. Her name means 'ginger,' because that is what color she is. She will not lay her eggs in the coop with the other chickens. I think she believes she is a person, so I allow her to go where she pleases, and she has never run away. Mariposa, she is my pet too. She was an orphaned cub when I found her three years ago. Her name means 'butterfly' because she is very gentle, like a butterfly."

Sawyer thought of his extensive injuries, wounds that were going to take quite some time to heal fully. If Mariposa's attack had been gentle he hated to think what she could do when in a violent mood. "She's your guard cat?"

Nodding, Zafiro reached out and tenderly pinched Mariposa's nose. "And sometimes she brings fresh meat to us. We become tired of eggs and fish, so we are always glad when she shares her catch with us. I cannot kill Pancha or Blanca, Rosa—"

"Who?"

"Pancha is my cow and we need her milk. Blanca and Rosa, they are some of my other chickens. We also have Rayo, our burro. He is in the barn with Pancha."

Sawyer listened to her tone of voice and studied her actions. She seemed calm, relaxed, as if she were truly enjoying the conversation.

He decided to keep her talking before she remembered she was supposed to kill him. Then, if and when she recalled her murder plans, he'd . . . Well, he wasn't sure what he'd do, but for now he'd just keep her talking. "Why don't you eat your chickens?"

"When there were many, we did. But now I have only eight. One cooked chicken will make only one meal. But a live chicken will continue to provide eggs."

"How do you keep Mariposa out of the chicken coop?"

Zafiro shook her head, remembering the day Pedro shot the chicken house apart. She'd tried to rebuild the fowl house, but the flimsy thing she'd made wasn't going to hold the chickens for long. "When I first found Mariposa I poured vinegar all over the hens and then let her smell them. She did not like the smell at all, and she has never gone near them since."

Sawyer silently congratulated her on her ingenuity. "So you get meat when Mariposa brings some. Why can't you hunt for yourselves?"

Zafiro sighed. "I do not have a gun that will work. The one I was going to shoot you with is not mine. I have tried to fashion traps to catch the rabbits who eat my garden, but they take one look at my traps and laugh. It is very irritating."

"Yes, I've heard rabbits laugh before," Sawyer answered in all seriousness. "And you're right. It's an irritating sound."

She gave him a good, hard frown to show him what she thought of his sarcasm. "It is not a funny thing, Sawyer," she chided him. "We are six people here, and we have animals too. If not for the nuns we would be hungry and so would our animals. The area farmers and villagers, they give food and supplies to the sisters in return for the sisters' prayers. And the nuns, they share with us what little provisions they have. Sometimes they bring meat. Sometimes sugar, flour, fruit, or salt. They even bring hay and grains for our animals when they can get it. But though the good sisters are very generous, the food and supplies they bring to us never last long enough. And the sisters, they do not have much themselves. No one does."

She retrieved the tray of food and set it on the table beside his bed. "Your fish."

His stomach growled and his mouth watered, but as he glanced at the bowl of hot stew, he couldn't help wondering if she'd laced it with a bit of strychnine. "You take the first bite."

"I have already eaten."

"I'm not asking you to eat the whole bowl, only a bite."

"Why?"

"Uh . . . Well, I want you to make sure it's not too hot. My injuries hurt bad enough. I don't want to burn my mouth too."

Zafiro smiled, sudden comprehension dawning upon her. "You think I have put poison in this food."

Her smile captured his full attention. She had full, sensuous lips, a captivating dimple in her left cheek, and her grin was so bright that it illuminated her striking blue eyes.

God, she was even more beautiful when she was happy.

"I asked if you think I've poisoned your food," Zafiro repeated.

"Are you kidding? Why would I think you'd try to poison me? You offered only to shoot, stab, hang, suffocate, or drown me. Poisoning was not among my choices, so I have no reason to believe that you—"

"I have changed my mind. Mariposa likes you, so I am not going to kill you."

He saw not a speck of dishonesty in her eyes, but remained wary. "Oh, and I'm just supposed to take your word for it."

Zafiro's first impulse was to tell him in no uncertain terms that if she said she wasn't going to kill him, then she wasn't going to kill him. She reconsidered, however, when she took a moment to put herself in his place. "I will prove to you that I mean what I say, but this is the last time I will do so. From now on you will believe me when I tell you something."

He watched her bend over the bowl of stew and slip a heaping spoonful of the fish stew into her mouth. All right, so the fish wasn't going to kill him. "What about the bread?"

Zafiro swallowed the stew, then ate a bit of the bread. She also munched into the apple and drank some of the milk. "There," she said, wiping her milk mustache off with the back of her hand. "Now sit up and eat."

Sawyer tried to sit up, but found the task impossible. Not only did Mariposa remain stretched out over half his body, but he was tiring again and his wounds were aching fiercely. Dammit, he hated feeling so helpless, so weak.

"You must eat, Sawyer Donovan."

"Why do you always have to call me by my full name?" he asked irritably.

"It is your name, isn't it?"

"Yeah, but you don't have to use both—"

"Why are you so angry?"

"I'm not angry."

"You are."

"All right, I'm angry."

"Why?"

"I'm hungry, dammit!"

"Then sit up and eat."

"I can't! For God's sake, woman, I've been torn up by a mountain lion, who's now draped over me like a damn afghan!" Carefully, he moved his body out from beneath Mariposa, whereupon Jengibre promptly got up and pecked at his arm as a punishment for disturbing her.

Sawyer rubbed the stinging chicken bite. "I don't feel good." He stared at the ceiling. "I'm hurting all over." He took a deep breath. "I can't eat." He closed his eyes. "Can't eat because I've been torn up by a mountain lion. I'm hurting too much to sit up, and there's a man-eating chicken in my bed."

"Men are such babies."

He opened his right eye. "Well, pardon the hell out of me. How stupid of me to complain. I've only been slashed to ribbons—"

"But you have been sewn up, and you will live."

"Only because the mountain lion who tore me up in the first place decided to like me. If it wasn't for Mariposa I'd be dead right now because you'd have killed me!"

"But I did not kill you." Before he could object, Zafiro began to feed him, pushing a spoonful of stew into his mouth. He'd barely had the chance to swallow it when she fed him another spoonful, another, and another.

"There," she said, dropping the spoon back into the empty bowl. "Now you are not hungry anymore. Are you still angry?"

Dribbles of fish stew all over his chin, he glared at her. "I'm wearing my meal."

She ignored his complaint, certain that Mariposa would ease it.

Sure enough, the cougar quickly and neatly cleaned Sawyer's chin of every trace of the fish stew.

"I am glad that I did not kill you, Sawyer Donovan."

"That makes two of us."

Zafiro cut the apple and popped a sliver into Sawyer's mouth. "How does it feel not to know who you are?"

He didn't want to discuss his memory loss. It was frustrating enough just to think about it. "How long have I been here?"

"It will soon be eight days. What is it like to have no memories?"

She wasn't going to give up. And he wasn't going to answer.

"Why do you not want to touch your trunk?" Zafiro asked. "The nuns said you did not like to be very near it."

Sawyer squeezed a handful of sheets. The trunk. Truth was, he didn't know why he didn't want to look at it, touch it, much less open it.

All he knew for sure was that every time he saw it he felt almost blinded by a crushing sort of pain. A horror that he didn't know how to overcome.

And yet he could not make himself get rid of the trunk. Whatever was inside seemed vitally important for him to keep.

He would not, however, look at it. Not now.

Someday. Maybe.

Maybe.

"Sawyer? What is it like not to have memories?" Zafiro continued to press.

"I have memories. I just can't remember them."

"Why?"

His irritation rose like steam from a kettle. "How the hell should I know? That's what this forgetting stuff is all about!"

For a few moments Zafiro chewed on her bottom lip, wondering whether or not to voice the thoughts in her mind. "Sawyer . . ." She reached up to fondle her sapphire, moving the large jewel between her fingers and finally clasping it in her palm. "While you were with fever you spoke . . . spoke about a big house with white curtains. You said there was blood in the house. Do you think . . . I . . . well, maybe the house is a memory you have forgotten and now it is trying to come back to you."

He didn't answer.

But she saw his body stiffen, and from his eyes spilled an agony that pulled at every compassionate part of her. "I am sorry," she whispered.

"For mentioning a house I know nothing about?"

He'd growled the question at her, and she knew then that if indeed he remembered as much as a fragment about the house with the white curtains, he wasn't going to discuss it. The urge to pursue further the subject of the bloody house was almost irresistible, but she instinctively realized that for Sawyer to speak about it, to try to remember, would cause him pain a thousand times worse than that of his physical injuries.

Perhaps in time, as the weeks passed, she would mention the house again. "You have strong legs."

He frowned, wondering what his legs had to do with the white-curtained house.

That house. He'd seen the house in his mind before, while he was awake. Now, apparently, he'd been talking about it in his sleep.

But where was the house? Had he lived in it? And why all the blood? God, so much blood.

Whose blood?

He couldn't think about it anymore. Though the thought of the house was much like a wisp of smoke that vanished almost as soon as it came to be, the mere notion of it filled him with pain he couldn't stand or comprehend.

"Sawyer?"

He took a deep breath and struggled to assume an ordinary expression. "I have strong legs. So what?"

"Maybe you are a ballet dancer," Zafiro explained, relieved by his normal tone of voice. "I saw a ballet once many years ago. The dancers, they had legs like yours, full of muscle. When you are well enough, you will dance for us and we will tell you if you are any good."

He still didn't want to talk about his memory loss, but he for damn sure didn't want her believing he was some pansy ballet dancer. "I am not a ballet—"

"How do you know?"

"I know because . . . because I just know!"

His shout got him another chicken bite on the arm. "Ow!" he yelled, glaring at Jengibre. "I can't believe I'm in bed with a mountain lion and a damn chicken, and it's the *chicken* who's trying to eat me! Get her off me!"

Zafiro gently placed Jengibre on the floor.

And Sawyer handed her the egg the hen had laid in the sheets.

She slipped the egg into the pocket in her skirt. "You do not know for sure that you are not a ballet dancer, Sawyer. When you dance for us, then we will know."

Zafiro pulled up a chair, sat down, and crossed her legs. "For now, though, all we know is your name and that you have ballet dancer legs."

Before he replied, Sawyer took a moment to appreciate the fact that she was barefoot and that her skirts fell in such a way as to afford him a tantalizing view of her shapely legs.

She had pretty feet. Dainty, and with tiny toes. Her ankles were slim, but her calves were well-rounded with sleek muscle.

"Do you like my legs as much as my breasts?"

He raised his gaze to hers, intrigued again by her candor. "I do."

His answer pleased her. "How many other breasts and legs have you seen?"

He grinned. "You know, we're talking about a lot of intimate things here, and I don't even know your name."

"Zafiro Maria Quintana."

He took a second to think about the way she'd pronounced her name: *Za-feer-oh*. "Zafiro. How do you spell it?"

She spelled it for him.

"Nice name. I like it."

"It means 'sapphire' in Spanish."

"You're named after the jewel you wear. It's the biggest sapphire I've ever seen. Nearly as big as your fist."

"I am named for the color of my eyes."

Sawyer stared at the large gemstone. "You know, if you sold that stone you'd get enough money to last a long time. Then you could buy the supplies you need. The villagers and the nuns might be hurting, but I'm sure the mercantiles around here are stocked with the things you need."

Zafiro picked up the sapphire and rubbed it over her cheek. "I cannot."

"Why?"

"My grandfather gave me this jewel when a grasshopper was as tall as my knee, and I have worn it ever since."

"When you were knee-high to a grasshopper."

"That is what I said. My sapphire, it was once the knob on a walking stick that belonged to a very rich man in Puebla. One day Grandfather saw the man beat a dog with the cane, so he stole the cane from the man. Grandfather, he was a wonderful thief."

"So you keep the sapphire for sentimental reasons. Because your grandfather gave it to you."

She'd never heard of anything so selfish in all her life. If she could have sold the jewel she'd have sold it years ago and used the money to care for her charges.

But she dared not. The sapphire, large and unique as it was, would surely rouse a lot of talk. Word of the magnificent jewel would travel quickly through the circle of thieves, and the news would eventually reach Luis, who would know exactly who owned the gem.

And then he'd track her down.

She couldn't sell the gem. Not for all the money in the country. Even in the world.

"Zafiro?"

"Yes?"

Sawyer wondered what caused the intense look in her eyes, then decided she was remembering her grandfather. "You must have loved your grandfather a lot."

"What? Oh. Yes, I did. I thought I would be with him forever. But, as time is supposed to do to all of us, Grandfather became old. So did the rest of the gang. It is a very sad thing to think about. Maclovio was the best horseman in the world, Sawyer. There were times when I

thought he worked magic on the horses. He even taught
Grandfather's horse to come when he heard Grandfather
whistle. And Pedro never missed his target with his gun.
Not once. Lorenzo could open any lock invented. But
. . . well, when the men became old . . . Pedro began
to believe he was Saint Peter, Maclovio started drinking
heavily, and Lorenzo lost his hearing. Tia became more
determined than ever to find her little boy, Francisco,
who had died even before Grandfather met her. And
Azucar—"

"She's the old woman who tries to ravish me every
night."

"Yes," Zafiro said, smiling. "Time caught up with her
body, but not her mind. She still thinks she is the young
seductress she once was. Anyway, when age began to slow
down the men, Grandfather brought us all here to these
mountains and built La Escondida. We are very alone
here. Only the convent and a few tiny villages are close
by. Piedra Blanca is the nearest real town. That is where
there is a big store. But Piedra Blanca, it is too far from La
Escondida."

"This place is hidden, isn't it? I remember seeing you
slip inside a concealed—"

"La Escondida means 'The Hidden.' My grandfather
fashioned the hidden entrance to keep us from being
found. The men, they helped, but it was Grandfather
whose cookie was clever."

"He was a smart cookie."

"How can a cookie be smart?"

Sawyer shrugged. "It's only a saying."

"You Americans say strange things."

"Maybe, but they sound even stranger when you say
them."

Zafiro chose to overlook his criticism, especially since

he tempered it with a smile and continued to shower Mariposa with affection. "My men, Sawyer. The Quintana Gang. You still do not think you have ever heard of them?"

He brushed his fingers through his hair. "Maclovio said they were famous. I guess I might have heard of them."

"But you do not remember. Well, it has been ten years since they rode together."

"And you've been hidden away here for ten years with them." Hidden, Sawyer thought. No men, save the gang and maybe a priest or two down at the convent, had ever seen Zafiro in those ten years.

His finding her was akin to discovering a rare and radiant jewel in the crevices of a hidden mine. No wonder she was so bold of tongue, so totally candid when speaking about sexual things. It was more than likely that no one had ever taught her differently.

He certainly wasn't going to be the one to enlighten her either.

"I will pay you if you tell me your thoughts, Sawyer."

"A penny for your thoughts," he translated. "So La Escondida is truly a den of thieves, huh?"

"That does not bother you?"

"If I said it did, would you try to kill me again?"

His answer made her laugh.

And Sawyer thought her laughter the softest, prettiest sound he'd heard in a very long while. "Whatever your men did ten years ago doesn't bother me in the slightest. I don't think I'm a lawman, but even if I were, I wouldn't turn them in. What purpose would it serve to put three harmless old men behind bars?"

There was no mistaking his sincerity. It shone from his golden eyes like sunshine through a crevice, and Zafiro's relief was of such depth that she reached for his hand, brought it to her mouth, and kissed his knuckles. "Whoever you are, I think you must be a very good man, Sawyer Donovan. Maybe you are a priest?"

He slid his thumb across her chin and smiled again when he saw her sapphire eyes darken to a dusky blue. Just as she'd been hidden away from the world for ten years, a wealth of passion was hidden away within her.

A pity he'd be leaving soon. He'd have liked to be the man to free her passion.

The thought convinced him he was definitely not a priest.

"Sawyer?"

"Hmm?"

"You know, although it is possible that you are a ballet dancer, you could be a farmer. The nuns said you knew a lot about gardening. You could also be one of other strong people. A logger, or a horse rancher, or a—"

"Fence builder," he interrupted. "Or a riverboat captain, or a miner, or a cattler breeder, or a soldier. Or maybe," he said, his eyes wide with mock excitement, "just maybe I'm Santa Claus!"

Before Zafiro could address his ridiculous guess her men entered the room.

"He could be a traveling salesman," Maclovio said. "A schoolmaster, or maybe a gunsmith. But I wish he was a fighter. If he was, I would enjoy smashing his face and—"

"Whoever he is, he is like Abraham," Pedro commented. "A man of brawn."

"Fawn?" Lorenzo asked, looking at Zafiro and licking his lips. "Did Mariposa bring us a fawn? Will Tia be making meat pies tonight?"

Zafiro didn't answer; she barely heard Lorenzo's question. Instead, she concentrated on what Maclovio had said about the possibility of Sawyer being a gunsmith.

Gunsmith.

Guns.

Her mind spun with thoughts that hadn't occurred to her before now. Was it possible that Sawyer knew anything about guns? But why wouldn't he? Most all men did, didn't they? Even Rudolfo, the nuns' farmer neighbor, possessed a pistol.

Excitement welled within her, causing her to smile a smile so broad that she felt her ears move.

Sawyer was not the danger she anticipated, that she knew. Rather, he was the miracle she'd pestered God to send her.

It would be a long while before his wounds were completely healed, but when he was well Sawyer Donovan was going to turn her men back into the fearsome gunmen they'd once been.

four

"I'm well. I want to get up now."

Tia clucked. "You are not well, Francisco. You only wish you were. The wounds on your chest and shoulder are much better, but your leg still hurts you. I do not think you could even walk on it yet."

Sawyer did, indeed, admit that his thigh injury still ached, but there was no way in hell that he was going to make the admission out loud. "I've been stuck in this room for months—"

"Barely three weeks have passed since Mariposa attacked you. You will stay put in this room."

As if he could leave, Sawyer complained silently. The door was always locked. Opening it would require kicking it down, and he couldn't do that because his injured leg simply wasn't strong enough to use for kicking or for supporting his body weight while he kicked with his good leg.

Besides that, every time he as much as turned over in the bed, Jengibre squawked loudly enough to shatter glass. And each time the hen sounded the alarm Tia would soon appear to see what was the matter.

Sawyer spent a lot of time thinking about the many ways he could possibly get back at the spiteful hen.

There was fried chicken. Chicken and dumplings. Roasted chicken. Chicken soup. Chicken potpie . . .

"I will let you get out of bed in one more week, my little Francisco," Tia said.

Lying on his side and facing her, Sawyer clenched his fist and punched it into his pillow. "I've been in this confounded bed for almost three weeks already! A gunshot to the head doesn't take this much time to heal! And I'm not your little Francisco, dammit!"

Quick as her stoutness would allow, Tia leaned over him and delivered a resounding smack to his bottom. "Who taught you to talk like that, *niño*? I will not hear another nasty word come out of your mouth, do you hear me?"

Sawyer clenched his fist again. This wasn't the first time the woman had spanked him. She'd done so the day before yesterday too, when he'd refused a spoonful of castor oil. "Don't hit me again!"

"I will spank you whenever you need a spanking, Francisco, and do not yell at me. As your mother it is my duty to make sure you know right from wrong. Now, open your mouth and take this medicine."

He watched her pour thick liquid into a spoon. "No. I hate that stuff."

"It is good for you. Castor oil will make you strong." Before he could resist, she pinched his nose closed and shoved the spoon into his mouth.

His insides rolled, and it was only with the greatest of effort that he managed to keep down the potato soup she'd given him for lunch.

"Good boy," Tia praised him, then leaned down to kiss his cheek. "Now, go to sleep. And stay in the bed."

He stayed in bed. Stayed in bed and stayed in bed. During the following week he didn't know what was worse: his memory loss, the maddening fact that he had still not regained the full measure of his strength, his all-consuming boredom, or the group of people and the chicken whose bizarre eccentricities threatened what precious little sanity his mysterious past had left to him.

Day after day he tried to convince Tia he was not her little boy, fended off Azucar's sexual advances, shouted so Lorenzo could hear him, untangled Pedro's twisted Bible stories, listened to Maclovio threaten to smash his face, and fished out Jengibre's eggs from within the folds of his covers. Once she even laid one in his navel while he was sleeping!

He saw little of Zafiro. From what he gathered, the chores around La Escondida kept her busy from dawn to dusk. On a few occasions, late at night, he heard her making noises in the yard. He'd get up and watch her throw armloads of kindling into the woodshed, toss hay to the horse in the paddock, and haul water into the barn. She hung wet clothes by moonlight, chased night-raiding rabbits from her garden, and tried to fix whatever Maclovio had smashed during the day.

Sometimes she'd suddenly stop whatever she was doing and stare into the distance for a long while before finally finishing whatever last chore demanded her attention. During those times it seemed to Sawyer as though she was looking for someone, waiting for someone.

Every now and then she came to visit him after completing her work, but after the first few minutes of telling him what she'd done that day she'd fall asleep in the chair beside his bed. Tia would then come in and escort her to her own room.

Something about Zafiro's heavy burdens struck a chord

in Sawyer's memory. Something about the way everyone depended on her to take care of them and La Escondida. He had endless hours to wonder why her hard work and her caring for her charges pricked at his buried recollections, but no answer would come to him.

The vague scrap of memory didn't merely bewilder him, however.

It haunted him with dark feelings that he couldn't name no matter how hard he tried.

"You are strong enough to leave your bed now, my sweet Francisco," Tia announced one sunny day as she arrived with an afternoon snack for him. "Zafiro brought your bag of clothes from the convent and washed them all for you. So you will have clean clothes to wear. Zafiro also brought your mule and your trunk. But your trunk, it is locked, and the nuns made her promise not to ask Lorenzo to open it. The sisters, they say that when you want to open the trunk, you will open it. I agree. Besides, I am sure that the trunk holds more of your treasures, the little things you so love to find and collect, like your pinecones and rocks."

Sawyer tried to snatch the thought of his trunk from his mind, to no avail.

That trunk. What was inside?

God.

Just wondering set him afire with pain. An inner pain that felt like it would kill him.

He wasn't going to open it. He couldn't.

But he would keep it. Surely one day he would find the

courage, the strength to open it and see what it contained.

For now, however, just the notion filled him with wrenching dread.

"Francisco, eat your raisin bread, drink your milk, and I will let you sit outside in the sunshine."

Sawyer had never eaten so quickly. He even swallowed his castor oil without arguing. It occurred to him that he was acting exactly like the small boy Tia thought him to be—a child who chose to be obedient so he could have a treat—but he didn't care.

Finally, after more than four long, tedious weeks of staring at the ceiling and watching spiders spin their webs, he was going to escape the bedroom. And soon—when his leg was sufficiently healed so he could ride—he would leave La Escondida and its eccentric inhabitants altogether, and . . .

And what? Wander again?

"Careful now, my son," Tia said when she handed him his clothes. "Your injuries and the weeks in the bed have made you weak."

"I am not weak." *And I am not your son!* He grabbed his pants from her plump hands and started to stuff his right leg into them.

But a sudden attack of dizziness forced him to slow down, and he admitted that irritating though the old woman was, Tia was right about his physical condition. While she helped him dress, he vowed that he would begin exercising his muscles as soon as possible.

Outside, Tia sat him down on Pedro's large rock in the yard. "Stay here, Francisco, and I will bring you some apple cider. Then I am going to make noodles because you like them so much. Lots and lots of noodles! I will dry them so that whenever you want some I will have them."

When she disappeared into the house Sawyer lifted his face to the late-afternoon sunshine. He then began to survey his surroundings, taking careful note of the fact that most of what he saw was in sad condition. There were several large holes in the roof and the sides of the barn. He could hear a cow lowing from inside the shabby structure. There was a burro in there too, he remembered. Pancha the cow, and Rayo the burro. He wondered how the poor animals stayed warm and dry in the winter.

A rickety wagon sat near the bottom of one of the slopes that helped conceal La Escondida. Surely Zafiro didn't use the conveyance. It looked to be older than the mountains themselves. The thought made Sawyer wonder what she did use when the need to transport heavy things arose.

Of course, she rarely left the hideaway. But still, how and where did she obtain supplies? Did the nuns provide everything for her?

Still pondering his mental questions, Sawyer continued to look around. All the fences around the place were falling down, including that which penned the stallion Zafiro called Coraje. The beautiful steed cantered around inside the paddock, bucking and rearing every so often and then disappearing into a tumbledown shed that was supposed to—but probably didn't—keep him sheltered from severe weather.

There was a wildness about Coraje, a feral disposition that alerted Sawyer to the fact that the stallion was a mean one. He wondered how Zafiro fed the horse, then remembered that she threw his food over the broken down fence.

He looked around again, noticing that the cabin porch

was missing a few planks and one of its front steps, and the woodshed door was attached by little more than a prayer. The door appeared to have been yanked from its hinges. A bit of Maclovio's handiwork, probably.

Most of the vegetables in the garden were nibbled down to the ground, and the chickens were stuffed into some sort of enclosure made of pieces of broken fence and tree branches. The pen looked to have been built by a three-year-old child, and two of the chickens had already escaped its flimsy confines and were now heading happily toward the woods that surrounded the yard.

Still, the place was as tidy as it could be, swept and raked clear of all leaves, sticks, and other manner of debris. Pots and barrels of lemon-yellow marigolds and scattered beds of red and white roses brightened the area, and not one weed existed within the thick emerald grass that circled the cabin.

Although Zafiro could not accomplish everything by herself, she'd done an excellent job with those tasks she could handle.

"Sawyer!"

He looked up and saw her walk out of the woods, a big basket of clothes in her arms. Sunbeams kissed her night-black hair, making those tresses look as though they were sprinkled with diamond chips. And though she was still a good distance away from him, Sawyer couldn't miss the sparkle of her smile. So much time had passed since he'd last seen it that he'd forgotten how beautiful that grin of hers really was.

"Tia is sure you are strong enough to be outside?" she asked as she approached.

The question in his mind was if *she* was strong enough to carry the large basket of clothes. It was obviously heavy; her gait, her straining arms, and the slight grimace of exertion on her face attested to that.

Disregarding Tia's orders to stay on the rock, he rose and limped out to meet Zafiro. His thigh throbbed, but he willed the discomfort away with grim determination. When he reached Zafiro he couldn't miss the dark rings under her eyes. "Give me that basket." He reached for the woven container of clothes.

"No." She pulled it out of his grasp. "You do not look strong enough to—"

"I'm a man, for God's sake! I can carry a stupid basket of clothes easier than you—"

"But I am not recovering from Mariposa's—"

"Give it to me." Swiftly, he tried to yank the basket out of her arms again, but she refused to relinquish her burden. With all the tugging back and forth the basket toppled out of Zafiro's hands, spilling the freshly washed clothing straight into the dirt.

Zafiro stared down at the damp, soiled laundry. "Look what you have done. It took me all morning to wash, and I was just about to hang these clothes on the line. I told you to let me carry the basket, but you are just like a donkey! You will not give in!"

He realized she was trying to say that he was as stubborn as a mule, but now was definitely not the time to correct her.

If fury had another name it would be Zafiro Maria Quintana.

He reached up to pull at his bandanna before he remembered he wasn't wearing it. Instead, he massaged the back of his neck. "I'm sor—"

"Your apology will not get these clothes clean."

"Look, I said I was sorry. You look tired, and I was only trying to help—"

"Carrying a basket of clothes is not the kind of help I need from you, Sawyer Donovan."

Remembering all the broken things he'd noticed earlier—the barn, the fence, the cabin porch and step, the woodshed door, the chicken coop—he became instantly wary. "Zafiro, are you going to ask me to fix every cracked, missing, falling-down, poorly built, eaten-down, hanging-off thing around here?"

He sounded incredulous, she mused. As if the very idea of making a few repairs was the most outrageous thing he'd ever thought of. "You helped the nuns," she pointed out.

"But I didn't rebuild the entire convent, which is what the work here at La Escondida would require. Besides, I was only there a few days and was going to leave—"

"Oh? And where were you going to go?"

He opened his mouth to form a snappy retort, but couldn't think of what to say. "That has nothing to do with anything. The point is that—"

"I was not going to ask you to make any repairs, Sawyer, even though making them would be a nice thing for you to do for the people who have looked after you all these weeks. We have twisted ourselves backward for you—"

"If you didn't own a guard cat I wouldn't have needed any of you to *bend over backward* for me."

She noticed that he was standing with most of his weight on his good leg and realized that his thigh injury was still aching. "Go sit down before you fall down."

He watched her get to her knees and begin putting the dirty clothes back into the basket. "If you weren't going to ask me to make any repairs, what kind of help do you want from me?"

"I will tell you when you are well enough to give it to me."

"When I'm well enough I'm leaving, Zafiro."

She finished stuffing the clothes back into the basket and stood. "That is what you think."

"Zafiro, I can't stay here—"

"The nuns said you were just wandering when you arrived at the convent. You might have thought you were wandering, but you were not. You were brought here. God sent you here to help me."

Oh, so she'd decided to take the religious route, had she? he mused.

"I have prayed for the answer to my problems for a very long time, Sawyer. God answered my prayers with you."

"Yeah? Well, God forgot to tell me anything about it. Listen, Zafiro, I—"

"God forgets nothing, Sawyer. His mind is like a snare made of iron."

"God has a mind like a steel trap." For a moment Sawyer pondered what he'd said. God had a mind like a steel trap?

He'd never heard himself say anything so strange. "I'm going crazy," he muttered, raking his fingers through his hair. "This place and all of you loonies are driving me stark raving mad."

"You—"

"There's Tia with her kisses, her spankings, and her blasted bottle of castor oil. I'm hoarse from screaming at Lorenzo, Pedro told me yesterday that the Angel Gabriel fed a multitude of hungry people with two tortillas and a pork rib, and Maclovio has threatened to smash my face so many times that I almost wish he'd go ahead and do it to get it over with! Oh, and let's not forget Azucar, who comes into my room night after night to take off her clothes and grope at my groin! What a desirable bit of female flesh *she* is!

"And what about that feathered fiend, Jengibre? She's laid enough eggs in my bed to feed the entire country, most of which I've accidentally rolled onto and smashed! And look at my arms!" He pushed up his sleeves and showed her the numerous chicken-peck marks scattered up and down his arms. "Then there's you, Zafiro. You, telling me to please drown myself in a bucket of water. Telling me I'm some sissy ballet dancer. Jumbling every expression known to man. And now you think I'm staying here to help you because you say I'm heaven-sent?"

"You have punched the nail head."

"I have *not* hit the nail on the head, because I am *not* staying here!"

Calmly, Zafiro hoisted the clothes basket off the ground. "Since you are obviously well enough to scream at me, you are well enough to follow me back to the stream. While I wash these clothes again, I will explain to you the reasons why I need your help. I am sure that once you understand why I need you, you will stay. Now, come."

She headed toward the woods again, leaving Sawyer the choice as to whether to follow her or go sit on Pedro's rock.

If he followed her he'd be obeying her orders. "Now, come," he mocked her, inflecting just the right touch of haughtiness in his voice. What did she think he was? Some dog whose purpose in life was to do her bidding whenever she whistled or snapped her fingers?

He'd rather sit on the rock. Turning, he started toward the cabin, but stopped when he saw Pedro.

"Come join me," Pedro called, sitting on the rock with

his net spread over his legs. "Come, and I will tell you the story of how King Solomon parted the Red Sea by tossing forbidden fruit across the waves."

"Caves?" Lorenzo asked as he tottered off the porch and into the yard. "Yes, we used to hide much of our stolen booty in caves. Come here, Sawyer, and I will tell you about the adventures of the Quintana Gang. Did you know I broke Ciro, Jaime, Pedro, and Maclovio out of jail once? It was up somewhere in the Oklahoma Territory, I think, and they would have hanged the next morning if I hadn't saved them. I—"

"Care for a little snort?" Maclovio shouted as he lurched out from behind a thick garden of roses. He raised his bottle to his lips, but tripped over his own feet and dropped the flask. "My . . . my whiskey," he seethed, staring down at the bottle. "You made me drop my whiskey, Sawyer, and now I will smash your face!" His eyes narrowed in anger, he balled his fists and started toward Sawyer.

Sick to death of Maclovio's threat, Sawyer prepared himself for a fight, standing straight and tall, until he felt two hard little things press into the backs of his thighs. He spun around and saw Azucar. Rotating her shoulders seductively, she smiled up at him.

"Lover," she whispered, now pushing her hipbones into the fronts of his thighs. "Come into the barn, and I will show you exactly why a man needs a woman."

Quickly, she slipped her scarlet gown off her shoulders, and Sawyer saw that her breasts hung down her chest like two long socks with a few stones in the toes.

He headed for the forest as fast as his sore leg would allow him. Finding the worn path he figured Zafiro had taken, he followed the winding trail through the woods and soon heard the splashing and bubbling sounds of a stream.

"I knew you would come, Sawyer Donovan."

Breathing heavily from his flight through the forest, Sawyer massaged his aching leg, looked around, and saw Zafiro kneeling in front of the rushing creek, rewashing the soiled clothing.

Bent over the way she was, her bottom was a fetching sight to behold, especially since her skirt was damp and clinging to her in all the right places.

Places on his own body warmed and stiffened. His leg might still be weak, he mused, but the rest of his parts were in fine working order.

"See, Sawyer?" she said. "It is not so hard to do as I ask, is it? I told you to come, and here you are."

His irritation with her returned full force. "I'm not here because you told me to come, Zafiro. I'm here because if I'd stayed in the yard I'd have been raped or smashed."

She smiled. "It is pretty, my stream, isn't it? I come here not only to wash and bathe, but also to think when I need to think. I find peace here, especially at night when the moon lights the water and the cool breeze sings a song through the tree branches."

She leaned over the shirt she was washing, acting as though she was totally absorbed by her task, but in reality peering at Sawyer through the veil of hair that curtained the side of her face.

He'd lost a substantial amount of weight, and he appeared to be fatigued from his walk through the woods. But he was still the most powerfully built man she'd ever seen. The mere thought of all the power locked within his body sent a shiver of pleasure through her.

Giving a little sigh, she thought about all the many

early mornings she'd sneaked into his room to watch him sleep. He'd never awakened during her visits, and she'd stood beside his bed staring at him just for the pure delight the sight of him gave her.

He was so handsome. So . . . so masculine. So—

"I see you looking at me through your hair, Zafiro," he said smugly.

Yanked out of her reverie, Zafiro struggled to invent a lie that would convince the arrogant man that she was not looking at him. But before a suitable falsehood came to her, she spied a snake slither out of the woods and stop behind him.

She dropped the shirt into the water. "*Cascabel.*"

Sawyer saw the shirt float down the creek. "What?"

"*Casca-cascabel.*"

It sounded to Sawyer as though she was calling him a dirty name in Spanish. "What the hell is a *cascabel?*" he asked, wondering just how profane her name-calling really was.

"Snake. Rattlesnake. They crawl all over these mountains, Sawyer, and one . . . one is right behind you."

He looked over his shoulder. There, only inches away from his heels, lay a five-foot rattler.

He turned back to Zafiro, saw her fear, and couldn't resist playing with her just a bit. "If I had an ax I could chop off his head."

"I will go get an ax. And I think I saw a stick of dynamite in the barn one time."

He smiled. If she thought she needed dynamite for one little snake, he couldn't imagine what form of weaponry she'd use when faced with true danger. Besides that, if her dynamite was as old as everything else at La Escondida, a damn forest fire wouldn't light it. "You mean to tell me you don't have a cannon stashed away somewhere around here?"

"Do not talk, Sawyer." Slowly—so as not to agitate the dangerous reptile—Zafiro rose to her feet and turned toward the path that led to the cabin.

"He's not going to hurt me," Sawyer stated quietly. "In fact, if I ignore him he'll go away."

She gawked at him. "You are either the bravest man in the world or the stupidest."

Slowly, Sawyer reached up and snapped off a long, sturdy twig from the tree branch that swayed above his head. "The snake's not coiled up, Zafiro. He's not rattling his tail either. In fact, if he were any more relaxed he'd be dead. He's only sunning himself, and he's not at all upset that I'm standing beside him. *He's* the one who approached *me*, remember? Snakes don't go around looking for people to bite, you know."

She stared at him again, unable to believe what she was hearing. "My ears are telling lies."

"You can't believe your ears," he translated. Without a sound Sawyer turned around and looked down at the snake. Then, with equally slow and silent movements, he stuck the twig beneath the middle of the snake's body.

Wide-eyed and incredulous, Zafiro watched him flick the snake back into the woods as if the creature were naught but an earthworm. The resulting crackle of leaves told her that the snake's landing had been a soft one.

"There," Sawyer said, tossing the stick into the stream, "he vanished."

The snake might have vanished, but Zafiro's amazement did not. Never in her life had she seen a man confront danger with such aplomb. Not even her grandfather, the brave Ciro, had ever demonstrated such total control when faced with peril.

"You are really and truly him," she murmured.

"Him? Who him?"

"The man God has sent."

"You've been around Saint Pedro too long."

"I was sure before, but now I am more sure than ever. You will reteach the men their lost skills, Sawyer. After weeks of practicing with you, they will once again be the proficient men they used to—"

"Wait," Sawyer said, holding up his hand to stop her flow of chatter. "Wait just a minute. Are you saying you want me to turn back time? Transform your men into the young, strong, and able outlaws they used to be? *That's* what you need me for?"

She didn't speak, but he saw her answer in her eyes, eyes that had become luminous with pleasure and relief. She *did* expect him to do the impossible!

The drunk Maclovio. The deaf and sleepy Lorenzo. And the holier-than-thou false apostle Pedro.

She really and truly believed the aged outlaws could skip back over the decades!

Sawyer smiled. And then, within a split second, he threw back his head and laughed out loud. He couldn't remember the last time he'd laughed, but the amusement he felt over her plans was so great that he could not stem it no matter how he tried.

"You think I am teasing," Zafiro said. "That your leg is stretched."

A while passed before his laughter faded sufficiently for him to speak. "That you're pulling my leg?" He chuckled again. "Listen, I know you well enough now to know you're dead serious, but if you think for one minute that I'm going to try and turn those three bumbling grandsires back into skilled gunmen . . . For that, you don't need a man sent from God, Zafiro, you need God *Himself*!"

With a wave of her hand she brushed away his words as if they were nothing but bothersome insects. "You are making hills out of mountains of moles."

"Making mountains out of molehills is exactly what it would be like to turn your gang back into able-bodied—"

"You will make us all ready. Not only the men, but Tia, Azucar, and myself too. There is no reason I can think of why the women and I cannot learn to protect ourselves.

"Oh, Sawyer," she whispered, holding out her hands in a gesture of extreme gratitude, "you will take care of us. Finally, at last long, someone is here to make sure that no harm comes to us."

For many moments he merely gawked at her. No words would come to him, not a one.

He was too busy concentrating on what she'd told him.

Finally, at last long, someone is here to make sure that no harm comes to us.

From deep, deep within him rose a vehement aversion to the idea. He almost felt sickened by it. Indeed, his stomach pitched, his forehead beaded with sweat, and his pulse quickened.

"No. I can't take care of anyone, do you understand? I can't . . . can't keep any of you from harm." Battling to quell the horrible and incomprehensible emotions that festered inside him, Sawyer returned to the trail in the woods that led to the cabin.

Zafiro traipsed along right at his heels. "You would disobey God?" she demanded, speaking to his back. "He sent you to—"

"Look," Sawyer said, spinning around and stopping so quickly that Zafiro ran straight into him. He grasped her shoulders and aimed his gaze straight down into hers. "I—"

"You are a heathen, Sawyer Donovan, that is what you are! To ignore heavenly orders—"

"Heavenly orders?" Sawyer rolled his eyes.

"You are a sinner of the worst sort!"

"And only last month *you* were going to commit cold-blooded murder."

For a moment, she felt taken aback, unable to dispute his reminder. "Well . . . Horses come in different colors."

He had to think for a second. "That was a horse of a different color?"

"*Sí.* That is what I said. I was going to kill you for good reason. I believed you were going to hurt us. But your refusal to help us is selfish and mean. You have been chosen by the highest power to—"

"Chosen? For God's sake, all I did was chase you from the convent when I thought you'd stolen—"

"Meeting and chasing me was meant to be!"

"Really? And did God also mean for me to be half-killed by Mariposa?"

"I am sure that is the only way He could think of to get you inside La Escondida. And do not forget that He did not allow you to die."

"Oh, of all the . . ." Sawyer rammed his fingers through his hair. "All right, fine. Okay. If I get a sign from heaven . . . some sort of holy proof that I'm your . . . your *knight in shining armor*, then I'll stay and perform every chivalrous and valorous deed you ask of me."

"How long will you wait for the sign?" She prayed for

God to hurry up. He could be so slow sometimes in her opinion.

"Five minutes."

"What? But—"

"God made the whole world in only six days. Do you think He can't get some silly little sign to me in five minutes? Actually, He could probably give me my sign within the next few seconds, but seeing as how it's God I'm dealing with, I'll be generous and give Him the full five minutes. After all, He might be busy right now, sending more knights in shining armor to other damsels in distress."

When Zafiro fell into silence he realized he'd finally beaten her. She knew as well as he did that no heavenly sign was going to arrive within the next five minutes. Assured of his victory, Sawyer turned back around and quickly followed the trail out of the forest.

He'd leave that very afternoon, he decided. True, his leg continued to ache and he wasn't strong enough to ride a great distance, but surely he could make it to some small town or village.

Because there was no way in hell that he was going to stay at La Escondida and take care of Zafiro and her feeble-minded friends.

That thought in mind, he quickened his pace through the forest. As soon as he stepped out of the glade, he stopped.

Stared.

And couldn't believe what he was seeing.

"*Santa María*," Zafiro whispered, she too, stopping and staring at the sight in the yard. "Your sign. There it is. You *are* my warrior dressed in sparkling steel, and there is your weapon to prove it! What do you say now, Sawyer Donovan?"

Hoping the vision would disappear, Sawyer blinked his eyes several times.

But the dazzling apparition remained.

Its tip stuck in the ground, its jewel-studded hilt pointing toward heaven, a magnificent silver sword shone in the bright sunlight.

five

"I don't care what you say, that dumb sword is *not* a
sign from God." Sitting in a rickety chair at the
table in the kitchen area of the great room, Sawyer threw Jengibre off his lap and glared at the ancient
blade in Zafiro's hands. "You act like it fell straight out of
heaven and landed in the yard."

"It—"

"Look, Zafiro, you said yourself that that blade is one
of the convent's treasures, some sword used in the Holy
Crusades—"

"It is also the sign you asked for." Smiling, Zafiro
leaned over in her chair and placed the gleaming weapon
on the table. "Your heaven-sent sign."

"It is not!" Sawyer slammed his fist down on the table.
"Tia said that Sister Carmelita and Sister Pilar brought
the sword while you and I were still at the stream! The
nuns told her they thought I might be able to figure out a
way to use it bring down fresh meat."

"Yes, that is what Tia said the nuns told her."

"I can just see myself running through the mountains
chasing animals with a sword."

"Sawyer, *who* do you think made the nuns think of bringing a warrior's weapon?"

"What?"

Zafiro smiled more broadly. "God told them to bring it."

"That's stupid!"

Zafiro gasped and clutched at her sapphire. "Do you say that God is stupid?"

"I didn't say God was stupid, and stop twisting around my words!"

"He is yelling at you, Zafiro," Maclovio slurred from across the room, so drunk that his eyes were crossed. "Do you want me to smash his face?"

"Grace?" Lorenzo asked. He looked up and watched Tia remove a fried lamb chop from a pan of hot grease. "Yes, let's say grace so we can eat. I am hungry for the lamb the good sisters brought to us." He bowed his head, but instead of praying, he fell asleep and would have fallen out of his chair had Sawyer not reached out and pulled the old man into his lap.

"Hold him, Sawyer," Zafiro entreated when Sawyer began to put Lorenzo back into the chair. "He will wake up in only a minute. If you sit him back up now, he will only fall out again."

Sighing with irritation, Sawyer leaned back in his chair, holding the frail Lorenzo in his arms like a baby. Just when he'd adjusted himself comfortably, he saw Azucar leave her chair and walk around the table toward him. The satin-garbed hag ran her bony fingers across her sagging breasts then lifted her gown to show Sawyer her sticklike leg.

Dammit, there was no way in hell he could hold Lorenzo and fend off Azucar at the same time. "Get her away from me, Zafiro," he demanded.

Zafiro quickly complied, taking hold of Azucar's arm and leading the old woman back to her chair. "Sawyer does not have any money, Azucar. Would you give yourself to him for free?"

Azucar frowned fiercely. "No. Men pay me with full bags of gold."

Listening to their exchange, Sawyer wondered why he hadn't thought of the poverty-stricken idea. "Sorry, sweetheart, but I'm fresh out of gold."

"Tomorrow you will have some gold," she told him. "Then you will be able to afford the pleasure you will find in my arms." To make sure that he understood her promise of sexual ecstasy, she closed her eyes and slowly ran her tongue across her bottom lip.

"Tomorrow it is." Sawyer went along with her because, after all, he wouldn't be here tomorrow.

"I am ready for my lamb chop," Lorenzo said, twitching while he awakened and yawned. "Ready for . . ." His voice trailed away when he realized he was in Sawyer's lap. "Why are you holding me, Sawyer?"

"Because you—"

"Dinner," Tia announced, placing a platter of sizzling meat on the table. Roasted potatoes, black beans, a stack of hot corn tortillas, and a bowl of green chili-laden sauce accompanied the succulent lamb. "We must remember the good sisters in our prayers tonight," she said, wiping her hands on her apron. "Not only did they bring us the fresh meat, but they also brought tea and a big batch of apple tarts that they baked this morning. We should enjoy this wonderful meal because no one knows when we will get another like it. Apple tarts, they are your favorite, aren't they, my sweet Francisco?"

Sawyer didn't bother to reply. Lifting Lorenzo from his lap, he placed the man back into his chair. "You almost fell on the floor!" he shouted into Lorenzo's hairy ear. "Try not to go to sleep at the table anymore!"

"Any whore?" Lorenzo said. "No, Azucar is not just *any* whore. She is a whore with a heart of gold, Sawyer. Do you know that she sold her little pearl ring to buy me a birthday present? That was years and years ago, but I still have the pair of small scissors she gave to me. I use them to cut my toenails, and they are the best scissors—"

"Where is Pedro?" Tia asked, setting his plate on the table in front of his empty chair. "I told him only a little while ago that supper would soon be ready."

Instantly alarmed, Zafiro crossed to the window and scanned the yard. When she didn't see Pedro anywhere, her anxiety deepened, especially since the sun was sinking fast. "It is not like Pedro to wander out of the yard."

"Maybe he ascended into heaven," Sawyer quipped. "Or it could be you'll find him at the stream walking on water."

"You are in my chair, Sawyer," Maclovio said, frowning. "If you do not get up and let me have my chair, I will smash—"

"Gladly." Sawyer rose from his chair and assisted the intoxicated Maclovio into the seat.

"Francisco, sit down and eat your dinner," Tia ordered.

He decided to indulge her fantasy just this once because, after all, he was leaving. "I'm not hungry, Mama. I promise I'll eat later."

She studied his face. "You do look tired, my son. Go to bed, and I will bring you your meal in a while, all right?"

"Yeah, all right." He wondered how his departure would affect the old woman. After having finally "found" her long-lost son, she'd probably be devastated when she learned he'd left again.

He hoped she wouldn't be too sad for too long. It

wasn't that she truly mattered to him, but . . . well, she *had* taken good care of him.

And what about Lorenzo? he thought, glancing at the old man who was happily and industriously gumming a piece of lamb. Would the day come when Lorenzo fell out of a chair and seriously hurt himself?

Sawyer hoped not, just as he hoped Maclovio would not systematically destroy what little of La Escondida was still standing.

He wondered if Maclovio would ever stop drinking, wondered if Azucar would ever have one last romp between the sheets before she withered away, and wondered, too, where Pedro was. Surely he'd come straggling home soon, none the worse from his jaunt away from the house. Then Zafiro could stop worrying about him.

Zafiro. Sawyer stared at her back, for she was still standing in front of the window looking for Pedro. She had such small, delicate shoulders.

How long would they be able to bear the weight of her worries? Another year? Six months? A few weeks?

A matter of days?

"I must go," she said suddenly, whirling away from the window. "It is almost dark, and Pedro, he could be in trouble. I will lift every rock I see until I find him."

"You'll leave no stone unturned," Sawyer corrected her.

"Yes, that is what I said. I will be back in a while, Sawyer, and then we will continue to discuss the sword."

In a flurry of silky black hair and ragged cotton skirts, she disappeared through the front door. Sawyer had a mind to call her back and make her understand that he was leaving, but decided against the idea. She'd only try to talk him into staying.

What was the matter with him anyway? For a full five

minutes he'd been standing here wondering about and worrying over the six people who had done their level best to drive him insane during the past four weeks!

He was leaving. Leaving, and that was that. Zafiro's problems were not his own, dammit. He had his own troubles, for God's sake, and possessed neither the time nor the inclination to solve hers or anyone else's.

Cursing the ache in his leg, he left the great room, ascended the staircase, and soon reached his bedroom, where he quickly packed his belongings into his satchel. Once downstairs again, he saw that Maclovio and Lorenzo had both fallen asleep at the table and that Tia stood in front of the oven with her back turned to him.

Only Azucar saw him cross to the front door. He put a finger to his lips to ask for her silence, then blew her a kiss when she nodded. His gesture of affection so delighted her that a few tears appeared in her bleary eyes.

It sure didn't take much to make the old woman happy, and for a few seconds Sawyer watched her tears slide over and disappear into the maze of wrinkles on her face. The sight compelled him to send her not just one more airy kiss, but three.

Her joyful giggle—which sounded more like a cackle—was the last thing he heard as he stepped outside and shut the door. In only moments he found his mule, Mister, and his trunk in the dim barn. After bridling the animal, he reached for the trunk.

Instantly, he drew his hands away. He didn't want to touch the trunk.

Something horrible was inside. He knew it.

But he needed the trunk, he told himself. For some reason he knew he needed it.

Gritting his teeth against the almost overwhelming sense of dread that pounded through him, he lifted the trunk from the floor and attached it to Mister's back. But many long moments passed before his emotions returned to normal.

He led the mule out of the barn. Moonlight showed him the way out of La Escondida and out of the confines of the hideaway. After closing the concealed doors he spotted Mariposa, who was feasting upon a big fat rabbit. Zafiro had said that the cougar sometimes brought fresh meat to her and her charges, but the great cat sure didn't show any signs of sharing the rabbit.

He wondered when Tia would again have meat to prepare. The lamb the nuns had brought was only enough for one meal.

Instantly, he tore the thought from his mind and mounted Mister—a difficult task considering the fact that his leg was now hurting fiercely. Urging the surefooted mule down the pebbled slope, he prayed he'd make it to a village or even some small farm before pain forced him to stop.

But before he reached the bottom of the foothill the acrid smell of smoke stopped him. Twisting upon Mister's back, he spied the source of the smoke: a small fire burning in the near distance. Although nighttime had fallen, he could also see a white-garbed figure moving around the fire.

Flames shot up around the person, and Sawyer realized immediately that he or she was soon going to catch fire. "Get away from the fire!"

His warning echoed through the mountains, but the person on the hill made no move to obey. He or she began to jump up and down and finally fell to the ground.

Sawyer drove Mister back up the mountainside. When the animal arrived a few feet away from the blaze, Sawyer slid off its back and hurried to assist the groaning man on the ground.

He gasped when he saw that the man was Pedro and that the hem of Pedro's white robe was burning. Instantly, he grabbed Pedro's shoulder and hip and began to roll him all over the pebble-strewn dirt, thereby suffocating the fire that would have soon consumed the robe and Pedro.

"For God's sake, Pedro, what the hell—"

"The bush," Pedro said raspily, hoarse from breathing too much smoke. "I saw the burning bush on the side of the mountain and knew I was being summoned."

"What?" Confused, Sawyer studied the fire that still blazed nearby. His bewilderment disappeared when he saw that the flaming object was, indeed, a bush. The scripture-preaching Pedro had more than likely set the bush afire himself in an effort to bring the Bible story to life.

Sawyer examined Pedro's feet and legs, frowning when he saw several burned places on the old man's wrinkled skin. "You could have burned to death, crazy old man! Zafiro's looking all over for you, and here you are on the side of the mountain setting bushes on fire!"

"Leave me in peace, my brother," Pedro requested. "This is the garden of olives, and I must pray here. I lost my coat of many colors, you see, but after I pray I will find it."

Sawyer's lips thinned in a tight line of irritation. His leg hurt so badly now that he could hardly stand to use it, but he gathered the old man into his arms and placed him on Mister's back. He couldn't leave Pedro here alone. The elderly lunatic would more than likely pitch himself off the mountain and call to the angels to save him.

The mule's bridle reins clutched tightly in his hand, Sawyer limped his way back to La Escondida, and by the time he reached the hidden entrance to the hideaway, he knew that he could travel no further tonight. He had exhausted what little strength he had going up and down the mountain and would have to spend one more night in the concealed den of batty bandits.

So frustrated was he with the maddening turn of events, he failed to see the thick tangle of vines that covered the ground ahead of him. When he reached the mass of thorny vegetation, his right foot disappeared into the twisting stems, which wrapped around his ankle as if alive.

He let go of the bridle reins, and down the slope he rolled, head over heels, until a crash into the rattletrap wagon stopped his fast and painful descent.

The old, unsound cart immediately splintered apart, and Sawyer soon found himself buried beneath a pile of rotten wood.

"Sawyer!"

He heard Zafiro call to him, then heard her footsteps as she approached the wagon. "Here," he managed to tell her.

She looked at the mountain of wood that used to be a wagon. "Are you all right?"

Gingerly, he moved away a rusty nail that bit into his neck. "Oh, I'm just fine, Zafiro. In fact, falling down that rocky slope, crashing into a one-hundred-year-old cart, and being buried alive beneath a heap of worm-eaten wagon planks was so much fun that I think I'll get up and do it again."

His caustic reply assured her that he'd survive his little accident with the wagon, so she turned her attention to

Pedro, who was struggling to dismount from Mister. "Pedro—"

"I am very angry at Sawyer, Zafiro," the old man said, wincing when his scorched feet hit the ground. "Righteously angry, because I was just setting out to find some blind, paralyzed, and demon-possessed people to cure, when he came and got me! If I was not a saint, I would—"

"He was setting bushes on fire, Zafiro!" Sawyer yelled as he battled his way out from under the rotten wagon wood. "Then he set *himself* on fire!"

"On fire?" Tia repeated as she arrived at the scene, holding her skirts above the ground as she waddled along. "Pedro, come into the house this second and let me tend to your burns. And you, Francisco, get out of that wood before you get splinters in your little bottom!"

Splinters in his "little bottom" were the least of his problems. His leg was hurting so badly now that he actually longed to be back in the bed in his bedroom. Stumbling out of the pile of broken wood, he glared at Zafiro, who in his frustrated mind, was the indirect cause of every infuriating thing that had happened to him since the day he'd chased her from the convent.

He felt like yelling at her and decided to give in to the temptation. "Zafiro, I swear to God that from the second I laid eyes on you, my life has been—"

"Thank you, Sawyer," she said, walking toward him and taking his hands into hers. "Thank you for going out to look for Pedro the way you did."

"What? But I didn't—"

"Pedro has never left La Escondida before, so I did not think to look for him on the mountain the way you did. You are intelligent like a switch."

"If I were smart as a whip, I wouldn't be here! Look, Zafiro, you don't understand. I didn't—"

"If not for you . . . Oh, Sawyer, if not for you, dear sweet Pedro would have burned to death! I knew you were sent to me. I knew in my heart that you—"

"Would you stop?" Sawyer blasted. He yanked his hands from her grasp. "I didn't go looking for your dear sweet Pedro! I had left La Escondida, got that? Left, and I was already almost at the bottom of the mountain when I smelled the smoke from Pedro's burning bush! I found him by accident and would be on my way to the nearest village by now if not for him!"

She drew away from him; her fingers trembled around her sapphire. "The nearest . . . village?"

He saw the shock and hurt in her pretty blue eyes, and lowered his voice. "I *told* you I was leaving. Told you, but you didn't believe—"

"Azucar is on my rock!" Pedro shouted from across the yard, resisting Tia's attempts to escort him into the house. "I do not mean to be disrespectful, Tia, but a soiled dove has no place on the rock that I am to build a church upon! Now, tell her to get off."

"I will get off when I am finished brushing my hair," Azucar announced, shaking her brush at him. "Sawyer is back, and I am sure that he has brought gold with him. I must be beautiful for him when I go to his room."

"Broom?" Lorenzo asked from his spot on the cabin porch. "I will get you a broom, Azucar." Turning, he reached for the broom that leaned against the wall by the door, but just as he took hold of the handle Maclovio burst out of the cabin and knocked him down on the porch.

"Who ate all the apple tarts?" Maclovio demanded, holding the heavy silver sword the nuns had brought from the convent. In a drunken frenzy he lurched off the porch and began swinging and stabbing the sword at various objects in his path.

One sharp blow left a gaping hole in the side of the woodshed, wherepon the door promptly fell off. Another vicious swing of the blade cut a swath through one of the rose gardens, and then Maclovio walked into the chicken coop.

The feeble cage broke open, and the hens quickly squawked, flapped, and scooted their way to freedom.

"*Santa Maria*, Maclovio, look what you did!" Zafiro started to race toward him, but stopped when Sawyer grabbed her arm.

"Are you insane?" he barked down at her. "He's a drunk with a sword! A combination like that could get you killed!"

"What do you care?" she shouted back at him, struggling to remove her arm from his hold. "You are leaving! Now, let go of me before Maclovio destroys everything we have!"

Sawyer saw that Maclovio was now using the sword to hack through a row of throw rugs that Zafiro had beaten clean earlier in the day. The rugs hung on a rope strung from oak tree to oak tree, and in only a few moments two of them were slashed beyond repair.

He let go of Zafiro's arm. "I'm going to knock him senseless," he seethed.

"Do not hurt him, Sawyer!" Zafiro cried when he began limping toward Maclovio. "*Dios mío*, please do not hurt—"

"In his state *nothing* could hurt him!"

When he saw Sawyer coming at him, Maclovio raised the sword and smiled. "At last we will fight, eh, Sawyer

Donovan? I have been waiting for a very long time to smash your face, and now I will do it!"

Knowing that his leg would prevent him from participating in a long fight, Sawyer realized he had precious little time to subdue the man. Gritting his teeth against the pain that flared through his thigh, he lunged toward Maclovio. His head rammed into Maclovio's stomach while his hand yanked the sword from Maclovio's grasp. He tossed the weighty blade into the nearby rose garden.

Both men crashed to the ground. Stunned, Maclovio lay still, blinking up at the stars and smiling the ridiculous smile of a man thoroughly overcome by liquor. "Yes, Sawyer," he slurred, "they came from all around to see me gentle the horses. Those were the days, my friend, but now . . . now they are over."

Sawyer staggered to his feet and glared down at the inebriated old outlaw, his anger quickly waning when he saw that Maclovio's entire face was wet with tears.

"You have gold now, Sawyer?" Azucar asked from her seat on the rock.

He looked up and saw she was still brushing that dry and brittle-as-straw hair of hers as if it were the longest, most luxurious set of tresses ever to grace a woman's head.

And Tia, he noticed, continued trying to get Pedro into the house, a fairly impossible task as Pedro lay prostrate on the ground in front of a small tree that he swore was the True Cross.

Snorting sounds then took Sawyer's attention to the porch, where Lorenzo lay sleeping. The porch was hard, and Lorenzo's head had fallen halfway into the hole where the missing plank had once been. But the old man was sleeping as soundly as he would have had his bed been made of a multitude of down-filled mattresses.

A wave of pity came over Sawyer, and the feeling intensified as he saw Zafiro chase several chickens into the dark woods. If she didn't catch the fowl there would be no eggs.

She and her people needed those eggs.

God, they needed so many things.

He resisted going soft, however, reminding himself repeatedly that if he stayed at La Escondida, not only would he be forced to deal with his loss of memory, but a loss of his sanity as well.

Still, he reckoned he could perform one good deed for Zafiro and help her find her chickens. She and her companions needed those eggs. He'd stay and find her chickens, and then he'd leave.

His walk through the woods went slowly because he could hardly see where he was going, but he finally approached the stream. Weeping sounds melded with the gentle rush of the water. With naught but the silvery moonlight to aid him, Sawyer looked around the area.

There on the creek bank sat Zafiro, crying into the feathers of the two flapping chickens she held in her lap. She was the most pitiful sight Sawyer could ever remember seeing. Her small shoulders shook with her sobs, she made deep, choking sounds, and even from where he stood, Sawyer could see that her chickens were wet with her tears.

He joined her at her spot by the water. "You're going to drown those chickens if you don't stop crying all over them."

She hadn't heard him approach. The sudden sound of his voice scared her so badly that she jumped up off the ground, dropped her chickens, and almost fell into the stream. Her pulse pounding in her ears, she looked up at Sawyer.

He was leaving.

She'd lost her chickens.

Maclovio had destroyed half of La Escondida.

And Luis . . . The deep, cold knowledge that he was soon going to find her . . .

Zafiro felt her knees buckle and would have fallen to the ground had Sawyer not reached for and caught her.

"The danger," she wept into his shirt. "It is coming."

"What?"

"And my chickens are gone. Now we will have no eggs. The barn is going to collapse on Pancha and Rayo, the fences are all . . . Oh, Sawyer, what am I going to do? I try," she said, sniffling, "but I cannot do everything all by myself!"

When she began to sob again, her slender body quaking in his arms, Sawyer didn't know what else to do but hold her. Gently, he rubbed her back, his fingers slipping through the midnight silk of her hair.

"Your chickens are all around here somewhere." He tried to comfort her. "They'll probably come home when they get hungry enough. You know how chickens are— always on the lookout for grand adventures."

He glanced down to see if his silly chicken story had made her smile and saw that it had not. "Zafiro—"

"I wish my grandfather was still here. He would know what to do. And my father too. My father, he died when I was very small. I held his head in my lap when he died."

Sawyer's sympathy toward her tripled. "I'm sorry. About your father."

She nodded miserably. "I was so little when he died that I do not have many memories of him. That is a very sad thing to me, so I understand how you must feel when you cannot remember your own father. Or your mother.

You do not even know if they are alive. I am very sorry that you do not have your memories, Sawyer."

That she could grieve over his loss of memory when she had so many troubles of her own touched Sawyer very deeply. A while passed before he spoke again. "What happened to your father?" he asked gently.

Zafiro slipped out of his embrace and turned to face the stream. For a long moment she watched the moonlight spill over the water like glitter pouring down from the sky. "A very horrible man shot and killed him."

Luis. His very name caused her to shudder, but she would not tell Sawyer about him. What was the use?

Sawyer was leaving.

Her boots digging into the soft sand of the creek bank, she spun away from the water and trudged toward the path in the woods. "I will look for my chickens by myself," she said when she heard Sawyer's footsteps behind her. "You want to leave, and I will not ask you to stay."

As he followed her out of the woods and into the yard, he tried to feel relieved that she'd accepted his decision to leave. But worry pestered him like an itch he couldn't reach. "Zafiro—"

"You do not have to be my warrior in shining steel," she said, stopping and turning to face him. "Go now. I will pray that you find your memories and much happiness, Sawyer."

The squeak in her voice and the glimmer of desperation in her wide eyes seemed to reach out to him as if with hands and fingers, for he could almost feel the trembling caress of her despair.

Shoving his fingers through his hair, he turned, walked a few feet away from her, and saw something shining within the mass of red roses.

The sword.

He retrieved the great weapon. Its fine hilt felt cold and hard in his hands.

Was it really the sign he'd required of heaven?

He didn't know. But something—whether it was a damn set of infuriating coincidences, his own maddening conscience, or the power of a higher being—something had brought him here in the first place and taken him back when he'd tried to leave. No bewildering or painful emotion he possessed disputed that fact.

Holding the sword out in front of his chest, he turned the blade and watched moonbeams frost the steel with silver.

Finally, at last long, someone is here to make sure that no harm comes to us.

As he held the sword, Zafiro's statement came back to him.

She didn't understand. Didn't know.

It wasn't that he *wouldn't* keep her and her charges from harm.

He *couldn't*. If he tried, he'd fail. Some deep-down horrible place inside him knew that he would.

But hidden away from the world as Zafiro and her companions were, what harm could come to them anyway? he asked himself. The two most dangerous beings around the place were Jengibre and Maclovio, neither of whom posed any real threat to Zafiro or the rest of her charges.

Still holding the sword out in front of his chest, Sawyer deliberated. Maybe he could make a few chivalrous repairs around the place, he mused. And perhaps he could get Zafiro some livestock from somewhere and teach her to breed the animals so she and her charges would always have fresh meat.

Yes, he could do those things. And then she could take care of herself. Herself and her gang.

Maybe he could be her knight in shining armor after all.

Smiling as broadly as a man could with a realization that he was probably going to regret his actions and a leg that felt as if it were about to fall off, he faced Zafiro again, held the sword against his chest, and bowed.

"Sir Sawyer Donovan, milady. Your knight in shining armor."

six

A fter a full week's worth of rest, Tia's doctoring,
and several hearty meals of venison—thanks
to Mariposa's deer-hunting skills—Sawyer's
physical condition was much improved. Despite Tia's insistence that he was much too young to tackle heavy
chores, he began preparations for all the many repairs
needed around La Escondida.

He found an array of tools in the barn, all of which
Ciro and the men had once used to build the hideaway.
Some of the instruments were too old to be of use, but
most of them needed but a bit of cleaning and sharpen-
ing.

Still, he could use a few new things, namely a big sack
of nails. He knew he could probably find the things he
needed in one of the nearby villages, but with no money
and nothing with which to barter, he stood no chance of
obtaining new tools.

If only Zafiro would consent to sell her sapphire, he
thought. The money from the sale would not only buy
the things that would facilitate making the repairs, but a
great deal of other needed items as well.

But if Zafiro had wanted to sell the sapphire she'd have

done so a long time ago. He would make do with the tools he'd found in the barn and think no more about it.

The first thing he did was fell trees. He found the task exceedingly difficult. Not only had he not yet recovered the wholeness of his strength, but the old outlaws would not stay out of the forest. The men welcomed a chance to break their monotonous routines and help with the work, but when one towering oak almost fell on Lorenzo, Sawyer refused to continue his work until Zafiro had locked the men in the cabin.

"You could give them *some* little job to do, Sawyer."

"Keeping them out of the woods is for their own good."

Zafiro was far from finished with the conversation, but first she took a moment to admire her handsome adversary. Standing in the woods beside Sawyer as he stripped leaves and bark from a long, thick branch, she watched cords of muscle bulge and relax in his arms and coil beneath the skin on his chest like big, thick snakes. Not even the scars left by his injuries detracted from the magnificence of his body.

Cool though the forest was, she warmed as if standing in the blistering sun. "Do you know something, Sawyer? Watching you work without your shirt on makes me feel very hot. And I do not understand why."

He snapped up his head so quickly that a sharp pain ripped down his neck. "I thought you said Azucar told you about lovemaking."

"Lovemaking?" She leaned her head toward her shoulder. "What does lovemaking have to do with my feeling so hot?"

Apparently, Azucar hadn't gone into much detail about what desire felt like, Sawyer thought. The old soiled dove had probably skipped explaining that important part and plunged right into the physical aspects of the act itself.

So Zafiro didn't know as much as she thought she did.

Sawyer almost smiled. "Those warm feelings of yours have everything to do with lovemaking, Zafiro."

His voice had changed, she noticed. Had gone from a normal sound to a deep and husky sort of tone that made her feel as though he were touching her.

Caressing her bare skin.

She felt even hotter then and unbuttoned a few buttons on her blouse to cool herself off. "I . . . I will have to remember to ask Azucar about this hot feeling. She will know."

"I could tell you," Sawyer offered. "Better yet, I could show you." His gaze dipped down to her chest. Now that she'd unfastened a few of her buttons, he could see the soft swells of her breasts.

"Sawyer, you are looking at my—"

"I know."

"Stop it."

He didn't stop it. "You didn't mind when I did it before."

"But today you are making me feel so hot that I can hardly breathe."

She wasn't exaggerating, he knew. Her chest was fairly heaving, and each time she drew in a breath the opening of her bodice stretched open even wider, revealing yet more of her charms.

Sawyer's own breathing became a bit labored.

He wondered if she would let him kiss her. Wondered if she'd allow him to touch her.

He wondered if there was anyone else around who might see what he was about to do, and began scanning the area for any would-be voyeurs.

"I locked the men in the cabin, just as you told me to do, Sawyer," Zafiro said when she saw him looking around the woods. "But you know, there are many things they could help you do if you would only let them."

Her announcement thoroughly dampened his heated thoughts and feelings. Damn those three old men! Even when they weren't around they got in his way!

He wiped sweat off his forehead with the back of his arm. "That tree would have driven Lorenzo into the ground like a mallet hammering a nail into butter. And what about Pedro's so-called help? He could barely lift the ax in the first place, but when he finally managed to swing it toward the tree, he almost cut Maclovio in half. I need their help like I need a hole in the head, Zafiro, so keep them in the cabin while I'm working. Keep Azucar away too, for that matter. A man can't get much done while being ravished."

"*Muy bien*," she flared, taking a seat on the tree trunk and casting him a good, hard glare. "Fine. But you are trying to do a lot of work for just one man."

"I need this exercise, Zafiro. I don't want any help, got that? I want to do everything by myself because while I was lying in bed for all that time, I got weak."

"All right! Do every single little thing by yourself! But do not show me your tears when you have gone up the stream without a boat."

He stared at her, wondering why in the world she even attempted to use expressions that were not at all familiar to her. "I won't come crying to you when I'm up a creek without a paddle. But I won't be up a creek without a paddle, because even though the work I've stayed here to do for you is a lot, it isn't impossible. Dealing with your three men *is*."

His last statement made her wonder if the time to talk

to him again about helping her men with their forgotten skills had come. Irritated and impatient with them as he was now, he wouldn't laugh as he'd done the first time she'd broached the subject.

He'd shout. He might even leave, especially since he believed that he was staying only until he'd finished the repairs around La Escondida—a belief he'd made clear to her on numerous occasions since the night he'd agreed to stay.

It wasn't that she didn't deeply appreciate his willingness to rebuild La Escondida. But broken fences, a shabby woodshed, a rickety barn, and a missing porch step were not going to kill anyone.

She had to tell him about Luis. Had to somehow convince him to practice fighting skills with her men.

"Sawyer, about my men . . ."

"Yeah?" He watched her carefully, not caring for the look of hesitancy on her face. She was up to something, he realized. Something that was going to irritate the hell out of him. "What about your men?"

"Well," she began, then gave him what she hoped was a pretty smile, "they might be across the mountain, but—"

"Over the hill."

She wasn't about to argue with him. Not when she had such a monumental favor to ask of him. "Over the hill? Yes, that is how it goes. You are right, and I was wrong."

Her quick admission of her error deepened his suspicion that she was up to no good. "Zafiro, what exactly are you getting at? I already know your men are old."

"Old, yes, but just because ice is all over the fire does not mean the roof's cold. I mean . . . well, what I mean is that under their wrinkles they are still on fire."

"There may be snow on the roof, but inside the fire's still burning?"

"Yes, and my men still have much fire inside. Well, maybe not fire, but they still have embers that can be fanned into flames."

A long while passed before Sawyer finally understood what she was talking about. "You still want me to work with your men, don't you? Turn them back into the skilled, able-bodied outlaws they used to be."

When she nodded and gave him another of her pretty smiles, he shook his head and gave her one of his terrible frowns. "No."

"Sawyer, let me explain why I need you to—"

"I don't care why! My answer is no!"

"But you do not under—"

"No, no, no, no, and *no*! I mean it, Zafiro. I only stayed to patch up this crumbling castle of yours."

"You are the filth of the world!"

"Or the scum of the earth. Take your pick. But either way I don't want anything to do with those three bumbling bandits."

"All right!" With that, Zafiro stormed out of the woods and marched straight into the cabin, slamming the door behind her.

And long hours later, when nighttime fell and Sawyer entered the cabin and trudged wearily toward his own room, too weary to even nibble at the supper Tia had prepared for him, he saw light seeping out from beneath Zafiro's door.

He stopped in front of the door and thought he heard a sniffling sound. Was she weeping? And if she was, had she been crying all day, ever since he yelled at her in the woods?

He told himself to ignore her sad little sounds. Told

himself that women always cried when they didn't get their way.

Told himself he didn't care if she cried all damn night. He'd been working since dawn and was too tired and sore to bother with female tears.

He told himself to open the door. And so he wrapped his hand around the knob.

But what if she was indecent? What if she was naked?

So what if she was? She'd seen him naked before, many times.

She'd seen *him* naked, but he'd never seen *her* naked. He told himself that fair was fair.

The wooden portal creaked softly as he swung it into the room. And there on the bed, with an array of miniature paintings spread all around her, sat Zafiro.

Sawyer sucked in a breath so deep that his lungs ached.

She wasn't naked, but she might as well have been. Her wisp of a gown was so sheer, so delicate, that it made Sawyer think of a pretty blush upon a soft cheek.

He could see straight through the pale pink gown. Could see the dark roundness of her nipples and the dusky shadow between her breasts. And her extraordinary sapphire blazed there too, its fiery beauty highlighting the perfect breasts upon which it shone.

"I . . ." he said, still staring at her breasts, "I guess you're trying to breast—I mean rest. *Rest!*" He drove his fingers through his hair, damning her breasts and his own slip of the tongue.

He was acting like some adolescent confronting his first glimpse of female sensuality. "I guess you're trying to *rest.* I'll go, so you—"

"You can stay if you want to."

He didn't want to. Well, yes, he did want to.

But he couldn't. Shouldn't. It was getting late. She wasn't wearing much more than a blush and a sapphire. If he stayed, there was no telling what might happen.

No, he needed to leave. Needed to go, and that was that.

He stayed. "So," he said, shutting the door, "this is where you sleep."

Her room was as small as his own, maybe smaller, but more feminine. She'd filled numerous bottles and jars with small pine boughs and bloodred roses, and the plants' potent scents suited her—reminded him of her pungent, fiery character.

Mismatched throw rugs, yellow, red, blue, and green, splattered the wooden floor with wild splashes of color, and thin red-and-white striped curtains fluttered in the breeze that swept through the two windows. On one windowsill sat a tin candle holder coated with ivory wax.

The doors of her armoire were open; two tattered skirts, three worn blouses, and a red-and-yellow serape hung inside. The only other furniture in the room were a battered rocking chair with an equally old guitar resting on the seat, a wooden stand with a blue pitcher on it, a bedside table, and Zafiro's bed, which was covered with a spread that looked to be made of the same coarse, brown fabric that the nuns' habits were made of.

Store signs—the kind of circulars that shopkeepers posted in their mercantile windows—covered one entire wall of the room. The creased, yellowing posters advertised crackers, tobacco, saddle soap, weapons, and ammunition, flour, sugar, cornmeal, coffee, and additional dry goods. Other signs publicized a county fair, free kittens, a church social, and work for hire.

More circulars were in Spanish, and Sawyer couldn't

read what they said, but all the fliers had been folded and unfolded numerous times before being pinned to the wall.

He looked at Zafiro again and saw that she was gathering up all the little framed paintings and depositing them into an iron box that said WHISTLE CANYON BANK on the lid.

"What are those?" he asked, walking toward her bed. Glancing down, he noticed that every small painting was of a woman.

"They are paintings." She dropped the last one into the box. "Do you want some tea?" She pointed toward a half-empty cup of pale yellow liquid. "It is lemon tea."

He wondered how she could be so nice to him after he'd yelled at her the way he had earlier in the woods. "No, thanks." Sitting down at the foot of her bed, he allowed himself another glance at the absolutely gorgeous visage of her breasts, then looked at the pile of small paintings in her box. "I heard you crying. Were you crying over those little portraits?"

She closed the box's lid. "Yes. Sometimes when I look at them, I only look at them and wonder. Other times, when my mouth is down, I cry."

When her mouth was down, he repeated silently. "When you're down in the mouth."

"However the saying goes, I mean that when I am in a sad mood the paintings sometimes make me cry. Today I am in a sad mood because you will not—"

"You were crying over women you don't know?" he interjected, unwilling to discuss her men.

"Yes."

"Why?"

She brought her knees up to her chest and circled her arms around her legs. "Because I do not know who they are."

"I don't know who they are either, but they don't make me cry."

She rested her chin on her left knee. "They do not make you cry because they do not mean anything to you."

"Well, how can they mean anything to you if you don't know who they—"

"I do not want to talk about the paintings." Quickly, she slipped off the bed, crossed to her armoire, and shut its doors. "What did you get done today, Sawyer? Without the help of my men?" she added snippily.

He chose to ignore her irritation because reacting to it would only cause an argument. And bickering with her was the last thing he wanted to do tonight.

He studied her breasts again, then drew his gaze down lower. Now that she was standing up he could also see the patch of darkness between her thighs.

"Sawyer," Zafiro said, "you have been staring at my breasts since you came in here, and now you are looking at my—"

"Well, it isn't easy not to, Zafiro, especially since I can see straight through your night—"

"This used to belong to Azucar," Zafiro interrupted, totally unconcerned as she looked down at her gown and then picked up the sides to show Sawyer how full the skirt was. "One of her lovers gave it to her as a gift. I think its age has made it see-through."

He managed to lift his gaze back up to her face. "You really don't mind when I look at you, do you?"

"As I told you before, you cannot help giving your eyes a lot of food because you are a man."

"Giving my eyes . . . Oh, you mean I'm feasting my eyes on you."

"Yes, that is what I said." She ambled away from the

armoire, stopping by the window. There, she looked down at the yard, trying to see the work Sawyer had accomplished that day.

She saw nothing but the falling-down fences, the shabby woodshed. . . . "You did not do anything today!"

Every muscle in his body hurt, and she claimed he hadn't done anything? "For your information I got a few boards done, and—"

"A few boards?" She turned from the window, swiping at her hair as the night breeze rustled through it. "Then you have not even put a dent in the surface!"

"I have *so* made a dent in it *and* scratched the surface! Don't forget that I also felled the trees, stripped them, split them—"

"You—"

"The work is going to take me longer than a day or two, Zafiro."

"It wouldn't if you would let my men help."

"No."

"But—"

"Where did you get all those store signs?"

When he abruptly changed the subject she gave a loud huff and glared at the wall papered with the circulars. "I collected them."

"From where?"

She watched him stretch out on her bed and slip his hands behind his head. Never having seen a man on her bed before, she took a bit of time to savor the sight.

"Is it your turn to stare at me, Zafiro?"

"You're the first man who's ever been in my bed."

A shame she wasn't in it with him, he mused. He looked at her breasts again. They weren't large, but they weren't overly small either.

They were the perfect kind. Two perfect handfuls of softness, just right for holding, for tasting—

"Sawyer?"

He frowned, realizing she'd been talking to him and that he hadn't heard a word she'd said. "I'm sorry, what did you say?"

"You look like you are not on this planet."

"I look like I'm in another world," he translated. "I was just thinking. About . . . about your signs."

"I got them from all the little stores that were in all the towns the gang and I visited." She studied the circulars again, her gaze touching each of them. "Well, I did not go to some of those towns," she admitted softly. "The men, they stole many of the signs and brought them to me."

"What do you mean, they brought them to you?"

She left the window and walked to the sign-papered wall. "Grandfather would not let me go to the towns if he and the men were going to steal there. I had to wait far away from the town with Tia and Azucar."

Sawyer watched her touch a circular that publicized a cure for warts. "The infamous Quintana Gang is wanted in two countries for stealing mercantile advertisements?"

His ridiculous question coerced her to smile at him. "No, but before they robbed the banks, jewelry stores, or the various wealthy citizens, they took the signs for me. You see . . . I never knew what it was like to live in a real town. We were always moving. Escaping, staying as far ahead of the law as we could.

"But how I loved those towns, Sawyer," she continued, looking at her signs again. "I saw children playing in the streets with their friends and puppies, and I wanted to be a part of their games. Only one time did a few children invite me to join them. We sat in a circle in front of the church and took turns secretly picking out something in our surroundings. When we had picked it we would tell the others what color the thing was that we had spied. Then the others would try to guess what specific thing we'd seen by looking for the color we had named. I won the game by picking something green. The children guessed at every green thing they saw, but no one noticed the green circle around one girl's throat. Her necklace was of cheap metal and had made a green circle on her skin.

"I had never played that game before, and I liked it very much. I also liked to watch the storekeepers sweep their porches, the townspeople greet each other as they passed each other on the boardwalk, and I even liked to spy on the harlots who flirted with the men in the saloons."

"And that's where you heard the expressions you like to use, huh? In those little towns."

"Yes."

Sawyer decided she collected the colorful expressions the way she collected her signs. Since she'd probably heard the sayings only once or twice, that explained why she could never remember them correctly.

"I watched ladies pick out hats and gloves and handbags," Zafiro went on. "Their children grabbed great handfuls of candy out of big jars that sat on the counters in the mercantiles. Old men sometimes sat outside the barbershops, playing checkers or sitting in rocking chairs, talking about the weather or the last sermon they'd heard at church. I watched some sweethearts once too. It was almost nighttime, and there was a swing hanging from a tree in the shadows near a small café. The sweethearts sat in the swing, swinging, holding hands, laughing, and whispering to each other."

Sawyer watched her look toward the window with a faraway look in her eyes, and he realized she was remembering the happy times she'd spent in the little towns.

Her memories were familiar to him. Had he lived in a town like those she'd described? Or had he only visited various towns the way she had?

"And sometimes," Zafiro said, "when classes were over for the day I would watch the children come out of the little schoolhouse—"

"You never went to school?"

"No. But the gang taught me to read and figure numbers."

"But when you were in those towns watching the schoolchildren, you wished you could go to school with them."

"Yes. I'd even pretend I was one of them. I'd admire the little girls' pretty dresses and pretend that I had a whole closetful in my own house—a house that I always imagined was at the end of Main Street. I did have one dress though."

She paused a moment to remember the fancy frock that Lorenzo had gotten for her. "Lorenzo stole a dress off a clothesline once. He said he saw it blowing in the breeze and knew it would be just my size. It was a white dress with tiny pink ribbons going down the front, and the bottom of the skirt was edged with pink lace. I wore it to church whenever Grandfather thought it was safe enough for us to stop someplace on Sundays. But I grew out of the dress very quickly, and I did not get another dress until we came here and met the nuns. Grandfather, he was a very good man and he usually gave me everything I wanted. But he could not understand why I wanted dresses. Dresses, he said, were not made for riding.

And we were always riding, so I wore breeches all the time."

Sawyer glanced at her armoire. Zafiro still didn't have many feminine clothes. Only a few ragged skirts.

She'd be beautiful in a fancy dress, he mused. A yellow one, or maybe a blue one, sapphire blue like her eyes. "Can't you sew yourself a dress?"

"Not without fabric."

"Oh."

"Do you know that I still remember the town where Lorenzo stole that dress off the clothesline? I sat on a porch step in front of a doctor's office in that town, and a fat woman with a flowered hat on stopped and asked me if I had heard the latest news. When I told her that I had not, she looked up and down the street, bent down to me, and told me that Maggie O'Donald—who was an Irish Catholic—had run off and married Wade Simms, the son of the Baptist preacher. The lady tried to act very upset, but I could tell she was happy to tell me the news. Later, Lorenzo told me that every town had a town gossip and that the fat lady who had spoken to me was that town's gossip. After that I always wondered if Maggie and Wade Simms were happy together. I did not know who Maggie and Wade were, but I still hoped that they were doing well together."

Sawyer pondered her story for a long while before speaking. "So the signs reminded you of all the things you liked seeing in the towns. That's why you collected and kept them."

Folding her arms across her chest, Zafiro returned to the bed and sat down beside Sawyer's feet. "Yes, and I would take them out of my satchel all the time to look at them and to think about what it would be like to go to school and play with other children. I wanted to buy and eat candy out of the big jars at the stores and hear town gossip from fat ladies with flowered hats on. Since I could not do any of those things, the signs helped me to pretend that I was doing them. Sometimes the gang would pretend with me. Tia would be the fat town gossip, Azucar would be herself, Lorenzo would be a shopkeeper and sell me candy that he'd bought especially for our pretend times, and Maclovio and Pedro would sit around and play checkers while talking about the weather and church sermons. Grandfather, he would be the swing I saw near the café. He'd clasp his hands together, have me sit in his palms, and then he would swing his arms back and forth, just like a real swing."

The Quintana Gang had been good to Zafiro, Sawyer realized. Good as the gold they stole.

Newborn respect for the old people welled within him. Whatever they were now, however eccentric they acted, ceased to matter.

Maclovio, Lorenzo, Pedro, Azucar, and Tia had loved Zafiro as if she'd been their own daughter. They still did, he realized, and that fact did much to sway his feelings toward them.

Tomorrow perhaps he could find some odd job for the men to do. Something simple that wouldn't be dangerous to them. "You still think about life in a town, don't you, Zafiro?" he asked quietly.

She nodded. "Most nights I fall asleep looking at my signs and thinking about how nice it would be to live in a town."

When she fell into pensive silence Sawyer did the same, thinking about how much she missed out on as a little girl. Always traveling around, fleeing from the law, and camping out in forests or deserts or mountain coves with the gang, she'd never had the opportunity to enjoy a social life. Not as a child, a young girl, or even now as a full-grown woman.

Pondering her, he realized he really knew very little about her.

And he realized he wanted to know more. "How old are you?"

"I am twenty-five. You? *Cuantos años tienes?*"

He figured she was asking him how old he was. "I don't know."

"You cannot remember."

He sat up in the bed and thrust his fingers through his hair. "I . . . It's strange. I can remember some things, but . . . but not others."

When he ceased speaking she wondered if talking about his memory loss still bothered him. The possibility hurt her a bit, for she'd certainly been open with him tonight. "You do not have to talk about it if you do not want to, Sawyer."

He started to tell her that she was damn right that he didn't have to talk about it if he didn't want to, but stopped himself when he realized that she'd made her statement in a voice as soft and gentle as a child's sigh.

What the hell. He decided to talk to her. "Well, I understood everything you said about towns, so I've probably been to many of them. And not only since I lost my memory either. I remember—I don't know. I remember being in a mercantile when I was young. I remember dipping my hand into a candy jar like the one you described. I grabbed out a jawbreaker almost as big as my fist, and it took me almost two weeks to lick and suck it down small enough so that I could finally bite and chew it."

He leaned his head back and stared at the ceiling, summoning whatever other memories his anguished mind sheltered. "I remember a horse too, but I don't remember whose it was. He was a very unusual-looking horse. A white gelding with streaks of black in his mane and tail and a solid stripe of black that ran down the full length of the front of his left foreleg. I guess he sticks out in my memory because his markings were so strange."

Zafiro tried to imagine the horse he described. "He does sound unusual. I do not think I have ever seen a horse like that. Do you remember anything else?"

"Lots of things, but none of them tells me anything about who I am or where I'm from." He concentrated for a moment. "For instance, I remember sleeping with a puppy. She was female. I know she was really ugly, but I can't recall what she looked like. All I know for sure was that she was a hideous-looking animal, and her name was Pretty Girl. And I remember making her a collar out of the reins of some old bridles. I made it too big for her so she'd grow into it. It was made of braided leather strips tied together, and Pretty Girl . . . well, she wore the collar as if she knew it somehow helped her live up to her name.

"I remember insignificant things like that," he said, "but I can't remember how old I am."

Zafiro's heart felt so swollen with emotion that it seemed to have swept into her throat. She reached out and patted Sawyer's thigh. "You look like you are around thirty. Maybe thirty-one or thirty-two."

"That old?" God, her hand felt good on his leg.

"That is very young compared to the men I am used to being with." *Santa Maria*, his leg muscles felt good beneath her palm.

Trying to read her thoughts and knowing full well he was reading them correctly, Sawyer smiled. She liked touching him. "Was one of the little towns you visited called Whistle Canyon?" He picked up the iron box in which she'd put her miniature paintings of all the women.

"No, I never went to Whistle Canyon. The gang robbed the bank there though. Not once, but three times, and they were never caught. That box was once full of money."

"What did the gang do with all the money they stole? You didn't have any dresses. You didn't live in a home that had to be furnished and kept up. You had only your horses and yourselves to feed. So what happened to all the money?"

"We bought what we needed to survive. Things like food, sturdy clothing, tack for the horses. Grandfather gave the rest away."

Her announcement stunned him. "He gave it away? Then why'd he even bother stealing so much in the first place?"

"Poor people needed it. We met a lot of very poor people while we traveled, Sawyer, and do you know that it was the poor who helped us more often than the rich? They gave us whatever we needed. The rich people, they usually told us to be on our way, even when all we asked for was water for our horses."

Thinking about what she'd said, Sawyer realized that although the men in the Quintana Gang were criminals, they were benevolent ones. "Like Robin Hood and his Merry Men."

"Robin Hood and his Merry Men?" Zafiro tried to remember if she'd heard of the gang, but could think of no instance when her grandfather had mentioned the men. "I was with my grandfather and his men for many years, but I do not think we ever met Robin Hood and his Merry Men."

Smiling, Sawyer recalled that she'd never been to school. "None of you ever met him, Zafiro. Robin Hood lived a long time ago. He was this thief who lived in Sherwood Forest with his men."

She looked at him for a long moment. "I think you must have gone to school when you were little, Sawyer. You know many things."

He shrugged. "Maybe. Or it could be that I just heard the story about Robin Hood somewhere."

"His men were happy men."

"What? Oh. Yeah, I guess they were happy. Anyway, I think the forest they lived in is somewhere in England. Robin Hood used to rob from the rich people and give money and jewels and stuff like that to poor people."

Zafiro took a moment to deliberate upon the story he'd told her. "Yes, Grandfather was like Robin Hood. Lorenzo, Pedro, and Maclovio were too. Maclovio once gave his horse away. He loved that horse as if it were human, but he gave it to a young boy who did not have a horse. And I remember one time when the gang had just stolen several sacks of gold from a train. Grandfather pocketed what he thought we would need for a while and said we would give the rest to a man in a town called Candelaria. Years before, a man there had given the gang food and shelter on a stormy night, and Grandfather never forgot him. But before we arrived in Candelaria the Night Master found us."

She'd spoken her last statement with such awe in her voice that Sawyer was instantly intrigued. "The Night Master?"

"Night Master was the only thief in the whole world who was more skillful than the Quintana Gang. I was fifteen when I first saw him, and I remember him well. He rode a horse as black as sin. And everything he wore—his breeches, gloves, boots, and mask—was just as black. I remember his black satin cloak the best. Its big, round buttons shone like white fire, and Grandfather said that nothing in the world could shine like those buttons—except diamonds.

"Diamonds," she whispered, rubbing her eyes with her fist. "Shortly before Night Master became known, a royal lady from another country had been visiting in Texas. While she was traveling in her carriage her soldiers were attacked by a masked highwayman. He attacked so suddenly and made such noise with his guns that the soldiers' horses reacted violently. Before the soldiers could calm their mounts, the highwayman had slipped the jewelry from the royal lady's neck and ridden into the night!"

Sawyer noticed that while she told him the story she'd stopped caressing his thigh. Obviously, she was enthralled with her tale about the Night Master. More so than she was with his leg. "Sounds like something right out of a book of fairy tales to me. Kind of fanciful, don't you think, the mysterious, black-garbed highwayman?"

"What?"

"That Night Master guy was probably no more than some petty pickpocket. Someone told a story about him, and then the tale grew more and more elaborate with each telling. The story's just too fantastic, Zafiro. Too romantic to be true." He moved his leg a bit to remind her to keep caressing it.

"The story is true, Sawyer, and there is more." She began caressing his leg muscles again. "The next time the masked highwayman struck, his cloak glittered with diamonds. He struck again and again and again, each of his midnight holdups more daring and successful than the last. People soon started calling him the Night Master, and rumors went around that the diamonds on his cloak came from the necklace he stole from the royal lady."

Sawyer rolled his eyes. "This story is getting more far-fetched by the second."

"Sawyer—"

"All right, all right." Biting back a smile, Sawyer affected a dramatic tone of voice. "And then, one dark and stormy night, the romantic and fanciful Night Master stole from the Quintana Gang, too. Mounted upon his magical horse—who could probably fly—and wielding his trusty sword, he—"

"I am not going to finish telling you about our meeting with Night Master if you do not stop—"

"Sorry."

"As I said," Zafiro continued, stifling a yawn, "our gang stole gold from the train, and then they rode over the border into Mexico, where Azucar and Tia and I were waiting for them. From there we were to ride to Candelaria, but only minutes after the gang arrived, Night Master came. He rode straight into our camp . . . directly into the light of the campfire, showing no fear. The men, they drew their guns, but Night Master was faster. He shot their guns from their hands. Not even Pedro, who was like magic with a gun, could stop him. Night Master then demanded our gold. While watching him, I counted twenty-five diamonds sewn down the length of his cloak."

Sawyer swore he saw twin stars dancing in her eyes. He rolled his own eyes again. "And then Night Master smiled, and his smile was like a flash of bright white in the dark shadows of midnight. He threw back his head and laughed too, and the sound of his laughter sent shivers down everyone's spines."

"You are right. He *did* smile at me. Smiled and told me

that because my eyes were so pretty, he would never again take from the Quintana Gang."

Sawyer didn't miss her breathy little sigh. "I think you have pretty eyes too."

She seemed not to hear him, he noticed. Or if she did, she obviously wasn't as pleased with *his* flattery as she'd been with Night Master's. "You have a nice smile too, Zafiro."

"Later," Zafiro went on with her story, "while we sat around the campfire, Grandfather laughed and said that being robbed by Night Master had been an honor. He told us that none of us should forget it, not ever, because Night Master was just as his name implied—a master of the night, and his story would one day be a legend."

"Did you hear what I said?"

"What?" She gave another great yawn.

"About your smile."

"What?"

He saw that her eyes watered with sleepiness. "Never mind. Lie down."

When he got off the bed, she crawled into it and drew the covers up to her chin. "Night Master died."

"Poor guy."

"He was last seen here in Mexico. He shot down a group of men near a village. Witnesses say one of the men shot back at him before escaping. Night Master disappeared then. That was about six months ago. No one ever saw him again, and the people who watched what had happened said he'd been shot and that he'd died of his wounds. The nuns learned of his death from a few vaqueros who stopped at the convent. They told me about it when they heard."

"But his legend lives on."

She nodded and closed her eyes. "You can look at the paintings in the box if you want to."

"Why would I want to see paintings of women I don't even know?"

She rolled to her side. "One of them might be my mother."

"Your mother. I see." One of them was her mother?

Deeply curious now, he retrieved the iron box, lifted the lid, and looked at the painted faces. All of the women were fair-skinned and blue-eyed.

That explained the color of Zafiro's eyes. "Zafiro, how'd you get all these little paintings, and why do you think one of these women might be your—" He stopped speaking when he saw she was fast asleep.

He laid the box at the end of her bed and watched her for a while. Lamplight flickered over her face, highlighting her beauty, emphasizing the beautiful golden brown of her skin. The light also sparkled through her hair, which lay spread over her pillow. Her raven-black hair . . . the stark whiteness of her pillow . . .

The striking contrast of colors compelled Sawyer to reach down and hold one lock of her hair. So black that it almost appeared blue, the glossy tress felt thick and soft in his hand, like a ribbon of heavy ebony satin.

She made a small mewling noise in her sleep, and then another. Sawyer listened, deciding the little moans sounded contented rather than sad.

He wondered if the diamond-studded Night Master filled her sleep-induced fantasies.

Or maybe she'd found her blue-eyed mother in her dream.

Could be that she was dreaming about living in a little town, wearing pretty dresses and swinging in swings.

Or perhaps she was receiving her first kiss.

Her first kiss.

He fell into deep thought. She was twenty-five, he recalled. And she'd never had a beau. Had never enjoyed a courtship with a man closer to her age.

Sawyer couldn't remember if he'd ever enjoyed a courtship either, but his situation was drastically different from Zafiro's. He wasn't stuck here at La Escondida the way she was. When he left the mountain hideaway he could find a woman to court and marry if he so chose.

But such things were not going to happen for Zafiro. She'd spend the next ten or fifteen years hidden away here in the Sierras, and when all her dependents were buried she'd probably live the rest of her life at the convent with the nuns. She'd have nowhere else to go, no other friends or family to keep her company.

Maybe she'd even join the holy order and become a nun.

A perfect rose that budded, bloomed, and withered away without anyone ever beholding its beauty, he thought. Such was the life she would lead.

What a waste.

Thoughts of her tragic fate still lingering in his mind, Sawyer gazed at her mouth. Her lips were parted slightly, like two pink petals about to open and blossom. They shone, probably because she'd licked them before falling asleep.

They sure did look soft, he thought. Sweet like sugar too, and her breath more than likely still smelled like the lemon tea she'd been drinking when he'd come into her room.

Pink petals. Sugar. Lemon.

What man could resist sampling an exquisite combination like that?

Especially when no other man had ever sampled it.

He bent over her, and when his hair fell over her graceful shoulder, he waited to see if she would awaken.

But she only sighed again, a warm breath that still held a faint scent of lemon. Sawyer could barely wait to feel her petal softness and taste the sugar sweetness of her lips.

Closing his eyes, he pressed a kiss to her mouth, a kiss so light and airy that she didn't move as much as an eyelash.

But although the kiss might not have affected *her*, the sensuous encounter left Sawyer so thoroughly drugged with desire that it was all he could do not to pull her into his arms and steal a passionate, more penetrating kiss.

Passionate? More penetrating? He took a deep, shuddering breath, unable to even imagine what a more passionate, more penetrating kiss would do to him.

Quietly, he left her room and started for his own. But he stopped before he reached his door, stopped and looked down the dim corridor, down toward Zafiro's room.

He was tired, but not too tired.

Sore, but not too sore.

Downstairs he went, and then outside into the yard. Bright moonlight spilled down upon the small pile of boards he'd fashioned during the day.

Moonlight bright enough to work by.

And so he worked. And worked. All night.

And when Zafiro woke up the next morning and stepped out into the yard, the first thing she saw was a swing hanging from a tree, a single red rose lying on its seat.

seven

"It is such a wonderful swing, Sawyer!" Standing in the cool shadows of the forest, Zafiro grasped his upper arm, giving it a little shake in an effort to gain his attention.

"So you've said. About a million times since you found it." He examined the thick oak trunk into which he'd driven wooden wedges. The wedges would split the huge trunk into pieces that he would split again and again. "You know, this one oak tree is going to give me enough wood to replace every fence on La Escondida, including Coraje's paddock. I might even have enough left to—"

"I am talking about the swing you made for me."

"Yeah, you've been swinging in it all day. I guess that means you like it, huh?"

"I do, but I have realized that the swing means something. Something that has made me very happy."

Sawyer nodded absently, too preoccupied with his tree to concentrate on much else. "And you know what the best thing is about this oak, Zafiro? I don't have to season it. Not for fences, I don't. I can use it green, and that's going to save me a lot of time and—"

"I think that the swing also means that you have changed, Sawyer. That you feel nicer toward me."

"Uh-huh. Pretty good work, don't you think, Mariposa?" He hunkered down and rubbed the purring cat's ears.

"Sawyer, I am talking to you, but I think a post hears better than you!"

Finally, he looked up at Zafiro. "I am not as deaf as a post. I heard every word you said."

"So when will you help my men learn to shoot and ride again?"

"Shoot and ride . . ." He frowned. "I didn't hear you say anything about—"

"Because you were not listening. If you had been listening you would have realized that I was just about to tell you what the swing means to me. You see, Sawyer, I think that when you made the swing for me, it meant that you have put away the ax with my men. You will practice their lost skills with them."

Slowly, Sawyer rose from the ground. "Just because I made you a swing, you think that in regards to your men I've buried the hatchet?"

"Yes. That is what I think."

"Then you think wrong. My making a swing for you had nothing to do with my helping your men with their shooting and riding."

"But—"

"I gave them jobs to do, just like you asked me to."

"Tying strings around bundles of kindling is not—"

"It is so a job."

"But you are making them stay in the house to do it! They need exercise, Sawyer. They have to be strong, and tying strings around sticks is not going to build up their muscles! So you can just put that in your tobacco and chew it!"

"Or I could put that in my pipe and smoke it."

"Smoke, chew . . . I do not care what you do with it!"

He flicked a piece of bark off his arm. "I can't work with your men hanging around. Just last night you were irritated that I'd only finished a few boards, and now you're—"

"You should not have made me the swing. Such a nice thing made me believe—"

"Look, the only reason I made the swing is . . ." He broke off for a moment, unsure of what to tell her. He had to be careful because he sure as hell didn't want her thinking that he'd made the swing for any sort of romantic reason. "I made it because you might need it if you ever get a sweetheart."

The instant the words left his mind and lips he knew they'd been the wrong thing to say. Her crestfallen expression told him that. "I don't mean *if*." He tried to clarify. "I mean *when*. *When* you get a sweetheart you'll need a swing to swing in. It's what sweethearts do, Zafiro. Everyone knows that. You even said you'd seen sweethearts swinging in that little town you—"

"I am never going to have a sweetheart, Sawyer, and you know it."

He did know it, but he wasn't going to tell *her* that. "Sure you'll have a sweetheart. You'll—"

"You kissed me."

He glared at her. So she'd been awake when he'd kissed her last night, had she?

Damn her.

He drew himself up to his full height. "It was a good-night kiss. A plain and simple, everyday, run of the mill, nothing to write home about good-night kiss."

"You don't say good night to Tia or Azucar by kissing them on their lips."

Was there no end to her snappy rejoinders? "It was a damn peck."

"I liked it."

He wanted to know how *much* she'd liked it, but swore the earth would open and eat him up before he'd ask. "I'm glad you liked it, but I'm beginning to regret I ever did it in the first place. For God's sake, Zafiro, would you just forget it? It was just a stupid kiss. Hell, it was hardly even a real kiss!"

"No? What is a real kiss like?"

It took him a moment to answer. Not because he didn't know how to reply, but because his attention was centered on her mouth, her lips.

Pink petals. Sugar. And lemons.

God, how he would enjoy showing her *exactly* what a real kiss entailed.

"Sawyer?"

"I don't want to talk about kissing anymore. Kissing and fence building . . . They just don't seem to go together." He picked up his bag of tools and walked deeper into the woods, where he'd left several felled trees.

Zafiro trailed along behind him, her sapphire swinging upon her chest. "Sawyer, why would you kiss me and make me a swing if you didn't like me?"

"What? I never said I didn't like you."

"So you do like me?"

He arrived at the spot where the trees had fallen and dropped his tools onto the leafy ground. "I liked you five minutes ago." He found his saw and began lopping off a branch from one of the trees.

"Well, if you like me then why won't you help my men with their fighting skills?"

"Why do you think that one of the women in your little paintings might be your mother?" He didn't even try to make a smoother change of the subject.

"I do not want to talk about the paintings—"

"Yeah? Well, I don't want to talk about your men, so we're even."

She wondered how she could turn the conversation back around to her men. Her eyebrow arched high, she pulled a single leaf off the felled tree and twisted its short, slender stem between her fingers. "My father, he had many lovers. Sometimes he had their portraits done in miniature. Of course, I do not know if he had all his women painted, so there is a chance that my mother's likeness is not one of the miniatures I have."

Seeing that she had his attention, she smoothed the leaf across her cheek and continued. "My mother, she left me with my father and the gang when I was barely a month old. It was night, my grandfather said, and he and his men were sleeping around the fire in their camp. A baby's cries awakened them. They found me in a basket nearby. The note attached to the basket informed my father that I was his daughter. Except for the color of my eyes, I looked very much like my father, so he and the gang accepted and named me. The men, they took very good care of me while I was growing up, and they could still take care of me if you would only work with them and teach them—"

"Oh, for God's sake. I've had enough. *Enough*, do you hear me? You say one more word about my working with your men, and I'll—"

"If you would only listen to the reasons why I need you to help them, you would—"

"Protection. You already told me that the day you first mentioned this harebrained idea of yours. But what the hell do you need protecting from? Besides, you've got a guard cougar, don't you? And if Mariposa's not sufficient, you can always press Jengibre into service too."

For a moment Zafiro struggled with the deep fear that the thought of Luis always gave her. The man was coming, and she had to make Sawyer understand! "Sawyer—"

"No one can find La Escondida anyway, Zafiro. If I hadn't seen how you got in here that day, I'd never have even noticed the concealed entrance. Hell, the Fountain of Youth would be easier to find than this lair of loony lawbreakers."

She frowned, unable to understand what he was talking about. "The Fountain of Youth?"

He decided to capitalize upon her lack of schooling. Talking about the Fountain of Youth might possibly take her mind off her old men. "Yeah, the Fountain of Youth. There was this guy, see, and his name was Ponce de León. He sailed all over the seas, looking for this Fountain—"

"Stop it, Sawyer."

"—of Youth," Sawyer continued smoothly. "And he . . . Stop it? Stop what? I'm only trying to tell you the story about the Fountain of—"

"No, you are trying to make me forget about my men. You must think that I have birds in my attic."

He couldn't suppress a small chuckle over her idiotic choice of words. "No, but I've often wondered if you have bats in your belfry. Look, Zafiro," he said, laying aside his saw and reaching out to cup her warm cheek with his hand, "I really don't think you have a thing to worry about. If anyone ever *did* happen to get inside La Escondida, they'd need no more than five minutes here before almost breaking their necks trying to get out."

She stepped away from him and peered up into his eyes. "You hate us, don't you? You really and truly hate us."

"Yes. I saved Pedro from death at a burning bush because I hate you. I'm trying to fix your home because I hate you. I made you a swing because I hate you. I—"

"Anyone with half a heart would have saved Pedro from burning himself up. And you are fixing my home because you said yourself that the work will strengthen your weakened muscles. And you made me a swing because . . . because . . ."

"Because why?" He arched one eyebrow while waiting for her answer.

She didn't give him one.

"Because I don't hate you, Zafiro," he answered for her. "There's no reason in the world why I had to stay up almost all night making you that stupid swing. I made it because I thought it would make you happy, and it's as simple as that. Now, if you'll excuse me, I'm hot and dirty, and I'm going to take a dip in the stream."

Untying the bandanna from around his neck as he walked, Sawyer headed toward the stream. By the time he reached the splashing, sun-sparkled water, he'd undone the top of his breeches and pulled them halfway down.

Moments later he dove into the lively creek. As the water enveloped and cooled his hot, bare skin, he exhaled and felt a burst of bubbles rush over his face as they rose to the surface. Opening his eyes beneath the water, he saw a cluster of aquatic plants oscillating in the current like little green people swaying in rhythm. In a flash of silver, a school of minnows shot past his face, and then he saw pebbles float down all around him.

More small stones pinged through the surface, making

splashing sounds and drifting through the water all around the area where he swam.

Someone was throwing the pebbles at him.

He lifted his head out of the stream and looked toward the bank, where he saw Zafiro clutching a handful of tiny rocks.

She threw more at him, satisfied when a few popped off the top of his head. "If you think you can escape me by going for a swim, Sawyer Donovan, then something else is arriving."

On his knees in the stream, he swiped water out of his eyes. "And you've *got another thing coming* if you think I'm going to listen to another word about your men's long-lost abilities. Now, leave me alone."

"No."

"Fine. Stand there and watch then."

She did, and smiled appreciatively when he dove back into the stream and she saw his sleek, bare body skimming through the water right beneath the surface. His hair flowed behind him, over his back. It had grown since he'd first come to La Escondida and now fell well past his shoulders.

He came up for air then. Water sparkled on his skin, a few droplets sliding off his face, down his throat, and pooling in the hollow beneath his Adam's apple.

She looked at his eyes, his lion eyes, and saw that he was staring straight back at her with a bold and steady gaze that brought to life inside her that now-familiar feeling of need and yearning and warmth.

"Like what you see?" Sawyer asked, smug over the intense manner with which she examined him.

"I have seen you naked before, Sawyer. And yes, I liked what I saw then, and I like it now. That warm feeling of wanting something comes to me. I do not feel any satisfaction from the need you make me feel, but the feeling is not uncomfortable."

He decided then that her candor was one of the things he liked best about her. That, and her eyes, her smile, her breasts, her legs . . .

Her unique and absolutely captivating combination of innocence and passion.

Except for her obnoxious insistence that he work with her men, there wasn't much he *didn't* like about Zafiro.

"Are you getting in?" he asked when she pulled off her boots and peeled off her stockings.

"No." Hiking her skirt up to her thighs, she stretched her legs toward the water, wiggling her toes and ankles when the cool stream lapped over her feet and splashed over her calves. "I only want to put my feet in."

Sawyer formed no reply. Indeed, speaking seemed an impossible thing, and it wasn't only Zafiro's legs that stole his voice.

The woman wore not a stitch of undergarments!

Her knees were slightly raised above the sand, her legs opened just a bit.

But far enough open to afford Sawyer a tantalizing, heart-stopping, pulse-pounding view of her darkly shadowed pearly-pink femininity.

Moisture drenched his face, but it wasn't stream water.

It was sweat. The sheen of a desire so wild that if Sawyer had been standing, he'd have fallen into the water and drowned.

He moaned, a deep involuntary sound that rumbled from his chest like a roll of thunder from a distance.

"Sawyer?" Zafiro looked at him, alarmed when she saw an expression of pure agony on his handsome face. "What's the matter? I heard you groan. Are you in pain?"

Of the worst kind, he answered silently.

"Sawyer? What is wrong?" she asked again. "Is something biting you?"

The second she asked the question, fear and panic almost strangled her. She'd seen water snakes in the stream on more than one occasion.

There was no time to go for Tía's help. She had to save Sawyer herself.

She jumped to her feet and, wasting not a second to take off her clothes, she threw herself straight into the water, alternately swimming and walking on her knees to get to Sawyer. When she reached him she grabbed his shoulders and pulled herself next to him.

The feel of her soft breasts as they flattened against his chest sent Sawyer straight over the edge of restraint. Wrapping his arms around her tiny waist, he hauled her even closer and lowered his head toward her face, his lips toward hers—

"Do not fight me, Sawyer!" Zafiro cried, knowing in her soul that he was trying to save himself by hanging on to her. Desperately, she pushed at his chest, praying that he would cooperate with his own rescue. "I know what is wrong, but if you will just relax and let me pull you in—"

"Pull me in?" He smiled into her wide, blue-fire eyes. "Zafiro—"

"I am trying to save you!" *Dios mío*, the snakebite was making him crazy, she realized. He couldn't even understand what she was trying to do for him!

Again she tried to squirm free of his hold on her, to no avail. Flailing her arms, she then began to try to beat him away from her so she could pull him out of the water.

He fended off her puny attempts to subdue him as easily as if she were a child. Catching both her wrists in one hand, he used his other arm to hold her against him, close, close enough to force her to feel what her beauty, her blatant, yet innocent sexuality had done to him.

She gasped in horror when she felt the hard, round length of the water snake against her belly. And the stiff creature had situated itself right between poor Sawyer's thighs! Even now the scaly beast was injecting more and more of its poison into one of Sawyer's legs!

She had to pull the reptile off before more of its venom flowed into Sawyer's limb. With only a fleeting thought to her own safety, she pulled her hand from Sawyer's grasp and plunged it into the water. Taking hold of the horrible serpent, she pulled with every shred of strength she possessed.

"Dear God!" Immense pain shooting through his loins and filling his lower belly with fire, Sawyer let go of Zafiro and fell back into the water. His eyes squeezed shut, his shallow breaths hissing between his clenched teeth, he covered his groin with his hands, prayed for death, then staggered to his feet and doubled over at the waist.

"Sawyer!" Zafiro waded toward him, taking his head in her arms when she reached him.

"I'm dying," he moaned.

"Oh, Sawyer, I tried to get it off you! I pulled as hard as I could, but . . . Oh, *Dios mío*, the snake has killed you!"

Somehow, the word *snake* slithered past Sawyer's pain and registered in his mind. He managed to rise from his doubled-over position, and when he was standing he looked down at Zafiro.

But she did not look up at him. Instead, she gazed downward, toward his groin, where a flesh-colored, staff-like thing was poking out from between his hands.

It was the most peculiar-looking "snake" she'd ever

encountered. "Sawyer . . . I . . . What . . . That is
not a snake . . . That is your . . . *Santa Maria!*"

"What the hell are you talking about?" he thundered.
She didn't answer. She only stared.

And right before her very eyes the thick, flesh-colored
"snake" shriveled in Sawyer's hands.

"Sawyer, it is shrinking!"

"Well, what do you expect?" Sawyer roared. "You
damn near pulled it off!"

Although she comprehended precisely what she'd
done, she remained bewildered. "I . . . I did not know,
Sawyer! Your man part—I have not seen it look like that,
big and hard and tall. I have only seen it when it was the
way it is now, soft and limp and short—"

"Never mind!" he yelled, not caring at all for her less-
than-flattering description of his masculinity. He sank
back down into the water so she could only see his head
and upper chest. "Why the hell did you try to yank it—"

"I told you! I thought it was a snake! I . . . I thought
a water snake had gotten hold of your thigh and was
biting—"

"A snake?"

She saw that he was looking at her as if she were the
stupidest human being walking the earth. "You think that
my three loaded oxen do not have enough bricks, don't
you?"

A full minute passed before he figured out what she
was trying to say. "I think you're dumb as an ox and that
you're three bricks short of a load."

She bit her bottom lip. "You . . . You really do, don't
you?"

"What? No! I was only untangling the two expressions
you—"

"You are mad at me."

"Mad? What gave you that idea? You only tried to turn me into a woman! Why would that make me mad?"

"I am sorry."

"All right."

She could tell that he was still annoyed. "What else do you want me to do? Promise that if I *had* pulled it off, I would have gotten you a new one?"

Her ridiculous offer incensed him. That she could take so lightly . . . that she could stand there and make wisecracks about the fact that she'd almost gelded him . . .

Well, it was just too much for a man to bear. Turning from her, he dove into the water and swam downstream.

"I said I was sorry," Zafiro murmured. She watched him until he disappeared around the winding curve in the creek, then waded out of the water and picked up her boots and stockings.

As she walked into the woods she thought about Sawyer's man part again. Why had it grown so thick and big the way it had?

A sudden thought made her stop.

And then she began to run, hastening toward the house as quickly as her feet could carry her.

Only one person she knew of could and would answer the question concerning the strange change of Sawyer's man part.

Azucar.

—— ◆ ——

"Zafiro!" Azucar exclaimed, looking up from her hand mirror, in which she'd been admiring her reflection. "You scared me, coming into the house and slamming the door like that. What is the matter?"

Panting from her race through the woods and into the house, Zafiro gazed around the great room. "Where are Tia, Maclovio, Lorenzo—"

"Tia is ironing Sawyer's shirts in her room. The men finished making the bundles of kindling, and I helped them. Now Maclovio is passed out in the hall upstairs. He is too heavy to move, so we just left him there. Lorenzo is asleep in his bed, and Pedro is going through the house marking all the doors with lamb's blood."

"What?"

Azucar laid her mirror down on the table and smiled. "He says the Angel of Death will soon pass over the house, and the lamb's blood will keep her from killing all of us. But it is not really lamb's blood that he uses. It is only water that Tia colored with red berry juice. Pedro was happy when she gave it to him, and he is now very busy marking the doors. Pedro, he is only a crazy old man, Zafiro, and we must take good care of him. Tell me, do you like my hair up like this? I think my lovers will like it very much."

Zafiro saw that Azucar had twisted her brittle white hair into a knot on the top of her head and kept the arrangement in place by means of two tin forks. The handles of the utensils stuck out of her head like two shiny horns. "Your hair is very nice like that, Azucar."

"Yes, my lovers are going to be like rutting bulls when they see how very pretty I am." Azucar reached up and patted her hair. "Now, tell me what is the matter with you."

Zafiro dropped her boots and stockings by the door and peeked out of the window to make sure Sawyer hadn't followed her from the stream. When she didn't see him she turned back to Azucar. "I need to talk to you."

"Come," Azucar said. "Sit by me, and we will talk."

"It is about men. I want to talk about men."

"They are my favorite things to talk about."

"Their bodies . . . Their bodies change, Azucar. I do not think a woman's does. I have never seen my own body change."

Azucar smiled again. "Come here with me."

Zafiro sat down at the table beside the old woman. "A man's part . . . His private part . . ."

"That is the best part of a man. And you must believe what I say, Zafiro, because I have seen thousands of man parts." Azucar leaned back in her chair, recalling her many lovers of the past. "Man parts," she murmured. "Some thick, some skinny. Some long, some short. Some appear red, others are very dark. But *all* are wonderful."

"And they change? The man part, it changes?"

Azucar laughed. "It would be very sad if it did not."

Zafiro felt more confused by the moment. "But why does it change, Azucar? How is it possible for a man part to be soft and little and then hard and big? What does that mean?"

For a moment Azucar merely looked at Zafiro. "Why do you ask me these questions? You have seen a man part change like this?"

Zafiro formed her explanation carefully. It certainly wouldn't do for Azucar to know that she'd handled Sawyer's man part. Such knowledge might very well make the old woman jealous.

And upsetting the dear, sweet Azucar was the last thing in the world Zafiro wanted to do. "I saw Sawyer's man part change, Azucar," she said. "He was bathing in the stream, and I accidentally caught him there. He did not see me, but before I could leave, his man part went from little and soft to big and hard. I saw it change with my own eyes, and I did not understand."

"Poor Sawyer," Azucar cooed, smiling once more. "He is so ready to bed me. When you saw him in the stream he was probably thinking about me, about my body, and the arousing things I can do to him. I will not change my mind though. Only when he has the gold will I give him his night of ecstasy."

Zafiro allowed Azucar to fantasize for a few minutes. "But you did not answer my question, Azucar. Why did Sawyer's man part grow the way it did?"

"That is what happens when a man wants a woman, *chiquita*."

"But why?"

A smile still lingering on her lips, Azucar rose from her chair and crossed to Tia's cooking pot, which hung over the gentle flames in the hearth. With a spoon she removed a single cooked noodle from the pot.

She then hobbled to the pantry, where Tia kept foods that she'd dried and put up for the times when fresh food was scarce. There she found a large jar of dried noodles and picked one from the container.

Next she slipped a small key from the gaping bodice of her gown.

Zafiro frowned when Azucar placed the cooked noodle, the dried noodle, and the key on the table. "Why do you give me these things?"

Azucar sat back down in her chair. "There is a small hole at the top of the key."

"Yes."

"You have a soft noodle and a hard noodle."

"Yes."

"Push each into the hole in the key, and then tell me which noodle was the easiest to push through."

Zafiro stared at the two noodles and the hole in the key.

She smiled. "I do not have to try. The hard noodle will be easier to push through the hole because it will not bend or sag."

"That is why a man's body changes. So he can easily push his staff into the soft, warm tunnel between a woman's legs. If his man part did not harden—"

"It would be like trying to push this flimsy cooked noodle into the little hole in the key!" Zafiro picked up the cooked noodle, smiling with it drooped over her thumb and forefinger.

Sawyer's bodily change meant that he'd been ready to make love to her, she realized. He'd been ready to push his staff into her soft, warm tunnel the way Azucar had described.

It meant that Sawyer wanted her.

"Do you know when Sawyer will have any gold, Zafiro?" Azucar queried. "I have been waiting so long to pleasure that handsome buck. Maybe if I give him a free night he will do everything he can to get gold for another night. I know that once he has had me he will want me again and again and again. It is always that way with the men who experience my favors."

Zafiro could only imagine how Sawyer would react to Azucar's idea. The men irritated him enough. He certainly didn't need to deal with Azucar's antics as well. "No, Azucar. He is never going to have any gold, so it would be a waste of your time to give him a free night."

At that, Azucar laughed. "Lovemaking is never a waste of time, Zafiro. When have you ever heard me say that I did not enjoy being with the men I entertained?"

Ordinarily, Zafiro would have listened avidly to whatever titillating story Azucar was about to relate, but her discovery concerning Sawyer, his man part, and his wanting her occupied her every thought.

"And do not think that the men did not enjoy *me*," Azucar boasted again, patting Zafiro's hand. "They did. So much that many of them spent every *peso* of their work pay to have me."

"Yes, I am sure they did, Azucar." Zafiro rose from the chair and began to amble around the room, all the while marveling over the fact that Sawyer had wanted to make love to her.

"Men," Azucar said, and sighed a long sigh. "They are not like women. Sometimes a woman, she does not have the mood for lovemaking. I do not know why this is so, but it is not like that with men. They are always ready for a woman. Men will do almost anything for a good time between the sheets. Anything at all."

"Yes," Zafiro answered absently. "Anything at . . . Anything . . ."

By the stove Zafiro stopped and slowly turned toward Azucar, the old woman's words flowing through her senses like the scent of beautiful perfume.

Men will do almost anything for a good time between the sheets.

Sawyer, Zafiro thought. He wanted her. Wanted to make love to her.

She'd seen and felt the proof of his desire when she'd nearly pulled it off.

If she let him make love to her, if she gave her soft, warm tunnel to him, would he consent to listen to her story about Luis? Would he agree to help her men remember their skills?

Men will do almost anything for a good time between the sheets .

"Azucar?"

"Yes?"

Zafiro returned to the table and sat back down with the seasoned lady of the evening. "I know you've already told me almost everything there is to know about what men and women do in the bed, but would you mind very much telling me again?"

"Mind?" Once again, Azucar laughed. "Oh, Zafiro, my lovely girl, nothing would make me happier."

And when Azucar began to describe and explain the many aspects of lovemaking, Zafiro memorized every word.

eight

Her mind nearly bursting with all the information Azucar had imparted, Zafiro stood naked in front of the mirror that hung inside one of the doors of her armoire, and held the red gown up to her shoulders.

The black lace that trimmed the dress was rather droopy, but the scarlet satin still shimmered. And although the gown was a good four or five inches too short, Zafiro remembered that Azucar said men liked to see the turn of a woman's ankle.

It was the dress of a true seductress. "Azucar let me borrow it," she informed Jengibre and Mariposa, both of whom watched her from the bed. "I told her that I only wanted to see what it looked like on me."

While the animals stared at her, Zafiro slipped into the dress, amazed and delighted by how wonderful the soft satin felt against her bare skin.

The gleaming fabric clung to each curve and line of her body. Accustomed as she was to seeing the dress hang on Azucar's bony frame, Zafiro hadn't realized how snugly the gown was supposed to fit.

The lace-trimmed bodice hugged her breasts and

plunged low in the front, barely covering her nipples, and a high slit up the left side of her dress showed her leg all the way up to the top of her thigh.

"Do you think this dress will make Sawyer's eyes bulge?" she asked her pets. "Azucar said that men's eyes always bulge out when they see a woman dressed in such finery."

She studied her hair. Men liked to unpin a woman's hair right before lovemaking began, Azucar said. They liked watching it fall down a woman's shoulders, and then they liked to push their fingers into it. Trouble was, Zafiro didn't have any hairpins. And she didn't want to use forks, the way Azucar had. Deliberating, she looked around her room in search of some other kind of item that might work.

Finally, she spied the vase of freshly picked red roses that sat on her bedside table. Fifteen minutes later she finished twisting her long, thick hair into loose knots on the top of her head, all of which she kept in place by working the thorny stems of the crimson roses into and through strategic places.

Now for the cosmetics. Azucar had explained that colored cheeks and lips and dramatically lined eyes roused a man's appreciation of beauty, and so Zafiro had also asked to borrow Azucar's box of face paints, all of which Azucar made herself with whatever ingredients were available to her.

Zafiro opened a small pot and saw that it held a greasy, beet-red substance. Remembering how rosy Azucar's cheeks always were, she decided the red stuff was for her face. She smeared onto her cheeks two perfect circles. Then, so her mouth would match her cheeks, she smoothed a bit of the red grease on her lips.

It didn't smell very good. In fact, it smelled rancid, as if it had gone bad.

"Well," she said to Jengibre and Mariposa, "the smell will probably go away after a while. And I can always wear some scent to cover it up."

Next she found a matchbox full of black powder and a matchstick whose end was covered with the black powder. The black dust looked like soot, and she realized it was for the eyes. Using the matchstick as an applicator, she lined both the top and bottom lash lines of her eyes, then she stood back and examined her face.

It certainly was colorful, she thought, and her eyes certainly did stand out.

Sawyer's appreciation of her beauty would certainly be roused.

She decided to go barefoot. The only shoes she had were her boots, and they were old and covered with mud. Too, they made loud clodding noises when she walked, and tonight she had to be the very essence of grace and femininity.

Because Azucar said men liked light-footed women. Light-footed women whose hips swayed and breasts jutted out.

For a final touch, and with the hope that a bit of scent would overcome the unpleasant smell of the rouge, she sprinkled homemade rosewater over her neck and shoulders.

"I am ready," she murmured to her pets. "Ready to give Sawyer so much passion that he will not be able to say no to anything I ask of him."

She retrieved a scrap of paper upon which she'd jotted down a list of passionate things that Azucar said men liked to hear. Slipping the note into the bodice of her gown, she looked toward the window.

It was almost nighttime. Already she could see a few stars glimmering in the darkening sky. Sawyer would be in the barn soon. The last chore he performed at night was feeding and watering Pancha, Rayo, and Mister.

But he'd find more than the cow, the burro, and the mule in the barn tonight.

He'd find Zafiro.

And ecstasy.

＊＊＊

Sawyer tossed a pile of hay over Coraje's paddock fence, barely moving away in time before the ill-tempered stallion lunged his huge head over the railing and bared his teeth. "Son of a bitch!" Sawyer shouted, watching as the horse bucked and reared.

Why Zafiro kept the malicious animal was beyond Sawyer's comprehension. Who cared if the horse would come when he heard a whistle? No one could get near him, much less ride him.

Hearing Pancha, Rayo, and Mister calling from inside the barn, Sawyer picked up the two buckets of water he'd brought from the stream and entered the shabby stable. Ordinarily, he would have had to light the lantern that hung from a nail beside the door, but not tonight.

Soft light already filled the animal sanctuary. Bewildered, Sawyer saw a multitude of lighted candles scattered throughout the barn. He walked farther inside, wondering who had created such a fire hazard.

Probably one of the old outlaws, he thought. Maybe Pedro had decided that this night was the night of the Savior's birth, and the candlelight was supposed to be the light of the star of Bethlehem.

Ten or fifteen minutes more and the light of the star of Bethlehem would have turned poor Pancha, Rayo, and Mister into the biggest banquet of roasted meat La Escondida had ever seen.

Shaking his head, Sawyer approached the animals' stalls, but stopped when he saw his trunk lying nearby.

He closed his eyes against the instant crash of something horrible that grabbed at him, but a long while passed before the feeling released him.

Dammit, what was in the trunk?

He didn't know.

Didn't want to know.

Not yet.

Breathing deeply to steady himself, he poured the clean, fresh water into the animals' water troughs. He then gave the hungry beasts several scoops of grain, making a mental reminder that he had to somehow replenish the dwindling supply of feed.

Watching Pancha, Rayo, and Mister munch their oats, he rubbed the back of his neck and pondered the idea of fencing two pastures, one for Pancha and Rayo and another for Coraje. If they had an enclosed place where they could graze, they wouldn't need so much hay or grain.

He wondered if there was enough grazing area within the confines of the hideaway. Deciding to investigate the possibility in the morning, he began blowing out the candles.

"Do not blow them out, my handsome buck."

Startled, and with his mouth still pursed from blowing the candles, Sawyer turned around and saw Zafiro close the barn doors. She then slid into place the board that locked the two weathered portals.

"We must have our privacy," she explained, dusting

off her hands. "With the board barring the door, no one can come in and interrupt us."

Dumbstruck, Sawyer stared at her. If he didn't know better he would have sworn she was wearing one of Azucar's dresses.

The gown sure looked different on Zafiro.

"I know you must be hungry after your long day of work," Zafiro said huskily, remembering that men liked it when a woman spoke with a low, throaty voice. "But forget about dinner."

Still standing in front of the barn doors, she drew her gaze down the length of his body. He wore only his breeches and his boots. She'd seen his bare chest before. Many times she'd seen him completely naked.

But things were different tonight.

Tonight she would touch his bare body the way a woman touches her lover. And he, in turn, would do the same to her.

A yearning stirred within her, a hunger that filled her with a sweet, deep ache. Greedily, as if the sight of him were the first course of a splendid feast, she devoured him with her eyes, missing no enticing part of him.

Candlelight coated his skin like the mellow mist of a golden morning, playing over and seeping into every curve, bulge, and crevice of his torso. His long, thick hair drenched his shoulders and chest with drizzles of gold, and his eyes picked up the hue, the tawny hue, gleaming at her like those of a lion who knew he could have anything in the world if he so chose to have it.

And he wanted *her*. This lion of a man, Sawyer Donovan, wanted *her*.

Her heart flopped within her breast, like a fish out of water. "Tonight, Sawyer," she murmured, "you will have only dessert—me."

She walked toward him, swinging her hips as widely as she could get them to swing, and with her breasts jutting out as far as she could get them to jut. "You like what you see, don't you, buck?"

Sawyer still hadn't figured out what he was seeing. He could only gape at Zafiro in pure, unadulterated amazement.

"Your eyes, they are bulging, buck," Zafiro murmured. Finally, she arrived before him, stopping just far enough away from where he stood so that he could get the full view of her, from head to toe.

As he continued to stare at her with wide eyes, she tried to think of a few more sensuous lines to say to him, things that had worked for Azucar when she'd been in the harlot business. "I have not seen a man like you in a very long time, buck. Just looking at you makes . . ."

Having forgotten the rest of the line, she dug into the bodice of her gown, withdrew the scrap of paper, and quickly scanned it. "Just looking at you makes me burn with desire. I know that if I do not soon have you inside me I will burst into flames."

"What?"

Batting her lashes and smiling, Zafiro slipped the paper back into her bodice. "Your man part," she whispered. "It is growing long and hard now, isn't it?"

The only thing Sawyer felt grow was his confusion. "Zafiro, what—"

"We are wasting time with all this talking. Kiss me, buck. Kiss me." She smoothed her tongue across her bottom lip the way she'd seen Azucar do on occasion.

She grimaced. And trembled with a shudder that went all the way down to her bare toes.

The lip rouge tasted worse than it smelled! *Santa Maria*, it truly *was* rotten!

It didn't matter, she told herself. Kisses were nice, but what men *really* wanted was to push their man part into a woman's soft, dark tunnel. Azucar said that some men ignored kissing altogether and got straight down to the serious side of lovemaking.

Sawyer was probably one of those men, she decided. After all, she'd never seen him waste a second of time. On the contrary, when he had a job to do, he just plowed right in.

"Come to me, lover," she invited him, sliding her hand over her hip. "Come to me, and I will take you to heaven."

Before Sawyer had a chance to react, she threw herself at him, the strength and momentum of her lunge tossing him straight into the small mound of hay behind him.

Zafiro fell directly on top of him. As Azucar had described, she ground her hips into his, all the while making little mewling sounds at the back of her throat.

"Zafiro, for God's sake, what are you—"

"I cannot wait any longer, buck," she murmured, running her hand over his bare chest. "You and I know that what is about to happen is something stronger than both of us. Now, take down my hair."

"What?" He stared at her again, noticing a chicken feather stuck to one of the red circles on her cheeks.

"Take down my hair, buck. Watch it fall over my shoulders, and then push your fingers into it."

When he made no move to obey her command, she picked up his hand and thrust it to the top of her head.

"Dammit!" he shouted when something sharp pricked his thumb and two of his fingers. Pulling his hand down, he saw blood dotting all three stinging digits. "What the hell—"

Breaking off, he stared at her hair, seeing all the roses she'd stuck on her head. "You've got thorns—"

"Forget about my hair," she told him, silently scolding herself for not realizing earlier that the thorny "hairpins" were not conducive to lovemaking. "Just lose yourself in the burning pools of my eyes."

Frowning so hard that his entire face ached, Sawyer stared at her eyes. They were black, as if she'd been the loser in a fistfight. "There's black stuff all over—"

"Dramatically lined, buck," she explained. "Just the way you like them, that is right?"

Soot, he thought. The stuff on her eyes looked just like soot.

He stared at the crimson circles on her cheeks, the smeared scarlet stain on her mouth.

And he smelled her too. His nose crinkled. He'd smelled that god-awful smell before, but what was it?

He had no time to think. He only had time to feel.

And he felt pain.

"God Almighty, Zafiro!" he shouted when her teeth sank into his nipple.

"You scream with pleasure, don't you, buck?" she slurred, her mouth full of his nipple. "You like what I do."

"Having my nipple chewed off?" he yelled, pulling her head away from his chest.

"You would rather chew on mine?" Quickly, she freed her breast and pressed the soft globe over his mouth. "Open your lips, buck."

Shocked by what he was hearing, Sawyer tried to protest, but couldn't because her breast was smashed against his mouth. He couldn't breathe either, because her breast was also smashed against his nose.

With one smooth and powerful motion he rolled her off his chest and started to stand.

Zafiro pulled him back down into the hay. "I . . ." Frantically, she dug into her bodice again and yanked out the piece of paper. "I have been hoping and waiting for you to come to me," she read aloud, "because I knew you would be built like a stallion and that you would have strength enough to last an entire night."

Sawyer bolted to his feet. "What the hell is this all about, Zafiro?"

"I—"

"What have you done to your face and hair?"

"I—"

"And for God's sake, what is that stench you're wearing?"

She couldn't understand why he was so angry. Hadn't she done everything Azucar had described?

A failure. That's what she was. A total failure at seduction.

"*Lard!*" Sawyer yelled suddenly. "That's what I smell. Rotten lard!"

She rose from the hay mound and pulled several strands of the dried grass from her hair. "I was trying to give you a good time between the sheets, Sawyer."

"A good time—"

"Between the sheets."

"This is a damn barn!"

His shouting further deflated her spirits. "I wanted to seduce you."

"By bathing in rotten lard, rubbing red grease on your face, and smearing ashes on your eyes?" he blasted. "By wearing a damn rose garden in your hair and trying to nip my nipple off?"

His questions made her feel beyond silly. Beyond stupid.

Beyond mortified.

She raced to the barn doors, yanked the bar off, and dashed outside.

Sawyer set off after her, but stopped abruptly when he smelled smoke. Several candles had toppled over, their flames swiftly igniting the straw-strewn floor.

Smoke stinging his nostrils and throat, Sawyer grabbed Pancha and Rayo's water troughs out of their stalls and threw the water over the flames. He did the same with Mister's water, then, with an old, dusty blanket, he beat at the rest of the blaze until he extinguished the fire.

Covered with sweat, the black residue of the smoke, and the reeking grease that Zafiro had been wearing on her face, he led the animals out of the barn and tied them to a tree in the yard. Later, when all the smoke had dissipated, he would return them to their stalls.

Tired, hungry, and filthy as he was after a long afternoon of work and then an evening of beating out a fire, he was in no mood to confront Zafiro over her ludicrous attempt at seduction. What the hell had gotten into the woman anyway? If she'd wanted him to bed her, all she had to do was tell him and he'd—

His train of thought changed suddenly.

If she'd wanted him to bed her . . .

Still standing beside Pancha, Rayo, and Mister, Sawyer looked into the distant darkness, and smiled.

Maybe he'd been too hard on Zafiro. Sure, her efforts to rouse his attention had been absurd, but after all, she didn't know much about men. Only what Azucar had told her.

Only what Azucar had told her.

Full comprehension dawned on Sawyer then. Azucar. The ancient lady of the evening had had a hand in the seduction that Zafiro had attempted to pull off tonight. The way Zafiro had walked, talked . . . The skintight scarlet gown . . . All the face paint and the sexy words . . .

Tools of a whore.

He still didn't understand why Zafiro smelled like rancid grease, but he felt sure there was a rational explanation for that too.

She'd tried to be beautiful and desirable for him, and he'd embarrassed and hurt her.

Somehow, someway, he had to make amends.

And when she'd accepted his apology, when he'd made her feel better about her sensuous but mangled endeavors, he'd welcome her invitation for a good time between the sheets.

It was the very least he could do after having hurt her feelings.

* * *

Sawyer found Zafiro at the stream. He'd known he would. Had known she'd run to the water to wash off the face paint and the rotten lard and also to find a bit of peace in the moonlit glade.

She knelt in a shallow area of the creek, the water lapping beneath her chin. She was naked. He knew she was because she didn't wear any underwear and he saw the red dress hanging off a tree branch.

He waited to see if she'd look at him. When she didn't, he realized she hadn't heard him arrive. Still at the edge of the woods, he hunched down near the ground and watched her through a cluster of tall bramble.

She stood.

A proud and naked Mexican goddess, he thought. Her hair, blacker than the night sky, reflected moonlight and water glimmers, and it spilled over her bare, brown shoulders and breasts in wet waves that clung to her smooth skin like shadows with substance.

He couldn't remember ever having beheld a more perfect woman. The flawless shape of her breasts . . . her gently rounded hips . . . her small, firm bottom . . . and her long, lean legs . . .

The way she moved through the stream . . . with her supple arms dangling by her sides and her slender fingers trailing through the sparkling water . . .

She was so lissome. Like a swan. Moving through the water, but showing no means of propulsion, as if by graceful magic. Sawyer knew she was undoubtedly the loveliest woman he had ever known. No memory loss he sustained disputed that fact, for nothing, no trauma could erase such impeccable beauty from his mind.

She'd set out to seduce him tonight. She'd failed in the barn.

Now, at the stream, she'd definitely succeeded.

With the red rose he'd picked for her pinched between his fingers, he eased out from behind the brush and, his gaze still stroking her exquisite form, he started toward the creek, uncaring that his boots crackled through the leaves and broke brittle twigs as he walked.

He wanted Zafiro to know he was there.

But it wasn't Zafiro who greeted him when he neared the water. As soon as he felt a pair of small, bony hands clutch at his bottom, he realized that Zafiro hadn't been alone at the stream.

"Lover!" Azucar cried, her fingers moving firmly over the cheeks of his behind. "You are hoping for a kiss beneath the moonlight, yes?"

He spun in the sand and grabbed her gnarled hands. "I don't have any gold!"

Slight though she was, Azucar managed to slip one hand from his grasp. Instantly, she reached for and fondled his crotch. "It is a shame that you are such a poor man, but I am a generous woman. I will give you a kiss for free, and if you are a good kisser I will also let you feel my big, soft breasts."

Twisting his hips to the side, Sawyer moved his groin away from her hand. "Zafiro!"

"Yes?" Still in the water, Zafiro watched as Sawyer struggled to keep Azucar from pawing him. So he wanted her help with Azucar, did he? Expected her to come to his aid after the way he'd humiliated her in the barn, did he?

Ha!

"Is something the matter, Sawyer?" she asked, her eyes wide with feigned innocence.

"Tell her to stop!" Sawyer snatched Azucar's hand again, whereupon she leaned into him and began licking his bare chest. She then wrapped her leg around his calf, clinging to him like a skinny vine around a tree trunk.

Sawyer longed to throw her off, but hesitated to use his strength against her. Old and frail as she was, he might hurt her.

He continued to hold her hands still, but groaned loudly when she pushed her hips into his leg. "Dammit, Zafiro, *do* something!"

Calmly, Zafiro waded out of the water, pulled her gown off the tree branch, and slipped into the dress. "I am sure you want your privacy. What you are about to do—your kiss with Azucar and your feel of her breasts— well, it is not something that should be done in front of an audience. Isn't that right, Azucar?"

"That is right, *chiquita.* Go to the cabin now so that Sawyer and I can have our fun."

"No!" Sawyer gritted his teeth. Zafiro was leaving him at the mercy of the old, toothless strumpet out of pure spite! Because she was still upset with him over what happened in the barn! "Zafiro—"

"Have a nice time, Sawyer. You too, Azucar." Chin tilted and shoulders back, Zafiro plucked the rose from Sawyer's fingers. Leaving him to his fate, she marched into the woods toward the cabin.

"Kiss me now, lover," Azucar cooed. She raised her head from his chest and pursed her lips.

The sight made Sawyer think of a prune. "Uh . . . listen, Azucar," he said, his mind filling with possible lies he could tell her. "Let's go to my bedroom for our kiss. I . . . You . . . Mosquitoes," he blurted. "They're swarming all over me, and I . . . well, I can't enjoy our kiss with mosquitoes biting me."

She unwrapped her leg from around his calf and smiled up at him. "All right, my anxious stallion."

As soon as she turned and started toward the woods, Sawyer shot past her, having every intention of locking himself in his room as soon as he reached the cabin. Then, when everyone was asleep, he'd settle things with Zafiro.

"Sawyer!" Azucar called.

Sawyer continued to run. Just as he reached the edge of the glade, Maclovio stepped out of the woods.

"What did you do to Azucar?" the outlaw slurred.

It happened so swiftly, so unexpectedly, that Sawyer had not a second to react. Maclovio's fist smashed into his face, casting him straight to the ground and knocking every bit of air from his lungs.

For a long moment he lay on the ground with his eyes closed. Finally, when his lungs began to burn, he opened his mouth to suck in more air and almost choked when a foul-smelling, horrible-tasting liquid flowed over his tongue and down his throat.

"Francisco, you are a very bad boy," Tia scolded. She squatted beside him with a spoon and bottle of castor oil in her hand. "Your supper is cold, and now I find you playing down here at the stream in the dark! I have been looking everywhere for you!"

His face aching and his stomach pitching, Sawyer sat up and rubbed his throbbing cheekbone. "Get away from me," he growled. "Every one of you get the hell away—"

"Sawyer!" Pedro exclaimed as he exited the woods, followed by Lorenzo, who held Jengibre in his arms. "I see you are ready to be baptized, my brother! Come into the River Galilee with me and I will wash away your sins."

Dear God, Sawyer thought. They were *all* here. *Every single one* of the lunatics! And they were all crowded around him: Tia and her castor oil; Maclovio and his fist; Pedro and his baptismal plans; Azucar and her prune lips; and Lorenzo with the carnivorous Jengibre.

Sawyer almost wished he *was* the little boy called Francisco. If that were so he could lay down his head and cry without the slightest bit of shame.

Slowly, he got off the ground. He was surrounded, completely encircled by five deranged people and a cantankerous chicken. "Move," he said, his gaze meeting each of theirs in turn. "Now."

"Sow?" Lorenzo said, shaking his head. "No, we do not have a sow. We have only a horse, a cow, a burro, a cougar, and some chickens. Here, you can hold Jengibre."

Before Sawyer could object, Lorenzo thrust the hen toward him. Startled, Jengibre released a piercing screech, then pecked at Sawyer's chest.

"Dammit to hell!" Sawyer roared, throwing the frenzied fowl away.

Jengibre floated to the ground, but was by no means finished with her attack. Again and again she flew off the sand, continuing to peck at Sawyer's chest and belly as if his torso were covered with a bucketful of chicken feed.

Maclovio merely folded his arms across his chest and watched the scene. But Tia, Azucar, Pedro, and Lorenzo all tried to help Sawyer grab the frenzied bird, the old people surging forward and Sawyer staggering backward.

Toward the stream.

"Oh, he is ready, brethren!" Pedro shouted. "Brother Sawyer has neared the stream and is ready for his baptism!" He pushed Sawyer straight into the shallow water at the edge. Joyously, he then sat on Sawyer's stomach. "I baptize you in the name of the—"

"Get off me, you crazy—"

"Lazy?" Lorenzo asked, seated on the shore and watching the baptism. "We are not lazy, Sawyer. We have wanted to help you with all the work around La Escondida, but you have only given us string and kindling. Myself, I could open any locks that you might need open, and—"

"—Father, the Son, and the Holy Ghost," Pedro finished smoothly. He tottered off Sawyer's stomach and lifted his arms toward heaven. "Rise now, Sawyer Donovan. Your many sins are forgiven. From this day forward, you are a new man."

A new man, Sawyer thought, lying in the shallow water and staring up at the star-filled sky. After being bitten, pawed, beaten, and pecked, he felt more like an old man than a new one.

Wearily, he turned onto his stomach and dragged himself farther into the stream. Knowing the old people wouldn't follow, he swam across the creek, then waded to the shore on the other side.

There was no way in hell he'd sleep in the cabin to-night. He didn't want to be within two feet of the five lunatics and the hateful hen who stood watching him from the opposite bank of the stream.

He turned and walked into the forest, quickly finding a mound of leaves to sleep on. Stretching out upon them, he closed his eyes and felt sleep drift over him almost immediately.

The house filled his dream, the big house with the white curtains. A man with gray at his temples, dressed in dark brown trousers and a crisp white shirt, stood on the porch, waving at the group of children who played with a ball in the flower-splashed yard.

The door of the house opened and out walked a strikingly beautiful woman carrying a tray of drinks. Dressed in a bright yellow dress the same color as the sunflowers that grew near one side of the porch, she stopped and kissed the man on his whiskery cheek. Though age had turned her hair to silvery-white, her figure was that of a girl, and when she smiled, her pretty eyes sparkled with youthful freshness. With a clear, musical voice she called to the children, laughing when they abandoned their game with the ball and ran to the porch for a glass of cold lemonade.

And then, suddenly, the people, the lemonade, and the ball disappeared. The flowers in the well-tended gardens lay on the ground, broken and smashed.

Trampled.

Horror enveloped the house like a frosting of winter dew.

The man with gray at his temples, the woman with silvery-white hair, and two of the children lay inside on the floor.

Dead, and in pools of their own blood.

An agonized scream awakened Sawyer immediately, and as soon as he opened his eyes he realized the scream was his own.

nine

"Zafiro."

At the sound of Sawyer's voice, Zafiro looked up from the carrot patch and saw him standing at the end of the row, the soft light of early morning glinting off his long, gold hair. He held a red rose in his hand, and she knew he'd picked it for her.

Memories of the episode in the barn flamed through her mind, but she no longer felt the shame she had last night. After lying awake in her bed until dawn she finally realized the true reasons behind Sawyer's reaction to her sensual performance.

Poor Sawyer, she thought. Poor, poor Sawyer.

With a nod of her head she acknowledged his presence, then returned her attention to the badly eaten carrot plants.

"Zafiro, about last night," Sawyer began, walking toward her. "I'm sorry I made you feel so ashamed. I—"

"The shame is not mine. It is yours."

"What? Uh . . . All right, I'm ashamed of myself—"

"I have to weed around these carrots," she interrupted. "There are so many weeds. And the rabbits have—"

"I shouldn't have shouted at you the way I did." Arriving beside her, Sawyer reached for her hand.

She moved to the side, well away from him. "I have found eight small carrots, three tomatoes, and a long green squash. I am hoping to find a few onions and potatoes too. We will have vegetables and fried fish for dinner—"

"Why won't you listen to me? I'm trying to apologize for—"

"I know what you are trying to do, Sawyer, and I am trying to save you what little pride you must have left. There is no reason for you to say you are sorry to me. What happened in the barn last night, it was not your fault."

"I'm a man who can apologize when I'm wrong, Zafiro. Saying I'm sorry to you doesn't injure my pride. What happened in the barn last night wasn't your fault either. It was—"

"Of course it was not my fault." She bent down and pulled a few weeds, tossing them over her shoulder. "I am not the abnormal one."

He felt sure he'd heard her incorrectly. "Excuse me? *What* did you say?"

"I am normal, and you are not. The things that happened last night, they cannot be my fault because I am normal. But they cannot be your fault either, because abnormal people cannot be blamed for their actions. Do not forget that I have lived with Tia, Azucar, and Pedro for many years. All three of them are—how do you say it?—they should be in their rockers, but they got up. Maclovio and Lorenzo, their problems are only drunkenness and deafness, so they are not really like Tia, Azucar, and Pedro."

Again, he couldn't believe what she was saying.

"You're saying I'm off my rocker? Comparing me to Mother Tia, Madame Azucar, and Saint Peter?"

She walked down the vegetable row, stopping in front of a sad-looking patch of lettuce. Her sapphire swung and shone in the sunlight as she leaned over the vegetables. "Tia, Azucar, and Pedro, sweet and wonderful as they are, are never going to be normal again. But you, Sawyer . . . you might not be in your head right now, but—"

"*I'm* out of *my* mind? *Me?* *I'm* not the one who nearly set the barn on fire last night! *I'm* not the one who smeared rotten lard all over my face and lips or wrapped a damn bouquet of thorns in my hair, or—"

"Sawyer, please," Zafiro entreated softly. "Do not do this to yourself. I know and understand the reasons why you acted the way you did with me last night. You do not have to hide your abnormality any longer. I am your friend, and I will accept your problem just the way I have the problems of Tia, Azucar, and Pedro."

He stormed down the row of vegetables, stopping so close to Zafiro that the tips of her breasts brushed his lower chest. "What problem is it that you think I have?" he shouted.

He loomed above her, staring down at her face, and his hair fell across her cheeks and over her shoulders. He smelled of earth, she thought. And sun, and that musky, wonderful scent she now recognized as utterly male.

Laying her hand over his heart, she felt a sharp stab of regret that she would not experience his lovemaking. For although her sensuous plans of last night had been carefully calculated toward gaining his consent to help her men, she'd also anticipated learning about and understanding the physical relationship that could be had between a man and a woman.

But it was not to be.

Raising her hand, she slid her fingers over the deep
hollow beneath his cheekbone. "You do not know how to
make love to a woman," she told him, smiling tenderly.
"Before you lost your memory you might have known,
but you have forgotten, just as you have forgotten so
many other things in your life. Your shouting at me last
night . . . You were only covering up your own embar-
rassment, isn't that right, Sawyer? So that I would not
guess your secret problem, you only pretended to—"

"Forgotten . . . Secret problem . . . No!"

Still smiling tenderly, she patted his cheek. "Lie to
me, but do not lie to yourself. You could not make love to
me last night because you do not know how. You are the
same as I am, Sawyer: a virgin. Maybe not physically as I
am, but mentally, because you do not remember how to
do it. Azucar said that men take great pride in their lovemaking abilities, and for such a thing to happen to a
strong, young man like you . . . It is very sad."

When she walked down the row of vegetables away
from him, calmly pulling weeds here and there, fury exploded inside Sawyer like a boulder blown to smithereens
by a case of dynamite.

He couldn't talk to her. Couldn't convince her how
totally wrong she was.

His rage was of such an extent that he could barely
take his next breath, much less speak.

He threw down the rose he'd picked for her, stormed
out of the garden and straight into the woods. There he
picked up his ax and began swinging at the trunk of an
oak as if the poor tree were a bloodthirsty creature about
to kill him.

"I'm off my rocker, am I?" he shouted. Again his ax bit
into the tree trunk.

Fragments of wood flew into the air and around him like a swarm of angry insects. "I'm out of my mind, am I?"

He continued to do battle with the tree, swinging the ax so quickly and with such strength that in only moments he'd cut clear into the core of the trunk.

"A virgin! The wacky wench compared me to a virgin!" He hurled the ax into the woods, and pressing his broad shoulder against the tree, he began to push with every shred of might his body held.

As its moist and supple fibers bent and twisted, the tree gave forth a loud spintering sound and crashed to the forest floor, a thing defeated and killed by one man's potent anger.

Sawyer made quick work of the slaughtered timber, scraping, hacking, and dissecting its woody meat as if it might somehow come back to life and attack him.

He would complete every single repair he'd promised to make at La Escondida, and then he would leave, never setting foot near Zafiro's mountain again. Damn the woman anyway! he fumed inwardly. Damn her, her crazy companions, and her maddening menagerie of animals!

He labored clear through the morning and on into the afternoon, breaking only for water and the entire loaf of bread that Tia left on the table in the great room of the cabin. When night fell he did those chores that he could by moonlight, seeking sleep only when pure exhaustion forced him to it.

The next day was the same, as was the following day. A week passed, and then another, during which time he painstakingly avoided Zafiro and all her charges. Each day he did the work of several men, and by the time stars twinkled in the sky he had only enough energy left to eat whatever scanty meal Tia left in his room. He would then fall fast asleep and awaken long before Zafiro or the sun to begin the next day's worth of work.

He made steady progress with all the repairs. Not only did he build a new woodshed out of whole pine logs linked permanently together at all four corners by the dovetail notches he painstakingly carved, but he also figured out a way to keep rabbits out of the vegetable patch. By surrounding the garden with four high walls of tall, straight pine saplings, he created a barrier that could be entered only by means of a swinging door that closed with a wooden latch. Upon further thought he incarcerated Jengibre within the enclosure. The peevish hen so hated being penned that she squawked, cackled, and screeched continuously, making such never-ending racket that not a single rabbit dared attempt to breach the pine walls.

The garden problem taken care of, he finished and laid out to dry the long, sturdy boards he would need to fix the side of the barn. After that he fashioned a new and sturdy chicken coop, restored the missing plank in the porch, and fixed the smashed porch step, all of which he accomplished nicely with old, rusty nails he'd found scattered among the pile of wood that used to be the wagon. He then began to replace the falling-down fences, working so quickly, so tirelessly, that it seemed to Zafiro that the fences had sprung out of the ground as if by sorcery.

Sawyer worked like a man possessed, she thought one early evening while watching him rifle through the old wagon boards in search of more nails. She knew in her heart that he was plagued by the fact that she'd discovered he had forgotten his lovemaking skills and wished there were some way she could alleviate his anguish.

Still, his abilities between the sheets would not save her and her people from Luis. How many times had she almost begun to tell Sawyer about her cousin? And now the man would not even come near her, ducking out of sight the second she came into his view. Some nights he didn't even sleep in the house, but sought a place outside to bed down instead.

"If things keep going the way they are going now, I will have to write everything down and send him a letter, Mariposa," she told the cougar, who sat on the new porch step beside her. "Or maybe I should—"

"Zafiro," Tia called as she opened the cabin door and held out a small pail. "Take these apple peels and cores to Pancha, Rayo, and Mister, *niña*. I have used the last of the apples for applesauce, and we must not let a bit of the apples go to waste. The animals, they love apples. I only wish I had more to give to them."

Zafiro rose from the step and took the pail from Tia's chubby brown hand. "I know where there is a big berry patch, Tia. It is not inside La Escondida, but it is not very far away. If we are careful to stay low, no one will see us while we gather the berries."

Tia nodded. "Francisco, he likes berry tarts almost as much as apple tarts. But we do not have much sugar either, *chiquita*. Or lard. But the garden, it has never given us so many vegetables! This morning I gathered enough potatoes to make mounds of potato cakes for dinner. And I have already started drying the peas and beans for winter. And have you seen the corn? Soon we will have enough corn to make sacks of *masa* for tortillas! My Francisco, he is a smart boy to think of putting a wall around the garden, isn't he?"

Zafiro glanced at the garden, her heart warming with pleasure and gratitude.

"Go now, Zafiro," Tia said. "Give the animals their treat."

Heading toward the barn, Zafiro continued to ponder the garden, but also wondered when the nuns would have supplies to share. It was all well and good that the vegetable garden was doing better, but the little patch did not grow sugar, salt, fresh meat, or other food items that Tía needed in order to keep everyone healthy and well-fed. Nor did the garden yield clothing, candles, lamp oil, fish hooks, hairbrushes, needles, thread, or other numerous necessities.

What she wouldn't do to be able to buy what she needed in Piedra Blanca. Unlike the sleepy villages that dotted the foothills, Piedra Blanca was a real town with a big store that sold everything a patron could imagine. The nuns had visited the town once two years ago to hear Mass in the town's brand new church. When they returned, their stories about the town had filled Zafiro's dreams for nearly a month.

But Piedra Blanca was nearly a whole day's ride away. And there was still a problem with money.

She didn't have any.

It was just as well, she thought. Riding out in the open the way she would be forced to do to get to Piedra Blanca . . . What if someone spotted her during the trip or recognized her while she shopped? Someone who by some chance knew about Luis and the fact that her cousin had sworn to hunt her down?

She couldn't take the risk.

Luis.

Her mouth went dry; her heart raced. She couldn't swallow, could barely think.

Santa María, he was coming. When, she didn't know, but he would come.

She gazed at the mountaintops. Even now was Luis somewhere near.

Taking deep breaths and forcing herself to concentrate on other matters, she managed to pull her emotions back together. A sigh gathering deep within her, she stopped beside Coraje's corral. The stallion's eyes filled with violence as soon as he noticed her.

"Grandfather loved you, Coraje," Zafiro whispered to him. "You were always spirited, but perhaps you are mean now because you miss him as much as we do."

She tossed several apple cores into the paddock, watched Coraje devour them, then entered the barn and divided the rest of the apple cores and peels between Pancha, Rayo, and Mister. When the gentle animals began chomping into the sweet treat, she wandered around the barn, noting the next-to-nothing mound of hay, the holes in one wall, and Sawyer's trunk.

It sat in a corner of the stable, its top coated with dust and bits of straw. She ran her fingers over the lock, wondering over and over again what the trunk contained.

She understood why Sawyer wouldn't open it. Understood that its contents were somehow connected with the memories he was loath to remember.

But her understanding did nothing to quell her curiosity. She stared down at the trunk for a few moments longer, then looked around the barn again and spied a row of tack that her men had once used on their mounts.

A wave of nostalgia surged through her. One of her earliest memories was that of her grandfather and his men cleaning and oiling their tack to keep it soft, supple, and gleaming.

But now rust coated the bridle bits and the stirrups. Cobwebs and thick layers of dust covered the stiff leather of the reins and saddles. As she examined the riding equipment, Zafiro knew a sharp stab of sadness.

Suddenly, it didn't matter to her that the bridles and

saddles would never be used again. They were treasures from the past, the same as Tia, Azucar, and the men. As such, they deserved whatever special care she could give them.

She hurried back to the house and gathered supplies: a bit of lard, some vinegar, a bucket of water with a small measure of soap in it, and several freshly washed rags. Armed with the cleaning supplies, she returned to the barn and sat in the middle of the floor with all the old, dirty tack spread around her.

By the light of the two old lanterns she'd lit, she wiped away all traces of dust and cobwebs from the riding equipment. Vigorous rubbing with the vinegar removed the rust from the bridle bits and other iron trappings. She then set about cleaning the dirty leather with the soapy water. A while later, when the tack had dried, an application of the lard gave the leather a luxurious gleam.

Tired, but pleased with her work, Zafiro sat back against Rayo's stall door. As she relaxed she looked at other objects in the barn: an old shovel, a few empty barrels, a stack of discarded burlap bags, and several wooden boxes.

She rose from her seat on the barn floor and opened the wooden containers. Inside them she found a handful of old bullets, a belt buckle, a dented tin cup, a wadded-up red kerchief, a deteriorated piece of dynamite, a coiled black whip, and a pair of handcuffs.

She shut the boxes, then spied another, a long wooden crate that sat in a pool of shadows next to the barn wall.

Her gaze rested on the crate. Years had passed since she'd last looked at its contents. Lingering nostalgia compelled her to look at them now.

The hinges on the wooden box creaked as she lifted

the lid. Inside, cloaked in the bloodstained serape he'd died in, lay her father's guns, two pistols and a rifle.

Wrapped and boxed though they'd been, the heavy weapons were still badly rusted. Zafiro seriously doubted they were even serviceable. But it didn't matter. They'd belonged to her father, and she handled them as though they were wrought of pure gold and studded with diamonds.

Lost in her reverie, she started when Sawyer's heavy footsteps broke through the musty silence of the barn. "Sawyer!"

He didn't even acknowledge her presence with a glance, but merely walked to the back wall of the barn and placed his ax and his saw on the shelf where he'd found them weeks ago.

"Sawyer, wait," Zafiro called when he headed toward the barn doors to leave. Quickly, she laid her father's guns back in the wooden crate. "I have been trying to tell you something very important for weeks, but—"

"I'm busy," he flared, stopping for a moment to turn and glare at her. "Busy rebuilding your home. I'm nearly through now, Zafiro. All I have left to do is fix this barn wall and fence in two pastures—"

"Yes, and I am very thankful for everything you have—"

"Consider it a promise kept." He growled the words at her, then proceeded toward the barn doors again.

"For more than two weeks you have evaded me, disappearing the second you see me, and now you are trying to escape me again. You do this because you are ashamed. But, Sawyer, I have not and will not tell anyone that you have forgotten the sexual talents you might have possessed before losing your memories. The loss of your lovemaking abilities, it does not matter to me, because that is not the reason why I need you."

He felt a muscle in his jaw begin to twitch. Renewed anger narrowed his eyes, clenched his teeth, and balled his fists.

He raked his gaze down the length of her body, not missing the way her breasts pushed at the thin fabric of her blouse, the way her skirt clung to her rounded hips and lean legs . . .

Or the way she licked her lower lip when she saw how he looked at her.

"There's more than one kind of need, Zafiro," he gritted out, barring the barn door with the board. "I know you're familiar with many of them, but now, right now, I'm going to show you one need in particular. A need that will prove beyond a shadow of a doubt that I have *not*—I repeat, *not*—forgotten the skills you think I have."

Before she could begin to understand what he meant, she saw a predatory gleam leap into his eyes, and then he started toward her. The broad-shouldered, hard-muscled power of him seemed a perilous thing to her now, for his quick, purposeful, and silent stride was that of a man who knew what he wanted . . .

. . . and had every intention of taking it.

ten

"Saw-Sawyer?"

His shadow fell over her. Like a live thing it consumed her, swallowing her wholly into him. And their bodies had yet to touch.

She took a step backward, both wanting and fearing his advances. "What—"

He gave her no chance to finish speaking. Rather, he whipped her into his embrace as though she were made of nothing but breath and pulse. Circling his right arm around her back and dragging her next to his chest, he heard her sharp intake of breath and saw her breasts rise. Whether she gasped with shock, anger, or excitement, he didn't know.

Nor did he care.

He threaded his fingers through the velvet cascade of her hair and held her steady for his kiss. One corner of his mouth rose in a slight smile, a slow, crooked smile that he knew would tell her exactly what he was about to do.

A smile that told her he knew exactly what she was about to feel.

He kissed her not like a man who had no knowledge of how to kiss a woman, but like a man who craved and now drank fully of a sweetness too long denied him. Parting her lips with his tongue, he prepared to show her that he was about as lacking in sensual skills as a fire was its searing heat.

She sighed into his mouth, and he felt a strong tremor surge through her soft body. He smiled again, this time inwardly, and then he plunged his tongue between her lips, penetrating her mouth with a motion and rhythm that he willed her to understand was but a hint of the deeper, more intimate invasion to come.

His hand dipped down her back to cup one firm cheek of her bottom. His fingers kneading her firm flesh, he pushed her snugly into him so that his hips cradled hers, so she could feel the turgid length of his arousal.

So she could begin to imagine what else he was going to do.

And still he kissed her hungrily, his senses further provoked when a moan of pleasure escaped her lips, the soft and beautiful melody of a woman's desire.

"I was right," he murmured, his mouth still clinging to hers. "I knew you'd be like this. So soft, sweet, so full of passion. I knew it, Zafiro."

In answer she pressed herself even closer to him, grinding her hips into his, taking his hand and squeezing his fingers over her breast, and trying desperately to remember the many other things Azucar had described.

"Not so fast, sweetheart," Sawyer whispered, removing his hand from hers. "This time we do it *my* way, not Azucar's."

"But I want—"

"I know what you want, and I'm going to give it to you."

At that she pulled her head away from him so she could see into his eyes. The absolutely smoldering expression she saw in them nearly caused her knees to buckle. "You . . . you have forgotten nothing."

He flashed her a satisfied smile right before he claimed her mouth for another kiss. Grasping a handful of her skirt, he lifted the coarse cotton up over her legs until he felt the bare skin of her trembling thighs beneath his palms. Her skirt now bunched up around her waist and kept in place by the pressure and weight of his own body, he attended to the buttons on her blouse, finding the fastenings delightfully easy to open.

While he slipped his hand inside her gaping bodice and molded his fingers around one full breast, he ceased the sensual plundering of her mouth and planted a trail of warm kisses over the graceful slope of her throat and down the silken expanse of her upper chest, finally taking her nipple between his lips and flicking the tip of his tongue over the stiffening peak.

Her sapphire grazed his cheek. Her breasts were warm and supple. The blue jewel was hard and cold.

The contrast awakened more excitement within him.

"Sawyer," Zafiro breathed. Hot rushes of feeling shot through her veins. She threw back her head and arched her back.

He felt the ends of her long, black hair brush the top of his hand as he continued to rub and massage the globes of her tight, sexy bottom. His own need blistered, melting through him and testing the very boundaries of his control.

Wanting more of her—all of her—he lowered his hand down to the back of her thigh, and then around.

Around to the front, to the patch of ebony silk at the juncture of her legs. She stirred restlessly against him, against his chest and his palm, but he knew that her ardent response was only the beginning of her ultimate surrender to his touch.

Before this encounter came to its end he would have her writhing beneath him, murmuring hot incomprehensible words into his ear, and he would see her eyes burn with the full knowledge and understanding that he had, indeed, retained his ability to bring to life and satisfy a woman's desire.

Those ends in mind, he skimmed his fingers through the soft nest that covered her feminine mound, and he found her hot, wet, and slick.

"Sawyer!" Zafiro cried, stunned with surprise and pleasure at this unexpected thing he did to her. She felt his fingers slide between the petals of her sex, toward the very center of her womanhood, and then he withdrew them, not completely, but to the hidden apex of her nether lips.

Over the most sensitive spot she ever imagined her body possessed. The pebble of flesh quivered beneath and seemed to push at the thick pad of his finger, like a form of life bursting forth from a tight little seed.

Only vaguely aware of her own actions, she clutched at Sawyer's massive shoulders, thankful for his strength, for if he so chose to release her from his embrace at that moment, she would have tumbled to the floor in a heaving heap. Her entire body felt gloriously alive with exquisite sensation that engulfed her with a need so sweet and fierce, she felt she would come apart like a string of beads if she did not somehow find the means with which to appease her hunger for him.

She raised her head and placed her hands on his cheeks, her nails biting into his temples. "Faster," she whispered.

He knew she didn't understand her own command.

Didn't have the slightest idea what she was demanding he do. On the contrary, her order was innocent. Ignorant.

Releasing the hardened crest of her breast from between his lips, he lifted his face to hers. What he saw excited the hell out of him.

Her face sparkled and her eyes glowed with unqualified passion. He'd thought her beautiful the first time he'd seen her.

But now . . . the way she looked now . . . with her lips swollen from his bruising kisses, with her thick tumble of sable hair falling around her gorgeous face in wild disarray, and with her fresh, never-assuaged female need emanating from her every pore . . .

Faster, she'd said.

He obeyed her and lightly pressed his thumb against the sweet jewel of her femininty, circling the tiny pearl in such a way as to sire deeper pleasure within her slender, straining body. "How do you feel, Zafiro?" he murmured.

"I . . ." she panted, "I am almost on the seventh cloud."

He smiled at that. "Or could it be that you're somewhere in between cloud nine and seventh heaven?"

"Yes, that is where I am going."

"Well, let me make sure you arrive." Sensing that her release was but a heartbeat away, he eased her to the floor of the barn, his hand never leaving its spot between her thighs. When she was lying on her back with her knees slightly bent, he stretched out beside her and took her lips in another searing kiss.

He swore he could hear the thunder of her heartbeat. Wanting to intensify her pleasure even further, he penetrated her, first with one finger, then with two.

"Sawyer!" With one strong action Zafiro clapped her

legs together, imprisoning his hand between her thighs. "Azucar did not tell me—"

"Then Azucar left out a lot. A whole lot." Unmindful of the way she'd squeezed her legs together, he moved his fingers within her, his breath coming in pants when he felt her virgin passage begin to tighten and pulse. She felt so good to him, so small, hot, and so wet that he felt as though he were drowning in the pure sensuality he'd found within her tremulous body.

He felt the first quivers of her climax even before she gasped and called out his name again.

Dammit, he was hot for her, so hot that no reason he could think of effectively dispelled the notion to have her then and there. Her body, her sweetness . . . He wanted everything she had to give him.

With his free hand he worked at the confines of his breeches, freeing his swollen manhood and feeling an almost uncontrollable urge to thrust himself inside her.

"Oh, Sawyer," she whispered. "Sawyer." Bright and blazing bliss shimmered through her limbs, her belly, her womanhood. Almost unendurable in its shattering intensity, the pleasure was the strangest, most wonderful experience of her life, and she hoped it would never end.

But it gradually began to lessen, calming from flames that licked through her to mellow sparkles that left her sated and so completely relaxed that she felt she would fall asleep within moments.

She blinked up at Sawyer, but she was too filled with wonder to speak. Instead, she gave him a smile, then slipped her fingers through the thick mass of his dark gold hair.

Sawyer had just manuevered himself over her hips when he saw her looking at him.

His entire body stilled, his heartbeat the only part of him that moved.

Her eyes looked like those of a young doe, full of gentleness, sparkling with happiness.

Glowing with trust.

Somehow, her tender expression broke the fever of his desire for her.

He knew she wouldn't stop him if he proceeded with his sensual intentions. On the contrary, she'd welcome the opportunity to experience the full circle of sexual intimacy.

But this was no harlot he'd found in some saloon or brothel.

This was Zafiro.

In the space of only a moment he remembered and pondered all the many things that had never been hers. Things she'd not had as a little girl and would never have as a woman.

A mother or a real home in a town. Proper schooling. Friends her own age, pretty clothes, or a sweetheart.

She'd never had a man make love to her either.

Make love to her? This—what he was about to do—it wasn't lovemaking.

It was rutting, pure and simple. A quick roll on a hard, hay-strewn floor in a mice-infested barn.

Zafiro deserved better.

Quickly, he readjusted his breeches. She might have learned a great deal from a whore, but she wasn't one, and he'd be damned if he was going to treat her as though she were.

"Sawyer?"

He sat up and moved his hair out of his face. "Zafiro, I'm sorry. Things got out of hand."

"They could have gone further. Why didn't they?"

He pulled her skirt down over her legs, reminding himself that she couldn't help being so bold. Not only was her openness a part of her character, but as far as he'd been able to determine no one in her life had ever taught her that good girls demonstrated modesty in everything they said and did.

Good girls? He shook his head.

It was Zafiro's profound goodness that enabled her to take such wonderful care of her elderly companions.

And *he* was one to talk about the carefree attitude she had toward her body and lovemaking! he chided himself. Hadn't he enjoyed her lack of modesty on more than one occasion?

He certainly had today.

"Sawyer?"

"Button your blouse."

She heard a hard edge to his voice, as if he were angry with her. Buttoning her blouse, she tried to think of anything that might have irritated him.

When a possible answer came to her, she bowed her head and stared at her lap. "I am sorry if I . . . did not do everything right. If I did not make your socks fall off."

"You're not supposed to know how to do everything right." A slight grin on his face, Sawyer stood, clasped his hands over his hips, and looked down at her. "And you *do* knock my socks off, Zafiro. But you need to understand that no matter how many things Azucar has told you, you don't know what you think you know."

"I—"

"What I'm talking about is your little performance a few weeks ago right here in this very barn. I know you were trying your best, but I'm not the one who didn't know what to do that night. As a maiden, there was no way in hell you could have even understood what you—"

"I did not know any more today than I knew then. What is the difference?"

"The difference is that today you weren't going by the things Azucar has described. Today you were responding to your own feelings, and believe me, today was a hell of a lot more pleasant than that night a few weeks ago."

"For you too? I mean . . . I made you happy, Sawyer?"

He wasn't blind; he saw the hope spilling from her eyes. Her desire to please him . . . Well, that in itself pleased him.

God, he thought. She would have made some lucky man an exquisite mate.

Part of him, some deep-down part, wished he could have been that lucky man. Zafiro was outrageously bold, obnoxious at times, a bit on the wacky side . . .

But she was a very caring woman. A sensitive woman. Passionate and generous.

And so damn beautiful that sometimes the mere thought of her was sufficient to play havoc with his heartbeat.

Reaching down to her, he pulled several long strands of straw out of her hair, then outlined the curve of her upper lip with the tip of his finger. "Yes, Zafiro, you made me happy."

His answer satisfied her at first, but a new thought replaced her pleasure with confusion. "How could I have made you happy?" She frowned, certain she was correct in her thinking. "Sawyer, you did not put your man part into my—"

"It made me happy to make you happy. I—" He broke off, wondering how to explain the way of things to her. "I know you've never known a man . . . I mean, well . . . There's never been a man in your life who was close to your own age. A woman like you—a naturally passionate woman who's been listening to Azucar's tales for so long—were bound to be curious about things. It made me happy to be the man to show you a little bit. To please you in such a way for the first time."

She understood what he meant. She enjoyed making people happy too. But the fact remained that Sawyer had not found the same sort of physical pleasure that she had. "You should have finished, Sawyer."

He watched a mouse scurry across the floor near Pancha's stall door. "If I had, I would have regretted it."

"You would regret making love to me?" Grabbing Sawyer's hand, Zafiro pulled herself off the floor and stood before him. "What a compliment, Sawyer Donovan. You have put music on my face and laughter in my heart."

"Music on your . . ." What was she trying to say? "Music . . . Oh. I've put a smile on your face and a song in your heart."

"I am being sarcastic," she clarified in case he didn't understand.

"Really?" He looked down at the ground and grinned. "You misunderstood, Zafiro. I didn't mean that I didn't want you. I meant that I would have felt bad about it later. Taking your innocence on a dirty barn floor . . . I doubt seriously that'd be the greatest experience of my life, not to mention yours."

Mulling over his explanation, she watched as he crossed the barn and threw bundles of wilted grass into the animals' stalls. "You . . . you care about me, don't you, Sawyer?" she murmured, her realization almost stealing her voice. "If you did not, you would not have thought two times about having a romp between the sheets here on the dirty barn floor. Your consideration, it means you truly and really care about me."

Oh, damn, he thought. What sort of romantic notion was going through her busy little mind now?

"Sawyer?"

"I've been cutting fresh grass for the animals." He skirted her question. "The hay's gone, but I've found some good grazing area on the other side of the stream. Like I said, I'm going to fence in a few pastures and—"

"Are you falling in love with me?"

"What? Hell, no!"

His sudden shout startled her so badly that she let out a little shriek. And his vehement denial to her question embarrassed and hurt her.

Was it such an awful thing to fall in love with her? she wondered miserably. Were other women in some way better than she was?

She had no way of knowing. Besides Tia, Azucar, and the nuns, there weren't any other women around with whom she could compare herself.

Looking at everything in the barn but Sawyer, she rubbed the back of her left calf with the top of her right foot. "So," she managed to say, "you are going to make pastures for the animals."

"Yes." He knew he should leave it at that, but he couldn't. He just couldn't do it to her.

Because he knew exactly what she was thinking—that there was something wrong with her. That she wasn't good enough for a man to love. She couldn't help thinking such things. There'd never been a man around to convince her otherwise.

"You're wrong, Zafiro."

She still couldn't look at him. "Wrong? About what?" she asked as if inquiring about the weather.

"About what you're thinking." He walked over to

where she stood across the barn. "Zafiro, look at me, please."

Affecting what she hoped was a nonchalant expression, she raised her face to his.

He hated the hurt he saw in her eyes and etched across her beautiful features. "I can't fall in love with you, sweetheart," he said, using the endearment on purpose to ease the sting of his own words. "I can't stay here at La Escondida. You know that. I . . . I have to leave. Have to find . . . who I am. If I can."

He pushed his fingers through her hair and curled them around the back of her neck. "But if I could love you, Zafiro, it wouldn't be hard to do. It wouldn't be hard for any man."

She felt her lips tilt into a shy smile. "Real-really, Sawyer?"

"Really," he said, relieved by her smile and the return of the light in her eyes. "And I do care about you. About you and your friends. I don't want anything bad to happen to any of you."

His announcement hit her ears like a burst of beautiful music. "You don't?" she asked just to make sure.

"Why's that so hard to believe? I'm not a monster. It's true that you and your people have done your level best to drive me insane, but I've never wanted anything bad to happen to you. Why do you think I stayed to help you out around here?"

"Oh, Sawyer!" Her arms open wide, Zafiro threw herself straight into him. "You do not know how glad you have made me!"

Instantly, suspicion permeated his senses like a powerful smell. She was up to something again. "Zafiro, what—"

"You do not want anything bad to happen to me or my

friends!" She wrapped her arms around his neck and covered his cheeks with loud kisses. "Now I *know* you will help my men!"

"Dammit to hell," he muttered. "You never give up, do you, Zafiro?" He jerked her arms off his neck and stormed toward the barn doors.

"Sawyer, wait!" She grabbed his hand and tried to keep him still. "You—"

"No! Do you hear me? No! I might not want anything bad to happen to any of you, but that sure as hell doesn't mean I want to go along with your harebrained schemes! I can't believe you, you know that? Not only won't you quit begging me to do something I've already told you I won't do, but you can't seem to get it through that head of yours that your idea is stupid! *Your men are too old to be young and skillful again!*"

"You cannot know that for sure, because you have not worked with them!" She pulled his arm once more. "If I have to knock you out and tie you up with ropes, you are not going to escape me again! I—"

She broke off suddenly, her gaze flying toward one of the wooden boxes she'd rummaged through earlier. Letting go of Sawyer's hand, she raced toward the box, lifted the lid, and snatched out one of its contents. Hiding the item behind her back, she caught up with Sawyer just as he reached the barn doors.

In the space of only a few seconds he heard a jangling sound, then felt something cold and hard circle and snap around his left wrist.

"There!" Zafiro shouted, holding up her right hand. "Now you cannot escape me!"

He stared at the pair of old, rusty handcuffs that bound him to her. "What—"

"Even if you walk out of this barn right now, you will

have to take me with you, Sawyer. Wherever you go, I go, so you might as well listen to what I have been trying to tell you for the past—"

"Take these damned things off—"

"No. Not until you listen—"

"Take them off right now!"

"No."

"Zafiro—"

"Will you listen to me?"

He glared at her so hard that his eyes began to sting. Had it really been only moments ago when they'd been in each other's arms, warmed by the heat of passion, and he'd caressed her to the point of sensual bliss?

Now he felt like wringing her slender little neck.

"Sawyer?"

He closed his eyes and started to count to ten, but he was so angry that he only got to number six before opening his eyes and glaring at her again. "If you don't open these cuffs, I'll—"

"I will release you as soon as you have heard what I have to say. All right?"

He didn't answer.

"All right?" she asked again.

He still didn't answer.

"Sawyer?"

"All right, dammit, all right! Say whatever the hell it is you have to say then get these blasted cuffs off!"

"Luis is coming." The words trembled from her lips, and she felt both relieved and frightened to say them. "Luis."

She was looking at him as if she expected some sort of effusive reaction from him. "Luis." He nodded a slow nod. "What do you want me to do? Cry? Dance a little jig? Wring my hands?"

She continued as though she hadn't heard a word of his sarcastic reply. "He is going to come to La Escondida and steal me away so that I will always be there to tell him and his gang when danger is coming. Then he and his men can escape the danger, you see."

"No, Zafiro, I don't see," Sawyer snapped. "I don't understand a damned thing—"

"And I am sure they will kill Azucar, Tia, and my men," she rushed on, determined to tell him the complete story before he found a way to stop her. "He would not want to leave any live witnesses to—"

"Kill?" God, the story was becoming more convoluted with each word she uttered! "Kill . . . as in to do something to make someone die?"

"Yes, that kind of kill. That is why I need you to help my men with their shooting and riding skills, Sawyer. So that when Luis and his gang come we will be ready to defend ourselves from them. Luis, he is good with a horse and a gun, but my men were better. Once you have practiced with them we will find a way to fill their mouths with guns, and then—"

"What?"

"Yes, you know. Fill their mouths with guns."

He felt so confused that he was almost dizzy. "Do you mean we'll arm them to the teeth?"

"Yes, that is—"

"That is not what you said."

"Well, it is what I meant to say. Luis will—"

"Stop." Sawyer held up his hand, dragging Zafiro's along as well. "Stop." With his free hand he shoved his fingers through his hair, all the while staring at Zafiro. "I'm going to ask you one simple question, and I want you to give me one simple answer. Get straight to the point, and don't get off the subject. Who . . . is . . . Luis?"

Relief coursed through her. Finally, after all these weeks, he was showing some interest in her dilemma. "Rogelio Luis Gutierrez. He did not like his first name, so he had everyone call him by his middle—"

"Who the hell is Luis?" Sawyer roared.

"I am trying to tell you!"

"Well, tell me then!"

"A sheep can wag its tail three times faster than I can tell the whole story, so we'd better sit down." Tugging him along, she walked back into the barn and sat down on a pile of burlap sacks.

Completely aggravated, Sawyer had no choice but to sit down beside her. "It's three shakes of a lamb's tail," he flared.

"What?"

"Three shakes of a lamb's tail. That means fast."

"I meant that I could not tell my story fast."

"I know, but you said it wrong. You said . . . Never mind. I'm waiting."

"Waiting?"

"For the story about Luis!"

The story, pent up inside her for so long, tumbled from her lips. "Luis is my cousin, the son of my father's sister. She and her husband died of a fever when Luis was sixteen. That is when he began to ride with us. But he was never like Grandfather and the rest of the men. Grandfather used to say that the best outlaw is the outlaw who does not use violence. But Luis was always trying to use his gun, even when it was not necessary. And Luis did not like to share the money the gang stole either. Because Luis was family, my grandfather tried to have patience with him, but in the end . . ."

When she faltered Sawyer realized the rest of her story was extremely difficult for her to relate. "In the end?"

"Luis . . . He . . . Luis is the very horrible man who killed my father."

Sawyer saw a tear appear at the corner of her eye. Though it was only one tiny droplet it overwhelmed him with sympathy for her. "I'm sorry," he whispered.

She nodded, closed her eyes, and felt her tear run warmly down her cheek. "It was late one night. Everyone was asleep around the fire. I woke up suddenly because I knew something dangerous was about to happen. What I did not understand was that the danger was about to happen to me. As soon as I opened my eyes I felt Luis's knife at my throat. He covered my mouth with his hand and dragged me toward his horse. Minutes later we were riding away from the camp.

"He hit me while we rode," she said, "and I remember that my cheek stung as if he had burned it. Then he told me that I would be using my gift for him and the band of men he would soon form. He—"

"Gift?"

Failing to remember she was handcuffed to Sawyer, Zafiro rose from the ground, then had to wait a moment for him to get up with her.

He followed her around the barn while she paced.

"I do not know if my gift is a blessing or a curse," she explained, passing the animal stalls. "It saved us from danger more times than I can remember, but it was also the reason why Luis stole me away that night. And," she said, bowing her head, "if not for my gift, my father might still be alive. My father, he woke up and followed Luis that night. When Luis saw him, he let go of me, pulled out his gun, and shot—"

"Zafiro, wait," Sawyer interrupted, taking her arm and forcing her to stand still. "What gift are you talking about?"

"I know when something bad is going to happen. Something dangerous. It is a terrible feeling that makes my heart pound, my mouth go dry, and I can hardly breathe. It will even wake me up if I am sleeping. There were many times when I told my grandfather and the gang about my feelings of a danger that was coming. We always had enough time to escape. The one and only time that my gift failed me was when Night Master found us and stole our gold. But I think that I did not feel danger from him because he was not going to hurt any of us. All he wanted was our gold. Once he got it, he left."

Sawyer wasn't sure if he believed in her sixth sense for peril, but the fear he saw in her eyes could not have been feigned. "This feeling you have for danger . . . I take it you feel it now?"

She fingered the handcuff; the rusty metal felt scratchy beneath her skin. "I have had the feeling for a long time, even before I first saw you at the convent. That is why I was going to kill you after Maclovio told you who we were. I believed you were the danger I anticipated. A lawman, maybe, or someone who would hurt us in some way. Now I know it is Luis who comes. It must be."

"But how do you know he still wants you? After all these years—"

"He swore to find me," Zafiro squeaked, more tears slipping down her face. "After he shot my father, Grandfather and the rest of the men arrived. Before they could even understand what had happened, Luis shouted an oath that he would find me if it took the rest of his life. He could not recapture me because I was already with my grandfather then. He left on his horse, and to this day I can still hear the way he laughed as he rode away. Maclovio, Pedro, and Lorenzo trailed him for days, but they did not find him.

"My father," she said, "he died in my arms, just as I told you. I held his head in my lap. With one hand I touched his cheek, and with the other I tried to stop the blood flowing from the hole in his chest. His last words were that he loved me, that he was sorry he had to leave me, and that he hoped I would have a very happy life. I remember that my tears fell onto his eyes just as he closed them and died."

When her shoulders began to shake, Sawyer gathered her next to him. "I'm sorry," he whispered, patting her hair. "So sorry."

His sympathy seemed to wrap around and hug her, his strength and warmth comforting her in a way that she had not been comforted in years, ever since she'd been a young girl and the Quintana Gang had all had their wits about them. The feeling made it easier to relate the rest of her story. "About three years later," she murmured into his shoulder, "we heard that a man fitting Luis's description had robbed a bank in a small town in Mississippi. Before he left the town he killed four people. One of them was a woman who ran into the street to keep her child from being run over by his horse. After that we began hearing more and more stories about him. He killed so many people, Sawyer, and Grandfather became more and more careful about where our gang went. At night Grandfather would have me sleep right in his bedroll with him, and Maclovio, Pedro, and Lorenzo would sleep beside us."

She drew away from him and peered up into his eyes. "So you see? Grandfather built La Escondida not only to hide his men, but me as well. From Luis. But he is coming, Sawyer. I—I know he is coming! I *feel* it, and that is why I need you to help my men recover their skills!"

Sawyer could actually feel her terror as it coursed

through her body. She shook uncontrollably. "Zafiro," he said softly, hoping his gentle tone of voice would soothe her, "I understand what you're saying, sweetheart, but what are you going to do about weapons and horses?"

"We have Coraje. When he hears a whistle, he—"

"You know as well as I do that that horse won't let anyone on his back. He won't even let me *feed* him without trying to bite me. And coming on the sound of a whistle doesn't make him any more useful."

"Well, maybe we will not need horses. I have weapons, Sawyer. They are old, but perhaps you could make them work again. If you could, then all we would need are bullets."

He followed her across the barn, where she opened the long wooden crate. From within the box she withdrew two heavy pistols and placed one of them in Sawyer's hand. "There are more guns somewhere around here, but this is one that belonged to my father. Do you think it will still work?"

Sawyer looked down at the gun, deeply disturbed by the way it looked in his hand. Tentatively, he curled his finger around the trigger. The hard, cold piece of metal felt horrible. Almost painful, as if it had teeth and was biting him.

An image came into his mind, blurry at first, but it quickly sharpened into clear focus, and he felt as though he were truly seeing it rather than remembering it.

That house. The one with the white curtains. And he saw the couple on the floor, the man with the gray at his temples and the woman with the pretty eyes and musical voice. They lay beside two children.

All of them were dead.

Sawyer felt sweat bead on his forehead and trickle down his face and neck.

Gunfire.

He heard it. It seemed to explode directly from his heart, but memory told him it had cracked straight through a silent night.

Agony thrashed through him. He felt like a live crab thrown into a pot of boiling water.

He threw the gun down to the ground and covered his eyes with his free hand. "No," he whispered. "I . . . I can't teach your men. I can't shoot."

"Sawyer—"

"Put the guns away."

"But—"

"Please. Put them away."

The unmitigated torment she heard in his voice induced her to grant his plea with no further argument. "Sawyer, did you remember something?" she asked, her voice almost a whisper. "The guns . . . What was it about the guns that made you—"

"I can't take care of you," he whispered raggedly. "Of any of you. Not with the guns. If I try . . . If I try, I'll fail."

"Fail? What do you mean? Sawyer, what—"

"Nothing." He thrust his fingers through his hair.

"It *was* something!" She grasped his shoulders and tried to shake him. "You say you do not want anything bad to happen to me or my people. Well, I do not want anything bad to happen to you either! Let's talk about what you remembered, Sawyer. If you talk about it, maybe—"

"Where's the key to these handcuffs?"

A moment passed before his question registered. "Key?"

"Key."

She hadn't seen a key in the box where she'd found

the cuffs, and belatedly realized there wasn't one. "I . . . Oh, Sawyer . . . "

"Oh, Sawyer, what?"

Closing her eyes and swallowing hard, she tried to prepare herself for the explosion she knew would follow her admission. "There is no key."

eleven

S awyer didn't say a word. He merely grabbed the
two lanterns and walked out of the barn and
into the night, uncaring that his long, quick
stride made it difficult for Zafiro to follow along.

Sensing that a volatile mood lurked just beneath the
surface of his silence, Zafiro quietly followed him into the
cabin, whereupon he marched straight up to Tia, who was
busy patting out potato cakes and slipping them into a
pan of hot grease over the fire. A platter of freshly fried
cakes sat on the table where she worked, and as the other
cakes finished cooking she continued to add them to the
platter.

"Where is Lorenzo?" Sawyer demanded.

Tia's patting hands stopped in mid-action. "I do not
like your tone of voice, *niño*." She set down the cake,
picked up a long wooden spoon, and pointed it at his
face. "If you talk to me like that again, I will—"

Sawyer muttered a string of profanities under his
breath and stormed toward the staircase.

"Do not go so fast, Sawyer!" Zafiro pleaded, the handcuff cutting into her wrist. "You are hurting—"

"You should have thought of that before you locked us

together!" At the top of the stairs he stopped and turned toward her. "If Lorenzo can't pick this lock how do you think we're going to get out of these? These cuffs might be old, Zafiro, but they're made of solid steel!"

"I would not have had to put them on you if you had listened to me when I first tried to talk to you! It was the only way—"

"You—"

"Step aside, Zafiro, and I will smash his face!" Maclovio boomed as he exited the room he shared with Pedro and Lorenzo. A bottle in his hand, he staggered into the hall, swinging his fist while still a good six feet away from Sawyer.

Zafiro quickly moved between the two men. Pushing the wobbly Maclovio aside, she pulled Sawyer into the room Maclovio had left and saw Pedro and Lorenzo inside.

"Lorenzo!" she shouted at the old man.

Curled up in a ball on the sagging bed with Mariposa, Lorenzo continued to snore.

"He is asleep," Pedro announced from his spot on the floor, where he was busy adding to his net. "Dreaming about a land flowing with milk and honey. Poor Lorenzo, he is afraid that I am going to turn him into a pillar of salt. I thought about doing that when he would not help me get my net up here. But I did not do it. Maclovio brought my net up here for me. To thank Maclovio for his help, I am going to wash his feet with my hair and—"

"Lorenzo!" Sawyer shouted. He pulled Zafiro to the bed and shook Lorenzo's shoulder.

The old man opened his eyes and smiled. "Tia is making potato cakes and she said I could have as many as I wanted. There is no one in the world who can make potato cakes like Tia—"

"Can you open this lock?" Sawyer shouted into the old man's ear.

"Clock? No, there is no clock in here, but if you want to know what time it is, I will teach you how to read the hour by studying the way the sun makes shadows on the land. It is a simple way to—"

"Lock!" Sawyer shouted again, his lips so close to Lorenzo's ear that the old man's hair tickled his nose. "I need you to open these cuffs because Zafiro can't find the key!"

"Pee?" Lorenzo scowled and pointed to a small pot in the corner of the room. "That is what Maclovio, Pedro, and I use, but I do not think you should use it in front of Zafiro because—"

"*Key*, not *pee*!" Sawyer yelled. "Dammit to hell!" So frustrated that he could barely see straight, he thrust his cuffed hand in front of Lorenzo's face, hoping the old man would understand the problem.

Lorenzo looked at the cuffs. "You are wearing handcuffs. Why?"

Sawyer's anger rose dangerously close to fury. "Take them off!" he shouted so loudly that he swore he heard his brain rattle.

"Cough?"

"Off!"

"Tia makes a good cough remedy with honey, lemon, and—"

"It's no use," Sawyer muttered. "I can't make him understand a damn word."

Zafiro quickly intervened. Using her fingernail, she pretended to pick the lock, knowing her simple action would help him to understand.

Lorenzo's face split into a smile. "You want me to open these cuffs? Well, why didn't you tell me? There is not a

lock, safe, or bolt in the universe that I cannot open."
Using Mariposa as a grip, he took hold of the powerful
cat's head, pulled himself into a sitting position, and
smiled when Mariposa licked his hand. "Ciro, he used to
say that the Quintana Gang could not have survived
without my skills. I got the gang out of jail—"

"Just open the cuffs, for God's sake!" Sawyer blasted.

"Cake?" Lorenzo stood and ambled to a large chest of
drawers that sat between two open windows. "You will
have to wait for your potato cake, just like the rest of us,
Sawyer. I do not know why you think you can have yours
before we have ours. That is greedy."

"Sawyer, my handsome stallion!" Azucar exclaimed as
she hobbled into the room.

Sawyer smacked his own forehead when he heard her
voice. "God help me," he whispered. "The whore of
yore."

Sensing Sawyer's forbearance had almost reached its
limit, Zafiro patted his shoulder and shook her head at
him. "Try to be nice."

"Nice?" he yelled. *"Nice?* I'm handcuffed to you for
what might be forever, I'm trying to get a sleepy old deaf
man to cooperate, in only a few seconds I'm going to be
ravished by a walking antique, and you expect me to be
nice?"

"Heist?" Lorenzo removed a black leather case from
the top drawer of the dresser and returned to the bed.
"Yes, the Quintana Gang pulled hundreds of heists, and
only the Night Master ever got the better of us."

"Come with me, Sawyer," Azucar said, eyeing his
groin, "and I will grant your deepest desires, your wildest
fantasies." She ran her hands down the sides of her torso.

"Sit down, please, Zafiro and Sawyer," Lorenzo instructed.

"I have to sit down, Azucar," Sawyer told the old woman. He sat down on the bed with Zafiro and, his every instinct trained on the elderly prostitute, watched as Lorenzo opened the black case. A set of tools lay neatly inside: an assortment of metal picks, two pairs of pliers, several stiff cards, a variety of knives, and an instrument that looked to be a surgeon's scalpel.

Lorenzo picked up the scalpel-looking instrument. "A glass cutter," he announced, smiling a wide, toothless grin. "Thanks to this little blade I robbed jewelry stores without ever setting foot inside the establishments. I just cut a hole in the front window, dipped my hand inside, and helped myself to whatever jewelry was on display. One time I even did it in broad daylight during a town parade. I think that was somewhere . . . Well, I do not know where that was. Everyone was so involved with the festivities that no one saw me near the store."

He reached for one of the metal picks, a long, slender implement whose tip curved and resembled a cat's claw. "Of course, I did not keep all the jewelry," he hastened to explain, bending over the lock on the handcuffs. "Some we sold for money and some we gave to people who had nothing."

With trembling fingers he inserted the pick into the lock. "Once I gave a pearl bracelet to a poor farmer's wife who had served us all a chicken dinner. She and her husband both fainted. It was good chicken that she made, worth every pearl of the bracelet. Fried, if I remember right, with crispy crust—"

"Concentrate on the cuffs!" Sawyer exploded. "Not the chicken dinner!"

"Thinner?" Lorenzo continued to work the pick inside the lock. "Yes, I am thinner now than I used to be. I think it is because we rarely have any meat. Now, please be quiet while I open this lock."

He leaned over even farther, laying his head on the mattress while he continued to move the pick within the metal opening of the lock.

And then he began to snore. The pick fell from his fingers and clattered to the floor.

Sawyer felt a tic begin in the muscle in his jaw. "I can't believe this," he whispered. "I just can't—"

"He must have had to get back to his dream about a land flowing with milk and honey," Pedro ventured, still tying knots into his net. "He is a good man, Lorenzo is. I remember when he gave the pearl bracelet to the farmer woman. I also remember when he gave a solid gold pocket watch encrusted with rubies to a ragged little boy who was in a field calling in his goats. Lorenzo hid behind some rocks, caught one of the goats, and tied the watch around the animal's neck. Then he let the goat go and sat back to watch what would happen. The boy found the shiny watch and started to dance with joy. All the angels and saints in heaven sang on that day."

"Zafiro," Sawyer seethed under his breath.

"Yes?" she asked sweetly, maintaining her smile even when she saw Sawyer's terrible frown.

"We didn't come in here to listen to stories," he whispered harshly. "I want these cuffs off."

"Well, you will have to wait, Sawyer. It is story time right now. We do this every now and then, you know, so no one will forget the past."

He stared at her. He'd forgotten his own past, and she wanted him to listen to the daft old men's stories?

He started to stand, but felt a sharp pain shoot through his cuffed wrist when Zafiro yanked him back down again.

"Zafiro, I am not staying here to listen to age-old tales of adventure."

She looked directly into his eyes, wishing with all her heart that she could see what thoughts were going on behind them.

Something about holding her father's gun had reminded him of his own past. She knew he remained deeply upset over whatever he had remembered or even partly recalled.

He wanted to be alone. She realized he did. But she knew also that the lighthearted stories her men would soon relate would be good for Sawyer. The heartwarming tales would most likely take his mind off his problems.

At least for a while. "You will stay here, Sawyer, because *I* am staying, and that is the end of it."

Having scolded him, she turned her attention back to her charges. "I remember when you did a good deed too, Pedro. We were in Nuestra Señora de las Rosas, and you met those two little girls who were crying because their friends were making fun of them for believing in miracles."

"This is unreal, Zafiro," Sawyer snapped quietly. "We're handcuffed, and you want to tell stories?"

"Yes," she said without looking at him. "Pedro, do you remember the girls?"

Pedro smiled. "They were sisters, and they lived in a little hut made of sticks and mud. In the front of the hut they had planted purple flowers. Their mother had recently died, and their father worked on a nearby hacienda until very late at night. The girls, they made their own supper—nothing but tortillas with a bit of grease spread on them. They were the poorest of the poor. They did not even have shoes to wear, isn't that right, Zafiro?"

"Yes, but you changed that with a little miracle, didn't

you, Pedro?" She glanced at Sawyer again, suppressing a smile when she saw the expression of grudging interest on his face.

"Pedro told the girls to pray for help from heaven, Sawyer," she explained. "He said that with help from heaven their father would not have to work so much and that they would have more time to spend with him. They said their prayers right in front of him. He kissed them on their cheeks, then pretended to leave. But he did not leave. Instead, he sneaked into their little hut and placed a treasure map on their father's straw mattress. Then Pedro buried some gold and a few jewels near the river that ran near the town. The father found the treasure by following the map. The next time we visited Nuestra Señora de las Rosas, the family lived in a very nice house and the father owned his own shop."

Sawyer looked at Pedro and Lorenzo. A gold watch-bearing goat and a treasure map. The two old outlaws had certainly come up with unique ways with which to share their wealth. He wondered what sort of things Maclovio had done during the gang's days of riding together.

"Do not forget Maclovio's kindnesses," Tia said from the doorway, where she'd been listening to the exchange for the past few minutes.

Sawyer smiled. "I was just wondering about that."

"A mother always knows what her child is thinking, my little Francisco." Balancing two trays of food and drinks in her hands, Tia proceeded into the room and set the trays on top of the dresser. "Not only did Maclovio once give his beloved horse to a man who did not have one, but I once saw him risk his own life to save a kitten."

She interrupted her own story for a few minutes while she made the plates of dinner, filling hot tortillas with potato cakes, fresh sliced tomatoes and onions, and sprinklings of chopped green chilies.

"We had stopped by the seashore and were enjoying an afternoon near the water," she went on, passing out the plates as she talked. "There were rocks in the surf, and Maclovio and the other men walked out on them. While there the men heard a cry, almost like a baby's, and Maclovio soon spotted a tiny white kitten in the waves. Ciro, Lorenzo, Pedro, and Jaime, they tried to hold him back, but Maclovio jumped into the water. The sea was rough that day, and the waves dragged him down several times. But he saved the kitten."

"And you kept the kitten, Zafiro?" Sawyer asked, deciding that Maclovio had probably given the little animal to her. He picked up one of his potato-filled tortillas, bit into it, and closed his eyes in appreciation. Tia was certainly a bit touched in the head, but she was a damn fine cook.

He wondered if his real mother had been as equally skilled in the kitchen.

"Maclovio saved the kitten several years before we found Zafiro in the basket, Francisco," Tia said, passing out drinks of lemon-flavored water. "If I am thinking right, he gave the kitten to a kindly shopkeeper who was troubled with mice."

"That is right," Maclovio said as he lurched into the room. "I gave him to a shopkeeper. And do you remember what you did for that man, Tia?"

Tia waved her hand at him. "I did nothing for him—"

"You did." Shaking his head and rubbing his face in an effort to clear his alcohol-sodden mind, Maclovio sat down on the floor to eat next to Pedro. "He did not have a wife to cook and clean for him. You spent two days cleaning his house and shop, and you also made meals for him."

"I offered him a free night in my arms," Azucar stated proudly, taking a seat on the bed and pulling up her dress so she could swing her bare leg. "But he did not accept my offer. I think he was too shy."

"All of you were and still are wonderful," Zafiro claimed. "Don't you think so, Sawyer?"

Sawyer saw her gaze touch each of the old people in the room, including the sleeping Lorenzo. There was no doubt she loved them and they loved her. They might not be her blood kin, but the relationship between them was every bit as close and devoted.

He wondered if *he* had a family somewhere. People whom he loved and who loved him in return. If so, had they given up ever finding him?

He ran his free hand through his hair.

"There is a special place in heaven for all of my men, Sawyer," Zafiro continued, wondering what had caused the faraway look on his face. "My father and grandfather, they are already in their special places, but Luis will not have one. That is a man who will burn in hell for all of eternity."

"But he must die first," Maclovio said. Bowing his head, he looked at his half-eaten meal and set his plate aside. The sadness he felt both diminished his appetite and sobered him. "The past . . . When I think about the past . . . There have been many times when I have wished that things had been different. My good friend Jaime, gone. And all of us living here. Hidden away from the whole world."

"Are you saying that if you had it all to do again, you wouldn't be a thief?" Sawyer asked.

"No, that is not what I am saying. It is true that thievery is wrong, but we helped many people. For that I am not sorry."

Zafiro nodded. "All money has a top and a bottom."

"There are two sides to every coin," Sawyer corrected her.

"Yes, and that includes the coin of thievery," Zafiro said. "The Quintana Gang was never selfish."

"And we only robbed the rich," Pedro added. "But not even from the very wealthy did we take more than we needed."

"That is right." Maclovio exhaled a great sigh, then took a deep, shuddering breath.

Watching the big man, Sawyer realized this was the first time he'd ever seen Maclovio sober. The drunken slur had vanished, and Maclovio was actually making sense.

Sawyer wondered who the real man was inside Maclovio. Oddly enough, he found himself looking forward to meeting the true side of the outlaw. "What would you do differently, Maclovio?"

"Luis," Maclovio growled. "If I could do things in a different way, I would have killed him with my bare hands the day I first realized he was not like us."

"And when was that?" Sawyer queried.

Maclovio hoisted his large frame off the floor and began to walk around the room. "He had been with us for only two days and was sixteen years old. Young, yes, but old enough to know that baby birds need their mother."

"You did not tell me this story, Maclovio," Zafiro said. "What happened?"

"He shot a mother bird right out of her nest. I saw him do it, and I grabbed him straight off the ground. He said I was mad over nothing. That it was only a bird. It was then that I knew in my heart that he had no feelings. No compassion or consideration for anyone or anything. That is the day I should have killed him."

"You have never killed anyone, Maclovio," Zafiro stated.

"That does not mean that I will not. When Luis comes, I will kill him."

Sawyer took note of the fact that Maclovio said "when," not "if." "You're sure he's coming?"

"We all are," Pedro answered emphatically. "If Zafiro feels danger, then danger comes. It must be Luis. He swore to find her. Her gift is more valuable to him and his gang than anything he could ever try to steal, so do not think that he has forgotten her."

"I will kill him," Maclovio repeated, balling his hands into tight fists.

"And I will help you," Pedro promised. "Luis is the devil's doing, and we must not allow such evil to continue. It is every man's responsibility to destroy any evil he finds."

"I know nothing about killing," Tia said, "but I will do whatever I can to keep Zafiro safe from Luis. There have been many days and nights when I am afraid to even wonder where he is."

"Sometimes I see him in my dreams," Azucar admitted. "I remember him so well that it is almost as if I just saw him yesterday."

Watching a tear slide down Azucar's wrinkled cheek, Sawyer knew instant pity. Old women shouldn't have to be afraid, he thought. They should be allowed to spend their final days in peace. "Luis is probably miles and miles away from here, Azucar," he tried to comfort her.

No one in the room made a reply. By the looks on their faces Sawyer realized his comment hadn't reassured a single person.

They all believed—knew—Luis would come.

And Sawyer began to wonder about the bastard too. "But how can he find you?" he asked, hoping to dispel some of the gloom. "Ciro did a great job hiding this place the way he did. If no one else has found you—"

"The devil will find a way to tell him," Pedro said. "Even now Satan is probably whispering into Luis's ear."

"If you will just be still for a moment, I will open the lock," Lorenzo said, awakening from his little nap. "I—" He broke off when he saw the expressions on all their faces. The women appeared afraid. Maclovio and Pedro's eyes glittered with hatred. "Luis," he said. "You are talking about Luis. Only talk and thoughts about him cause all of you to feel such fear and hatred."

Everyone nodded at the same time.

Absolute silence crept through the room, heightening the sense of fear, the apprehension of pondering the unknown. Like a wicked sword that cut out tongues, the silence rendered everyone mute, challenging someone to break its unnerving power.

A sudden crack of thunder killed the quiet, its loudness much like a slap across the faces of everyone in the room.

Tia was the first to recover. Nervously, she began to collect the plates and glasses, and the tableware rattled as she piled it on the tray. "Bedtime, my Francisco. I should not have allowed you to be in here tonight in the first place. All this talk about Luis . . . I do not want you to be afraid, my son. Maclovio, Pedro, and Lorenzo, they will not let that bad man hurt you or any of us, do you understand?"

Sawyer glanced at the three outlaws. Even if he *were* the boy called Francisco, he'd still realize that the old men couldn't keep him safe.

"Francisco?" Tia pressed.

Sawyer felt Zafiro squeeze his cuffed hand—a gentle reminder to be nice to the sweet old woman. "All right," he said to Tia. "I won't be afraid."

"Muy bien," she answered, smiling at him. "Please tuck him in and tell him a story, Zafiro. I have some mending to do downstairs." The tray of plates and glasses in her hands, she left the room.

"I think we should all go to sleep now," Zafiro said, rising from the bed.

Her action forced Sawyer to stand as well. "Have you forgotten we're handcuffed?" He raised their bound hands.

"Well, there is no help for it tonight, Sawyer. We cannot get the lock open. Lorenzo is asleep again."

"I will put Lorenzo to bed," Maclovio offered. He waited for Zafiro and Sawyer to step aside, then lifted the limp Lorenzo into his beefy arms and placed the man on the mattress beside Mariposa. One friend taken care of, he turned to Pedro and helped him off the floor.

"You are like the giant Goliath," Pedro said, clapping Maclovio on the back. "Goliath married the Queen of Sheba, who bore him a son called Judas. Goliath and the Queen of Sheba were very proud of Judas because he defeated Ramses the pharaoh with the jawbone of an ass." Having related his story, Pedro headed for his own cot on the other side of the room.

"Good night to everyone," Maclovio said. He kissed Zafiro and Azucar's cheeks, then shook Sawyer's free hand. "I think you are a good man, Sawyer Donovan, and I will try not to smash your face again."

"I'll take your word until the next time I see you drunk," Sawyer answered.

"I am not going to drink anymore."

Zafiro clucked at him. "You always say that when you are sober, Maclovio."

"Want some help in keeping your promise, Maclovio?" Sawyer asked.

"What kind of help?"

Sawyer raised his right eyebrow and smiled. "I'm going to find and destroy your still. And once I do you'll never drink anything stronger than Tia's lemon water again."

Maclovio chuckled. "I invite you to try, Donovan."

With a nod of his head, Sawyer accepted the invitation.

"You will not succeed, Sawyer," Zafiro whispered as she led Azucar into the hallway and pulled Sawyer along too. After closing the bedroom door, she sighed. "I have spent years looking for his whiskey machine. Sister Carmelita has helped me. We have never found it."

Sawyer didn't comment. Obviously, he mused, Maclovio was leaving the cabin to tend to his still while everyone else was asleep or otherwise occupied. With a bit of careful vigilance, catching the man wouldn't be too difficult.

And once Maclovio became sober for good, Zafiro would have one less problem to worry about.

"Sawyer?"

The crackly voice seized Sawyer's full attention. "Go to sleep, Azucar."

"Good night, Azucar." Zafiro gave Azucar a quick hug.

"You would not turn me down if I offered you a free night of ecstasy, would you, Sawyer?" One hand kneading her own breast, Azucar reached for the bulge in his breeches.

He sidestepped her advance. "Zafiro, tell her—"

"Azucar," Zafiro pleaded, taking hold of the woman's

bony hand, "you said you needed privacy for such a thing."

Azucar nodded, her fingers still outstretched and straining in an attempt to get a feel of Sawyer's crotch. "You should go to your own room now, *chiquita*. I will go with Sawyer to his."

"But do you forget that I am handcuffed to Sawyer?" Zafiro held up the cuffs.

Azucar eyed the handcuffs and sighed. "Yes, I forgot. My mind is not as good as it was a few years ago when I was seventeen. But at least I still have my beauty, eh, Sawyer?"

He watched as she batted her scanty eyelashes and shook her flabby bottom. Her scarlet dress rustling and her bony hips swaying, she tottered down the hall, entered her own room, and shut the door.

"How can she not know how old she is?" Sawyer asked. "She has to see all her own wrinkles every time she looks in a mirror."

"You do not know who you are either, Sawyer." Zafiro reached up to his shoulder and slid her fingers through his thick, tawny hair. "You know, you really should give in to Azucar."

"*What?* She's one step away from being a mummy, and you want me to take her to bed and—"

"No," Zafiro replied, and laughed. "Just make her happy. Give her a kiss on the cheek every now and then. A hug. Some flowers. Any sort of romantic attention would make her happy. For the matter of that, you should indulge all my people. Call Tia 'Mother' sometimes. Ask Pedro for a blessing. Carry on a conversation with Lorenzo even though he hears nothing you say."

"Forget it. It's all I can do just to keep my patience

with them. I sure as hell can't cater to their fantasies and infirmities."

"But—"

"I'll be nice, Zafiro. That's all I can promise." With that Sawyer approached his room, opened the door, but stopped before entering. Looking down, he stared at the rusty pair of handcuffs. "Oh, this ought to be fun. How do you think we're going to sleep, Zafiro?"

"How?" She smiled. "Together, Sawyer."

twelve

Her answer hit his ears, traveled down from his mind, and licked through his loins like a tongue of fire. "Right. Together."

"Yes. These handcuffs have surrounded us with a hard, stony place."

He led her inside his room, and tried to decipher the expression she'd just mangled. "We're between a rock and a hard place, and that is not what you said, so don't tell me it was."

She closed the door and glanced at the bed. Strange. She'd seen that very bed hundreds of times, but the sight of it had never done to her what it was doing now.

Tonight she would sleep in it with Sawyer. Would cuddle up next to his big, hard body until morning. "The bed, it is so small."

"Yours isn't any bigger."

Her gaze met his, and she saw a roguish smile on his mouth. That now familiar heat melted through her.

I knew you'd be like this. So soft, sweet, so full of passion. I knew it, Zafiro.

The memory of what he'd told her in the barn intensified her feelings. "We will have to sleep very close together. With our bodies touching."

"That, or one of us is going to fall on the floor." Sawyer moved to turn down the lamp, then sat on the edge of the mattress to take off his boots.

Zafiro did likewise, and when they were both barefoot they looked down at the mattress.

"Do you sleep on your stomach or your back?" Sawyer asked.

"On my side. Why do you ask me that question?"

"Because of the handcuffs. We can't sleep any old way we want because my left hand is bound to your right hand." He looked at the mattress again. "All right, you crawl over there to the side next to the wall. That way we can sleep either on our sides or on our backs."

Zafiro glanced at the wall. "I cannot sleep next to the wall with you on the other side of me."

"Why not?"

"I like to hang my leg out of the bed if I get too hot at night."

"Oh. All right." Sawyer moved the pillows to the other end of the bed. "Now our heads will be at this end. That way I'll be next to the wall, and you can hang your leg out."

"Sawyer?"

"What?"

"I cannot sleep with my head at that end of the bed. I am used to having my pillow at the other end of—"

"Well, you can't have it both ways, Zafiro. Either you hang your leg off the bed or you have your pillow at this end."

Zafiro looked down at the handcuffs.

"Maybe you'll think twice before handcuffing yourself to someone again," Sawyer said.

His smile was contagious. She smiled back, then moved the pillows back to the other end of the bed. "I would rather have my pillow at this end than hang my leg off." She crawled into bed close to the wall, moving way over to give Sawyer the most room.

As soon as he laid down beside her, the warmth of her body and the faint scent of roses that clung to her skin aroused him almost to the point of discomfort.

You should have finished, Sawyer.

She'd spoken those words to him. In the barn, when he'd ended their passionate encounter.

His breeches felt so tight. If he were alone he'd take them off.

But the reason why they felt so tight was because he *wasn't* alone. "Comfortable?"

Zafiro wiggled a bit, then settled down. "Warm and comfortable. Like a spider in the carpet."

"Snug as a bug in a rug. It has to rhyme, Zafiro."

Before she could answer, she felt the fingers on his cuffed hand caress her wrist. The slight touch fairly took away her breath.

"So," Sawyer said, glancing at the ceiling. "Sleepy?"

A very long while passed before she made her reply. "Sawyer, we are not lying on a dirty floor in a barn with mice in it."

He felt as though his breeches would split wide open. "No," he whispered. "We're in bed."

"And there are sheets on this bed. Sheets to romp in."

He swore he heard the seams on his breeches rip apart. "Yes."

"Sawyer? Are you thinking and feeling what I am thinking and feeling?"

Before answering he pondered the situation. She

wanted him. Her breathing, the sound of her voice, and all the things she was saying convinced him of it.

God, it would be so easy to have her right now.

"Sawyer?"

"Yes. I think it's a safe bet we're both thinking and feeling the same things, Zafiro, but—"

"We cannot do the things we are thinking about with these handcuffs on?"

Her question made him smile. "These handcuffs aren't a problem, sweetheart. They might be a bit of a nuisance, but I promise you they aren't a problem."

"Then?" She turned to her side and rested her chin on his shoulder. "I would like to finish what we started in the barn, Sawyer."

So would I.

But he hesitated. She was so vulnerable. So fanciful. If he gave in to desire . . . if he joined his body with hers in the most intimate way possible . . .

What would it do to her emotions? "I can't love you, Zafiro," he told her abruptly. "I already told you that."

"What? But I did not ask for you to love me." Her palm on his cheek, she turned his face toward hers, forcing him to look at her. "I only want to *make* love. There is a difference, no?"

Her question deepened his hesitation. "Yes, there's a difference. At least in my book there is."

"You wrote a book?"

He smiled again and reached out to play with a lock of her silky black hair. "No. It's only an expression. Now that you've heard it I'm sure you'll mutilate it before long."

He smoothed the lock of her hair across her lips. "In my opinion, making love is something two people who are in love do. When the people aren't in love it's just mating. Just a sexual union. When it's like that, the partners want only the physical pleasure."

She took into great consideration what he said and found it made perfect sense. "That is what I want, Sawyer," she declared firmly, lifting her head from his shoulder and nodding. "The physical pleasure. It felt very good. And I will give you the same pleasure in return."

Her offer all but stopped his pulse.

"I know you cannot love me, Sawyer. But you have said that you like me. That you care about me. That is enough to have a sexual union of mating with me, isn't it?"

He felt sweat trickle off his forehead.

"You will leave me one day," Zafiro murmured, sliding her hand down to his lower belly. "When you go I will miss you very much. I . . . During the time you have been here I have liked being with you. When you leave, I would like to have beautiful memories of you. Memories of mating with you in a sexual union."

He felt her breast press against his upper arm, and her hand felt so good on his belly. His hunger for her rose to near starvation.

"You see, Sawyer," she continued, moving her hand lower, the tips of her fingers touching his groin. "When you are gone I will be able to remember how you taught me to mate. How you gave me pleasure, and how you showed me how to give you pleasure as well. How a man puts his hard part into the tunnel between a woman's legs. There will be no one else in my life who can teach me these mating skills. You are my one, only, and last chance to know."

Oh, God, he groaned inwardly. If she said one more word, he'd lose all control.

"Sawyer?"

That was the word.

He curled his arm around her. Before her breasts even met his chest he was kissing her. Hard. Deeply, as if she would disappear before he could get his fill of her sweetness.

And she returned his kiss with equal abandon, parting her lips for his sensual foray and meeting his tongue with her own when the invasion began. Wanting and needing to feel his bare skin against hers, she squeezed her hand between her body and his and began to unfasten the buttons on her blouse. "I want to feel you against me," she whispered.

Sawyer moved her hand away and saw to the task himself.

"Thank you," she murmured.

"What's a knight in shining armor for?" Deftly, he worked at the fastenings, and when they were open he helped her remove her blouse.

They both smiled when they realized they couldn't take the garment completely off, but had to leave it wound around their bound wrists.

"Well, at least we will not have this problem with my skirt and your pants, Sawyer." Zafiro cast a glance at his breeches. Her eyes widened when she saw the huge bulge beneath his pants. "Oh, Sawyer."

"It's not a snake, got that? Don't go grabbing at it again." When she didn't reply he wondered if she was afraid of what she was seeing. "Zafiro," he said gently, "if you're afraid—"

"I am not afraid. I . . . I am only curious about all of this."

He reminded himself to go slowly. Enthusiastic as she was, she was still a maiden.

And the last thing he wanted was for her first time to

hurt or frighten her. "Let's kiss for a while longer." He tried to pull her head down to his.

But she resisted. "I will kiss you some more, Sawyer, but I told you I wanted to feel your skin against mine. Will you take your breeches off now?"

He decided the best experience was hands-on experience. "You do it."

She sat up, and with her free hand, she began to unfasten his breeches. "You do not wear undergarments," she said when she saw the thick mat of tawny hair that covered his loins.

"Oh, and you do?"

His sweet sarcasm made her smile. "Only in the winter. In the summer, underwear makes me too hot. Why don't you wear any?"

He picked up her sapphire, held it for a moment, then curled his hand around her breast and began to knead the soft, lush globe. "I'm always prepared. After all, a man never knows when he's going to meet a crazy woman who handcuffs him to her and then wants him to bed her. Thinking of that, I figured it was probably safer not to wear any underwear. Makes things easier when you're hot and handcuffed, you know."

She giggled. "It is all right for people to laugh when they mate in a sexual union?"

"Sweetheart, it's more than all right. In fact, sometimes laughing makes it all the more fun. Depends on the mood, I guess."

His explanation pleased her; she smiled broadly and continued trying to release him from his constricting breeches. "I understand that you want me to do this myself, Sawyer, but I think you will have to help me by lifting your hips. Do you think it would be too much work for you to do that?"

Pretending the task was one of the most strenuous he'd ever performed, Sawyer grimaced with feigned exertion, flexed all his muscles as if lifting a great weight, and slowly raised his hips off the mattress. "Hurry," he panted between clenched teeth. "I can't hold myself up like this for long!"

Giggling once more, Zafiro pulled, yanked, and jerked at the waistband of his breeches, finally succeeding in slipping them over his hips and down to his upper thighs.

Her giggling faded instantly.

Sawyer lowered his hips back down to the bed. "Zafiro?" He tried to understand the reflective expression on her face.

"I . . . I am sure you have the biggest man part in the world, Sawyer," she murmured, still staring at his fully erect masculinity. "It is not a wonder that I thought it was a large snake."

Though he felt flattered by her words, he remained undecided about what she was thinking. "Are you afraid now?" he asked as softly as he could.

Her fingers trembled over the long, velvety length of him. "I will never be afraid of you, Sawyer. Or of any part of you."

Her answer wrapped around him like a pair of soft, warm arms, even as her gentle touch caused him to shudder with need for her. He kissed her again then, slowly, and with all the tenderness he felt for her.

And while his lips nuzzled hers, Zafiro deftly unfastened her skirt. As soon as she had pulled the garment down over her bare hips, she felt Sawyer's desire burn into her lower belly.

"Oh, Sawyer, I am—"

"I know," he answered, reading her thoughts as if from

a page. "Me too." He tugged her skirt off, then shed his breeches as well.

And when they were naked, heartbeat to heartbeat, Zafiro knew the most wondrous feelings she'd ever imagined could exist. Sawyer's skin was warm, his body hard. His size made her feel small, secure, and his scent of wind, pine needles, fresh wood, and hay played further havoc upon her emotions.

She noticed how very still he lay and realized he was giving her the opportunity to do as she wished. Tentatively, she began to explore the bare length of his body with her hand and her eyes.

And her thoughts. Slowly, she mused. There was no need to rush. "You were right," she whispered to him, her hand on his chest. "Azucar does not have a part in what we are doing now. Tonight is my night to learn, Sawyer, and I will learn by doing whatever my instincts lead me to do."

"Then I place myself in the hands of your instincts." Threading his fingers through her raven hair, he smiled at her.

Dios mío, she thought. His smile could melt the snow from the mountain peaks.

Mesmerized by his voice, his scent, the very aura of sheer masculinity about him, she traced his nipples with her finger, then with her tongue, surprised and pleased when the sensitive flesh pebbled beneath her touch. Pushing her knee between his legs, she felt his male parts on her thigh and heard his low moan of raw need. She moved her hand from his chest, down the side of his torso, and gently kneaded his firmly muscled buttocks.

Swearing she could hear his body calling to hers, she inched closer to him, closer still, and her own body moistened with the sheen of desire, trembled with the need for the same pleasure he'd given her in the barn.

But she wanted to please him too. Wanted to gift him with whatever bliss men were capable of feeling. The question was, how did she give it to him?

She wouldn't ask. She would experiment. Try a multitude of things until she sensed she'd found the right one.

The mere thought of what she was about to do excited her immensely, and she realized that Sawyer had been right when he'd said that giving sensual pleasure was pleasing all in itself.

Deciding that his ecstasy would most likely stem from the same place hers had, she drew her hips away from his and sat up to look at his man parts. She slipped her fingers through the tawny hair of his loins. It felt thick, soft, and wonderful, and she lingered there for a long moment before moving her hand lower, down to the soft pouch that lay beneath the base of his manhood.

"Careful," Sawyer murmured, stiffening slightly. "Do not even *think* the word snake while holding me there, all right?"

"This is a tender part of you?" She curled her fingers around the velvety-soft sac.

"Zafiro," he began, doing his damnedest to relax. "Uh—"

"You are at my mercy." Smiling, she began to examine the sensitive part of him she held. "There are two round things inside."

"That's so if some daft woman yanks one off, I'll have a spare."

Laughing at his apprehension, she bent over him and placed a gentle kiss upon the vulnerable pouch, then let go of him. "I am merciful."

Merciful? he thought. She was torturing him with her

innocent play! The hardly there kiss she'd given him there made him so hot that he could barely find a shred of control.

He wondered if she'd kiss him elsewhere. He hadn't taught her *that* aspect of sensual foreplay yet, but perhaps her instincts would tell her for him.

"I am doing well, Sawyer?"

"If you were doing any better this would be all over in only a few more seconds."

She struggled to understand what he was talking about. "What—"

"Never mind. Just listen to your instincts, sweetheart."

Obeying, she clasped his arousal. "Do not worry. I will not pull at it."

He stifled a chuckle. "A *little* bit of pulling there feels good." Tilting his hips, he slid his erection through the tunnel of her hand, then drew it down again.

Understanding what he wanted her to do, she grasped him a tad more tightly, then imitated the motions he'd just shown her, watching her hand glide up and down his hardness. The sight fascinated her. This was the movement a man used when he bedded a woman, her intuition told her. Yes, this way. In. And out.

A man stroked a woman inside, she realized. And in turn the woman stroked the man right back.

She continued to fondle him, her pleasure growing when he grew even harder. Hotter.

A bead of moisture appeared at the tip of his length. She stopped her caresses and stared at the shimmering droplet. "Sawyer?"

He saw the reason for her confusion. "It means I'm ready. That you've done a very thorough job of making me want you."

"But what—" She broke off when he pushed his hand

between her thighs and touched her intimately. When he withdrew from her she saw that his fingers glistened.

"See?" he said. "Women do it too."

"So I am as ready as you are."

"Come here, Zafiro." Hands at her waist, he lifted her over his body so that she sat on his thighs with her legs spread slightly. Her position affording him perfect access to her femininity, he took full advantage and began to stroke her as she had him.

In only moments Zafiro heard a moan escape her own lips. As her pleasure heightened, her hips began to rock back and forth, seemingly of their own volition.

"That's it, sweetheart, that's it," Sawyer urged her softly. He watched her face. Her eyes were closed and her mouth was set in a grim line of concentration and determination. Every muscle in her body that he could see was contracted.

But it was the low, throaty sounds that whispered from her that excited him the most. God, how he loved those involuntary sounds of desire.

And he wanted his own to mingle with hers.

Gently, he moved her back down to the bed again, and when she was lying on her back he knelt between her knees.

"Sawyer," Zafiro breathed when she saw him position his hard man part at the opening of her body.

No further words would come to her. She felt the tip of him probe at her, push at her.

Enter her.

His hands grasping her hips, Sawyer prepared to penetrate her further, fully. Every fiber of his being throbbing with need, he drew his hips back, and—

"Francisco?" Tia called from out in the hall.

"*Santa Maria*, Sawyer, Tia is coming!" Zafiro squealed

quietly. Frantically, she groped for the covers, her efforts hindered by the fact that she was handcuffed to Sawyer, who was groping for the blankets just as wildly.

"Be still and pretend you're asleep!" he hissed at her. With his right hand he jerked the blanket out from under her, then threw himself down beside her.

He'd just yanked the blanket up beneath his and Zafiro's chins when Tia opened the door and waddled into the room. "Zafiro?" she whispered. "You are still awake?"

Zafiro remained as quiet and still as a corpse.

"Francisco?"

Sawyer made not a move. He didn't even breathe.

"Oh, how sweet the two of you look," Tia murmured, smiling as she looked down at them. "Like two innocent angels, both of you."

Leaning over them, she kissed them on their foreheads, watched them for a few minutes longer, then left the room, closing the door quietly behind her.

Sawyer opened one eye, saw she was gone, and began to laugh. "Innocent angels!"

"How can you laugh? Do you know how upset she would have been if she had seen what we were doing?"

Sawyer gathered her into his arms and smiled into her hair. "But she didn't see us."

"What if she had adjusted the blanket and seen that we are naked? Oh, *Dios mío*, Sawyer—"

"But it didn't happen, sweetheart." Sawyer began kissing her cheek, her temple, her eyebrow.

"We were almost caught with our hands all red," Zafiro said, casting another glance at the door. "It was enough to put my teeth on the border."

Sawyer chuckled again. "Yes, we were almost caught

red-handed, and it was enough to set our teeth on edge. But it's all right now, sweetheart."

"We cannot—"

"Yes, we can. *You* can, anyway."

Before she could make sense of what he'd said, she felt his hand between her thighs, his fingers quickly finding her most sensitive spot.

Her nerves still a bit rattled, she wanted to resist him. But her pleasure began almost instantly, and all thoughts fled her mind. Arching her hips into his hand, she surrendered to his sensual skills and released a loud moan.

Sawyer smothered the sound with a kiss and continued caressing her. Her body stiffened for a moment, then began to tremble. "That's it, sweetheart," he murmured, his lips still pressed to hers. "That's it."

The bliss he fostered within her body was even more powerful now than it had been in the barn. Starting at the core of her womanhood, waves and waves of sensations coursed through her, the feelings so intense that she felt her eyes fill with tears.

Only after many long moments did the fierce ecstasy begin to wane. Only after long moments could she think clearly, dwell on anything but the absolute joy Sawyer had given her.

"You all right?" he asked when she opened her eyes and looked at him. "You look like you've been crying."

"I did. I mean, I have. But I did not do it with purpose. The tears, they came all by themselves."

"I know I didn't hurt you."

She heard a tinge of worry in his voice, and his concern felt warmer than sunshine. "No, you did not hurt me. I think the tears were happy ones. This is the very first time I have ever cried happy tears." She snuggled next to his chest. "You have made me happy, Sawyer.

Not only tonight, but on many other nights and days too. I . . . I hope that I have made you happy too. That you have liked to be here with me as much as I have liked you being here."

He thought for a moment. If he hadn't found his way to La Escondida, where would he be right now?

Wandering, that's where, just as he'd been before stopping at the convent.

"Yes," he said. "I've enjoyed being here with you, Zafiro."

Contentment ribboned through her. "Sawyer?"

"Yes?"

"Your mood, it is a good one right now?"

He ran his hand over the gentle curve of her hip. "Yes."

"All right." Zafiro sat up. "Do you remember anything about guns?" she blurted. "Any reason why my father's pistol made you feel such pain? I have been wanting to ask you, but was waiting for you to have a good mood."

Her reminder about the gun quickly darkened his disposition. "I don't want to talk—"

"But you must, don't you see? You must! It is the only way that you—"

"How the hell can I talk about something I don't remember?"

She leaned down to him, her breasts flattening against his chest, her hands cupping his cheeks. "Please," she whispered. "Please tell me whatever little thing you remembered."

He couldn't miss the genuine interest and concern in her startling sapphire eyes. But how could he explain something he couldn't understand himself? "Zafiro, I don't remember enough to tell you. If I did, I could—"

"But you remember pieces and bits."

Her backward expression tempered his emotions. "Yes, I remember bits and pieces."

"Tell them to me, Sawyer. I do not ask this because my nose is big, but only because I want to try to help you as you have helped us."

Her ridiculous referral to her nose further softened his mood. "You aren't being nosy."

She nodded.

He nodded back.

"Well?" she asked.

Sawyer urged her back to his shoulder, and when he felt her warm breath wisp across his chest, he closed his eyes and began to speak in an even, hushed tone of voice. "You know about the house."

He waited for the heinous feeling to come to him, the feeling he always had when thinking of the house. But he felt another feeling instead, that of Zafiro's arm as she slipped it around his waist. The sweetness of her action helped him continue.

"I see a house with white curtains," he said. "In the yard, flowers are growing and children are playing. A man is on the porch, and he's soon joined by a beautiful older lady whose voice sounds like music. She kisses the man on his cheek, then calls to the children."

"The children," Zafiro said, "they are little ones?"

"Some are. A few are older."

"Could the lady be their mother?"

Sawyer pondered her question for a long time. "You know, now that you ask, I don't think so. She's a very pretty woman, but she seems too old to have such young children of her own."

"Maybe she is watching them for her neighbors."

"Yes, maybe she is."

Is? he repeated silently.

Was. Not *is. Was.*

He stopped for a moment then, struggling to quell the familiar horror that finally returned to him. "I see the house in another way too," he continued, his voice cracking. "Inside the house, a man, a woman, and two children are lying on the floor in their own blood."

"They . . . they are the same man and same woman you see on the porch?"

"Yes."

Zafiro tightened her hold around his waist and tried desperately to understand his fragments of memory. "And the gun, Sawyer?" she asked softly. "When you held my father's gun what did you remember? What did you think?"

Instantly, he pictured the gun in his hand. "I . . . It felt cold. Looked . . . looked horrible in my hand. Staring down at it made me think of the four dead people in the house again." He paused again, a mixture of panic and dread burning through him. "And then I remembered the crack of gunfire in a silent night. The explosion of guns. I—"

When he stopped speaking so abruptly, Zafiro raised her head from his shoulder and saw horrified disbelief in his eyes. "Sawyer, what is the matter?" she asked loudly. "What are you remembering now?"

"Dear God," he rasped. "Dear God."

"What?" Truly frightened for him now, Zafiro bolted upright into a sitting position, curled her hands around the muscles in his shoulders, and squeezed hard. "Sawyer, you must tell me! You must speak of this, do you understand? You cannot continue to bury these things inside you or you will never be free of them!"

He yanked her hands off his shoulders, sat up, and

stood, uncaring that his swift actions almost jerked Zafiro's arm out of its socket.

"Sawyer!" She crawled out of the bed and stood beside him. "What—"

He spun on his heel to face her, grabbed her upper arms, and shook her. "The people! The four dead people in the house! Don't you understand? The gunfire! The blood! Can't you see?"

"They were shot?" she answered. Gently, she pulled his hands off her arms to stop him from shaking her head off her shoulders. "They were shot and killed?"

She watched him lift his gaze from her face, over the top of her head. He stared intently, as if he could see the story of his past in pictures upon the log wall behind her. "Sawyer?"

His shoulders slumped; he exhaled every bit of breath from his lungs and sat back down on the bed.

Zafiro sat down beside him.

"I understand now," he whispered raggedly. "I know what happened."

His voice was filled with such indescribable pain that Zafiro knew nothing on earth could ease his torment. Prayers to heaven on his behalf swirled through her mind like hundreds of petals blowing in the wind.

"I killed them, Zafiro." Sawyer bowed his head, and bringing her hand along with his, he held his face in his hands. "Whoever that man, woman, and two children were, I shot them down and killed them in that house."

Though his pain was silent, Zafiro swore she could hear its chilling scream as it roared through him. She said nothing. Her heart and mind brimmed with horror and shock, but she said nothing.

She merely urged him back down to the bed. And

when he turned toward her and buried his face in her hair, his huge body shuddering with his grief, she wept.

Time held no meaning for her as she continued to embrace and caress him. Indeed, when he fell asleep upon the cushion of her hair, all she knew for sure was that dawn had pinkened the sky.

Four people, two of them children. Her heart twisted at the thought.

He'd killed them. Shot them down and killed them in the house with the white curtains and the flowers in the yard.

Her grandfather and the gang had never taken a life. Had rarely even drawn their guns.

But Sawyer . . .

Having no more tears to cry, Zafiro wept inside.

The man she loved was a murderer.

thirteen

Zafiro thanked all the angels and saints in heaven that Sawyer was bound to her with the handcuffs. If he hadn't been, she knew he would have left her and La Escondida hours ago when he'd awakened in her arms.

As it was he was forced to take her along wherever he went. She accompanied him to the barn and to the corral, where he saw to the animals. She went with him to the garden, where he checked to see if the plants and Jengibre were faring well. She tagged along behind him when he returned to the cabin and grabbed a loaf of bread, a wedge of cheese, and a bunch of freshly picked carrots.

Now she sat in a secluded glade near the stream with him, a pretty spot she'd visited only on occasion because it was so far from the house. "Do you come to this place often, Sawyer?" she asked, knowing full well he wouldn't answer her.

He hadn't spoken a word all day. Not to her or to anyone else. He'd drawn into himself, shutting everyone and everything out of his thoughts and emotions.

The sole thing upon which he could concentrate was the realization that he had murdered four people.

And Zafiro knew in the heart of her soul that even if God Himself commanded Sawyer to talk about the murders, Sawyer would not comply.

She blinked back tears, as she'd been doing all day. Although she could only imagine the torment that boiled inside him, his pain had become her own. But she felt so helpless. So useless. Sawyer had done so much for her, and now—when he was in need himself—she did not know what to do for him.

Turning her head away from him so he wouldn't see her tears, she wiped her eyes dry. "You brought lunch out here. Are you hungry now?"

He picked up a pebble and hurled it into the stream.

"I think we should eat, Sawyer. We did not have breakfast." She handed him a carrot.

He ignored her hand and the carrot.

"Why did you bring all this food out here if you are not going to eat it? Was it just for me?"

For a moment he watched a sparrow fly from branch to branch in a nearby tree. When the sparrow finally flew away, he threw a twig into the creek and watched it float downstream.

Zafiro tore off a hunk of the bread. "Well, if all this food is just for me, then at least I know that even if you are not talking to me, you are still thinking about me."

She slipped a morsel of bread into her mouth. "Sawyer? I . . . I know you are horrified by what you remembered last night, but—"

The stiffening of his body, the hard, cold glitter that suddenly iced his eyes, silenced her instantly.

She felt utterly uncertain about the man who sat beside her. He looked like the Sawyer Donovan she knew, but he was not that man.

The Sawyer beside her now was a complete stranger to her. His eyes, his body . . . everything about him was cold and distant, as if he'd been frozen and taken away to a place too far to reach.

Zafiro picked up another carrot, a small, slender one, and slipped its thickest end into her mouth. "When I was a little girl, I used to smoke carrots, twigs, pencils . . . anything that looked like a cheroot to me," she rambled nervously, the carrot waving up and down in her mouth as she spoke. "I did not light them though. I only pretended to smoke. Grandfather smoked sometimes. Once, he caught me with one of his cheroots in my mouth. He took it away from me and told me that smoking would make my hair smell bad."

Talk to me, Sawyer. Please do not be this icy way with me.

"Will you try to find Maclovio's whiskey machine today, Sawyer? I will help you if you want to go looking for it."

Clicking the toes of his boots together, he scared away a bothersome fly that buzzed around his legs.

"Sometimes I have wondered what it is like to be drunk," Zafiro continued. "Maclovio, he always seems to have a good time. At least he does before he becomes violent. He sings and he dances. He laughs at things that are not funny to anyone else. One day maybe I will get drunk. Just to see what is the feeling of being so silly and so happy."

She slipped a small piece of cheese into her mouth and let it melt on her tongue before she spoke again. "I promised Tia I would take her to gather berries today, Sawyer. There are no more apples. The berries, they do not grow inside La Escondida, but the patch is very near. You will have to come with me when I take her."

He wouldn't go with her to pick berries, she knew. The task of having to bend and straighten with her so many times to gather the succulent fruit would deeply irritate him.

How were they going to remove the handcuffs? she wondered.

Trying to stay busy, she pinched off another bit of bread, rolled it into a small, tight ball, then threw it into the creek. Quickly, dozens of fish began to snap at it, their silvery fins looking like clusters of watered stars. "Do you want to feed the fish?" She placed another ball of rolled bread into the palm of his hand, saddened when he made no move to toss it to the fish.

She neither said nor did anything more. What was the use? He responded to nothing.

It was only when a low snarl hissed from within the grove of trees to her left that Sawyer finally reacted. Jumping up from the sandy shore, he forced Zafiro to her feet as well. His eyes narrowing, he peered into the dark area of the trees.

A mountain lion crept out of the shadows, then stopped and crouched low to the ground.

Zafiro shrank back toward Sawyer. "It is not Mariposa. That cougar looks like he is starving. Look at his bones, Sawyer."

"He's a she." Yanking Zafiro along, Saywer waded into the deepest section of the stream, where the water bubbled around his chest and up around Zafiro's neck.

"She is very hungry," Zafiro said. "I know she will wait for us to come out of the water, Sawyer. I have watched Mariposa wait for hours for a rabbit she knew was in a hole."

Sawyer watched the great cat slink toward the bread and the cheese. The cougar sniffed at the bread and the carrots, then devoured the entire wedge of cheese. Licking its mouth, the animal then turned toward the stream and laid on its belly.

"We're going to float downstream," Sawyer said. "Just turn onto your stomach, keep your head above the water, and let the water take us along."

The swift current of the stream immediately carried them along on its journey.

On the shore, the mountain lion followed.

"Dammit," Sawyer swore, watching as the golden cat ran just as quickly as the water.

"She will get tired of running," Zafiro said, then choked as water filled her mouth and ran down her throat.

"But there's no telling when she'll stop or where we'll end up!" Sawyer shouted, spitting water as the stream splashed his face. "That cat could follow us for miles before stopping!"

As she continued to watch the mountain lion lope along the shore, Zafiro began to recognize the area of the woods that surrounded the stream. "Sawyer, we are home! The cabin is just beyond those trees!"

He stopped himself and her immediately, holding her steady until her feet met with the creek bottom. "We still can't get out," he said, noticing that the cougar stopped right along with them.

"We can call for Maclovio to bring the sword. Maybe he is sober and will hear us." She opened her mouth to call for Maclovio.

Sawyer clamped his hand over her mouth, suffocating her loud call. "What if he's *not* sober? What if he's falling-down drunk? There's no way in hell a drunk man can defend himself from a hungry mountain lion. A *sober* man doesn't even stand much of a chance. Or don't you remember how I met Mariposa?"

Zafiro pulled his hand from her mouth. "Then what are we going to do?"

"Wait."

They waited.

So did the cougar.

An hour passed.

The cougar, her dark yellow eyes never leaving her prey in the water, possessed a wealth of patience.

And her forbearance was soon rewarded.

Jengibre came scooting out of the forest, clucking and flapping her wings.

"Sawyer!" Zafiro cried, pointing toward the bank. "Jengibre! Oh, *Dios mío*, someone must have gone into the garden and let her out!"

The cougar turned from the stream and saw the fat chicken.

"*Santa Maria*, the lion is going to eat my sweet Jengibre!" Oblivious to the danger of her own actions, she started toward the shore.

Sawyer stopped her. "Are you crazy?" he blasted. "You can't fight that cougar, Zafiro! You can't—"

"Let me go!" Wildly, she twisted and turned in his arms, her heart pounding with fear for her pet chicken. "Sawyer, let me—"

"No!"

She pummeled at his chest, tried to kick him beneath the water, but her strength was no match for his.

Finally, she gave up. Turning her back to the lion and Jengibre, she laid her face in her hands and began to sob. "I cannot watch," she wept. "I cannot see my pet be killed."

Her cries of anguish filling his ears, Sawyer continued to watch the scene on the shore. The mountain lion crouched. Jengibre began to flee as fast as her scrawny legs and wings could carry her.

Sloshing through the water, Sawyer dragged Zafiro nearer to the shore, then began to splash water at the cougar, who stared at him momentarily before bringing her attention back to the squawking chicken.

"No!" Zafiro screamed when she saw the cougar begin to slink toward Jengibre. *"Sawyer, do something!"*

Terror for her pet forced renewed strength through her body. She wrenched away from Sawyer's side, falling into the water as she tried madly to reach the shore. "Sawyer!" she sputtered through the water and her tears. "For the love of God, please help me save her!"

Her piteous plea severed every fiber of logic Sawyer possessed. Without further thought of the fact that he was going to fight a mountain lion to save the stupid chicken who hated him, Sawyer stumbled toward the shore, pushing Zafiro back behind him every time she tried to reach the bank before he did.

Standing in shallow water, he reached for a handful of stones and dashed them at the cougar. Another handful of the rocks followed, and another.

Growling, the cougar turned toward the stream and crouched.

"Oh, God," Sawyer muttered when he realized the cougar was about to attack. He couldn't fight the animal. Being handcuffed to Zafiro made the notion impossible. As fast as he could and with as much strength as he had, he pushed Zafiro back into the water, hoping to reach deep water again.

But she fell in the shallow water, and when she toppled over he splashed right down beside her. "Crawl!" he screamed at her. "Get into the deep water!"

The moment he shouted the command, he knew it was too late. He saw the cougar wiggle its hindquarters and spring into the air, leaping directly toward where he and Zafiro lay.

Instinctively, Sawyer covered Zafiro's body with his own, curling his limbs around her in an effort to protect as much of her as possible from the vicious cat's claws and teeth. His own body contracted, every muscle hard with tension, every nerve stretched tightly as he waited for the starving cat to land on him.

But instead of feeling anything, he heard. Heard the tremendous sound of a growl, followed by another. Lifting his head and twisting around, he saw Mariposa meet the other cougar in midair.

The two lions landed loudly on the ground and began a ferocious fight that soon drew blood from both of them. On the leaf-strewn shore they rolled, locked around each other, their teeth bared, their claws unsheathed, their muscles bulging beneath their golden coats.

"Mariposa!" Zafiro yelled, trying to wade out of the water. "Sawyer—"

"Stop it!" With a grip that defied her every movement, Sawyer kept her right where she was, beside him in the stream. "What are you going to do, throw yourself in the middle of a cougar fight? You can't do anything, dammit!"

Powerless to aid Mariposa, Zafiro could only watch and pray as her tamed cougar battled the wild one. But so entwined were the animals as they fought, she could not tell which was Mariposa. All she knew was that both lions were bleeding.

And then—as fast as it had begun—the savage fight ended.

One cougar limped down the shore and disappeared into a thick grove of trees. The other cougar spat fur from her mouth, sat on the bank, and began to lick a wound on her shoulder.

"Mariposa!" Zafiro screamed.

The tawny cat trotted toward the stream, holding out her paw when she reached the water.

Finally, Sawyer released Zafiro, whereupon she lunged out of the water and threw her free arm around her pet.

"Zafiro!" Tia shouted as she waddled out of the forest, followed by the rest of La Escondida's inhabitants. "We heard Mariposa fighting! I think even Lorenzo heard the noise!"

Maclovio was the first to reach the stream. Sober, he clasped Sawyer and Zafiro's arms and led them out of the water. "What happened?"

Exhausted from her sleepless night, her swim down the stream, her struggles with Sawyer, and her unmitigated fear for Jengibre and Mariposa, Zafiro sank to the ground, bringing Sawyer down with her. "Tia, please see if Mariposa is fine."

"*Sí, chiquita.*" Tia made a quick but thorough exam of the cougar. "She is fine, Zafiro. I find only three scratches on her, and I will dress the wounds when we go back to the house. Now, you must tell us what happened."

Pushing her wet hair out of her face, Zafiro began to explain.

As she related more and more of the story of what had happened with the wild cougar, a variety of insights began to come to her, building upon each other until they formed a solid wall of realization.

She stopped her own story and looked up at Sawyer. "You tried to save Jengibre," she whispered.

He brushed sand off his wet breeches. "Don't remind me. It was the stupidest thing I've ever—"

"And then you covered me with your own body when that other cougar jumped at us."

He brushed more sand off his pants and shrugged.

Zafiro got to her knees and straddled his legs. Her hands flat on his chest, she gazed directly into his eyes. "You have never killed anyone, Sawyer. I know that as truly as if I had just read it in the Bible."

She saw the cold glitter return to his eyes, but heedlessly continued. "Sawyer, don't you see? A man who would risk his life to save a chicken is not a man capable of murder. And a man who would die for another is not a man capable of murder. Today you did both of those things. A cold-blooded murderer would do neither."

"Sawyer thinks he is a murderer?" Pedro asked.

Swiftly, and without Sawyer's permission, Zafiro told her people about the particles of memory that had come to him.

Maclovio sat down beside Sawyer, picked up a twig, and began drawing circles in the dirt. "Thinking of four dead people in a house does not mean that you are the one who killed them, Sawyer Donovan. When I first met Luis I knew in my heart that he was a bad one. But I have never felt the same way about you. I agree with Zafiro. You are not a murderer."

"I agree with her too," Azucar said. Her scarlet dress whispering, she moved to stand behind Sawyer, then began to massage his shoulders. "You are gentle, Sawyer. A strong, handsome, gentle buck. I sense such things, you know. I must, because I would never invite a killer into my bed. There are many women in my profession who do not possess the same sense that I have. Some of them have ended up dead."

"Zafiro, Maclovio, and Azucar are right," Pedro stated, reaching out and pressing the shape of a cross on Sawyer's forehead. "I am Peter the Apostle, the keeper of the keys and sentinel to the gates of heaven. By the grace of God Almighty, I recognize a sinner when I see one. But you, Sawyer, you have done many kind things for us. You have rebuilt our home and saved me from burning. With a hurt leg you fought with Maclovio to keep him from destroying our possessions. But most important of all, you have become a friend to our Zafiro. You have made her a swing, and you have made her laugh. I assure you, my son, nothing that might have happened in your past has taken away the place that our Father has prepared for you."

"What did everyone say?" Lorenzo wanted to know.

Maclovio, whose shout was the loudest, motioned for Lorenzo to sit on the ground beside him. "Sawyer thinks he's a killer!" he yelled straight into Lorenzo's ear.

Lorenzo nodded. "A pillar," he said, and grinned. "Yes, he has been a pillar of strength for us all. You are a kind man, Sawyer. Sometimes you remind me of Ciro. He was like you. Kind. Strong. Very smart. There is a big heart inside you."

"What is this talk of killing?" Tia chided, waving her hand as if to blow away the discussion. "Francisco, you would not hurt anyone or anything. Do you remember how angry Jengibre made you while you were in bed recovering all those weeks? You could have wrung her neck, my son, but you did not even swat at her. Now, stop this talk of killing. I do not like for you to speak of such things."

Before Sawyer could reply, he felt Zafiro and all her

people reach for some part of him to hold. The men took him by the arms and shoulders. Tia and Azucar both patted his hands, and Zafiro curled her slender fingers around his cheeks.

One by one he thought about each of them.

Pedro had lost his mind. Azucar had lost her youth, beauty, *and* her mind. Lorenzo had lost his hearing, and Tia had lost her son. Maclovio had lost the will to face reality and took refuge in the bottle.

And Zafiro . . . She'd been hidden away at La Escondida for ten years and probably would remain here for many more years. Zafiro had lost the entire world.

And *he'd* lost his past.

They'd all lost something important. Some of them might possibly regain what they'd lost, others never would. But the fact remained that they all had something in common, and the moment Sawyer realized and deliberated upon that truth, guilt coated him inside and out.

He'd tolerated the old people under Zafiro's care, but he'd never gone out of his way to be truly kind to any of them. They couldn't help being the way they were any more than he could help having lost his memories.

Whoever and whatever he was, these people accepted him, he realized. They not only doubted the bad that might exist within him, they saw and appreciated the good.

He looked into each of the six pairs of eyes that were staring at him and saw concern in all those unblinking gazes. Trust and confidence. He recognized kindness, loyalty, and affection.

Faith. He didn't miss their faith in him, either. The feeling shone from their eyes as brightly as diamonds on black velvet.

Sawyer closed his own eyes then, thinking, concentrating, sorting out his emotions.

And for the first time since he'd lost his past, he wondered if he'd found a present and a future.

At La Escondida.

fourteen

"The problem, you see," Lorenzo said, bending over Sawyer and Zafiro's cuffed hands as he wiggled the pick into the lock, "is that this is the quietest lock that I have ever come across." He scooted his chair closer to the table and practically laid his ear on the lock. "I would have to be a bat to hear the clicks I need to hear."

The thought of Lorenzo possessing the amazing hearing of a bat was one of the most ludicrous Sawyer had ever heard. Looking at Zafiro, he tried to tell her with his eyes that waiting for Lorenzo to remove the handcuffs was a waste of time. "Thank you anyway, Lorenzo!" he yelled into the old man's fuzzy ear. "But it's going on two days now already, and I have to think of another way!"

"Another day," Lorenzo replied. "Yes, I can try to pick the lock open another day, Sawyer. You are really anxious to see my skills, aren't you? I will show them to you soon."

Tired of shouting, Sawyer gave the man an affirmative nod. "Come on," he said to Zafiro, helping her to her feet as he stood. "There's got to be some way to get these cuffs off."

She followed him to the door, but stopped suddenly.

The beginning of fear crawled over her, like a big bug with a vicious bite. Her heartbeat quickened, her mouth dried, and she couldn't breathe.

Luis.

He was still looking for her. He still wanted and needed her to guard him and his men from danger. He still planned on keeping his promise to find her.

She could almost hear him whispering those things into her ear, could almost feel his hot breath upon her cheek.

"Zafiro?" Sawyer asked. "What—"

She silenced him with a shake of her head, then waited for the hideous apprehension to lessen. "I—"

"Francisco, where do you think you are going?" Tia wanted to know, turning from the hearth with a long wooden spoon in her hand.

Sawyer waited for the fear on Zafiro's face to fade away, then turned to Tia. In the old woman's eyes he saw an authoritative gleam, a sparkle that indicated she was about to exercise her motherly rights. "I—"

"You will sit down and eat this stew," Tia interrupted, and pointed to the pot with the spoon. "It is mostly vegetable, but there is also a bit of fish—"

"I can't," Sawyer told her. "I need to get these cuffs—"

"You would tell your mother no?" Tia asked incredulously. "Very well, if you will not eat, then you will go straight to bed. I know you are tired, so do not tell me you are not. You spent too much time swimming in the cold stream, you won't eat, so now you will go to sleep."

"I—"

"*Now.*" Tia came toward him with the wooden spoon,

holding the untensil in such a way as to give him a good smack on the bottom when she reached him.

"We are going, Tia!" Quickly and firmly, Zafiro dragged Sawyer to the stairs, pulling him behind her as she ascended the steps.

"Why'd you give in to her?" Sawyer flared when she entered his room and shut the door. "Zafiro, we have to get these cuffs off. I've been running around without a shirt on for almost two days, and your blouse is filthy. And now you've let Tia have her way—"

"You saw the look in her eyes."

"Yes, but—"

"You know that look means that she will not be defied, Sawyer. There is nothing else you can do tonight but what she tells you to do. If you do not, she will spank your—"

"Bottom," Sawyer finished for her. "I'm a grown man, for God's sake, and I'm still getting my bottom whacked!"

Smiling, Zafiro slipped her arms around his bare waist. "It is only for one more night, Sawyer. You will find a way to get the handcuffs off tomorrow. Besides, it is dark outside already."

Although he was in no mood for any sort of sensual play, the feel of her breasts upon his chest was difficult to ignore. "Zafiro—"

"Hold me." She laid her head on his shoulder.

He did as she asked, curling his free arm around her back and bending to catch the sweet fragrance of her hair.

She had faith in him, he mused. She truly believed he had not killed anyone. He wasn't wholly convinced she was right about him, but her trust in his innocence meant more to him than he knew how to describe.

"Francisco?"

At the sound of Tia's voice as she waddled down the hall, both Zafiro and Sawyer rushed to the bed. They'd just laid down when Tia burst into the room. "Zafiro, *chiquita*," she said, "just because my stubborn son will not eat is no reason why you should go to bed without dinner. Bound to him as you are, your day was just as busy as his. I have brought you a cup of stew." She set the cup on the table by the window, gave "her son" another of the frowns that only mothers know how to give, then left the room, shutting the door behind her.

"Well, here we are again, Sawyer."

"Yeah. Here again."

Lying in bed beside him, Zafiro turned to look at him. He was staring at the ceiling, his gaze unblinking, his chest rising and falling slowly, rhythmically, as he pondered whatever deep thoughts had suddenly occupied his mind.

Bright silver moonlight illuminated his face, making clear to her the ruggedness of his features, the sun-weathered texture of his skin, and the rich hue of his long, tawny hair. She felt her pulse skip as she continued to watch him. It was true that she hadn't seen any men besides her own three for quite a while, but she couldn't imagine another man as handsome and kind as Sawyer.

"You have not said much since the ordeal with the cougar," she murmured. "We've been back from the stream for hours already. You do not seem to be as upset as you were this morning, but you are not a laughing keg either."

He continued to watch nothing on the ceiling. "A barrel of laughs."

"A barrel of laughs. Yes, that is what I—"

"I'm thinking, Zafiro. And no, I don't want to talk about what I'm thinking."

She smiled, comforted by the fact that he knew her so well now. Asking him what he was thinking was exactly what she'd been about to do.

Still, she vowed he *would* talk about it before the night was over. For now, however, she would broach another subject entirely. "Are you going to kiss me tonight?"

At her bold query, a question he was totally unprepared to hear, he felt his lips twitch. The near smile was the first he'd experienced since realizing he might very well have killed four people.

Zafiro, he thought. She possessed the amazing ability to disturb him when he was happy and make him happy when he was disturbed. It was really the damnedest thing, the way she kept his emotions dancing on her palm.

"Sawyer?" When he didn't answer she became bolder and lightly placed her hand on his thigh.

"Tia's going to come back, Zafiro," Sawyer reminded her. "And you know damn well it doesn't matter if we lock the door or not. She has the key." His heartbeat began to race; he felt overly warm. Her caresses, slight though they were, made him want to do every sensual thing she suggested and more. "I'll bet you money she'll be back at least twice before going to bed."

"Yes, but she just left. It will be at least a half hour before she comes back. What kinds of things could we start and finish in a half hour?"

Sawyer didn't answer. He could only feel. Zafiro's fingers had now edged upward and she was slowly, gently stroking his masculinity to life.

"I wish there was a way we could hide from Tia," Zafiro said. "But her sight is like a bird's."

"She has eyes like a hawk," Sawyer corrected. God, Zafiro's hand felt so good that he could barely stem his rising need for her.

To hell with thinking tonight, he decided. He could think tomorrow. "You know, Zafiro . . . little boys like to sleep outside in the woods."

"What?"

Sawyer sat up. "All little boys like to camp outside. I think I want to camp outside tonight. In the woods."

Finally, Zafiro began to understand. "But she is punishing you, remember? I do not think she will let you."

"What if I asked her real nicely?"

Zafiro sat up beside him. "Maybe. Yes, maybe. She has apple eyes for you."

Sawyer chuckled. "I'm the apple of her eye."

"Yes, that is what I—"

"Yeah, that's exactly what you said, Zafiro." Sawyer got out of bed and waited for Zafiro to follow him to the door and into the corridor. Downstairs in the great room he saw Lorenzo asleep in a chair, Pedro and Azucar eating bowls of stew, and Tia sipping a cup of tea by the hearth. Maclovio was nowhere to be seen.

"Where is Maclovio?" he asked suspiciously.

"Francisco!" Tia said when she saw him enter the room. "What are you doing out of—"

"Maclovio said he had something to take care of, Sawyer," Pedro answered, then spooned more stew into his mouth.

Something to take care of, Sawyer mused. He looked out the window. Maclovio was off getting drunk. Two days of sobriety were as much as the man could take.

Well, Sawyer thought, there was nothing he could do now. It was already dark outside, and searching for Maclovio now would mean dragging Zafiro along as well.

"Sawyer, my handsome buck," Azucar said, licking stew off her bottom lip. "Come and sit beside me, and I will whisper sensuous things into your ear while you eat."

"Francisco?" Tia said. "I asked you why you were out of bed."

"Can I sleep outside?" Sawyer blurted in the best little boy voice he could muster. Hearing Zafiro's soft giggle behind him, he suppressed a grin.

"Outside?" Tia frowned.

"I want to sleep in the woods. Please? Please?"

Zafiro stepped out from behind Sawyer. "I will be with him, Tia," she said, lifting their hands and showing the handcuffs.

Tia set her cup of tea down on the table. "Francisco, I do not think that sleeping in the woods—"

"But it's warm outside," Sawyer argued. "I won't be cold. I promise I'll go to sleep as soon as I find a good place to make camp, and I'll take Mariposa along for protection."

Tia shook her head. "You did not eat well today, Francisco. You are being punished, do you forget that?"

Pulling Zafiro along, Sawyer strode toward the hearth, grabbed a cup, and dipped out a full ladle of the warm vegetable stew he'd not wanted to eat earlier. Quickly, he ate the stew, wiping his mouth with his lower arm when he was finished. "There. I ate. Now can I go camping in the woods?"

Tia tapped her cheek. "Well . . ."

"Please." Lifting Zafiro's arm as he lifted his own two, Sawyer hugged the plump woman. "Please, Mama. I love you so much, Mama. Please let me go."

His words of love brought tears to Tia's eyes. Smiling, she returned his hug, patting his back with her fingers. "Very well, my sweet Francisco. You may go. I cannot say no when you ask so sweetly. But you must be back early for breakfast."

Sawyer flashed a broad smile. "Thank you, Mama. But

don't look for me, all right? Part of camping is hiding
from the enemies. I'll be hidden."

Tia winked at Zafiro. "Yes, Francisco. You must hide
from the enemies. Zafiro? *Chiquita*, are you sure you do
not mind sleeping in the woods with him? It is something
only a child would want to do, so if you do not want
to—"

"It is only for one night, Tia," Zafiro replied, trying to
sound as though she'd been roped into doing something
she really didn't want to do. "It is all right. I will go with
him and make sure he is back early in the morning."

"Well, my little Francisco," Tia said, giving him a loving smile, "you have charmed Zafiro and me into letting
you have your way. I think you will have a way with
women when you grow up."

"A way with women?" Sawyer repeated, feigning innocence.

Tia nodded. "Yes, but you are too young to understand
that now. One day you will know what I am saying. And
you, Zafiro, one day you will know too. When you meet
the handsome man of your dreams, he will show you what
it all means."

"Yeah," Sawyer said, exchanging a secret glance with
Zafiro. "One day a man will teach you everything you
want to know and more, Zafiro."

At his promise Zafiro felt heat and excitement lace
through her. Anxious for him to show her the things she
wanted to know, she turned and headed for the door.

"Wait!" Tia called. "I will give you a few things to take
with you."

Ten minutes later, carrying a blanket, two pillows, and
a bag of food Tia had insisted they take, Zafiro and Sawyer left the cabin and entered the dark forest. True to his
word, Sawyer had Mariposa come along as well, and the

great cat began to lead the way through the woods, her eyesight being much better than that of her human companions.

After a short while Sawyer began to see better as well. He passed Mariposa and took Zafiro deeper into the woods until he found the perfect spot to spend the night. An open area covered with leaves, surrounded by gently swaying oak trees, and lightly scented by wildflowers, the place shimmered with the iridescent light of the moon.

It would be their bedchamber, he decided. Here, encircled by nature herself, he would show Zafiro what it meant to be a woman. "Here," he murmured.

Zafiro didn't think she'd ever seen the spot before. "How is it that you have come to know La Escondida better than I do, Sawyer?" she asked as she helped him pile up leaves for their bed.

He spread the blanket over the mound of soft leaves. "You forget I've spent most of my time in these woods. I've been all through them, looking for just the right trees to fell." He took the pillows from her and tossed them down to the blanket. "There's really only one place here I haven't been to. Behind the house there's a bluff that's covered with juniper. If I had all the money in the world, I'd bet it to prove that's where Maclovio keeps his still and it's where he is right now."

Zafiro sank down to the leaf bed, pulling Sawyer down with her. "I have looked there. I did not find his still. He has hidden it so well that I do not think God can even—"

"Zafiro?"

"Yes?"

"I'll take care of the still." He gathered her in his arms. "We have other things to talk about and do right now. And believe me, they have nothing at all to do with a little boy's wish to sleep in the woods and hide from the enemies."

His husky tone of voice and the words he murmured sent desire streaking through her like so many hot shooting stars. "You will not stop tonight, Sawyer," she said, her statement actually a question. "You will—"

"I won't stop tonight, Zafiro," he answered, sliding his hand down the side of her waist. "And in answer to your second question, yes. Yes . . . I will."

With the exception of Zafiro's shirt, their clothes fell away from their bodies as if by magic. With nothing but the night air and Zafiro's sapphire between them, they embraced, whispering each other's names, their need deepening with each caress and kiss.

And then, suddenly, Sawyer pulled out of Zafiro's arms and lowered his body downward. On his stomach with his face beside her hips, he looked up into her moonlit eyes.

The visage of her beauty captured his full attention like the vivid flash of an exceedingly valuable jewel. He could feel her, feel her warmth, her affection, and the genuine kindness that made her who she was.

Her scent swirled around him, not of roses, nor of sun or wind. She wore the perfume of femininity, a glorious fragrance of womanly softness. It was a fragrance of tenderness, too, and understanding. Of acceptance and concern, of all the things he so needed in his life right now.

He heard her as well. Her breathing, her heartbeat, and although she said nothing he could hear the sound of her voice sing through his memory. She made music when she spoke, a melody that no instrument could play as beautifully.

He saw her, felt her, smelled and heard her.

And now he would taste her.

At the thought of what he was about to do, desire slammed into him so forcefully, he began to sweat.

"Sawyer, what are you doing down there?" she asked, confused by his abrupt move.

He might have explained had he thought mere words could describe what he was about to do. Instead, he showed her.

She saw him raise his head and lean close over her thighs. She saw his eyes smolder with what she now recognized as desire, and she saw how her own body trembled with anticipation at whatever he was about to do.

When she felt the gentle pressure of his lips as he kissed the mound of her womanhood, she closed her eyes and gave in to the first tiny hint of pleasure. She'd never dreamed or imagined that a man would want to caress a woman in such a way, but as the exquisite sensations that Sawyer's sensual attentions created began to heighten, she realized he was showing her only one of the many ways that pleasure could be given and had.

Without even thinking she parted her thighs, wanting and needing more, and moaning from deep inside when she felt him accommodate her unspoken wishes. As his lips nuzzled into her softness, his tongue flicked across her nether lips. The moan inside her escaped then, filling the forest and telling Sawyer in no uncertain terms that while she was totally unfamiliar with the way he was loving her, she was not at all embarrassed by it.

That knowledge in mind, he moved his hand between her legs and easily slid two fingers inside her, all the while continuing to bring life to the sweet gem of sensitive flesh that swelled beneath his touch. With his tongue, his lips, his hot breath stroking her unceasingly, he realized instantly when ecstasy was upon her.

Her body tensed, strained, and her breathing began to

come in short pants. Out of the corner of his eye, he saw her hands clutch at the blanket, her fingers trembling.

His own fingers moistened further as the pleasure he gave skimmed through her femininity and traveled through her body, but he persevered with his endeavors until at last her body stilled, her breathing quieted, and a tiny smile appeared on her petal-pink lips.

Even then he continued to fondle her with his mouth, the essence of her joy a taste too sweet to deny himself.

"I did not know," Zafiro whispered, finally opening her eyes and seeing the silver medley of moonlight and star shine glint through the tree branches above. "You did not tell me."

"But you know now." His lips still moved upon her slick softness. The feel, the scent, the sound, the taste, and the sight of Zafiro . . .

Every single thing about the woman who lay upon his bed of leaves touched him in such a way that he felt filled to the brim with a contentment that had long eluded him.

"Sawyer." Zafiro turned to her side, patting the blanket in an indication that she wanted him to come to her. And when he did as she asked and stretched out beside her, she lowered her body downward, stopping only when her face was next to his hips.

So great was his need and excitement, he didn't dare take a breath, much less speak. Was she going to do it? The same thing he'd done to her?

But she didn't know how.

It didn't matter.

Whatever she did, however she caressed him . . .

It didn't matter.

He felt her silken hair flow over his hips as she raised her head above his belly. The beginning of pleasure swirled through his loins, causing him to take a deep breath and hold it inside his chest.

God, she'd yet to even touch him and he was already so worked up that the encounter was almost over before it had begun!

"Zafiro," he managed to tell her in a raspy whisper, "not much. Not . . ."

"Not much?" She spread barely there kisses over his belly, lingering at his navel and filling the small indentation with the tip of her tongue.

Sawyer squeezed a handful of her hair so hard that his thumb cramped. Mindless of the pain, he tried to sit up, frustrated and resigned at once when Zafiro pushed at his chest and made him lie down again.

"Wait," he said when he felt her lips nip at the hair that shadowed his groin. "You don't understand. I'm— Zafiro, I'm too—I want you too much to be able to stand—"

"You are not standing, Sawyer. You are flat on your back." With her free hand, she took hold of his turgid length and touched her lips to its hard, hot tip.

"Oh, God," Sawyer moaned. Already he felt himself throb; bliss rose steadily through him, making him painfully aware of the fact that if he did not stop her now, there would be no stopping at all.

He sat up again, but not quickly enough. As soon as his back left the blanket, he felt her take him between her lips, and her mouth was so soft, so warm, so completely wonderful that every thought of denial he'd entertained only seconds before vanished like shadows attacked by a burst of sunlight.

Completely unable to connect his rational thoughts with his body's demands, he began to move his hips, moving in and out of her mouth with a gentle, steady rhythm. And as he did so, he felt her suckle him.

The pressure her action imparted sent him straight over the brink of control. He surrendered to the potent need for release, no power on earth strong enough to overcome the all-consuming pleasure that was only seconds away.

No power but one.

And that was the acrid and frightening smell of fire.

He smelled the burning scent at the same time as Zafiro, who immediately raised her head and turned toward the direction from which the alarming smell drifted.

Whatever had caught fire was near the cabin, she realized. "Sawyer—"

"Get dressed!"

As fast as they were able they donned their clothes, then raced through the woods toward the house. Out of breath when they arrived in the yard, they stopped suddenly and stared at the blaze that devoured the wooden wall of logs.

"*Santa Maria!*" Zafiro shouted, tears of horror filling her eyes. "The garden! Sawyer, the food—"

He held her steady when she tried to move toward the burning vegetable patch. "It's too late, Zafiro," he said, hearing the disbelief and shock in his own voice. "The fire is too wild, too hot. We can't—"

"But Jengibre!" she screamed. "Jengibre—"

"Herè is Jengibre, Zafiro!" Tia shouted from her spot by one of the rose beds. Her own eyes blurred with tears, she held up the ginger-colored hen, then turned to comfort Azucar, who stood beside her with her face in her hands.

"What happened, dammit?" His every step roaring

with rage, Sawyer stalked toward the rose bed, dragging Zafiro along with him. "How—"

"We do not know!" Tia wailed. Completely undone by the tragedy, she buried her face in Jengibre's soft feathers and sobbed. "We will have no food for the winter," she wept piteously. "No vegetables to see us through the cold winter."

"It happened so quickly, Sawyer," Pedro announced. His chest heaving with exertion, he dropped an empty bucket and slowly approached the rose garden. "Lorenzo and I, we had just gone to bed when Tia and Azucar began to scream. As soon as I opened my eyes I saw the light of the blazes moving on the wall. I shook Lorenzo awake, and he and I did our best to douse the flames. But we had only the water in the kitchen, and as soon as we started for the stream to get more, the fire . . . It was like a live thing, Sawyer. Like a monster from hell, and it swallowed the wall you built within seconds. Lorenzo and I, we knew then that nothing we could do would help."

"I beat the flames," Lorenzo added, he, too, struggling to catch his breath. "I burned my hands." A single tear dripping down his face, he held out his hands to show Sawyer the blisters that splattered his palms.

Instantly, Sawyer put his arm around Lorenzo's bony shoulders. Trying in some way to comfort the old, distraught man, he patted Lorenzo's upper arm, then turned to stare at the flames that ate at La Escondida's supply of fresh food.

How had the fire started? he wondered. Only a short while ago, when he and Zafiro had left the yard and entered the woods, all had been well.

Bewilderment weighed on his mind like a boulder, until one tiny suspicion crept past it.

"Maclovio," he gritted out from between clenched teeth.

As if on cue, Maclovio stumbled into the front yard from behind the house, a bottle in one hand, a charred stick in the other, and the sword from the Holy Crusades swinging by his left thigh, its hilt stuck inside his belt. "Oh, there is Jengibre!" Stumbling over plants, mounds in the grass, and his own two feet, he crossed the yard and stopped in front of Tia. "Where did you find the little hen, Tia? I looked all over for her in the garden, but it was too dark to see. I finally made a torch, but even with the light I could not find her."

"A torch," Sawyer snapped, grabbing the burned stick from Maclovio's grasp. "Haven't you noticed what you did with your damn torch, Maclovio? Or are you as blind as you are drunk?"

"Blind?" Swaying precariously, Maclovio turned around and saw the wall of flames that consumed the garden. "Well," he said, "it is a good thing that Tia got Jengibre out of there, isn't it?" Smiling, he lifted the bottle and tilted it toward his mouth.

But he never tasted another drop of the homemade whiskey.

With one fast, smooth move, Sawyer knocked the bottle from his hand. "You've had enough, dammit!"

Maclovio narrowed his eyes and felt his nostrils flare. "You will pay for spilling my drink, Sawyer Donovan. I am going to smash your face!"

Quickly, Sawyer moved himself and Zafiro out of Maclovio's reach and watched the drunken man swing at thin air. He wanted nothing more than to knock Maclovio senseless and thus give the man an opportunity to sleep off his intoxication, but couldn't start a fight for fear of Zafiro getting hurt.

Damn the handcuffs to hell and back, he seethed silently. "Get out of here, Maclovio," he demanded, so angry that he felt the heat of his hot words burn his mouth. "Go back to your bluff behind the house and don't come back until you—"

"You do not tell me what to do, Sawyer Donovan." Maclovio stepped forward and drew back his arm again.

"No!" Without hesitation, Zafiro placed herself between Sawyer and Maclovio, her action so quick that no one could have stopped her.

With barely a fraction of a second to spare, Sawyer reached around her and caught Maclovio's punch in the palm of his hand.

Maclovio laughed and pulled back his other fist.

"Maclovio, you do not fight fairly!" Casting herself at his arm, Zafiro effectively stopped him from throwing another punch. "Sawyer cannot fight you! He is bound to me!"

When she held up their cuffed hands Maclovio stopped, rubbed his chin, then glared at Sawyer. "I will free you from the handcuffs, Sawyer Donovan, and then I will smash your face!"

With a quickness that belied his drunken state, Maclovio drew the sword from his belt and held it high over his head. "Hold out your arms, and I will cut through the chain!"

"God, no!" Instantly, Sawyer threw himself at Zafiro, knocking her to ground and well away from Maclovio and his sword.

She cringed when the tremendous sword sliced into the dirt mere inches from her face, then gasped when Maclovio raised the sword again.

"Keep your hands on the ground!" Maclovio demanded. "If you will just be still I will—"

"Get up," Sawyer commanded Zafiro. "Now!"

She bolted off the ground, following Sawyer when he dashed toward the house. "He is still coming after us, Sawyer!"

Looking over his shoulder, Sawyer watched Maclovio trail behind them, fending off Pedro and Lorenzo and swishing the sword through the air as if slaying a herd of fire-breathing dragons. Weaving and tripping, he tottered toward the house, then dropped the sword and fell down beside it.

The man was as drunk as Sawyer had ever seen him, so bad off that his eyes fairly rolled around in his head like two black marbles in an empty bucket. "I swear to God," he vowed, "as soon as I get these damn cuffs off, I'm going to find his still and tear it apart piece by piece! And then I'm going to tear *him* apart!"

"Sawyer!" Pedro shouted. Moving as quickly as his tired, worn-out legs would let him, he hurried toward the cabin steps, stopping in front of Sawyer and Zafiro. "I know that you want to see Lorenzo perform his skills at picking a lock, but he will have to show them to you another time. Right now we must get these handcuffs off so you can do something with Maclovio."

Sawyer and Zafiro watched in astonishment as Pedro lifted the string of keys he wore around his neck, selected one, and inserted it into the lock on the handcuffs.

In the next moment the handcuffs clattered to the porch step.

"The key," Sawyer murmured, staring down at the cuffs. "Pedro had it all the time, Zafiro."

She, too, looked down at the cuffs. "Pedro, why—"

"You can take care of Maclovio now, Sawyer," Pedro said, turning to watch as the groaning Maclovio heaved himself off the ground. "If I had known the trouble he would cause, I would have freed you and Zafiro two days ago. But of course, you did not ask me for the key, so I knew it was Lorenzo's skill at lock picking that you really wanted to see."

Sawyer had not a second to reply to Pedro's explanation. Maclovio wielded the sword once more, this time seemingly of a mind to throw it at one of the cabin windows.

It took only one strong, swift punch of Sawyer's fist to put the man out of his drunken misery. On one heel, Maclovio spun in the grass and toppled face first to the ground, his body as still as death.

But he wasn't dead, Sawyer knew. He would wake up in the morning and more than likely steal away for more of his whiskey to alleviate the pounding headache he would have.

Sawyer glanced at the house, thinking of the juniper-scattered bluff behind it. He then looked at the burning garden. The fierce flames had died down a bit, but the vegetable patch still burned.

Resolve oozed from his every pore. Dark or no dark, he was going to find Maclovio's still tonight. And by morning, he swore, the whiskey contraption would be nothing but a smashed heap of rubble.

"Go to bed," he ordered. "All of you. Maclovio won't do any more harm tonight."

"Sawyer," Zafiro called when he started around the house, "where are you—"

"To do something that needed to be done a long time ago," he answered. With that he disappeared behind the house.

Knowing he was going to find and destroy Maclovio's still, Zafiro longed to accompany him. Nothing she could think of at that moment would have given her more satisfaction than breaking apart the contraption that had caused so much grief at La Escondida.

But her people needed her. Tia and Azucar still wept beside the rose garden, Lorenzo's blistered hands needed attention, and Pedro was far too pale for her liking. The old man was clearly exhausted from his fight with the fire.

Struggling to tame her own sorrow, worry, and anger, she ushered her four elderly charges into the house, leaving Maclovio to sleep in the yard. Once inside she quickly tended to Lorenzo's hands, then made a pot of tea.

Overcome with sadness as she was, Tia could do naught but watch as Zafiro took charge. "We will be hungry this winter, *chiquita*," she said when Zafiro handed her a cup of hot tea. "Without the garden—"

"We have never had very many vegetables," Zafiro reminded the sniffling woman. "The rabbits have eaten them year after year. The fire destroying the garden is no different—"

"It is different," Tia argued. "The rabbits always left a bit. The fire has eaten it all."

Zafiro hugged Tia, then moved to comfort Azucar, who sat in her chair with a look of unmitigated stupefaction on her wrinkled face. "Tia, you forget the berry patch I told you about," she said, forcing herself to present a bright, encouraging smile while still hugging Azucar. "The berries, they are many and they are ripe for picking. And do not forget the good sisters. They—"

"The holy sisters must be in the same situation as we are," Pedro declared. Holding the keys he wore about his neck, he hobbled around the room, stopping here and there to shake his head before continuing his pacing. "They have brought us nothing in weeks. And Mariposa has brought no meat. There is not even enough for our animals. I have watched Sawyer bring in fresh grass for them, but he cannot continue to do that after the winter snows. The only thing I have seen in the barn is a bag of shriveled corn for the chickens."

"I am hungry," Lorenzo said, the thought of having no food causing his stomach to growl. "Zafiro, what are we going to do?"

A sigh collected within her breast, but she dared not release it for fear of further upsetting her charges. Still trying to smile, she dipped out a bowl of Tia's stew and handed it to Lorenzo. Her heart tripped when the old man devoured it as if it were the last food on earth.

"Zafiro, what are we going to do?" Azucar asked. "No food . . . And there is also Luis."

"Luis," Zafiro whispered. As if she could ever forget him. He remained in her mind like an ugly stain she couldn't scrub away.

She battled her fear, then after a long moment, she saw her people staring at her, looking into her eyes and hoping to find a bit of reassurance there.

Somehow she pushed down her apprehension. Her chin tilted upward in a gesture of confidence, she walked to the window and peered through the glass.

Eggs, she thought as she looked at the chicken coop in the yard. Eggs, fish, a smattering of dried berries, what little the sisters might provide, and whatever game Mariposa decided to share—that would be the extent of the winter food.

Asking Sawyer for further aid was useless. Strong, capable, and efficient as he was, he could not plant and cultivate another garden this late in the season. The first frost was only about a month away.

Nor could he hunt for fresh meat. The memories that haunted him would not allow him to handle a gun.

Sawyer had done and was still doing everything he was able to do for her and her charges.

Money was the answer, she knew. With hard, cold cash, she could buy everything La Escondida and its people needed to survive the harsh winter of the Sierra Madres. She wouldn't even have to take the risk of being seen in any towns or villages. Sawyer or the nuns could see to the task of shopping.

But there was no money. Gone were the days when her men could easily steal the money needed to survive and have enough left to share with the poor.

Finally, she released the sigh she'd kept captive within her breast. The warmth of her breath as it escaped her lips made a foggy circle upon the windowpane.

It was true what was said about life.

It was not roses to sleep on.

fifteen

Dawn was well on its way to becoming full morning when Sawyer finally returned from the dusty hills behind the house and walked into the yard. He looked filthy and felt dirtier, for he'd spent most of the night looking for Maclovio's still, then a good hour destroying the damn thing after he'd found it hidden in a drafty cave.

Even while breaking the still apart, he had to admire Maclovio's genius in making it. Simply designed, yet obviously quite serviceable, the whiskey-making contraption was skillfully fashioned with odds and ends Maclovio had found lying around La Escondida: a sturdy wooden barrel, a big copper pot and hollow coil and pipe, a glass jug, a cap and plug, and rags. Scatterings of animal feed and a few dried-up berries and roots told Sawyer that Maclovio had used whatever edible thing he could find to make his lethal brew.

But Sawyer hadn't seen any more of such odds and ends anywhere on La Escondida, and because he'd completely demolished the items Maclovio had found and used years ago, he doubted seriously that the man could make another still.

The man in question was no longer lying in the yard, where he'd passed out the night before, Sawyer noticed. Maclovio had probably awakened with a pounding headache and gone to the stream for a dip in the refreshing water.

Hunger gnawing at him after his busy night, Sawyer entered the cabin, but found no one in the great room. Strange. Tia was always doing something here in the kitchen.

"Zafiro!" he called.

In the next moment he heard someone descending the staircase. "Zafiro, where's Tia—"

"Sawyer!" Azucar greeted him as she wobbled off the last step and started toward him. "It is a perfect time for you to have returned. Tia and Zafiro have gone to gather berries. Mariposa went with them, but then she returned and is now cleaning herself upstairs in your room. Maclovio has left to bathe, Pedro is in the woods praying, and Lorenzo fell asleep in the barn when he went to visit the animals. We are all alone, my handsome buck. Free to indulge in all the many pleasures of the flesh."

In no mood for her advances, Sawyer began to step away from her, but suddenly remembered his decision to be kinder to all the elderly inhabitants of La Escondida. Smiling down at the crimson-draped hag, he took her frail shoulders into his hands and bent to place a tender kiss on her wrinkled cheek. Her gasp of pure joy told him he'd made her truly happy. "We'll have to talk about this later, Azucar, darling," he murmured into her ear. "Right now I've got to make a much needed visit to the stream."

Azucar drew away and examined him, not missing all the dirt and sweat stains that coated his clothing and skin. "Yes, I see you are very dirty. All right, my anxious stallion, go wash, and then we will go to my bedroom for a little morning delight."

Gently, he tweaked her nose, grabbed a bar of soap from a basket attached to the wall, then crossed to the door. Outside, he headed straight for the stream.

And met Maclovio in the forest.

"Sawyer," Maclovio said, blinking as water dripped from his clean hair into his bloodshot eyes.

"Maclovio."

Maclovio bowed his head and watched his feet shuffle in the brittle leaves. "I saw what I did."

Sawyer remained silent.

"I am sorry," Maclovio muttered. "I do not even remember doing it. It was Pedro who told me when I woke up. I cannot believe—"

"You won't do anything like that again, Maclovio."

Maclovio had no need for further explanation. The sound in Sawyer's voice was sufficient. "You found it."

"And destroyed it."

"I cannot build another."

"I know."

Maclovio lifted his head. "I am sorry, Sawyer. If I could undo what I did, I would."

As Sawyer looked into the old giant's eyes he felt compassion surge through him. "I know you would, Maclovio."

"We will be hungry this winter."

"Maybe not."

Maclovio's eyes widened. "No? What are you going to do then?"

It was Sawyer's turn to bow his head. While absently looking at the toes of his dusty boots, he ran his fingers through his hair. "I don't know. I just don't know yet."

Maclovio wrapped his hand over Sawyer's shoulder. "I

will help. Now that I cannot drink anymore, you will see
how I can help."

"I appreciate that."

"Money is what we need, Sawyer," Maclovio said,
then wiped a dribble of stream water off his neck. "With
money we could buy—"

"But we don't have any, Maclovio."

"I could steal again. About ten miles south of here
there is a road that is well-traveled by wealthy people on
their way to Mexico City. And to the north of here are
several fine haciendas owned and lived in by wealthy
Spaniards. I could—"

"And how would you get there?"

Maclovio smiled. "There is Coraje. No horse I have
ever known could run as fast as he."

Alarm flashed through Sawyer's mind as he imagined
the old man trying to mount Coraje.

The horse would kill him. "If I catch you anywhere
near that monster I'll smash your face, Maclovio. And
that's not an empty promise."

At Maclovio's crestfallen expression, Sawyer tempered
his next words. "I just don't want anything to happen to
you."

On impulse, Maclovio reached out and gave Sawyer a
quick, strong hug, then released him. "You are a good
man, Sawyer Donovan. It is an honor to call you my
friend."

Sawyer clapped Maclovio on the back before resuming
his trip to the stream. Once at the bank he swiftly took
off his clothes, and with the bar of soap in hand he dove
into the rushing water. After soaking for a few moments,
he rubbed the soap between his palms to create a lather,
then began to wash.

A flash of red in the woods suddenly stole his attention.

"Sawyer," Azucar called as she exited the forest and tottered toward the stream. "I have brought you a towel."

He sank low into the stream; water flowed beneath his chin. "Uh . . . Thank you, Azucar." Watching her warily, he wondered if she would soon rip off her gown and join him in the creek.

"Oh, I see you did not bring clean clothes with you, my handsome buck." Laying the towel on the shore, Azucar picked up Sawyer's dirty clothes. "I will take these away and bring you back some clean ones."

When she doddered back into the woods with his dirty clothes, Sawyer relaxed and smiled. She really was a kind person, he thought. Insane, but kind.

Insane. The word made him wonder where Zafiro was, where she'd gone to pick the berries with Tia. Well, wherever she was she'd be back soon, he decided, lathering his hair.

He could hardly wait to tell her he'd found and destroyed Maclovio's still. She needed to hear some happy news.

Yes, today would be a good day for Zafiro.

— ◀✦▶ —

"See, Tia?" Zafiro asked, standing in the midst of a lush patch of vegetation. "I told you we would find berries here." She looked around the area, a small grassy field that was about a ten-minute walk away from La Escondida. "Are you happier now?"

"I am happier, *chiquita*," Tia answered, bending over to strip another hill of plump red berries. "If I can get enough sugar I will make jams and jellies. And I will dry the berries too, and make berry candies, and of course we will have fresh berry pies."

"But you will need more flour, Tia." For a moment Zafiro glanced over the landscape, frowning without really understanding why. She wondered where Mariposa was, then decided the cougar had returned to the cabin.

For some reason she wished the mountain lion was near.

She shook the peculiar feeling off. "I will see if I can get flour for us. I have not visited the nuns in a while, so perhaps I will . . ."

Her voice trailed away when she detected what sounded like a distant rumble of thunder. Strange. Not as much as a whiff of clouds broke the blue of the vast Mexican sky.

"It is too bad that we cannot pick other foods off plants the way we can with these berries," Tia said. "Imagine if we could go pick a pig off a bush or shake flour, salt, and sugar from the trees."

Zafiro barely understood a word Tia said, so intently did she concentrate on the faraway noise that continued to hit her ears. It wasn't thunder. She didn't know why she was certain that it wasn't, but she knew it was not thunder.

The mountain wind whined past her, picking up her hair and blowing it all around her face. Her cheeks stung as the tresses whipped at her skin, and still the remote noise taunted her comprehension.

A fine shiver crawled over her, not one of cold, but of apprehension. Her heart seemed to tumble, as if missing its rhythmic footing.

"Tia," she whispered.

"I think we should bring Azucar, Maclovio, Pedro, and

Lorenzo to this patch tomorrow morning," Tia continued merrily, dropping another handful of berries into her basket. "There are so many! And we will ask my sweet Francisco to take some to the good sisters at the convent. The nuns, they will enjoy—"

"Tia."

Slowly, Tia straightened from her hunched-over position. A slight frown wrinkling the wrinkles on her forehead, she looked at her young companion. "Zafiro." She, too, looked in the distance, in the same direction as did Zafiro. "What do you see?"

Zafiro parted her lips to answer, but stopped suddenly when her throat began to close. "Run," she whispered.

She struggled to breathe, to take in enough air to be able to shout. Deep foreboding caused her to drop her basket.

Finally, she gulped in air. "Run! Tia, run back to La Escondida!"

Tia's basket flew into the air, spilling berries everywhere as she turned and fled toward the entrance of the hideaway. Hearing Zafiro's racing footsteps behind her, she prayed they would find safety before the coming danger caught up with them.

"Faster, Tia, faster!" Zafiro yelled. The noise became louder, her fear deeper. She turned to look over her shoulder.

And stifled a scream of terror.

Three mounted men followed on horseback, their mounts ripping up great clods of dirt. The horses ran at a breakneck gallop, their riders leaning low over their necks.

Without a hint of hesitation Zafiro changed her course, turning to her right toward a grove of oak trees. Panic tore at her insides at the thought of the men following her into the woods, but she did not know what else to do.

It was the only thing she could think of that might save Tia.

"Run!" she shouted again, hoping the wind would carry her instructions to Tia. "Run to La Escondida, and do not stop, Tia!"

Tia did as bade, scrambling toward the safety of La Escondida as fast as her fat legs could move. When she was but several yards away from the entrance, she turned and reached for Zafiro with the intention of pulling her into the hideaway.

She clutched at handfuls of air. Shock struck inside her breast, burning her into near collapse. Dazed by fear, she scanned the area where she'd last seen Zafiro.

The mountains repeated her scream many times over.

But the men who had captured Zafiro rode on.

The scream Sawyer heard was like a live thing. An invisible monster, it clawed into his ears, lunged through his mind, and began to eat at his gut.

He lunged out of the stream and grabbed up the towel from the shore. Dread pumped steadily through his veins, but even as his apprehension mounted so did his strength. He bolted through the forest as if blown and guided by the unerring breath of the wind herself and finally ran into the yard in front of the cabin.

What he saw bewildered him and deepened his alarm.

Tia stood by the barn, jumping up and down, screaming and weeping, Azucar by her side doing the same. Lorenzo was dragging a box out of the barn. When he opened it, Pedro began searching frantically through its contents, throwing various items every which way until he found what he'd been looking for: two pistols.

Sawyer watched Pedro thrust one of the guns into Lorenzo's hand. The weapon promptly fell apart and spilled pieces of iron onto Lorenzo's feet.

Lorenzo hurried back into the barn just as Maclovio emerged with a saddle and a bridle in his hands. Thrust into one of the saddle trappings was Jaime's rifle.

"Maclovio, no!" Knowing full well that Maclovio was about to try to mount and ride Coraje, Sawyer raced toward the barn. Just as he reached the old man, Lorenzo came out of the barn again.

Sawyer's mouth formed a wide O.

Lorenzo rode the little burro, Rayo.

But Lorenzo rode backward, with his back facing Rayo's head.

Sawyer had to force himself out of his state of disbelief and confusion. "For God's sake, Lorenzo, what the hell are you—"

"Sawyer!" Azucar cried. "They have taken Zafiro!"

Her information chilled Sawyer's blood. "Taken—"

"Do not bother Sawyer with this, Azucar!" Maclovio boomed. "He cannot shoot because he cannot make himself handle guns! Zafiro told me so herself!" Saddle and bridle still in his hands, Maclovio turned to Sawyer. "Stay here and keep Tia and Azucar calm, Sawyer. I will go after Zafiro."

A shred of logic stabbing through the chaos in his mind, Sawyer grabbed the tack out of Maclovio's grasp. *"What happened to Zafiro?"* he roared.

"We were gathering berries right over that hill!" Tia pointed to the bluff, behind which grew the berry patches. "Three mounted men arrived out of nowhere,

and one of them caught Zafiro as she ran into the forest!
She . . . She . . . Oh, I know she led them there to
keep them from catching me!"

"Caught Zafiro." The words escaped Sawyer's lips like
a shot of flame.

She was in danger. She could be killed.

In danger. Killed.

Hadn't other people been in danger and killed?

In his mind he left La Escondida and went back. Back
to Synner, Texas, where the house with the white curtains stood.

He remembered them. Everything about the people
lying on the floor in the house.

They'd been murdered.

Because he hadn't been there to save them.

Every memory he'd killed and buried made a violent
resurrection. He dropped the saddle. And the bridle. He
thrust his fingers through his damp hair, and he gritted
his teeth. He wanted to scream, but the scream clogged in
his throat, thick, awful, too big to choke down, too horrible to release.

He hadn't been there to save them, and they'd died.

He wanted to crumble to the ground. His knees began
to shake.

And then into his mind, shining through all the darkness, appeared a pair of sapphire eyes. They weren't
closed in death, but danced with vibrant life.

Zafiro.

With a will he'd never realized he possessed, he fought
himself free from the crushing grip of grief and ran into
the barn. There he found his trunk. He didn't have to
open it to know what was inside.

He knew now.

Lifting the chest, he felt along its splintery bottom

until his fingers found a crack in the wood. From the fissure he pulled out a key, then quickly opened the trunk.

Inside lay his Colts. They gleamed in the dim light of the barn, and he knew they were fully loaded.

He reached for them, then suddenly remembered that he wore only a towel. There was no time to go to the cabin for clothes. He would have to wear the clothing in the trunk.

In only moments he was fully dressed, his feet and calves encased in shiny black boots, his Colts lying alongside his thighs.

He grabbed a coiled rope off the floor in the corner of the stable and quickly fashioned a lasso. As he left the barn and strode outside, his sable cape flowed behind him.

Maclovio, Pedro, Tia, and Azucar gaped at him. Lorenzo fell off Rayo's back and tumbled to the ground, but never took his gaze away from Sawyer.

Maclovio groped for a fence post. "Saw-Saw-Sawyer—"

Ignoring the stuttering man, Sawyer climbed over Coraje's paddock fence, tied the end of the rope to a post, and silently commanded the stallion to come to him.

And Coraje did. With his ears laid back flat on his head, his nostrils flared, the black horse charged straight toward him.

Sawyer stood as rigid as frozen steel, then tossed the rope toward the racing animal. Neatly, the lasso fell around Coraje's neck, whereupon Sawyer shot across the paddock to the other side.

Coraje stopped, turned, and started forward, intent on hurting the man in his pen.

The rope halted his progress. He fought the rope, muscles bulging in his neck and hindquarters. And then he stood still for a moment, pawed the ground, and began to run in the directions the rope would allow—to the left and to the right.

Sawyer crossed the paddock again and grabbed the rope. Walking his hands up the heavy twine and pulling with all his might, he shortened its length and gradually made his way nearer to Coraje.

The horse stood motionless, watched warily as Sawyer approached, then lunged out his neck to deliver a vicious bite.

But Sawyer was ready and faster. His motion a blur, he reached out, caught Coraje's bottom lip, and firmly twisted the bit of flesh. He knew his action didn't actually hurt the horse; it only delivered enough of a sting to render the animal incapable of concentrating on anything else.

Coraje stilled instantly, his only movement the shudder of his nostrils.

"Maclovio, bring me the tack!"

Maclovio didn't move. He simply stared.

"Maclovio, *now*, dammit!"

Pedro was the first to come out of the spell of astonishment. He snatched the bridle and saddle off the ground, opened the paddock, and took the tack to Sawyer. His eyes never leaving horse or man, he then backed out of the enclosure. "Do I shut the gate?"

Working quickly, Sawyer made no reply. He slid the bit into the horse's mouth easily, then drew the straps of leather over the horse's ears and buckled the fastenings securely. Just as quickly, he saddled the steed.

A pair of sapphire eyes glowing in his mind, he grabbed Coraje's thick mane and swung himself onto the horse's back.

Dumbfounded, Maclovio, Lorenzo, Pedro, and the women watched Sawyer subdue Ciro's savage stallion, unable to comprehend how Sawyer would manage to stay on the bucking, rearing, and totally enraged horse.

But Sawyer did stay mounted, and Coraje soon realized he'd been mastered. The horse surrendered to Sawyer's skills, pawing the ground gently and letting out a soft nicker.

Sawyer glanced at the gate and saw that Pedro had closed it. His long legs wrapped around the steed's barrel, Sawyer pressed in with his thighs and sent Coraje soaring over the fence.

The powerful horse cantered out of the yard and began to climb the steep, pebbled hill that led to the hidden exit. Once outside La Escondida's confines he responded to his rider's commands, veered sharply to the left, and headed down a slope that spilled into an open meadow surrounded by oak and pine trees.

Sawyer leaned low over the stallion's neck, giving him his head and urging him into a ground-eating gallop. He knew exactly where to go.

The riders who'd stolen Zafiro away had left a trail of beaten earth in their wake.

A long time had passed since Sawyer had handled a gun.

But as he continued to follow the path to Zafiro, he vowed that he would kill the men who'd taken her.

Zafiro lost all sense of time as her abductors rode through the mountain passages. Her capture seemed to have happened only minutes ago, and yet La Escondida seemed hundreds of miles away.

The man who held her next to him, his arm fairly crushing her ribs as he kept her in place on his thigh, wore his long, reddish-brown hair tied back with a strip of frayed rawhide. A filthy black hat on his head and streaks of dirt striping his face and neck, he'd narrowed his eyes against the sting of the wind and the lash of her hair, and he kept licking his thin, cracked lips.

He smelled of roasted meat. Obviously, he'd eaten recently. She wondered where he'd gotten his meal, wondered if it had been good, and wondered if he'd consumed large portions.

She didn't understand why such trifling thoughts occupied her mind and tried to summon back her terror. She'd fought the man wildly when he'd caught and lifted her from the ground in the forest, but he'd subdued her instantly with a sharp blow to the side of her head. And now the fingers on the arm that held her were tangled in her hair. Every time she moved he yanked so hard that her scalp felt as though it was on fire.

I am afraid, she told herself, and she knew that deep down she really was. But she couldn't think properly, couldn't concentrate on what might happen to her as soon as the men stopped their horses.

It was as though she'd buried her fear. Laid it away beneath thoughts that were easier to bear. Insignificant thoughts like what her captor had eaten.

The noise of the horses' hooves as they sped over the ground drummed into her ears, but in her mind she heard only one thing.

The sound of Sawyer's voice.

One day a man will teach you everything you want to know and more, Zafiro.

Like a fist, sorrow bashed into her heart. Sawyer would not teach her everything she wanted to know.

She would never see him again. Nor would she ever see Tia, Azucar, Lorenzo, Pedro, or Maclovio. No one would find her. No one could save her.

Because no one at La Escondida could ride or shoot.

"Here!" she heard one of the other men shout, and the sound of his voice made her feel as though he'd poured ice water down her bare back. She began to shiver, and shiver by shiver her fear returned.

The men stopped their horses, and the animals panted wildly, their necks lathered with the white foam of exertion. One horse, a pretty chestnut mare, seemed to be in serious distress.

Zafiro wondered if she would die along with the abused horse.

Her captor released her suddenly. She slipped to the rocky ground, bruising her knees and cutting the palm of her left hand. The air jarred from her lungs, she remained on her hands and knees trying to breathe until one of the other men grabbed her arm and hauled her to her feet.

His handsomeness surprised her. Although not as handsome as Sawyer, his features were pleasing, his hair was a rich shade of dark brown, and his body was well built with muscle.

His cool green eyes roamed the length of her frame, finally settling upon her sapphire. He reached out to touch the large jewel, running his finger around its sides.

"I've never seen a sapphire like this," he declared, and when he spoke Zafiro noticed his straight white teeth.

"I've never seen a *woman* like this," another man said.

She watched the second man approach her and could not quell a shudder of revulsion. While the man who touched her sapphire was handsome, the man walking toward her now was the ugliest human being she'd ever seen.

He looked like a hog. A wide pug nose, thick lips, eyes like dark, round stones, and fat all over his face made him truly hideous.

She didn't want him to touch her, but he did. Her stomach pitched when she felt his hand on her breast.

"I get her first."

The man who announced his place in line was the man with whom she'd ridden, the man who'd caught her as she'd fled through the woods. He was the biggest of the three, as big as Maclovio.

The men would rape her. The big one would be first, then the other two would fight over who would be second.

She flinched when the big man pulled a button off her blouse. Then he pulled off two more.

Her mind blinded her to what was happening, and in her thoughts, her heart, her soul, she pondered the fact that she'd offered her virginity to Sawyer. He hadn't taken it in the barn, the dirty, mouse-infested barn.

And now she would lose her innocence on a bed of rocks. To three men she didn't even know.

She didn't know when her tears began, but by the time she noticed them, her face was wet with them.

The big man pushed her back down to the ground, and while she laid there on the stones she watched him fumble with the fastenings of his breeches. The reality of her situation burst through the daze that clouded her mind.

And when he knelt on the ground beside her and began to lift her skirt, the instinct for survival jolted through her. Quick as a cat, she swatted at his face, her nails scraping into his filthy flesh.

His blood stained the tips of her fingers, and the sight

of the red fluid incited fury within her. She'd never hurt anyone or anything in her life, but now, as she stared up at the three men who would ravish her, her entire body shook with the need and the want to kill.

Deep growling noises coming from her throat and sounding horrible even to her own ears, she kicked her captor in the groin, almost laughing with satisfaction when he screamed and doubled over.

Instantly, the other two men were upon her, one on each side, both holding her down. Somehow she managed to notice they'd opened their breeches.

Their straining man parts sickened her so thoroughly that she gagged. Valiantly struggling to control the desire to retch, she twisted her neck toward her shoulder and bit the hairy hand that held her there.

"Dammit! You bitch!" He drew back his hand, preparing to hit her hard.

But in the next moment the hand he balled into a fist burst into a mass of bleeding tissue and splintered bone, shattered by the sheer speed and force of a bullet.

All three men looked up from the woman on the ground and saw a black-garbed horseman galloping toward them.

Their eyes widened with recognition and shock, and for a moment they could do nothing but stare in abject astonishment.

Another explosion of gunfire, followed by a second carefully aimed bullet, instantly killed the man with cool green eyes. An expression of disbelief his final action on earth, he fell, a neat hole right in the middle of his forehead.

Zafiro almost lost the will not to retch when his body slumped over her. With his face pushed into her chest, she could feel his blood warm her breasts, but before she had time to push him off and run, the third thunder of gunfire blasted through the mountain air.

The man whose hand was destroyed died at once, his heart as shattered as his hand.

With one tremendous flash of strength Zafiro pushed the two dead men away and staggered to her feet. Just as she stood she saw the third man, the one who looked like a pig. He jumped onto his horse and rode as if the master of hell himself was after him.

Shaking so badly that she could barely stay standing, Zafiro turned and looked in the direction from where the gunfire had erupted.

What she saw nearly sent her to her knees.

A broad-shouldered man upon a coal-black stallion galloped toward her. His long gold hair whipped behind him like a gold banner, a striking contrast to the ebony hue of the cape he wore.

He held a gun in his hand, and she saw another hanging from his hip. Even from where she stood she could see the brutal fury in his eyes. It glittered like sun-washed ice.

The stallion stopped as soon as his rider tugged on the reins.

Zafiro watched the man dismount, his motions so fluid and easy that he seemed to be made of air. He tied his raven mount to the trunk of an oak and strode toward her, his black boots crunching into the mass of pebbles.

"Zafiro."

She counted the buttons sewn down the front of his black satin cloak. Twenty-five.

Twenty-five diamonds.

She looked into Sawyer's eyes.

And when she spoke it was with a voice stunned with amazement and awe.

"Night Master."

sixteen

S awyer stared at the scarlet bloodstain on her blouse and in the valley between her breasts. More blood splattered her face. "They hurt you."

She heard the dread in his voice, saw it reflected in his tawny eyes. "No."

"But—"

"It is not mine." She touched her bloodstained blouse. "It is theirs. The men you killed."

Sawyer's first impulse was to take her into his arms.

But he didn't. Now that he knew she was all right, that he'd saved her from harm, the full impact of his remembered past slammed into him.

He turned away from her, not so much because he didn't want her to see his pain. She'd sense it whether he tried to hide it or not.

But he didn't know how to tell her about it. She'd ask; he knew she would. She'd pester him without mercy.

One part of him would welcome her curiosity, her concern, and the succor that might be had from her caring.

Another part of him shied from putting words to such

agony, such grief, such guilt. It seemed to him that to voice such emotions would be to intensify them.

But a third part of him—an empty part he'd only realized existed since Zafiro had come into his life—longed to be filled with whatever emotions she spilled into it.

Only hours ago he hadn't known who he really was at all.

And now he identified and admitted to three separate sides to himself.

"Sawyer?"

He felt her hand on his back. Her skin was warm, her voice was warmer.

"Sawyer, you are Night Master."

Astonishment laced her words. He wondered if the caring he wanted from her could get past her obvious incredulity.

"Sawyer?" Zafiro moved around his black form, needing to see his eyes.

When she saw them she almost shrank away.

Never, not ever, in all the time she'd known him, had she seen his eyes express such profound misery.

She no longer saw the black cloak he wore. The glitter of the diamond buttons eluded her, and the gleam of his lethal guns dulled, then vanished.

There was another man behind the somber clothes. Not Night Master. Not the Sawyer Donovan she'd come to know either.

The other man was the real man. The man who'd been lost to him for so long.

In her mind Zafiro didn't know what to do. Would he reject her concern? Would he continue to keep his thoughts locked away from her?

It was her heart that banished the notions. Her heart that brought a kind and caring smile to her lips.

Her heart that pushed her to curl her arms around his back and press the side of her face onto his shoulder. "Finally," she murmured, "I am meeting the man I have longed to know."

She looked up at him and saw him gazing down at her with an expression of hope, expectation, and yearning. "Not Night Master," she clarified softly, her hands stroking the muscles in his back. "But you. The man I have not met yet. The man with all the memories. As I have told you about all the things I remember as a child, now you—"

"They aren't only childhood memories," he interrupted her. "It's the others . . . The ones that . . ."

When he stepped out of her embrace she made no objection. Confused did not begin to describe how he felt inside, she knew. Sawyer still felt the torment, more so now than before.

Biting back all the many things she wanted to say and ask, she watched as he crossed to where the two dead men lay. He stared down at them for a moment, shook his head, then walked toward the dead men's horses.

He watched the little chestnut mare, ran his hand down her sweat-drenched neck, and picked up her reins. Leading her, he began to walk slowly all around the area.

"I remember the horse now," he said. "The one I told you about the night I came to your room."

"Yes," Zafiro replied, realizing she was going to hear his stories in bits and pieces and not necessarily in proper sequence. "The horse with the strange markings. A white gelding, no?"

"With streaks of black in his mane and tail," Sawyer added, still walking the ailing mare. "And a solid stripe of black down the front of his left foreleg. His name was Apple Lover, and he belonged to my father."

Zafiro could almost feel the strain in her ears as she listened and clung to his every word. "Your father."

Sawyer handed the mare's reins to Zafiro. "Yes."

"Apple Lover."

"Not my father's choice of names. One of the orphans named the horse when my father bought him."

Orphans? Zafiro repeated silently. *Santa Maria*, her bewilderment deepened steadily with each word he uttered!

"Can you ride, Zafiro? Ride the gelding over there and lead this mare along? Coraje won't tolerate the gelding and won't be able to leave the mare alone."

Zafiro looked at the other horse, a big Appaloosa who was biting at small clumps of grass growing in the rocky ground. "Yes." She approached the Appaloosa and took hold of his reins, while Sawyer saw to the task of divesting the dead men of their guns and other weapons.

"Will you bury them, Sawyer?"

Sawyer thought about how the men had abused Zafiro. "No."

The coldness in his voice froze solid all thoughts of arguing with him. With silent acceptance of his decision, Zafiro simply nodded.

"Up you go now." Sawyer lifted Zafiro into the saddle. He then adjusted the stirrup straps to the length of her legs. "We'll go slowly. You're not used to riding, and the mare is close to exhaustion. She's nearly been ridden into the ground and is going to need a lot of rest and good food if she's to survive."

"Shouldn't we let her stand still for a while then?"

"No." Sawyer returned to Coraje and untied the stallion's reins from around the tree trunk. Murmuring soft words to the agitated horse, he mounted. "She's got to keep walking so she doesn't get chilled and her muscles don't cramp."

Impressed by the knowledge she never realized he had, Zafiro nodded again, then gently urged the Appaloosa toward Coraje. "We're going back to La Escondida now?"

Sawyer kneed Coraje into a languid walk. He knew Zafiro was overcome with curiosity to hear what he'd remembered about his past, knew that she didn't want to wait until they'd reached the hideaway.

But he wasn't going to delay their return. "You know they're worried, Zafiro. Your people. Every one of them was frantic over your abduction."

She realized Sawyer was right. Tia, Azucar, Maclovio, Pedro, and Lorenzo were probably completely panicked. She hadn't thought of that. Sawyer had.

His concern for them caressed her heart.

"Small world," Sawyer said, keeping his eyes straight ahead, but knowing Zafiro could hear him plainly as she followed along behind. "I've met you. Years ago. I remember that now."

She couldn't miss the nervousness in his voice. He wanted to tell her everything, but wasn't certain how or where to begin. Instead, he was speaking whatever thoughts came into his mind, and he was struggling to keep from surrendering to the grief and horror his returned recollections had brought to him.

He was trying to be brave.

"Zafiro?"

"What? Oh. Yes." She recalled the night he'd stolen the gang's gold. How he'd smiled at her. "Yes, you stole our gold. But because you thought my eyes were pretty, you swore not to steal from us again."

"And I never did." Sawyer guided Coraje down a steep slope, over a large area covered with thick brush and huge gray rocks, and finally into a cool glade of juniper.

Two fat rabbits scampered out of his path, startling Coraje.

Sawyer quickly brought the stallion under control. "I'm not going to be able to stay at La Escondida, Zafiro."

His sudden announcement nearly caused her to fall out of the saddle.

"I have to go back," he continued, swiping at a few juniper branches as Coraje walked past them. "I'm from Synner, Texas, and I have to go back."

"Synner?" Zafiro repeated absently.

She couldn't concentrate on the name of the town, couldn't remember if she'd ever been there.

"Zafiro?" He knew his news had shocked her, but he wasn't going to keep the truth from her. "I left brothers and a sister there, Zafiro. It's been months. Almost eight months since . . . since I left them."

Zafiro made no answer. She couldn't. Too many things to think about crowded her mind, each vying for her full attention.

His father's horse, Apple Lover. Who were the orphans who named the oddly marked steed?

His father. Was the man still alive?

The brothers and the sister in Synner. How many? What were their ages? Who had he left them with?

She waited for him to tell her more, but he said nothing else. Watching his black satin cloak ripple behind him in the breeze, she followed him out of the juniper woods and into the meadow where she'd first seen the men who had captured her.

He passed the berry patches and took Coraje up the hillside in which the entrance to La Escondida was carved. As they entered the hideway his name whispered through her senses.

Sawyer.

The loss of his past had brought him to her.
The return of his memories would take him away.

⊷ ⚏✦⚏ ⊷

With as much patience as she could muster, Zafiro allowed her elderly charges to fuss over her. Their happiness and relief over her safe return even overcame their persistent awe over Sawyer's earlier revelation of being Night Master, and each of them took turns hugging and kissing her.

"I am fine," Zafiro assured them for the hundredth time. She'd bathed and donned clean clothing and now felt close to normal again as she sat at the table in the great room and allowed Tia to finish tending to the bruise on her face and the scratches on her hands and knees. "Sawyer arrived before anything bad happened to me."

At the mention of Sawyer's name everyone save Lorenzo began talking at once.

"I am so proud of my Francisco," Tia said. "Imagine a little boy so smart that he thought of a way to dress like Night Master and save our Zafiro!"

"When he came out of the barn dressed as Night Master, I could not believe what I was seeing," Maclovio said. "He—"

"And you should have seen him tame Coraje, *chiquita*," Tia added. "The stallion—"

"All this time he has lived with us under our roof, and we did not recognize him," Pedro declared. "We—"

"And to think that the legendary Night Master yearns for the night when he can share my bed!" Azucar exclaimed.

Lorenzo rose from his chair and hobbled over to the window. "Where did Night Master go?"

Zafiro wondered the same thing. After their arrival into La Escondida Sawyer had instructed Maclovio to see to the two new horses and had then ridden into the forest.

He'd been gone for over an hour now. Zafiro realized he probably needed to be alone, but she could not help but wish he would hurry and come back.

"There he is!" Lorenzo shouted, the power of his own yell nearly making him lose his balance.

Everyone in the cabin hurried out into the yard to welcome the return of their hero.

But Sawyer had no intention of answering the many questions the elderly people put to him in such rapid succession as they crowded around Coraje. Still mounted, he lifted the deer he'd just hunted and killed from around his shoulders and handed the game to Maclovio. "Mama, meat for your table," he told Tia.

At the sight of the deer, Tia burst into tears. "Oh, my sweet Francisco!"

Turning to Pedro and Lorenzo, Sawyer gave the old outlaws the knives he'd taken from the two men he'd killed. "Help Tia butcher the deer," he told Pedro, knowing Lorenzo didn't hear a word he said. "We'll be back later."

"We?" Zafiro asked.

Sawyer held out his hand to her. When she laid her palm across his, he pulled her into the saddle and quickly took Coraje out of La Escondida again. He didn't stop the horse nor did he speak until he'd reached a sheltered cove bursting with long swaying grass and white and red wildflowers.

"Here," he said. Gently, he lowered Zafiro to the

ground, watching as her tattered skirt disappeared into the depths of the lush vegetation. He then dismounted and secured Coraje to the thick, woody stem of an overgrown bush.

"Here?" Zafiro asked.

He ran his fingers through his hair and looked around. "I found this place a few weeks ago. This is where all the grass I've been feeding the animals has come from."

"I see." She wondered when he'd begin to talk, then decided she'd waited long enough for him to start. "Tell me everything you remember."

Her bluntness and the insistence he heard in her voice didn't surprise him. Indeed, he was surprised she'd waited this long to start her interrogation. He thought she'd begin attacking him with questions as soon as he'd returned to La Escondida with the deer.

But she'd been silent as he'd take her to this pretty, flower-sprinkled meadow. Not typical of Zafiro by any means. "Are you sure you're all right?"

She felt tears sting her eyes. "My body is fine."

But her emotions were not, he knew. "You don't understand the whole story yet, Zafiro. I haven't told you."

He took her hand and walked through the grass with her. "I did kill them," he said, his voice almost, but not quite, a whisper. "The four people in the house."

Disbelief staggered through her. "No."

"Yes." He stopped by a large, weather-smoothed boulder and sat her down there. "But four are still alive. That's why I have to go back."

"Yes. Of course. I see." But she saw no sense at all in what he was saying. "Sawyer—"

"Pretty Girl's there in Synner too," he blurted, sitting down in front of the boulder. "But Apple Lover's not."

Zafiro felt like shaking him for making so little sense. "I am trying to understand, but—"

"Then I'll start at the beginning." One by one Sawyer picked the red and white flowers, laying the blossoms on his thigh. "When I was twenty-one the minister in Synner asked my parents if they would take care of an orphan girl until a permanent home could be found for her. They ended up loving and keeping her. Her name was Minnie, and she was the one who named my father's horse."

Zafiro took careful note of the fact that he'd said the girl's name *was* Minnie and realized Minnie was one of the children who'd died. "Your parents had kind hearts," she murmured.

Sawyer picked more flowers, adding them to the pile on his thigh. "Rumors began to spread that my parents had opened an orphanage in our house. One thing led to another, and they soon found themselves with five other children. Tucker was an infant when they accepted him. He's ten now. Jenna and Jesse are twins. They're twelve. Ira's the oldest. He's sixteen. And Nathaniel . . . Nathaniel was three when he came to live with us. He died when he was thirteen."

Minnie and Nathaniel, Zafiro thought. They were the children who'd been killed in the house with the white curtains.

And the man and the woman shot down with the children had been Sawyer's parents. "Your parents . . ."

"Russell and Mercy Donovan." Two at a time, Sawyer tied the red and white posies together, making a flower chain. "They'd been getting on in years when they adopted Minnie. Father was a farmer and did well by selling his produce in Synner, but when the rest of the children came along things got harder. Even when my mother started taking in seamstress jobs and I contributed the cash I made by breaking and training horses at a nearby ranch, there was never enough money to provide for the nine of us."

The flowers trembled in his shaking fingers. "That's when I began to steal. At night. Like the Quintana Gang, I robbed the wealthy, but I never took more than my family needed. I told my parents I'd earned the extra money by teaching boys from rich families how to shoot and ride. Since I'd always been good with horses and weapons, my parents believed me.

"I usually had to steal only every two months or so. I liked taking gold because it was so easy to spend in towns where people didn't know me. Jewels were a little more difficult. I had to sell them, and a few of the jewelers who bought them asked questions about where I got them. Somehow I always had an answer that satisfied them. Most of them didn't ask anything at all, though, because I always sold the jewels for far less than they were worth."

His flower chain broke. "You're wrong about the diamonds, Zafiro," he continued as he repaired the break in the string of blossoms. "The ones attached to my cloak. They didn't come from any lady of royalty. I have no idea how that story was invented. The diamonds were a pleasant surprise I found in the false bottom of a hatbox. I'd just robbed and let go an elegant carriage that I'd trailed since it had left Synner two days earlier. As the coach sped away the hatbox fell off the top. I took it with me, but didn't look inside until I'd almost reached Synner. When I took the feathered hat out, the box still felt heavy. That's when I found the false bottom and the loose diamonds. They'd been fashioned into buttons, so it wasn't difficult to sew them right on."

"Why?" Zafiro murmured. "Why did you want them on your cloak?"

Sawyer took a deep breath and looked up at the sky as he sighed. "I didn't like stealing, Zafiro. I had to force myself to make those midnight raids. As I kept doing it, it got harder and harder, and times came when I didn't go at all for months. Then things would get so bad at home that I had to return to thievery whether I liked it or not."

He fingered one of the blossoms in the posy chain. "The diamonds helped me. They glowed like my mother's eyes. Her eyes would do that when I brought home money to her. They'd glow. So whenever I'd set out to steal, I'd look down at the diamonds and remember how happy and relieved she was when I gave her money to feed the family. Thinking of that, I could do what I had to do."

No longer able to be apart from him, Zafiro left her seat on the boulder and moved to sit down beside him.

Her nearness encouraged Sawyer to remember and relate the heinous memories of his past. "I continued to steal from the wealthy for ten years. Finally, I remember the last time I rode as Night Master."

This was it, Zafiro sensed. He was about to tell her what had happened that had caused him to forget his past. She took his hand between her own, hoping he would feel, understand, and accept her support and concern.

"I rode into the yard just before dawn one morning, and knew instantly that something was wrong." Sawyer tightened his fingers around her hand, but couldn't meet her gaze. "In case I returned, my mother always left a lamp burning in the parlor. This time, when I rode up to the house, I found it dark."

He tried to swallow, but couldn't. "I drew my guns and went inside. I couldn't see, so I lit the lantern my father always kept in the entryway. That's when I saw the house had been ransacked. Mother's little silver cream pitcher was missing from the table in the foyer. It was the only piece of real silver she had, and I knew then that every other valuable thing in the house had also been stolen."

With his free hand he picked up the fragile necklace of wildflowers and crushed several of the colorful blossoms. The red petals left a crimson stain on his palm. It reminded him of blood, and he squeezed his eyes shut before speaking again. "I went upstairs. To the bedrooms. I found my parents in their room. Minnie and Nathaniel were with them. They were all on the floor, shot to death, lying in their own blood, and the white curtains at the window made moving shadows over their bodies as the breeze swept inside."

"Sawyer." Zafiro felt his horror. It seeped into her, sickening her to such an extent that she felt physically ill. "But," she whispered achingly, "you did not kill them. You are not the one who murdered—"

"I am!" Listening to his own shout thunder through the mountains, he bolted off the ground and stormed through the sea of grass and flowers. "I wasn't there, can't you understand that? I wasn't there to protect them! If I'd been there—"

"But you did not know! You—"

"I killed them, same as if I shot them myself! It's what I made myself forget! It's why I couldn't look in the damn trunk!"

"The trunk—"

"The clothes and the guns were in there!" Sawyer clenched his fists, gritted his teeth, and sucked in a deep breath. "I killed my family!"

Deeply disturbed by his twisted belief, Zafiro stood and marched toward him. "You are wrong! You cannot believe—"

"I can believe anything I damn well want to believe!"

She reached for his arms, holding them tightly. "Sawyer, listen to—"

"There's more." He yanked her hands off his arms, and stalked away from her. "I found Tucker, Ira, Jenna, and Jesse in the barn. They were in the hayloft. When they saw it was me who'd come looking for them, Jenna fell out of the loft and broke her arm. She screamed with pain, and the others screamed with fear and horror. My own screams mixed with theirs, and if I live to be a thousand years old, I know I will never hear the sound of such grief and pain again."

For a full five minutes Zafiro watched him pace through the meadow, kicking at the grass and flowers, and throwing stones and sticks as he found them. The brutality of his memories had crazed him, she realized.

She could do nothing but wait until he calmed sufficiently to speak again.

"My brothers and my sister . . . They told me what they knew about the men who'd broken into the house. A gang of five, they said, two Mexicans and three white men. One of the white men wore gold earrings, and one of the Mexicans stole Apple Lover. That's all the kids could remember.

"After they told me what they knew I heard a whining sound." He cast another rock as far as he could throw it. "Pretty Girl, my dog . . . She came limping into the barn then. She'd been shot in the leg, and I knew she'd been shot while trying to save my parents, Minnie, and Nathaniel. I don't know where I found the reasoning or how I summoned the patience, but I hitched up the wagon and got all the children in it. Pretty Girl too. Then I ordered Ira to drive to the Ames's house. Mr. and Mrs. Ames lived about five miles away, and Bonnie Ames was my mother's best friend. I knew they'd be safe there. Before Ira drove away I gave him the gold I'd stolen two nights before and made all four of them swear not to tell anyone how they'd seen me dressed or where they'd gotten the gold. I . . . I sent the money with them because I didn't know how long I'd be gone. It was for their support and for . . . to pay for my parents', Minnie's, and Nathanial's burials."

His emotions so ragged that he could barely stand, Sawyer drew one of his Colts. Sunlight glinted off the weapon and for a moment he allowed the flashes to mesmerize him.

"I set off to find the killers then," he went on, quiet fury making his words sizzle as if made of fire. "It didn't take long to find their trail."

He raised his arm, holding the Colt out in front of his face and sighting along the gleaming barrel. "I found them on the fourth day. They were just heading out of a small town past the border in Mexico. In front of God and everyone in the town, I shot and killed four of them."

The sudden, deafening crack of gunfire made Zafiro shriek. Her nerves stretched so tightly that she feared they would break, she rubbed her hands briskly up and down her arms in an effort to calm her jangled emotions. "Four of them."

"I got them before they even saw me." Sawyer lowered his gun, his arm dangling at his side. "But the man who'd taken Apple Lover escaped. He emptied his guns at me, but he didn't hit me. As I saw him ride away on my father's horse, I could taste the flavor of hatred. It's a metallic taste, Zafiro. Like sucking on a piece of rusty iron.

"I tracked the bastard deep into Mexico, but I lost his

trail. I . . . I don't know how I lost it. I was tired. Hadn't eaten much. I couldn't stop thinking about my parents and the children. I . . . I lost the son of a bitch somewhere in Mexico, and then suddenly, in the middle of nowhere, I didn't know anything anymore. I couldn't ride my horse. The sight of my guns turned my stomach and filled me with a horror I couldn't understand, couldn't name. I took off my clothes, the satin clothes of a night raider, and I changed. My trunk . . . It was still on my saddle. The trunk of extra clothes I always took with me when I went out thieving as Night Master."

Slowly, he placed his gun back into his belt. "I sold my horse in the next town I came to and bought my mule. I wandered for months, doing odd jobs to support myself and trying to understand why such feelings of strange sorrow and pain came to me at such odd times. They even filled my dreams. I saw the house. The white curtains. The flowers in the yard. My parents, and my brothers and sisters. But even as I thought of all of them, I didn't know why or how I knew them."

Hesitantly, as if Sawyer might turn on her, Zafiro walked toward him. "And then you found the convent."

"And you."

She wanted to touch him, but dared not. She couldn't read his expression or the sound in his voice. "Eight months. You have been away from your brothers and sister for a long time."

He felt his eyes begin to sting. "They've probably given up on me by now. Lost hope that I'll be back."

The moist glitter she saw in his eyes drowned her with compassion. "Children are not like that," she tried to make him understand. "Children hope when there is no hope. I am sure that Ira, Jesse, Jenna, and Tucker—"

"No." Sawyer gave her his back so she wouldn't see

the spill of his emotions. "If the news of Night Master's death reached you all the way up here in La Escondida, then Synner has heard the news as well. Ira, Jesse, Jenna, and Tucker saw me that night, Zafiro. They knew who I was. And they have no way of knowing that the reports about my death are false."

Zafiro longed to argue, but couldn't. Sawyer was right. If his siblings had heard the rumor about his death, they'd have no choice but to believe their big brother was dead.

"I understand now," she murmured. "I understand why you refused to take care of us when I first asked you."

"Yes."

"Something in your mind, or perhaps in your heart, it remembered the deaths of your parents and Minnie and Nathaniel. You felt you had not taken care of them, but you did not know why you felt that way. And so you had the same feeling about us. And again, you did not know why."

"Yes. And there's more. You. When I first came to La Escondida the sight of you taking care of your people caused me to slightly remember doing the same. I didn't know why I remembered taking care of people, of being the sole means of support for them, but I remembered. Your caring for your men, Tia, and Azucar seemed familiar to me somehow."

His ragged whispering tore at her. Her vision blurred as tears filled her eyes, but she would not let herself cry. It was Sawyer who needed to weep. To release all the grief he'd held inside for so long.

She touched his hair and felt its sun-warmed softness caress the tips of her fingers. "You have not mourned, have you, Sawyer? Since the night you discovered that your parents, Minnie, and Nathaniel had been murdered, you have not grieved."

He kept his back to her. "It won't bring them back, Zafiro."

"No." *Dios mío*, how she hurt for him. "No, it will not bring them back, but mourning their deaths will heal you, Sawyer. Only when you allow yourself to grieve will your pain begin to lessen."

He didn't answer her, but she saw his shoulders shake. He was trying to battle his sorrow. Still trying to keep it locked inside.

She walked around him, took his cheeks into her hands, and aimed her gaze straight into his. The harsh words she would tell him were almost impossible to speak, but she knew in her heart he had to hear them. "You try to be brave by holding in your feelings. But you are not showing courage, Sawyer. You are being a coward."

Stung by her brutal accusation given in the face of his torment, he spun on his heel and headed for Coraje.

"I am not going back to La Escondida until I see you grieve, Sawyer!"

He untied the horse and mounted. "Fine. Stay here then."

She watched him canter out of the meadow and out of sight, his black cloak and golden hair whipping behind him. With more calmness than she felt, she returned to the boulder and sat down to await his return.

Five minutes passed.

Ten.

Fifteen.

But she refused to believe Sawyer would not come back for her.

Her faith proved true.

Sawyer galloped back into the meadow, then tugged Coraje's reins so quickly that the horse reared to a stop. "I came back to tell you that you aren't the woman I thought you were, Zafiro," he bit down at her. "I thought you had a heart, but you—"

"I do have a heart."

He glared at her, needing to strike out at something, someone. "I am not a coward, damn you."

"You have a lily for a liver," she goaded him on, returning his glare with a good hard one of her own.

"Lily-livered," he gritted out.

"That is what I—"

"It's not what you said! You never say anything right! You're insane, you know that, Zafiro Maria Quintana? Insane!"

Her feelings began to tremble, but she reminded herself that Sawyer's pain was far worse than any injury he chose to deliver to her now. "And you are afraid. Afraid to face, deal with, and fight your grief. That makes you a coward. Your belly is all yellow, Sawyer."

"Yellow-bellied."

"Your whole body is yellow. Even your lily liver."

Rage rattled inside him like rocks in a tin can. He flew off Coraje's back and pulled Zafiro off the boulder, his fingers digging into the tender flesh at the backs of her arms. "Why are you doing this?" he flared.

"They're dead," she returned. "They were murdered."

He felt her words slash inside him like so many swords. "I know they're dead!"

"You will never see them again."

As if he'd turned around and around too many times, he felt dizzy. Unbalanced by the sheer force of his tumultuous emotions.

He pushed Zafiro away.

She staggered backward, but managed to remain standing.

And Sawyer's scream shook the Sierra Madre Mountains. The noise sounded as if hell itself had suddenly erupted from inside the earth and was destroying every good thing in the world with fire and evil.

Then it stopped.

Sawyer sank to his knees, bowing his head so low that his chin touched his chest. Tears poured down his face so quickly that his shirt was soon wet with them. "Gone," he whispered thickly.

"Yes, gone, Sawyer." Her own face shining with tears, Zafiro knelt in front of him and gathered as much of his huge body as her arms could hold.

"They . . . they died." He lifted his head and hid his face in the warm nest of her hair. "I couldn't save them."

"It was a tragedy you could not prevent, Sawyer," Zafiro cooed. "It was not your fault."

Sawyer wrapped his arms around her tiny waist and squeezed her so hard that he heard her sharp intake of breath.

And then he began to sob, his frame shuddering so violently that Zafiro's body shook as well.

She held him. Whispered caring words to him. She wept with him, kissed his hair, his tear-salted face, and she willed him to know that if her heart could somehow repair his broken one, then she would freely tear it from her breast and give it to him.

Dusk shadowed the meadow when Sawyer's tears finally ceased, when his body finally stopped shaking. Zafiro still in his embrace, he laid down in the grass, in the flowers, and he turned to her, into her softness, next to her chest, where he could hear her tender heart beating a soothing sound that further eased him.

He felt her take a deep breath and knew she was about to speak.

But he was unprepared for the words she told him.

"Sawyer, I love you."

seventeen

S awyer raised his face from her breast and looked
into her eyes. The whisper-soft sheen of adora-
tion he saw tinting those beautiful sapphire orbs
echoed her declaration.

He didn't know how to reply. To have gone from soul-
wrenching grief to unmitigated surprise stole all reason
from him.

But Zafiro saw no need for words. Surrounded by the
fragrance of the flowers and the masculine scent that was
Saywer's alone, she touched her lips to his.

Her gentle caress and the powerful caring Sawyer
sensed flowing from her into him . . .

He couldn't remember ever wanting anything or anyone as badly as he wanted Zafiro now.

A man in vital need of and too long deprived of the
sweet succor she offered, he took her lips in a kiss that
demanded everything she had to give. His fingers lacing
through the wind-kissed silk of her hair, his right leg
lying over her hip, he held her still and steady as he
prepared to induce and accept her full surrender to him.

But what he sought, Zafiro had relinquished to him
long ago. She gave what he craved with joyous abandon,

smiling into his kiss and pressing her body into his so closely that to be any nearer to him would have been to be inside him.

Together and swiftly, they removed each other's clothes. The grass and flowers were cool on their skin, and yet all they could sense was the fierce heat of their need for each other.

A low, feral sound rumbled from Sawyer's chest when he felt Zafiro take his straining length into her hand and try to position it at the entrance to her body. Male instinct told him she needed no further preparation to accept him, but he would not join his body with hers until he was certain. He slid his fingers over her feminine mound and into the warmth of her womanhood.

He found her slick. Wet. She arched into his hand in silent supplication.

There would be pain, he knew, but there was nothing else he could do to ready her for it.

She was already so eager that even the slight touch of his fingers had set her thighs and belly to trembling.

He knelt between her thighs and lifted her legs, glad when she wrapped them around his waist. Tunneling his hands beneath her firm bottom, he raised her hips off the ground and positioned her so that the crown of his manhood kissed the dewy passage to the sweetness inside her.

He hurt to have her. His loins felt like sunbaked stone. But he hesitated, unable to rid himself of the regret of giving her pain. "Zafiro."

Maiden though she was, she read the expression in his eyes as if words were written within them. He knew something she did not.

But she wanted to know.

And there was only one way for her to learn.

She tightened her legs around his waist.

And whispered to him.

"I love you, Sawyer."

He folded her words into his heart, and with one sure, swift stroke he took her from her maiden's world and made her a woman in the most intimate of ways.

"Sawyer." His name burned from her throat on a heated breath as she struggled to understand and conquer the sharp pain his penetration had caused.

After a moment she convinced herself that it was not *her* pain she felt, but *his*. He would pour it inside her, and she would gladly take it into herself and never let it hurt him again.

She smiled up at him, telling him with her eyes that she wanted the full circle of his lovemaking.

"Zafiro." This time when he spoke her name, his voice thrummed with the sound of relief. Lowering his body gently down to hers, he slanted his mouth across hers and groaned when she slipped her arms around his neck and locked her feet together behind his back.

He began to move within her, slowly at first, but then with faster, steadier strokes when she moved restlessly beneath him.

She cried out his name, but his mouth swallowed her voice even as his body consumed hers.

Nothing or no one could have prepared her or helped her to fully understand the exquisite sensation of being so sensuously possessed by a man. Holding a part of Sawyer inside her, squeezing him as he plunged in and out of her, went far beyond mere physical pleasure.

Her emotions danced and flickered like a handful of sparkle upon a sunlit breath of breeze.

He murmured something to her, his lips moving upon hers. She couldn't understand what he said, but the sound of his husky voice increased her excitement, deepened her need, and heightened her yearning for the full burst of pleasure to come.

And as she tried to match the rhythmic pumping of his hips, she realized that her actions delivered to Sawyer the same wonderful bliss that his offered to her. Amazed and delighted by her discovery, she concentrated on harmonizing with his motions, relying on her instincts and his guidance to tell her what to do.

"Oh, God," Sawyer murmured. Her innocent, slightly tentative attempts to please him flooded his loins with glorious sensations he knew he could not contain. Wishing he possessed further strength to continue fostering her own rising pleasure, but knowing that his wish was not to be granted, he relented to the powerful force of his release just as he felt the first tiny flutters of hers.

Their shared ecstasy brought them together in full awareness, and they felt the world they knew fall apart. Clinging to each other, savoring and memorizing each tingle of bliss, each deep shot of pleasure, they floated in another world, one their passion had created especially for them.

And when at last they left that world of exquisite sensual joy, when the last sparkle of rapture faded away, Sawyer slipped to the ground. With a gentleness that belied his earlier and almost savage demands of her, he gathered Zafiro into his arms.

And he thought about how right it felt to have her there.

"You were right," Zafiro murmured to Sawyer as she lay within the warm, comforting shelter of his brawny arms. "No one could have explained this to me. What it is like when a man and a woman join their bodies in such a way."

She pressed a graceful trail of tiny kisses up his chest, over his throat and chin, and finally to his mouth. "Thank you, Sawyer Donovan. Thank you for showing—"

"No." He touched a finger to her lips to silence her. "I'm the one who should thank you. You were made for loving, Zafiro. Made to be cherished and taken care of. If it were possible I would stay and be the man to love, cherish, and take care of you."

His last statement hurled her straight into the bitterness of reality. "When will you leave?"

The squeak in her voice made him hurt. But he could not ease her sorrow. He had to leave La Escondida and return to Synner. "Tomorrow."

"You will take Coraje with you. He is faster than your mule, and no one but you can ride him anyway. We will keep the Appaloosa and the little chestnut mare."

There it was again, he mused. That squeak in her voice. He hurt for her again. "Zafiro, I—"

"You are better now." Loath to continue discussing his departure in the morning, she changed the subject. "About your parents. Your brother and your sister."

"I'll always miss them." He looked into her eyes, then peered up at the full and glorious moon.

He found the moon lacking. Zafiro's eyes held beauty that far surpassed the glowing orb of night.

Joining his gaze with hers again, he toyed with a tendril of her ebony hair. "My parents. Minnie. And Nathaniel. And I'll always wish I could have been there to . . . to keep them safe."

He plucked a single red wildflower and brushed it

along the hollow between her breasts, then twirled the crimson petals over the intricate facets of her sapphire. "But I wasn't there, and I can't skip back over eight months to make it so. I thank you again, Zafiro. For taunting me into meeting sadness head-on. If not for you . . ."

He left his statement unfinished as he pondered what she meant to him.

If not for Zafiro he would still be wandering. He doubted seriously that he would have stayed with the nuns for long.

If not for Zafiro he would not have gained a sense of purpose. Rebuilding her home had not been easy, but the strenuous work and knowledge this his skills were needed and appreciated had made him feel worthwhile again.

If not for Zafiro he would not have laughed. The daft woman had him smiling almost at every turn.

If not for Zafiro he would not have found his past. True, she hadn't meant to be captured by the men who'd taken her, but her being in the wrong place at the right time and his subsequent fear for her safety had effectively returned his memory.

And last and perhaps most important of all, if not for Zafiro he would not be lying in this blossomy meadow, beneath the mountain moon and speaking of his acceptance of his family's deaths. She'd pushed him into releasing his horror, his grief, and for that he would remember and thank her for the rest of his days.

"Sawyer?"

"Mmm?"

"About Luis . . ."

Apprehension almost turned him inside out.

Luis.

With all the many things that had happened today, he'd forgotten Zafiro's fear of her cousin.

"Sawyer," Zafiro murmured, "I just wanted to tell you that the feeling of danger I had—that sense of something bad about to happen—it is gone now."

He frowned when she turned her face away from him. "Gone?"

She gave a slight nod and nervously ran her hand through the billows of grass and flowers. "I think . . . I think the feeling came from the men who caught me today. Now that they can no longer hurt me or anyone else at La Escondida, the feeling of danger has gone. I . . . I thought at first maybe they were Luis's men, but I know now they were not. I am not afraid anymore."

She was lying through those perfect white teeth of hers, and he knew it. The feeling she had of coming danger wasn't gone. It followed her like an evil phantom that took his ease in her shadow.

She was lying so he wouldn't feel guilty when he left in the morning. So he could return to his brothers and sister free of worry.

But her attempts to reassure him failed. Sawyer still wasn't sure he believed in her sixth sense for danger, but his own beliefs didn't matter.

It was the fact that Zafiro believed them that was important. After he left she would continue to be afraid. Would continue to gaze at the mountain ridges, wondering when Luis would find and steal her away.

Himself, Sawyer didn't believe Luis would find La Escondida. The hideaway more than lived up to its name: "The Hidden."

But she would worry, he knew.

There was also her problem of providing for her charges. He could bring down more game for her in the morning, but the meat wouldn't last through the winter. Before the cold had ended she and her people would again be hungry.

But he couldn't stay. He just couldn't. He'd left four children in Synner, Texas. Children he loved every bit as much as he would have had they been the natural offspring of his parents.

Zafiro, Tia, Azucar, Maclovio, Lorenzo, and Pedro needed him, yes.

But Ira, Tucker, Jesse, and Jenna were his family. And he owed it to his slain parents to take care of them.

His mind spun with possible solutions to his dilemma, and in only a moment an answer came to him.

Money.

With money Zafiro could purchase everything she needed to provide for herself and her elderly dependents. If she remained wary of leaving the hideaway, she could ask the good sisters to do her shopping for her.

Yes, money was the solution.

And Sawyer knew exactly how to acquire the money she needed.

Night Master was going to ride again.

⊷⊶⊷

Her stomach full after having eaten Tia's delicious meal of fresh venison, Zafiro fought to keep her eyes open. She sat at the table with Tia and Sawyer, the others having gone to bed hours earlier.

The aftereffects of her day made her limbs feel leaden. The abduction. Her battle with her captors. The shock of learning who Sawyer was. The overwhelming compassion and need to help that she'd felt when he'd refused to give in to his grief. Their lovemaking.

And the all-consuming sorrow she felt over his impending departure.

She wanted to stay awake all night with him. Talking. Holding him. Hearing and branding into her heart the last things he would ever tell her.

But try as she did, she could no longer fight her exhaustion. Her mind as weary as her body, she began to nod off to sleep right in her chair.

"*Pobrecita,*" Tia said, watching Zafiro. "Poor little thing. She is very tired, Francisco."

Having been wondering when Zafiro would finally give in to her fatigue, Sawyer smiled and rose from his own chair to lift her into his arms.

"I do not want to go to bed, Sawyer," she mumbled into his shoulder. "I am not sleepy one bit."

"Yes, Zafiro, I can see that you're wide awake," Sawyer answered when she promptly fell back to sleep.

"I will help you put her to bed, Francisco," Tia said.

He followed the plump woman up the stairs and into Zafiro's room, where Tia lit a candle and pulled down the bed covers.

"I will undress her," Tia stated. "You go to bed, Francisco. And leave your Night Master costume at the end of your bed. It is dirty. I will wash it so you can play in it again."

He made no move to leave. Rather, he watched as Tia began to unbutton Zafiro's blouse.

The memory of their sensuous evening in the meadow came to him in a vivid flash. He felt himself becoming aroused.

"Francisco, do as I say."

Tia's sharp command irritated and amused him at

once. Reminding himself that he had no time to dally
with Zafiro anyway, he headed out the door. "Night,
Mama," he called over his shoulder.

In his own room he loaded his Colts and waited until
he heard no sounds save the whine of the night wind as it
rushed past the windows and the occasional clucking of
Jengibre, who sat comfortably in the middle of his pillow,
presumably laying an egg. He left the room then and
quietly checked the other bedrooms.

Everyone, including Tia, was fast asleep.

Downstairs, a glance at the clock on the shelf above
the hearth told him it was almost midnight.

He had little time, for the herald of dawn presented a
mighty enemy to a highwayman.

For the third time that day, he rode Coraje out of La
Escondida. He headed north, where Maclovio had said
the wealthy Spaniards lived, and he followed a twisting
path that soon led him away from the foothills of the
Sierras.

An hour later he came upon a hacienda. It rose from
the ground and stretched toward heaven, a sprawling for-
tress made of all things old and beautiful. Washed in the
silver glow of night, the ancient home fairly reeked of
wealth.

A brisk breeze picked up Sawyer's ebony satin cloak,
and the sound of the lustrous, rippling fabric stimulated
skills that Sawyer hadn't used in eight long months. With
the experience that had made him a legend in two countries, he laid down his plans in his mind.

Quickly but quietly, he urged Coraje toward the majestic estate. When the horse arrived into a shadowed
area beneath a cluster of swaying trees, he withdrew from
the hidden pocket on the inside of his cloak a black velvet mask. He hadn't thought to use the mask earlier,

when he'd rescued Zafiro from the bastards who'd taken her.

But he would need it tonight.

With the mask tied around his face he dismounted and slipped Coraje's reins beneath a small stone container filled with miniature roses. If Coraje pulled back gently, the stallion would think he was well-secured.

But Sawyer knew that if the horse was intent on escaping he could do so with little problem.

Not making a sound, Sawyer approached the front of the house. Night creatures buzzed and chirped in the trees and bushes, and an old yellow dog crept out from behind a marble statue of St. Francis that stood near the door.

Sawyer watched the dog carefully, ready to bolt should the animal begin to bark. When the beast merely stared back at him, he held out his hand, smiling and whispering softly when the dog licked his fingers.

Reaching into the pocket inside his cloak once more, Sawyer took out a long metal pick. He couldn't remember the last time he'd used the device and hoped he hadn't forgotten how.

He ascended the seven stone steps that led to the huge, richly carved door and eased the pick into the brass lock. Concentrating intently on sounds and sensations, he listened for the clicks and quivers that would tell him he'd opened the lock.

He sensed he'd succeeded before any click or quiver reached his ears or fingers, and dropped the metal pick back into the pocket in his cloak. Slowly, he twisted the knob, pushed the door open, and stepped inside.

His eyes quickly adjusted to the dark, and when his vision improved he knew he'd struck gold.

The house not only reeked of wealth, it glittered with it as well. Everything Sawyer saw, from the richly papered walls and elegant furniture to such trivial items as the small rug in front of the door and the hat stand, spoke of money.

He made his way through the house quickly and silently, finding expensive objects such as gold candlesticks, silver tableware, and bejeweled sit-arounds in various rooms. He didn't touch the valuable household objects, however, for they would have to be sold.

What he wanted was cold, hard cash. Money Zafiro could spend immediately.

He found a handful of currency in a clay jar in the kitchen. He also found two dozing maids in the room, neither of whom so much as twitched in their sleep as he searched.

Much like a maze, with connecting corridors and rooms that opened into others, the hacienda offered countless places to investigate. Sawyer found more bills in a desk in an office, inside a velvet reticule he found in one of the salons, and in two pockets of a coat lying on the back of a chair in the dining room.

He then ascended the staircase. The first room he came to sheltered a baby and the infant's sleeping nanny. The baby stirred restlessly in his cradle, making small whimpering sounds that told Sawyer he was about to cry and wake up the woman responsible for his care.

Sawyer made great haste to pick the baby up out of the cradle. Patting his little back, he walked the child around the room until the infant fell asleep again. Gently, he put the baby back in his bed and left the room.

He found nothing in the next five rooms he searched, but at last came upon the one bedroom he'd been looking for.

The *patrón* and *patrona* of the hacienda slept peacefully in their bed, which was canopied by a dark green swath of satin. Making not a sound, Sawyer crept into the room and swiftly found money in the dresser drawers, in several purses, and even a handful of coins scattered on the top of a vanity.

But he knew there was more. And his finely honed instincts told him exactly where to look for it.

He crossed the room and looked at the huge, magnificently framed portrait of a distinguished gentleman that hung on the wall above a satin settee. After taking the portrait down he didn't see a safe in the wall.

But then, he hadn't expected to.

He felt along the back of the heavy portrait, triumph soaring through him when he found a small slit in the velvet backing. Sliding his hand into the opening, he felt an object and pulled it out.

The flattened leather pouch was full of crisp bills, which he promptly slipped into his cloak.

One more place to look, and he would be done and gone.

He approached and knelt beside the bed. His movements slow and steady, he pushed his hand beneath the mattress, right under the sleeping owner of the hacienda. The man mumbled something in his sleep and rolled over closer to his wife.

The wife let out a loud snore that nearly stopped Sawyer's heartbeat.

Perspiration trickling from his forehead, he pushed his arm farther between the two mattresses, smiling when he felt a hard container. Carefully, slowly, he pulled it out.

The money box brimmed with gold coins.

It was time to leave.

He exited the room and made his way down the dim corridor. As he neared the top of the staircase he heard a noise at the other end of the hall and turned to look.

Two people stared back at him, a young man wearing only a pair of ragged breeches and a young woman dressed in a gossamer night rail edged in fine lace.

The *patrón's* daughter and some servant lad were obviously lovers.

And they'd caught him. The girl began to scream.

Sawyer whirled away from the stairs and dashed into one of the bedrooms he'd investigated earlier. The one with the doors that opened onto a balcony. He yanked the doors open, stepped out on the balcony, and whistled loud and long.

He then climbed onto the railing, and with one tremendous burst of strength he threw himself into the air.

He caught the tree branch neatly. As the branch bowed with his weight he whistled again.

Out of the night came Coraje, who stopped beneath the tree and snorted when Sawyer fell to the ground in front of him.

Sawyer scrambled to his feet and mounted. "You could have come a little closer so I could have landed right on your back," he mumbled to the stallion.

With that he urged the black horse into an easy canter that soon became a thundering gallop.

And the inhabitants of the hacienda poured out of the estate just in time to see the legend who'd come back to life.

※ ✦ ※

Zafiro and her people stood in the great room, unable to speak as they stared at the small mountain of currency and gold Sawyer had dumped on the table.

Tears filled the eyes of the old outlaws, each of them

remembering the days when they, too, had enjoyed midnight forays such as the one Sawyer had committed only hours ago.

Tia dabbed at her eyes as well. The money her dear Francisco has somehow acquired meant that her kitchen would soon be filled with every supply she could ever wish to have.

Azucar's gaze bounced from Sawyer to the gold and back up to Sawyer. Now the handsome devil had money to pay for her services. Finally, at long last, she would lie beneath his muscled body and give him the ecstasy she'd yearned to give him since the first day she'd seen him.

Sawyer saw plainly everyone's emotions and thoughts. Everyone's save Zafiro's.

No expression whatsoever touched her features or glimmered in her eyes. She simply stood by the table staring at the money, her only movement the gentle rise and fall of her breasts as she breathed.

Was she angry that he'd returned to pillaging? he wondered. But why would that anger her? She'd spent most of her life with thieves, and she adored them, defended them, understood why they did what they did.

"Zafiro?" he said.

Finally, she looked up from the money.

And finally, he realized what she was feeling, thinking. Sadness burned in her eyes, a deep sorrow that could only have come from her heart.

She knew. Knew that the money was the last thing he would ever do for her. The last duty he would perform as her knight in shining armor.

Delaying his departure would only prolong her grief, he decided. Although he'd slept only a few hours after his return to La Escondida, he would gather his belongings and leave. With any luck he would reach Synner, Texas, in two weeks' time.

"You are leaving now," Zafiro said.

Her voice shook; he knew she was holding back tears. "You know why I have to go."

"Yes." Sorrow squeezed around her very soul. "Yes, you must go."

"Why must he go?" Pedro asked, his question echoed by everyone except Lorenzo, who had sat down in a chair and fallen asleep with a gold coin in his hand.

"Zafiro will explain," Sawyer answered. "Now I've got to get my things together."

When he disappeared upstairs Zafiro told her people everything Sawyer had remembered and everything he now had to do. Only Tia saw no sense in the story. Lost in her fantasy world, she vowed to spank Sawyer if he so much as set foot out of the cabin much less out of La Escondida.

But when he came back downstairs Sawyer quickly ended her protests. "Mama, I'm not a little boy anymore," he said gently, rubbing his finger over her fat cheek. "You can see for yourself that I've grown into a man now. I can't stay with my mother forever. You know that. I have to go out and make my own way in the world. It's what sons are supposed to do, you know."

Slowly, reluctantly, Tia understood his reasoning. She stepped away from him, looked at him up and down, and her eyes widened. "A man," she whispered. "You have become a man now, Francisco. Oh, my son." Her hug of farewell lasted so long that Sawyer was forced to pry her arms from around him. And when he drew away from her his shirt was damp with her tears.

He turned to Azucar then. Reaching out, he caressed her cheek, played with her brittle hair, then bent down to give her a quick peck right on her lips. Her gasp of joy induced him to give her a sad smile.

Odd. But he realized he was going to miss the old strumpet.

Next he faced the old outlaws and embraced each of them in turn. His throat closed a little as he held them, and he knew he would miss them as well.

The hug he gave to Lorenzo awakened the old man, and Lorenzo promptly returned to the subject about which he'd been speaking before falling asleep. "Yes, the Quintana Gang stole our share of gold too, Sawyer. And we will never forget the night you robbed us. A thief robbing thieves. It was an honor, you know."

"Yes, well, good-bye to you all," Sawyer said. Each old person, in his or her own way, had become special to him, and his voice was thick with emotion as he bade them farewell.

His bag of clothing slung over his shoulder, he picked up Zafiro's hand and led her outside toward the barn. There, he quickly saddled and bridled Coraje and attached his bag and small trunk to the saddle.

The last thing to do was to say good-bye to Zafiro.

She looked so miserable standing beside the barn door. Like a little broken thing that couldn't be repaired.

He'd broken her. He hadn't meant to, but he had.

He pulled her into his arms, and in only seconds he felt her hot tears further wet his shirt and warm his chest. "I wish I didn't have to go," he murmured to her. "I'd stay, you know. If I could, I'd—"

"But you cannot." Closing her eyes as tightly as she could, she squeezed out the rest of her tears and willed herself to stop crying.

This was not how she wanted Sawyer to remember her.

She lifted her face from his chest and smiled for him. "Thank you for all you have done, Sawyer Donovan. If not for you I do not know what would have happened to us. I, too, wish you could stay at La Escondida, but life, it is not roses to sleep on."

He smiled a sad smile, knowing he was going to miss her mangled expressions. He'd miss the sound of her voice, the song of her laughter, the pretty sparkle of her smile, and the beautiful glow in her sapphire eyes.

He would truly miss Zafiro Maria Quintana.

Bending slightly, he kissed her. This was the last time he'd ever kiss her. Hold her. Feel her.

The moment he realized that, something inside him emptied and became a dark void. And he knew no one could ever fill or illuminate it again.

It belonged to Zafiro. Without her it would be empty and dark forever.

What an ironic twist of fate, he mused. He'd come to La Escondida with a dark emptiness inside him, and he was leaving with another.

Zafiro was right.

Life was not roses to sleep on.

"I will pray for you," Zafiro said when he lifted his head and ended the tender kiss. "I will think of you every single day for the rest of my life, Sawyer. I promise."

"And I won't forget you either, sweetheart." Seeing that she was about to lose her valiant battle with tears, he released her from his embrace and mounted Coraje.

She watched him slide his black hat onto his head, and for a moment she did nothing but stare at the contrast of the black against the gold of his hair. "Be safe," she whispered.

"I will. You too."

"Sawyer?"

"Yes, Zafiro."

She moistened her lips, lips still warm with the gentleness of his kiss. "I love you."

He tucked her love into his heart, where he would shelter the tender emotions forever. With a nod of his head and a flash of his smile, he bid her a final farewell and quickly urged Coraje out of the boundaries of the hideaway called La Escondida.

Giving Coraje his head as the stallion carefully picked his way down the rocky slopes, Sawyer dwelled on the woman he'd left behind.

Anything musical would remind him of her voice, her laughter. A song. A sweetly played instrument. A whistle. Even the sound of a gentle rain.

He would think of her smile when he saw something bright. Sun-kissed dewdrops. The happy twinkle of a star. A sudden and beautiful sizzle of lightning.

And her hair . . . God, she had gorgeous hair. The velvet black of midnight would never let him forget her hair.

Her thoughts. Her ideas. Sawyer smiled. Anything outlandish in the world would have him remember that wonderful daftness of hers.

An hour passed. He continued to think of Zafiro. Another hour passed. He found a road that headed north, and he followed it.

It would lead him into Texas. Toward Synner and his brothers and sister.

He felt as though he were two men. One knew he had no choice but to return to his family, to the children who needed him.

But the other man yearned to return to Zafiro, in whose arms he'd found such pleasure and in whose outrageous company he laughed and shouted on the same breath.

A sigh rushed from his chest, and he leaned his head back over his shoulder and looked at the wide-open azure sky.

Zafiro's eyes were bluer.

Her eyes shone even more brightly than her sapphire.

Her sapphire.

The large and unusual jewel appeared in his mind so clearly, he felt as though it were truly inside his head.

Her sapphire.

He jerked on the reins, forcing Coraje to an abrupt halt on the dusty road. His mind pounded with realizations.

She was right. Zafiro was right.

Danger *would* arrive to La Escondida.

He turned Coraje around and quickly sent the stalwart animal into a full gallop.

Why hadn't he thought of this before? he chastised himself. How could he have been so blind to such obvious peril?

In a little over an hour a very tired Coraje entered the stony confines of the hideaway. "Zafiro!" Panic edged Sawyer's voice as his gaze swept through the yard searching for her.

Zafiro almost fell out of her swing when she saw Sawyer return.

He leapt off Coraje's back and met her halfway as she ran across the yard.

They stopped in front of each other, each of them breathing hard.

"I had to come back," Sawyer told her. He stared at her sapphire, which glimmered between her breasts.

"You did?" Joy danced through her.

Sawyer picked up her sapphire. "The man that got away yesterday," he began, rolling the blue jewel around in his hand. "He saw Tia run into La Escondida, didn't he?"

"What? I . . . Yes. Yes, I think he did. Why?"

"He saw your sapphire too, Zafiro."

She looked down at her gem, then back up at Sawyer, suddenly sensing all was not right. "Yes. He saw it."

"He won't forget it. If he tells anyone about it . . . If he mentions it even in passing . . ."

"If he tells?"

"Luis is going to hear about the sapphire, Zafiro," Sawyer explained, careful to keep his voice low and even so as not to unduly frighten her. "When he hears about it he's going to know who was wearing it. And it won't be hard to find out where the sapphire was last seen. The man who got away yesterday knows where La Escondida is."

Fear stole Zafiro's voice and her every thought but the one of Luis.

He was coming. But of course she'd known he was. Had known for months.

It's just that she never expected her sapphire to be the cause of his arrival.

Sawyer was right. News of her sapphire would travel quickly through the tight circle of thieves, and then Luis would know exactly where to find her.

"That's why I came back," Sawyer rushed to tell her as he watched panic fill her eyes. "I'll be here, Zafiro. I won't let anything happen to you."

The need to believe him consumed her. But he didn't know Luis the way she did. Didn't understand the lengths Luis would go to to acquire what he wanted.

"Zafiro?" Sawyer stared at her face. Right before his eyes her coloring paled. "Zafiro—"

"You are not enough."

"What?"

She took her sapphire into her hand, squeezing it so hard that her hand began to ache. "I mean that you will need help," she said, the shiver she heard in her own voice deepening her apprehension. "You cannot face Luis alone. He is too—"

"Sawyer, you are back!" Maclovio shouted as he, Pedro, and Lorenzo came out of the cabin and stepped into the yard.

With a nod of his head, Sawyer acknowledged the three men, then turned back to Zafiro. "Listen. I can—"

"No," she whispered. "No!" Spinning away from him, she looked beyond the stony walls of La Escondida, imagining Luis and his gang riding toward the hideaway. "You do not understand, Sawyer! Luis will—"

"All right, I can't face him alone," he cooed. Folding his arms around her, he smoothed her hair and caressed her cheek. He wasn't afraid to face Luis and the man's gang alone, but knew he had to somehow set Zafiro's mind at ease before true panic set in. "I'll have help, Zafiro."

She struggled to comprehend what he was telling her. "Help?"

He couldn't believe he was really going to tell her what he was going to tell her. "I'm going to attempt the impossible. I'm going to work with your men."

She blinked up at him. "What?"

Sawyer gave her a smile, one he hoped would further ease her distress. "Yes, I think it's time the Quintana Gang came out of retirement."

eighteen

It took some doing, but Sawyer was finally able to convince the nuns to do his shopping. He'd have gone for the supplies himself, but dared not take the risk of leaving Zafiro and her people alone.

Four days later, the nuns brought the needed provisions to La Escondida.

But the Reverend Mother remained highly displeased. "We took our habits off and wore skirts and blouses when we went to Piedra Blanca to buy these things for you, Sawyer," she said, sitting at the table in the great room and gratefully accepting the cup of tea that Tia handed to her. "It would not do for a group of nuns to march into a store and buy things such as guns, ammunition, daggers, and dynamite."

Doing their best to ignore the Mother Superior's irritation, Sawyer, Zafiro, and all the old people examined the supplies. Not only had the nuns brought the weaponry, but also enough food and other household provisions to last a long while.

"We borrowed the clothing from a few of the village women," Sister Inez explained further. "We told them we needed the clothing to use as patterns because we were going to start trying to make apparel to sell."

"Lies," the Reverend Mother muttered. "We have told falsehoods to get you these things. Oh, may God Almighty forgive us our sins."

Sister Carmelita smiled broadly. "And when we were inside the store in Piedra Blanca, a few men flirted with me!"

"Sister!" the Mother Superior flared. "Remember yourself!" She sent a sharp gaze Sawyer's way. "And to think we bought these things for you with money you stole, Sawyer. If indeed we go to hell when we die, I imagine we will see you there."

Because he heard the tiniest hint of amusement in the holy sister's voice, Sawyer smiled at her. "Thank you for doing us this favor, Sisters. I promise you that your efforts and all the lies you told will help keep Zafiro and her people safe."

Zafiro nodded and smiled. "You have rescued us from the day, Sisters."

"They've saved the day, Zafiro," Sawyer corrected her.

"Yes. They have saved the day! Roses are growing everywhere now!"

Sawyer rolled his eyes. "Everything's coming up roses."

"That is what I meant to say, Sawyer."

"Of course." He smiled into her eyes.

Their happy and obviously affectionate exchange effectively eased the Reverend Mother's earlier misgivings concerning the stolen money. Sawyer was providing for Zafiro and her people the only way he knew how.

And Zafiro was in love with Sawyer. The Reverend Mother knew.

She prayed that Zafiro would not be hurt. Sawyer would leave one day. He would have to.

When that day came, what would become of Zafiro?

"Reverend Mother?" Zafiro asked. "Is something wrong?"

The Reverend Mother shook her head, but prayers for Zafiro still lingered in her heart. "Sawyer, with the money you gave us we also bought food and other supplies for the convent," she announced, tilting her chin up. "We knew you would want us to do so."

He threw back his head and laughed. "Of course, Reverend Mother. Of course."

"Your brothers and your sister, Sawyer," Sister Carmelita began. "They will be fine where they are while you are here to help Zafiro?"

The nun's query quickly sobered Sawyer. "As I told you, Sister, I left them with good people," he answered softly, then ran his fingers through his hair. "Mr. and Mrs. Ames won't let anything happen to them. I . . . It's just that I hope the money I left with them hasn't run out. No one in Synner would let the kids go hungry, but I don't like thinking of them as charity cases. And . . . Well, I don't like them thinking I'm dead either."

The Reverend Mother rose from her chair and laid her palm on Sawyer's chest. "But you are helping Zafiro, my son. The good Lord above knows this. You must have faith that He is repaying your goodness by watching over your brothers and your sister. He does not let any good deed go unrewarded."

Although Sawyer had never been overly religious, he found that the Reverend Mother's words did, indeed, give him solace and hope. "Thank you," he murmured.

"And we can send the children a letter for you, Sawyer," Sister Inez offered. "The mail, it is very slow and unreliable, but we could try."

"I'll write it tonight, Sister," Sawyer replied, thinking

her suggestion a very good one. "For now, though, let's start polishing up some shooting skills."

Maclovio and Pedro both reached for pistols, anxious to return to their past selves. Zafiro picked one up as well.

Sawyer took it away from her and gave it to Lorenzo. "No, Zafiro. Not you."

"But why? I can learn to shoot—"

"I don't even want you around when Luis shows up," Sawyer stated firmly. "In fact, I already know where I'm going to send you when he comes. You, Tia, and Azucar are going to hide in the cave where I found Maclovio's still. Only a pack of bloodhounds could find you there. And besides, I'll keep Luis too busy to look for you."

Sensing his adamancy, Zafiro didn't argue.

But she wasn't going to hide in any cave when Luis and his gang showed up.

She'd thought about it long and hard. Luis had killed her father and had filled almost her entire life with chilling fear. The man sowed anguish as if throwing it like seed.

Horrible as it sounded, she wanted to watch him die.

Sawyer summoned the last dregs of his supply of patience as Lorenzo toppled to the ground. Every time the man shot the pistol, the force of the explosion threw him straight off his feet.

Pedro was no better. His hands shook so badly that he kept dropping the gun.

And Maclovio couldn't have hit the bottle on the fence post if his very life depended on it. He'd shot several saplings in half, put a bullet through one of the flower barrels, and almost killed Coraje. His shooting skills were not only rusty.

They were dead.

And Sawyer began to wonder if he should send the three old outlaws into the cave with the women when Luis arrived.

But he continued to humor them, practicing with them each day. Especially with Maclovio, hoping that daily practice would somehow improve the man's awful aim.

And later, when daytime surrendered to night, he practiced with Zafiro. Practiced skills of an entirely different sort.

Long walks in the woods, by the stream, and over the mountain paths offered them time and privacy as well as an escape from Tia's watchful eye. Beneath the smiling moon and within the stony arms of the Sierras, they surrendered to their passion for each other, each sensual encounter teaching each more about the other.

And it was during one of their nightly strolls that Zafiro asked Sawyer the question she'd been keeping secret in her heart.

"Have you fallen in love with me, Sawyer?"

His hand stilled upon her bare breast, and he shifted in the soft sand by the stream.

"Sawyer?" Zafiro moved to lie on top of him, and the feel of his nakedness beneath her caused her a delicious shimmer of pleasure.

"Zafiro . . ." He clasped her waist, his fingers smoothing over her back. "I . . . You know I can't stay here with you," he tried to make her understand. "I have to leave—"

"I know," she answered softly, "but do you love me?"

"I'm not going to let myself love you."

There. He'd said it. He'd told her bluntly and perhaps he'd hurt her feelings, but he could think of no other way to make her understand. "I have to leave. I have to return to Synner. If I loved you, Zafiro . . ."

If he loved her, leaving her would be the hardest thing he'd ever done in his entire life. And so he wasn't going to love her. No matter how difficult it was to do, he was not going to allow his feelings for her to deepen.

"No," he said softly. "I have to leave."

She didn't like his answer one bit. "But you know, I have been thinking. You could bring your brothers and sister—"

"Do you think I haven't already thought of that?"

"You have?"

"Yes. But I can't do it."

"But why?"

"Think about it, Zafiro," he said gently. "Think about what taking them away from Synner would do to them."

His reasoning hit her like a blast of wind. "The town," she whispered. "All the things I never had, but wanted. School. Friends. A store. A place where I knew everyone and everyone knew me."

"And where you could stick your hand into the jaw-breaker jar, watch lovers swing on the swings, and hear about who ran away to marry who."

Her watched her as she dwelled on what he'd told her. She, of all people, would understand.

And he counted on her kindness, her loving heart to help her accept his decision.

She didn't disappoint him. "You are right, Sawyer. There is nothing for your brothers and your sister here at La Escondida. They would miss many things. Things that are very important to children. It would be unfair for you to bring them here."

He picked up a handful of sand, then let it sprinkle from his fingers. "Yes."

"And I . . . Even if you invited me I could not go to Synner. My men, they might be old, but they are still wanted for their crimes. I could not take the risk of someone realizing who they are."

The sad resignation that suddenly appeared within the depths of her beautiful sapphire eyes deepened Sawyer's own profound regret. Given the liberty, he would freely open himself to her, allowing his every feeling for her to grow, intensify, and strengthen.

No, he told himself. *No.*

He decided to turn her attention elsewhere. To give her and himself something else to think about.

Tenderly, leisurely, he began to make love to her. Kissing her sweetly, he took full advantage of her position on top of him, opened her legs, and slid easily into her.

Never having made love in the manner Sawyer was showing her now, Zafiro wasn't exactly certain what to do. But her confusion vanished when Sawyer grasped her hips and began to move them for her. He moved them in small circles, then moved them up and down, and as soon as she caught the cadence and motions he'd set and began to imitate them on her own, the first hint of pleasure caught her unaware.

"Oh, Sawyer," she breathed. "This way is the best we have done it so far!"

Her delight made him smile. The truth was that every position he'd taught her had been the best one they'd done so far. She said the same thing every time he showed her something different.

Yesterday he'd had her lie on her stomach and had entered her from behind while bringing her to climax with his hand. She'd said that had been the best way so far.

A few nights ago he'd made love to her while she sat in his lap facing him. That, too, had been the best way so far.

He'd loved her while they were lying on their sides, chest to chest, hips to hips. The best way so far, she'd said.

The position for lovemaking never mattered to her. She loved having him inside her every bit as much as he loved being there.

Love.

God, it would be so easy to love this wonderful, beautiful girl.

"Sawyer."

In the sound of his own name he recognized what she was telling him. He felt it too. She pulsed around him, the rhythmic proof of her climax hugging his length.

But he wasn't going to give in to his own desire. Not yet.

He wanted to give Zafiro a second gift of pleasure. One he would share with her.

He took her hips and moved them again, all the while pumping into her depths with the strong and steady strokes he knew would bring her straight into the same swirl of bliss that had taken hold of him.

And he knew he'd succeeded when her body trembled in his arms, when she moaned incomprehensible words into his shoulder . . . and when her heart began to beat so wildly that it felt as though it had jumped into his own chest.

He yielded to his own release then. White-hot ecstasy bolting through him, he plunged into Zafiro so deeply that he touched the mouth of her womb.

And there he spilled his seed.

When she felt him flood her with his essence, Zafiro wondered about the possibility of a child. To have a part of Sawyer in the form of his son or daughter filled her with joy.

And yet she hoped it would not happen. Raising his child in La Escondida presented the same problems that bringing his brothers and sister here had. The mountain hideaway, beautiful as it was, was no place for children.

The pleasure Sawyer had given her swiftly faded, replaced by an overwhelming sadness.

She couldn't have Sawyer, nor could she have his child.

All she would have when he was gone were memories.

* * *

Sorrow lingered within Zafiro's heart for days that spilled into weeks. A month passed. Nothing she thought of could temper the grief she felt over the coming of Sawyer's departure. She stayed by his side all through the day and all through the night, memorizing everything he said and everything he did.

When he was gone she would summon the recollections and relive them. And so, to make sure she had enough to last her a lifetime, she clung to his every word, his every action, and even attempted to read his thoughts.

He continued to spend many hours each day with the old gang. Pedro and Lorenzo were hopeless. Nothing he did helped them to shoot.

But thanks to his skills and perhaps a bit of help from heaven, Maclovio's shooting had improved. Five times

out of ten Maclovio managed to hit the targets Sawyer set
up for him. For that, Zafiro was exceedingly grateful, for it
meant that Sawyer would have a bit of help with Luis at
least.

Even Sawyer was forced to admit that Maclovio might
very well prove to be of value when Luis appeared. Eventually, he concentrated solely on Maclovio and made the
firm decision to send Pedro and Lorenzo into the cave
with the women when the day of danger arrived.

But one morning Maclovio didn't show up for practice.

"I just saw him an hour ago," Sawyer said, standing in
the yard and looking all around. "He was in the loft in
the barn. Said he was looking for something he thought
he'd left up there."

"Lorenzo and I saw him there too," Pedro said, standing with Lorenzo beside one of the rose beds.

"I am sure he will be along in a minute, Sawyer,"
Zafiro said. Seated on the porch step with Tia and Azucar, she swatted at a bothersome insect. "Maclovio would
not miss a practice on purpose. He will be here even if he
has to meet the devil and go through a flood."

Sawyer frowned. "Meet the devil . . ." It took him a
while, but he finally deciphered what she'd said. "He'll be
here come hell or high water."

"Yes, that is—"

"What you said," he finished for her. Laughing, he
began to load the guns Maclovio would use when he arrived. "Rabbit stew, right, Tia?" he asked, smelling the
fragrant meal as it wafted from the open window in the
cabin.

Tia beamed. "I have made enough rabbit stew for us all
to have three bowls if we want that many. And Zafiro,
she is going to help me make a spice cake with the cinna-

mon and cloves the nuns brought to us from Piedra Blanca. Isn't that right, *chiquita?*"

Tia turned to smile at Zafiro. One look at the girl's face quickly turned her smile into a deep frown. "Zafiro," she murmured. "You . . . you feel something."

"Tia." Suddenly, Zafiro's heart fluttered, missed several beats, felt as though it would stop altogether, then began to hammer. She raised her hand to her throat, knowing what symptom was coming next, dreading its arrival.

It happened quickly. She couldn't seem to breathe; her mouth went completely dry, preventing her from being able to swallow.

Her wide-eyed gaze flew to the hidden entrance of La Escondida, and she stared at the portal so hard that her eyes watered and stung. No longer could she stay seated on the porch step beside Azucar and Tia.

Her legs shook with the need to run. To escape. She rose from the porch step as if an explosion from hell had thrown her off.

Panic seized her. Absolute fear.

The terror was upon her.

"Luis." She whispered his name, afraid that speaking it aloud would suddenly make him appear in front of her. Wildly, she tried to sense where he was, how long it would be before he arrived.

Soon, she realized. Today.

Now.

"Sawyer!"

Her scream turned his blood to ice. One glance at her face told him she was about to collapse.

He rushed toward her, taking her into his arms just as she began to crumble. "Zafiro, what—"

"He's here!"

Her scream was so horrible and loud that even Lorenzo

heard. Everyone save Zafiro and Sawyer began running around the yard, picking up weapons, snatching open boxes of amunition, and running into each other.

Their faith in Zafiro's warning seeped into Sawyer like water through a crack.

And suddenly, quite unexpectedly, he knew in his heart that Luis and his gang were only minutes away from finding La Escondida.

He squeezed Zafiro's shoulders and shook her slightly. "Listen to me," he seethed. "At the top of the bluff behind the house, beyond a group of junipers, is a cave. Take Tia, Azucar, Lorenzo, and Pedro, and—"

"No!"

"What do you mean *no*? You do as I say—"

"I want—"

"I don't give a damn what you want, Zafiro! Take the women to the cave right now!"

She jerked herself out of his hold on her. "Tia! Azucar! Pedro and Lorenzo!"

The four old people hurried toward her, their faces ashen with fear.

Zafiro ushered them behind the house. One look over her shoulder at Sawyer told her he believed she was following his orders.

Once at the back of the house she told her charges where to find the cave, then watched as they started toward the bluff. When they'd disappeared from her sight she did her best to conquer her terror, then she crept around the side of the house and peeked around the corner.

She saw no one. The yard was empty.

Sawyer was hiding in preparation for Luis's arrival.

She would do the same. Returning to the back of the

house, she opened the window that led into the great room and crawled inside.

Her nerves screaming with apprehension, she ascended the stairs and headed directly for Sawyer's room. From there she would see the yard, where she figured the fight would take place.

She could barely wait to watch Luis die. To see years of fear be killed before her very eyes.

Still struggling to contain her dizzying fright, she made her way to the window and peered down at the yard below.

All was quiet. No one was about.

The tension that filled her caused her stomach to pitch. Her hands shook as she pushed her hair away from her face, and her heart beat so fast, so erratically, that she wondered if it would soon burst and kill her.

Footsteps in the corridor nearly caused her to scream. In the next moment she heard Tia and Azucar calling her name.

The two old women entered Sawyer's room. Tia wielded an iron skillet, and Azucar held the large, smooth stone Tia used to grind corn for tortillas.

"What are you doing here?" Zafiro demanded. "I told you to go to the cave—"

"We are here for the same reason you are," Tia answered.

"We want to watch Luis die," Azucar added. She raised the rock, its weight causing her arm to tremble. "Pedro and Lorenzo, they did not go to the cave either. They came back to help Sawyer and Maclovio."

"Yes," Tia said. "Lorenzo, he is downstairs in the great room. But I did not see where Pedro went."

Zafiro parted her lips to argue, but didn't have the chance to utter a word.

A voice.

From the yard shouted a voice, one she'd prayed she'd never hear again.

"Zafiro!"

Luis.

He was here.

She turned to the window and looked through the glass.

And she saw him, the object of her many years of hatred and fear.

He'd hardly changed. His black hair was longer, and he'd grown an ugly mustache. But other than that he looked the same.

An arrogant smile touched his lips, and his dark eyes snapped with the glitter of danger.

He wore evil, Luis did. Like clothes. Like a hat.

Four men accompanied him, each as heavily armed as he, each almost as sinister-looking as their coldhearted leader.

Sawyer's image flashed into Zafiro's mind. She saw his guns, remembered his abilities.

Luis and his men made five.

Sawyer was only one.

Luis and his men were highly proficient.

But Sawyer was Night Master.

Zafiro prayed that he would live up to the skills that had made him a legend.

— ◆ —

From the shadows in the forest Sawyer watched as Luis and his men entered La Escondida and rode into the yard.

Shock and a violent need to kill consumed every part of him.

The horse. Luis's horse.

It was Apple Lover.

Memories of his slain father slammed into him.

Luis had killed his father. His mother. Minnie. And Nathaniel.

And Zafiro's father as well.

He'd never felt such sickening hatred in all his life. Deeper resolve sifted through him. With single-minded purpose and absolute steadiness of the hand, he raised his Colt and sighted down the barrel.

He aimed straight at Luis's chest, wanting to know that his bullet shattered the piece of ice that existed inside there.

But a sudden movement near the barn caused him to lower his gun.

Every profanity he'd ever heard of filled his mind as he watched Maclovio stagger into the yard with a brown bottle in his hand. In an instant he realized that when he'd seen Maclovio in the hayloft earlier, the man had been searching for a hidden bottle of whiskey.

"Luis!" Maclovio shouted. Still weaving, he dropped the bottle and fumbled for the gun stuck in the waistband of his breeches. "I am going to kill you, you damn son of a bitch!"

Sawyer bolted out of the forest, firing both his guns just as Luis and his men drew their own weapons. Sawyer killed the outlaw who aimed at Maclovio. "Maclovio, hide, dammit!"

While Maclovio stumbled toward the barn, Luis and the other three men scattered. One raced into the cabin, another ran around the side of the house. The third man found shelter inside the woodshed.

Luis simply disappeared. As if into the mountain air.

Instantly, Sawyer ducked behind one of the barrels of flowers at the edge of the yard. He knew exactly where Luis's three remaining men were hiding and would make quick work of them the second they made a move.

It was Luis who worried him. Having no idea where the bastard had concealed himself, he could only pray he'd find Luis before the man had the chance to live up to his evil reputation.

Thank God Zafiro, Tia, Azucar, Lorenzo, and Pedro were safely hidden in the cave on the bluff, he thought.

"Sawyer!"

At the sound of his name Sawyer stared at the cabin, from where the shout had come. "Lorenzo?" he whispered.

No. It couldn't be. Lorenzo was in the cave!

"I got him, Sawyer!" Out the cabin door Lorenzo wobbled, holding the Holy Crusades sword high into the air so Sawyer could see its bloodstained tip. "I killed him!"

Sawyer gritted his teeth. The daft old man stood on the porch in open view for anyone who cared to shoot him down. "Lorenzo, get down!" he shouted, but he knew the deaf thief couldn't hear him.

He dashed out from behind the barrel, shooting at the woodshed and zigzagging across the yard as a barrage of bullets whizzed past him. Several feet away from the porch, he threw himself straight at Lorenzo, knocking the man through the open door and into the great room.

As he and Lorenzo landed on and slid across the floor, Sawyer suddenly saw the man Lorenzo had wounded with the sword. The outlaw was not at all dead, but stood in front of the staircase holding the flesh wound on his arm with one hand and pointing his gun at Lorenzo with the other.

Frantically, Sawyer tried to untangle Lorenzo's scrawny limbs from around his body so he could lift his gun and fire. He did manage to perform the feat, but before he could pull the trigger, he heard a scuffle on the stairs, then a loud metallic bang.

Tia's frying pan knocked the outlaw into total oblivion. His eyes rolling into the back of his head, he slumped to the floor, whereupon Azucar commenced to beat at his body with her large, smooth stone.

"What the hell are you doing here?" Sawyer shouted at the two old women. He jumped to his feet. "I told you to go to the cave—"

"We are here to help, Francisco!" Tia shouted right back at him. "And it is a good thing we came back! This man was about to shoot you!"

"Where's Zafiro?" Sawyer demanded.

Azucar pummeled the unconscious man one more time, bringing her stone down upon his shoulder. "Zafiro is—"

"Sawyer!" Maclovio slurred loudly from outside. "I lit the dynamite!"

"Dear God," Sawyer muttered, so angry that he could barely think or see straight. "Get back upstairs!" he told the women. "And take Lorenzo with you!"

Quickly, he reloaded his guns, then crossed to the window and looked through the sparkling glass.

Fury and panic forced him back outside. Again dodging gunfire, he raced toward the front of the barn, where Maclovio was calmly lighting a third stick of dynamite. Two more of the sizzling explosives smoked in front of his feet.

Sawyer tore the dynamite from Maclovio's hand, snatched the other two burning sticks off the ground, and with all the power his arm held, threw them toward the woodshed.

They exploded within seconds of each other, one sending the shed into the air within a bright burst of fire and splintered wood. A body likewise flew into the air, landing in the midst of the burning wood with a dull thud.

"You killed the bastard who was hiding in there, Sawyer!" Smiling, Maclovio clapped Sawyer's back in a gesture of congratulations, then reached inside his shirt and withdrew the bottle of whiskey he'd found in the hayloft. "Remembered I had one more bottle left. I found it in the hay—"

Sawyer gave him no chance to finish his statement. He forced Maclovio into the barn. Knowing that only the state of unconsciousness would keep the man from being killed, he knocked Maclovio out cold with one mighty blow to the side of the head.

When he left the barn and prepared to tempt Luis out of hiding, he failed to see the last man alive from Luis's gang.

But from his spot at the window in his bedroom, Pedro saw the man. Saw him slink out from behind the cabin, stop directly beneath the window, and aim his pistol at Sawyer's back.

With a strength that contradicted his frailness, Pedro opened the window, then lugged his knotted fishing net off the floor. His muscles straining with exertion, he lifted the heavy net to the window and pushed it into space.

The man's surprise as the giant net fell over him, caused him to drop his gun. Frenzied with shock and the desperate desire to escape, he pulled, tugged, and yanked at the net, but his efforts only tangled the net more tightly around him.

Sawyer's bullet put a swift end to the man's struggles. The dead outlaw dropped to the ground, his body twitching within the intricate patterns of knotted rope.

Only Luis was left now.

His body as straight and rigid as the sturdy fence post he stood beside, Sawyer held his Colts in perfect readiness. "Luis!" he shouted, and the man's name sounded horrible as it chanted through the mountains. "Come out of hiding and face me, you slimy son of a bastard and his whore!"

His nerves taut with tension and pent-up rage, Sawyer walked through the yard, silently daring Luis to make even one wrong twitch. Every instinct he possessed pulsed with vivid awareness, and no sound, feeling, sight, or smell escaped him. He swore that when he got near enough he would even taste the rancid flavor with which Luis's foulness sullied the air.

His search ended with Zafiro's horrified scream. The sound reached into Sawyer's very soul, setting aflame the very essence of what made him who he was.

He didn't remember his flight across the yard, his bursting into the cabin, or his breakneck trip up the staircase.

But all of a sudden he was there. In his bedroom.

Where Luis restrained Zafiro by holding her next to the front of his body. In one hand he clutched his gun; in the other he held a dagger poised at Zafiro's throat.

The beast of fear bit at Sawyer like a rabid dog, but he quickly tried to tame his alarm. Fear could have no part in a confrontation such as this one with Luis.

He looked away from Zafiro's wide, horror-filled eyes and concentrated on Luis's ugly, black, laughing ones. His hatred toward the man effectively tempered the last of his apprehension.

"You look familiar to me," Luis declared. Smiling, he spat a blob of spittle on the floor, then bent his head down to wipe his wet mouth on Zafiro's shoulder. "Who are you?"

"Your killer," came Sawyer's icy response.

Luis pressed the tip of his knife into the tender flesh of Zafiro's neck. Her sudden gasp and a quick glance at the thin rivulet of blood that trickled down her throat made him chuckle. He looked up at the big golden-haired man who stood on the threshold. "I will kill her before you can kill me. I might even have time to kill you. And then I will see to the four stupid old people who just came in behind you."

Sawyer didn't need Luis to tell him that Pedro, Lorenzo, Tia, and Azucar stood behind him. He'd heard the shuffling of their footsteps as they'd entered the room.

Dammit to hell, he cursed inwardly. Now not only did he have to see to Zafiro's safety, he also had to worry about four of her elderly charges as well.

"So," Luis snapped. "Who will be the first to die? Will it be my beautiful cousin, Zafiro?"

"You won't hurt her," Sawyer sneered. "You need her, remember? You need her sense for danger. It's what you came here for, isn't it? To take her away with you so she can warn you before any harm comes to you?"

Still keeping his Colts fixed in his steady hands, Sawyer forced himself to smile. "You, Luis Gutierrez," he scoffed. "The most feared outlaw in two lands. And he needs a woman to protect him."

Luis frowned and pushed the tip of his blade into another part of Zafiro's throat, slicing a second nick into her skin. "Who are you?" he demanded. "I know I have seen you somewhere before."

Sawyer raised one tawny eyebrow. "You killed my father, my mother, my sister, and my brother."

Luis shrugged. "I have killed many fathers, mothers, sisters, and brothers. What you say means nothing to me."

Sawyer's fingers tightened around the triggers of his guns. "The horse you ride belonged to my father. It was I who followed you from Synner, Texas, and found you outside that Mexican village."

At that information Luis recoiled, taking a few steps backward and pulling Zafiro along with him. He tried to wet his lips, but his tongue felt like something parched. "Night . . . Night Master," he murmured.

"So I've been called on occasion," Sawyer replied.

"I . . . I thought I killed you."

"It would seem you aren't as good a shot as you believe you are," Sawyer continued to taunt the man. "Surely you didn't think I'd let you kill me, Luis. I had to stay alive so I could find and punish you for what you did to my family. And while I'm at it, I'm going to avenge Jaime Quintana's death as well. You've killed too many loved ones to be allowed to live."

The Night Master spoke with deadly confidence, Luis thought, his anxiety intensifying. Realizing he had to escape before dread poisoned him with cowardice, he edged Zafiro toward the bedroom door, taking great care to keep a wide distance from the gunman whose skills he knew far exceeded his own.

Nodding his head to the side, he gestured for Tia, Azucar, Pedro, and Lorenzo to move farther into the bedroom. When the four people obeyed, he dragged Zafiro into the corridor, leaving his adversary inside the room. His back against the hall wall, he stopped.

And stared at Night Master.

Sawyer stared straight back.

"Sawyer."

At the unmitigated terror he heard in Zafiro's voice, Sawyer knew an inexorable desire to swiftly put an end to her fear. He raised the barrels of his Colts slightly, aiming for Luis's forehead, the only truly vulnerable part of the man's body that was not shielded by Zafiro's shaking frame.

He pulled both triggers at once.

But Luis had already doubled over at the waist, nearly bending Zafiro in half. The two bullets smashed into the wall, causing several small paintings to fall from their hooks and crash to the floor.

Walking backward, and with his gun pointed toward the bedroom from where he knew the Night Master would soon emerge, Luis pulled Zafiro toward the staircase.

Sawyer did, indeed, come tearing out into the hall.

But so did Pedro, Lorenzo, Tia, and Azucar. The four terrified people ran straight into him, their combined weights knocking Sawyer to the floor. By the time he managed to pull himself out from beneath the heap of wiggling, wrinkled bodies, Luis and Zafiro had disappeared from sight.

He flew down the hall and the staircase, leaping over the unconscious man who still lay in front of the steps. As he raced out of the cabin he saw Luis drag Zafiro across the yard toward Apple Lover, who stood grazing at the edge of the woods with Jengibre pecking at the ground beside him.

Sawyer ached to shoot and kill the man who had caused such misery to so many people, but he dared not even make the attempt. Zafiro struggled in Luis's arms, her torso, arms, and legs twisting wildly.

Sawyer would not take the risk of hitting her instead of the scum incarnate who had her.

"Kill him!" Pedro shouted as he, Lorenzo, Tia, and Azucar poured out of the cabin. "Sawyer, he has almost reached his horse! You must kill—"

"Stay back!" Sawyer shouted at them. "Just stay back!" His every step whispering his fury, he stormed after Luis, praying for one solitary chance to kill him.

Jengibre answered his prayer. The ornery hen took extreme exception to the man who almost stepped on her. Squawking and flapping her wings, she halfway jumped, halfway flew off the ground and delivered a vicious peck to Luis's cheek.

Shock and the sting on his face caused Luis to lose his concentration. With the hand that had held the knife to Zafiro's throat, he swung out at the chicken, who continued to fly at his face, chest, arms, whatever part of him she could reach.

Zafiro took full advantage of Jengibre's surprise attack, throwing herself out of his hold and lunging toward the ground.

Gunfire sounded through the mountains like a thousand cracking whips.

And Zafiro got her wish.

Luis collapsed to the ground, Sawyer's bullets lodged within the ice of his frigid heart.

nineteen

While a very contrite Maclovio collected the bodies of the four slain men and dragged them one by one out of La Escondida, Sawyer saw to the member of the gang whose head had met with Tia's iron skillet. After gagging the man he wrapped a long length of rope around the man's torso, pinning his arms to his sides. Unable to stand the sight of the bastard inside Zafiro's home, he then dragged him outside and tossed him on the ground.

From the porch, Zafiro, Tia, Azucar, Lorenzo, and Pedro watched.

"He still lives," Zafiro said. Her fingers wrapped around her sapphire, she stared at the man who littered her yard. He began to moan and move as he slowly came out of unconsciousness.

"I'm going to hand him in to the authorities," Sawyer answered, wiping sweat from his forehead with the back of his hand. "He'll be hanged for his crimes, Zafiro."

"Yes. He will be hanged, but first he will tell on my men. It will be his last crime on earth, but he will commit it out of revenge before he hangs. And then they will come here. The lawmen will find La Escondida and arrest Maclovio, Lorenzo, and Pedro."

Slowly, Sawyer looked up from the groaning man on the ground and met Zafiro's gaze. "What do you want me to do?" he asked softly.

Zafiro narrowed her eyes and tried to suppress the revulsion her reply brought to her. "I want you to kill him."

Sawyer had never shot at a defenseless man before, much less killed one. It was one thing to fire at a man who was shooting back.

It was entirely different to shoot a gagged, bound, and barely conscious one.

But he didn't argue. Indeed, there was nothing he could think of that he wouldn't do to put a final end to Zafiro's years of terror.

Closing his mind to the cold-blooded murder he was about to commit, he slid his Colt from his gun belt, cocked it, and aimed the gleaming weapon at the man's head.

"*No!*" Zafiro flew off the porch and into the yard toward Sawyer, pushing him with all her might when she reached him.

"Zafiro, what the hell—"

"I cannot," she squeaked miserably. "Afraid as I am that this man will tell on my men, I cannot let you kill him like this! He is tied up and gagged, lying on the ground without a single way to defend himself. I . . . It is wrong. It is wrong to murder him this way, Sawyer."

At that moment, as her words sang through his thoughts, Sawyer realized he loved her. No heart in the world beat the way Zafiro's did, with such compassion, such mercy, such extraordinary goodness.

She was an angel. And he knew it to be so just as surely as if God had just whispered it into his ear.

His gun still dangling in his hand, he started to reach for her, wanting her in his arms so badly that he had to subdue the urge to grab and crush her to him.

But the man on the ground stopped him.

Squinting his eyes against the vicious pain in his head, the man rocked himself into a sitting position, then staggered to his feet. Glancing at Night Master's Colt, he knew he was going to die.

But he wasn't going to meet his Maker before trying to escape. Impossible though he knew getting away would be, he turned and began to run.

At the edge of the woods Mariposa met him. The great cat sniffed the air, recognizing his scent as a strange one. With one graceful leap she brought the man down, then sank her teeth into his throat.

He never even had the chance to scream before he died.

＊＋≡＋＋

In her own bed, Zafiro lay beside Sawyer. The hour was late, and there was no chance Tia would catch them together. All five of the elderly people were so exhausted from a day filled with fear, horror, and overwhelming relief that they'd sought their rooms and gone to sleep as soon as the first hint of dusk had pinkened the sky.

This night with Sawyer would be her last. No longer was there a reason for him to stay. He'd succeeded in accomplishing every last thing she'd asked him to do.

But she wasn't going to let her sadness ruin these final hours with him. There would be time enough to grieve when he was gone.

A lifetime.

"Sawyer."

He moved above her, lowering his body down upon hers and holding her sapphire gaze steady as he stared into her eyes.

She felt his masculinity slide between her legs. It was hot. She wanted it to set her afire.

He entered her slightly, then withdrew completely, teasing her into wanting more . . . all he could give her.

She responded to his actions with a kiss so full of passion and sweetness that he almost admitted that he'd fallen in love with her.

But he didn't.

Instead, he told her with his body what he could not tell her with words.

He loved her more tenderly than he ever had before, lifting her slowly and wonderfully toward the highest rapture two lovers can find.

And while he held her in his arms, drank of her exquisite kisses, and filled her with himself, he realized that for the first time in his life he'd made love to a woman. For his coupling with Zafiro was not mere mating. Was not only a sexual union.

She was in love with him, and he with her.

In its truest form, this was lovemaking.

I love you, he told her when she trembled beneath him.

I love you, he told her again when his own release melded with hers.

I love you, he told her once more when she snuggled beside him and began to kiss away the dampness on his face that their lovemaking had caused.

"I love you, Sawyer," she whispered.

He watched her lick her glistening lips, lips made moist by the dampness on his face that she'd kissed away.

And only he knew that the droplets of moisture she tasted were his tears.

Before Zafiro even opened her eyes the next morning, she knew Sawyer was gone. There'd been no need for another good-bye.

His tender lovemaking last night had been his farewell.

Her sorrow too deep for tears, her actions almost mechanical, she got out of bed, then turned to pull up the covers.

Her hands stilled before ever touching the sheet or the blanket.

Scattered all over the bed were roses. Their thorny stems clipped off, the red rosebuds filled her heart with memories of Sawyer.

How many, many times had Sawyer picked roses for her?

Too many times to count.

She gathered the fragrant blossoms from the bed and put them in a basket. Every night before she went to sleep she would look at them. Touch them. They would soon shrivel, blacken, and die.

But her love for Sawyer Donovan never would.

After making the bed, she dressed and left the room to awaken her companions and tell them the news of Sawyer's departure. For their sake, and because every one of them wept, she continued to hold her own tears at bay.

Days passed, and still she didn't cry. The days spilled into weeks, bringing the arrival of autumn, the first kiss of frost . . .

. . . and the discovery that she carried Sawyer's child.

Sitting in the swing he'd made for her, she glanced at the paddock in front of the barn. Coraje looked back at her.

Sawyer had taken his father's horse. Apple Lover. The wild stallion he'd tamed pawed at the cold earth.

She moved her gaze to the rose beds. Ice sparkled upon the velvety leaves, making the flowers seem coated with diamonds.

Roses. The very thought of the flowers Sawyer had picked and spread all over her bed the morning he left squeezed around her heart.

She laid her hand over her lower belly.

And her tears finally came.

—•— ▰◆▰ —•—

Bending over at the waist and pulling weeds from the thriving vegetable garden, Zafiro swiped at her moist forehead with her sleeve. Although a mountain breeze picked up her hair and teased her skirts, the summer sunshine beat down on her.

She straightened, admiring the fine wall of pine logs Maclovio had built around the garden. Copying the same design Sawyer had used, the gentle giant had built another enclosure to replace the one he'd burned down so long ago.

Maclovio had also fenced in two large pastures. Pancha, Rayo, Mister, and the horses now had wide-open enclosures in which to run, graze, and play.

With the money Sawyer had left them Zafiro had the nuns purchase livestock. Tia, Azucar, Pedro, and Lorenzo enjoyed taking care of all the pigs, sheep, and new chickens, and the money the animals fetched in the villages was enough to keep La Escondida well-supplied with needed provisions.

All was well, Zafiro thought, as she gazed at the beautiful ranges of the Sierra Madres.

All except her broken heart. It would never be whole again.

Not without Sawyer.

With a dirty hand she brushed away her tears, then continued to yank out the weeds that grew between the vegetable plants.

A while later a strange feeling passed over her. When she first felt it she named it fear.

But it wasn't fear, she realized. It was something else. A shiver, but not one of cold, not one of dread. It was more like a shimmer, she amended. A shimmer of expectation.

Bewildered by the unfamiliar sensation, she ignored the weeds she'd been about to pull and stood up straight.

Her aching heart took on a rhythm she hadn't felt in months. Its lethargic beat quickened—like some dying thing that had been kissed back to vibrant life.

She reached for her sapphire, her fingers curling around the ball of cold, blue fire. A smile tilted her lips, but even as she felt its presence she couldn't understand what caused it.

A feeling of anticipation caused her to lose her breath. She began to pant. Short little puffs of air that gradually made her giddy with a happiness she couldn't comprehend.

She stood still in the garden and listened. Listened not to any sound she could hear with her ears.

But to the whispered words of her soul.

And then she knew. Before any noise at all hit her ears, she knew.

She tore out of the vegetable patch. As she raced through the door a nail snagged her skirt and ripped the fabric, but she didn't care. Through the yard she fled, past Tia and Azucar, who were playing with a new litter of piglets. Past Maclovio, Lorenzo, and Pedro, who'd just emerged from the henhouse with baskets full of eggs.

She'd just begun to scale the rocky slope that led to the exit of La Escondida when the words she'd heard in her soul finally wafted into her ears.

"Zafiro!" the voice shouted loudly, ringing through the mountains. "Zafiro, I'm back!"

She staggered backward, catching hold of a leafy shrub to keep herself from falling. Her gaze centered on the wooden portals that opened into La Escondida, she felt the broken pieces of her heart come together as if some unseen hand had joined them again.

And then he was there. Mounted on Apple Lover, his long hair shining around his face like strands of burnished gold.

Sawyer.

She tried to call his name, but her joy was too deep to put to sound.

Silently, she watched him ride down the slope. A wagon followed him. A cart filled with children of various ages and the ugliest dog she'd ever seen.

Ira drove the wagon. She knew he did. He was a young man with black hair, blue eyes, and a bright smile. And Tucker, Jesse, and Jenna sat in the back. Tucker had red hair, green eyes, and thousands of freckles. The twins, Jesse and Jenna, both had yellow-blond hair, brown eyes, and buckteeth.

Pretty Girl sat beside Ira, wagging her stubby tail. The

mongrel looked as though someone had dipped her into at least ten different colors of paint, and she barked with the kind of happiness that only well-loved dogs have.

"Zafiro."

She looked up at him, at the man she loved more with each breath she took, with each beat of her heart, with each second more that God granted to earth.

"I'm back." Sawyer dismounted, let go of Apple Lover's reins, and held out his arms.

In an instant Zafiro felt his embrace close securely around her. Arms she thought would never wrap around her again warmed her with peace, security, and happiness once more.

"I've brought my brothers and my sister," Sawyer murmured into her hair, so overcome with emotion that he couldn't keep his thoughts straight. "Ira," he called. "Tucker, Jesse, and Jenna. Come meet Zafiro."

The children bounded out of the wagon, each of them shaking her hand and hugging her around the waist. She hugged them all numerous times, not stopping until Sawyer finally took her into his arms again.

"A town," he whispered, sliding his fingers down her cheek. "I've got the money. School's out. They aren't in school now. I've brought them, my brothers and sister. We'll build a town, Zafiro. With a store. It'll have a jar of jawbreakers."

She couldn't understand a word he was saying, but it didn't matter. He was here.

He'd come back to her.

"I've got the money," Sawyer tried to make her understand. "Night Master. I . . . Every time I went out on a raid I thought of you. Of your lifelong wish to live in a town."

Gently, he drew away from her, aiming his gaze into

eyes so blue they defied description. "La Escondida is going to be a town, Zafiro. We're going to build. We're going to bring people here. We're going to make it a town."

She struggled to understand, but couldn't. All she could dwell upon was the fact that he stood right in front of her. Sawyer.

Her Sawyer.

"I got a pardon for your men," Sawyer told her, her beauty so mesmerizing to him that he could barely explain. "I lied. Told Synner's authorities that I'd witnessed the deaths of Luis and his men with my own eyes. Told them I'd watched the old Quintana Gang shoot them down. I've lived in Synner my whole life, and my reputation there is spotless. The sheriff believed me. The charges . . . Zafiro, the charges against your men have been dropped. The authorities were so glad to know that Luis and his men were dead that they pardoned Maclovio, Lorenzo, and Pedro."

Somehow, through the daze of her happiness, his words finally took root. "Free," she whispered. "My men are free."

"Yes."

Sawyer brought her close to him again, so close that he could feel her pulse thrum against his body. "I love you, Zafiro. I think I've loved you since the day you told me to put my head in the bucket and drown. All the time I've been away I've been working for a way to come back. Back here. To La Escondida, where I fell in love with you."

Zafiro could hardly see him through the blur of her tears. "Sawyer," she whispered.

"Marry me, Zafiro. Say you'll marry me."

She gazed into the topaz eyes of the most wonderful

man in the world. "Yes," she murmured with all the love she'd ever imagined could exist. "Yes, I will marry you, Sawyer Donovan."

He bent to kiss her, but before his lips touched hers, Maclovio, Pedro, Lorenzo, Azucar, and Tia hobbled up the slope.

He frowned as he watched Tia struggle up the hill. In her plump arms was a swaddled bundle.

And it was moving.

"Zafiro, I have brought him," Tia panted.

Zafiro didn't miss the glow of pride in the old woman's eyes. After finally being convinced that her "dear little Francisco" had become a man and that he'd fallen in love with Zafiro, Tia believed the child to be her grandson.

"Sawyer," Zafiro said. She took the wiggling, blanket-swathed package from Tia's arms and gently handed it to Sawyer.

His arms shaking, he stared down at the golden-haired baby whose sapphire eyes were the exact shade of Zafiro's. Comprehension dawned on him like the first light of day upon the darkest hour of the night, but he could find no words to express his thoughts or feelings.

"Your son," Zafiro said proudly. "Jaime Russell Ciro Donovan."

Jaime Russell Ciro Donovan, Sawyer repeated silently. The name didn't blend, but it didn't matter.

His son was the most magnificent being he'd ever laid eyes on, and his heart was already so full of love for the baby boy that he wondered if it would burst.

Holding little Jaime close to his chest, he leaned over and touched his lips to Zafiro's.

Wild applause echoed through the Sierras as Zafiro's elderly charges and Sawyer's brothers and sister began to clap.

And Sawyer realized that the loss of his past had ultimately given him a future.

At La Escondida.

With the most beautiful, loving, and outlandish woman in the world.

Zafiro Maria Quintana.

Epilogue

Zafiro strolled out of the cabin, that sat at the end of Main Street. Smiling and waving at all the people walking along the boardwalks on either side of her, she looked around for her elderly charges.

In front of the mercantile Lorenzo played checkers with Maclovio. Jengibre sat on their table, pecking at the checkers. The two men waved back at her, then Lorenzo promptly fell asleep, not waking even when he banged his head on the checkerboard.

Zafiro passed the town stable and the saloon, where Azucar stood by the swinging doors kissing a man too drunk to realize he was fondling a woman old enough to be his great-great grandmother. The sight made Zafiro smile, then laugh.

She neared the whitewashed church and saw Pedro. Dressed in his white robe with his string of keys dangling from his scrawny neck, he was deep in discussion with Father Vasquez.

Father Vasquez waved to her. "Pedro is teaching me to speak Hebrew, Zafiro!" he called gaily, then winked at her.

Laughing once more, Zafiro returned his sly wink, then

continued down the well-swept street and approached
the town's café. A quaint blue and white structure with
terra-cotta pots filled with red geraniums scattered all
around its little yard, the restaurant was always filled with
the delicious scents of Tia's cooking. And the café was
always busy, too, for not a single townsperson could resist
the woman's kindness or her food. Even as Zafiro peered
into the sparkling window of the establishment, she could
see Tia fussing over a table full of smiling patrons.

Sawyer's brothers and sister, Ira, Tucker, Jesse, and
Jenna, helped Tia in the café when they weren't in
school. Indeed, they thought of her as their grandmother,
and Tia fussed over and spoiled them just as a grandmother was supposed to do.

Thankful and happy that Sawyer's brothers and sister
had found such love and happiness in La Escondida,
Zafiro walked past Tia's café and noticed Mariposa sitting
near a bush that grew in front of the blacksmith's. The
cougar still wasn't sure she liked everyone who lived in
the town, but she hadn't done a single thing to upset
anyone.

Well, Zafiro amended silently, the cat had sneaked
into the mercantile and knocked the jar of jawbreakers
off the counter one day. But considering what other
chaos the mountain lion could cause, a few spilled
candies wasn't much to fret over.

"Mariposa!" she called to her pet, then proceeded
down the street again with the cougar loping at her side.

Her destination came into view. Built of smooth, pol-
ished stones from the Sierras, the sheriff's office looked
professional and beautiful at once. And Zafiro especially
liked all the rose bushes blooming in front of the jail-
house. The bright and velvety flowers added just the right
touch in her opinion.

She opened the door of the office and stepped inside. There, sitting in his big leather chair with his son in his lap, sat the handsome sheriff of the town of La Escondida.

And she was married to him.

La Escondida had nothing to fear with Night Master as its sheriff.

"Zafiro," Sawyer greeted her and gave her a warm smile. "There better not be any crimes being committed in La Escondida right now because this rascal won't let me do my work."

Zafiro looked at her son, Jaime Russell Ciro.

A secret smile touched her lips as she thought of the news she'd come to tell the sweet boy's father.

"Mama, I locked Papa in the cell," Jaime said proudly.

"Jaime," Zafiro scolded gently. "How did you get out, Sawyer?"

Sawyer hugged his son. "I had to promise him a camping trip in the woods."

Smiling, Zafiro approached the desk and leaned over to tousle Jaime's mop of hair. "Sawyer, do I look like a cat with a bird in its stomach?"

He stared at her, knowing in his heart that no matter how many times he told her the correct way to use the expressions she loved so much, she would never learn. "A cat," he mumbled, his mind working furiously as he tried to decipher her meaning. "Do you look like the cat that swallowed the canary?"

"Yes. That is—"

"What you said. Yes, of course it is. Now, come here. I've got two legs, you know."

She walked around his desk and sat on his other knee, grinning when Jaime began to play with her sapphire. "I have a secret, Sawyer. I've come to tell you."

Sawyer caressed her cheek, her chin, her neck, and her shoulder. It didn't matter how many times he touched her, he never got enough of her. "What is this secret, sweetheart?"

She picked up his hand and laid it over her lower belly. "I am going to have another baby. Doctor Hernandez told me this morning."

Sawyer frowned, then smiled, then laughed. "When?"

"In January."

Two children, Sawyer thought. Unadulterated joy lit up his eyes as he pulled her down and embraced her. "Zafiro—"

"She will be a girl, Sawyer. I know it. And we will name her Mercy Carmelita Pilar Inez."

The sound of the name jangled Sawyer's mind, but he didn't care. Whatever Zafiro wanted, he gave. "Wonderful name, sweetheart. I couldn't have thought of a better one myself. Now, give me a kiss."

She lifted her face to his and gloried in the feeling of his lips upon hers. And when at last his tender kiss ended and she looked into his wonderful gold eyes, she pondered all the many things he'd done for her.

La Escondida was a real town now, complete with every single thing she'd never had as a child. Sawyer had even provided a town gossip, a Señora Morales, who made it her duty to know everyone's business and make sure the stories were thoroughly spread around town.

Living in the town with her magnificent husband and beautiful child had changed Zafiro's way of thinking about her very existence in the world.

Not every day was perfect, of course. Problems arose every now and then, yes.

But Sawyer solved each and every trouble.

Her heart bursting with emotion, Zafiro kissed her husband again. And as the warmth of his love flowed into her, caressing every part of her, a beautiful thought occurred to her.

Life with Sawyer was truly a bed of roses.